GEN Z BIBLE

The Gospel by Gen Z and other Bible Stories

Z-Verse Press

Table of Contents

GENESIS

Way back in the day, before anything cool existed, the Great Architect, aka God, decided it was time to start something epic. The earth was just chilling there, all dark and empty, with God's Spirit floating above like it was waiting for the party to start. Suddenly, He was like, "Let there be light," and bam, there it was. God took a look and thought, "Yeah, this is good." He divided the day from the night. Light got the name "day," and darkness got called "night." And that's how day one went down.

Next up, on day two, God thinks, "Let's add some air." So, He split the water into two – some below, some above, and called this space "sky." Pretty slick move. Day three gets interesting. God gathered all the water into pools so dry land could show up. He named the dry spots "earth" and the water spots "seas." Not stopping there, God turned the earth into a giant garden, popping up plants and trees everywhere. He stepped back, nodded, and thought, "Yeah, this is good." Day four is all about setting the mood. God rolled out the sun for daytime vibes and the moon and stars for the night. It wasn't just for looks – they were also the world's first

calendar. God was feeling pretty proud of this setup. Come day five. God filled the ocean with all kinds of fish and the sky with birds. The water was literally teeming with life, and the air had birds flying all over. God gave them a thumbs up, telling them to go wild and multiply.

Day six is the big finale. God brought out animals of all kinds to live on the land. But the real showstopper? Humans. Made to look like God, they were given the job to look after everything, from fish and birds to all the animals. Plus, they got an all-you-can-eat pass to every plant and tree out there. Looking over the week's work, God was like "yeah". Everything was just perfect. So, on day seven, God decided to kick back and relax, marking the end of a pretty productive week by making this day extra special and chill.

Back when the world was still fresh, God decided to make a guy out of dust, breathed life into him, and boom, we got our first dude, chilling in this lush spot called Eden. It was the original paradise, complete with mystery trees: one for life, and one for knowing too much – the good and the evil. God was like, "Eat from any tree you want, but HEY! The knowledge tree is off-limits. Touch that, and it's game over." But then, God thought,

4

"Man shouldn't solo this gig," so He crafted a woman from the man's rib, making the first-ever dynamic duo. Enter the crafty snake, throwing shade on God's one rule, tempting the woman with the fruit that was supposed to make them like Top G. She was sold, took a bite, and even shared with her man. Suddenly, they were like, "Whoaa, we're naked," and fashioned some fig leaf fits. When God strolled in for an evening chat, our first couple went into stealth mode among the trees. God was like, "Where you at?" And man was like, "Uh, hiding 'cause I'm naked and all that." God, knowing something was up, asked, "You didn't eat from that tree, did you?" The man passed the buck to the woman, who then blamed the snake. Classic blame game. So, God laid down the cosmic law: snake was now a belly crawler, woman was gonna have a rough time with childbirth, and man was sentenced to hard labor on the cursed ground till he would be dust again. And Eve, she got named 'Life' because she was mother to all living. But there's a twist – now that they knew too much, God was like, "Can't have them living forever," and sent them packing from Eden. To keep them from sneaking back in for eternal life, He put up some divine security: cherubim and a spinning flame sword.

And just like that, paradise was lost over a snack, teaching us all a lesson about temptation, consequences, and the importance of reading the fine print. After Eden turned into a no-go zone, Eve and Adam started their own little squad, kicking things off with Cain. Eve was pretty stoked, giving props to the Big Boss Upstairs for the assist. Then along came Abel, who decided sheep were cooler than plants and went full shepherd mode, while Cain stuck to playing in the dirt with his crops.

CAIN AND ABEL

Fast forward a bit, and both bros decided to throw some gifts God's way. Cain rocked up with some farmer's market specials, but Abel brought the premium, organic, free-range meat platter. God was all about that farm-to-heaven table, giving Abel the thumbs up and leaving Cain hanging. Not cool, thought Cain, getting all kinds of salty and throwing shade with his eyes. God, playing the celestial therapist, was like, "Dude, Cain, why the face? Step up your game, and you'll get a high five too. But heads up, sin's creeping

5

on you, ready to pounce like a cat on a laser pointer." Cain, missing the memo on brotherly love, invited Abel for a little field trip, then went full dark side and ended the brotherly bonding for good. When God's like, "Where's your bro Abel?" Cain hit him with the first recorded "Not my problem," but God was already on to him, laying down the ultimate guilt trip and cursing Cain to a life of eternal wanderlust, with farming now being a bust. Cain was freaking out, thinking he was now the world's target practice. But God, in a move of unexpected mercy, slapped on the first-ever "Do not disturb" sign on Cain to keep him safe from angry mobs. Cain bounced, heads to Nod, east of Eden, started a family, and even dabbled in some early city planning, naming a city after his kid, Enoch. Fast forward, and we meet Lamech, Cain's great-great-plus grandson, who decided monogamy wasn't his style and married two. His kids? Well, they were the ancient equivalents of a cowboy, a rock star, and a blacksmith. Lamech, perhaps feeling a bit too inspired by Cain's legacy, upped the ante on family feuds, declaring himself untouchable. Back at Adam and Eve's, they were not done adding to their brood and welcomed Seth, sort of a tribute band to Abel. Seth kept the family tree growing with Enosh, and that was when people really started dialing into the divine hotline. So, from the get-go, humanity's story is a mix of sibling rivalries, divine interventions, and the start of civilization with all its complications, proving even the earliest days were filled with drama, innovation, and the eternal quest for redemption. After the whole Eden episode, Adam and the crew started expanding. Adam was hitting triple digits when he had Seth, and then he just kept going, clocking in at 930 years before calling it a day. Seth took up the family baton at 105, adding Enosh to the mix, and the pattern just kept rolling. These guys were living so long they probably forgot their own birthdays, with lifespans hitting the 800s and 900s like it was nothing. They were having kids left, right, and center, making the family tree more like a family forest. Then there's Enoch, who broke the mold by getting tight with God. Instead of the usual "lived and died" story, Enoch went for a divine exit at 365 — just up and vanished because God was like, "You, come with me." Methuselah stepped up next, holding the record for the longest run at 969 years. Imagine the candles on that birthday cake. He had Lamech, who then had Noah, predicting he'd be the breath of fresh air humanity needed amidst all the cursed-ground drama. By the time Noah hit 500, he was already a dad to Shem, Ham, and Japheth, setting the stage for some serious flood-prep action. So, while everyone was living centuries and popping out kids like it was going out of style, the real game-changer was Noah, gearing up for his ark adventure. It's like the world's longest prequel to the ultimate survival story.

THE NOAH'S ADVENTURE

So, when folks started multiplying and daughters were hitting the scene, the sons of God caught sight and thought, "Earth girls are pretty cute," and started marrying them left and right. But then, God was like, "Alright, hold up. My Spirit couldn't stick around with humans forever, especially with them acting up. Their shelf life was now capped at 120 years." Oh, and those Nephilim giants were around, towering over everyone, the celebs of ancient times.

Fast forward, and God gave Earth the side-eye, not thrilled with the vibe – too much wickedness, like a party gone wrong. He regretted the whole human project but saw something special in Noah. God was like, "Noah, buddy, you're the lone bright spot in this mess. Whip up an ark, 'cause I'm about to give Earth a serious bath. Bring your fam and a mix of all creatures. We're hitting the reset button." Noah, the original DIY king, got cracking on the ark – a giant, floating zoo meets survival pod. Noah, at the ripe age of 600, watched as Earth turned into an endless pool. With his family and a pair of every creature on board, they followed God's blueprint to the letter. A week later, it was go time – the floodgates opened, and it rained buckets, non-stop. For forty days and nights, it poured. The ark just cruised, and every mountaintop was underwater. Total wipeout – every living thing not on the ark was toast. Only Noah and his ark squad were left standing after the waters decided to dial it back. After what had felt like an eternity on history's least luxury cruise, Noah and his floating zoo finally caught a break. God had remembered Noah and all the critters aboard, sending a breeze to chill things out, and the floodwaters started to peace out. The deep-sea spigots and heavenly showerheads had been turned off, and after 150 days, the water levels had dropped faster than the hype around the latest viral trend. The ark, done with its extended sea voyage, had parked itself on the mountains of Ararat on a crisp day in July. By October, mountain peaks had started popping up like unexpected guests at a party. Noah, getting a bit stir-crazy, had cracked open a window and sent out a raven, which turned into a feathery reconnaissance mission, scouting the scene until the earth was dry enough for a land selfie.

Still not convinced, Noah had sent out a dove, which came back empty-beaked, finding nowhere dry to perch. A week later, he tried the dove again, and this time it returned sporting an olive leaf – nature's olive branch, signaling land was near. Another week passed, the dove didn't return, and Noah was like, "Guess it found its own pad." By Noah's 601st year, on the first day of the year, the earth had finally ditched its soggy attire. Noah peeked out, saw the ground looking back to its old self, and by late February, Earth was ready for its close-up, dry and inviting. God then signaled to Noah: "It's time to hit the exit. Unload your crew and let them go forth and multiply." So, Noah, his family, and the entire cast of Animal Planet had disembarked from the ark, ready

to reboot Earth's ecosystems. Noah, feeling a mix of relief and gratitude, built an altar and turned grill master, offering up some clean animals and birds. The aroma had hit God right in the heartstrings, and He thought, "You know what, let's not do the whole flood thing again, even though humans have a knack for mischief. We'll keep the seasonal reruns, day and night on loop, for all time."

Post-flood life kicked off with God dropping a major blessing on Noah and his sons, hitting them with the "go forth and multiply" chat. He basically made them the A-listers of the animal world, with every creature on Earth vibing in fear of them. God was like, "Everything that moves is now your grub, but keep it classy – no blood in your steak, please." God also laid down some ground rules about life respect, saying if anyone gets violent, it's going to be a serious issue. He put a divine twist on "what goes around, comes around," especially for anyone messing with human life, because humans are made in God's selfie image. Then God got all official, making a forever promise with Noah and his crew, including every living critter that had ark tickets. He was like, "Flood's over, and we're not doing that again. My rainbow in the sky will be our no-floods-again contract." So every time God's up there painting rainbows after a rain gig, it's Him nodding to the no-destroy deal, making sure Noah and every creature remember the pact. Now, onto Noah's fam drama: Noah turned farmer, started a vineyard, and one day got so smashed he forgot the "clothes are cool" memo inside his tent. Ham, seeing his dad in the buff, decided it was prime gossip material for his brothers. But Shem and Japheth, being the MVPs, respectfully covered their dad without peeping. When Noah sobered up and found out what Ham had done, he was less than thrilled. He ended up cursing Ham's son Canaan, predicting a life of being at the bottom of the family pecking order. Meanwhile, he blessed Shem and gave a shoutout to Japheth for their MVP moves. Noah clocked in another 350 years post-flood, bringing his lifetime total to a whopping 950 years before he checked out.

ABRAHAM'S JOURNEY TO GLORY

Back in the day when everyone on Earth was vibing with the same language and slang, a bunch of people moved eastward and found themselves in the land of Shinar, where they decided to settle down. They got all DIY and said, "Let's whip up some bricks and use asphalt as glue." Next thing, they're plotting to build the ultimate city and a sky-high tower because they wanted to be Insta-famous and not just random dots on the planet. But then, God logged in to check out their project and was like, "Hold up, if they're all speaking the same language and can pull this off, they'll be unstoppable." So, God decided to mix things up and introduced the world to language barriers, making sure they couldn't understand each other. Just like that, the ultimate city project got canceled, and people got scattered all over the place. That's why it's called Babylon – the place where God turned the world's language settings from 'universal' to 'custom.'

Zooming ahead, we hit the genealogy express from Shem to Abram, which is pretty much "this guy lived a long time and had these kids." The highlight reel includes Shem kicking things off post-flood, and several generations later, we land at Terah, who had Abram, Nahor, and Haran. Haran had a kid named Lot but checked out early in Ur of the Chaldeans. Abram married Sarai, who couldn't have kids, and Nahor married Milcah. In a plot twist, Terah packs up the fam, including Abram, Sarai, and Lot, aiming for Canaan but ends up chilling in Haran instead. And that's where Terah's story wraps up, at the ripe old age of 205. God hit up Abram with a life-changing DM: "Ditch your crib, your fam, and head to a spot I'll show you." The promise was epic: fame, blessings, and becoming a major player in history. Abram, at the ripe age of 75, packed up with Sarai and Lot, grabbed all their stuff, and hit the road to Canaan, the promised land. Once they got to Canaan, Abram was touring the place, setting up altars like they were going out of style, basically marking his territory for God everywhere. But then, plot twist: a famine hit, turning their promised land adventure into a survival reality show. Abram's solution? Head to Egypt, where it's all about the Nile and not dying of hunger. Before crossing into Egypt, Abram was like, "Babe, you're too hot. If the Egyptians know we're married, I'm a dead man. Let's just say you're my sister." Classic ancient world problems. As predicted, Sarai's beauty caught Pharaoh's eye, and Abram ended up with a Pharaoh-sponsored goody bag: livestock, servants, you name it. But God wasn't about to let Pharaoh turn Sarai into his latest queen. Plagues hit Pharaoh's house hard, and he figured out the whole sister act. Pharaoh, feeling played, was like, "Why'd you make me the villain in your soap opera? Take your wife and get out!" And so, they did, leaving Egypt richer but probably banned for life. Back in Canaan, Abram and Lot realized they were too loaded to live together; their entourages were causing drama. Abram, ever the peacemaker, was like, "Let's not fight. There's enough MTV Cribs-worthy land for both of us. You pick first." Lot chose the lush Jordan plain, setting up camp near Sodom, while Abram stayed in Canaan. God then gave Abram another epic promise: land as far as the eye could see and more descendants than he could count, basically making him the OG influencer. Abram settled in Hebron, continuing his altar-building spree, staying tight with God. Back in the day, when kings were pretty much the influencers of their era, there was this epic showdown that sounded like it was straight out of a high-fantasy novel. King Amraphel of Shinar, King Arioch of Ellasar, King Chedorlaomer of Elam, and King Tidal of Goiim decided to throw down against King Bera of Sodom, King Birsha of Gomorrah, and a few other local rulers. It was like the ancient version of a celebrity battle royale, with everyone picking sides for the ultimate showdown in the Siddim Valley, aka the Dead Sea's front yard. For twelve years, these city-state kings had been chill under Chedorlaomer's rule, but then the thirteenth year hit, and they were like, "Nah, let's bounce." Big mistake. The fourteenth year rolled around, and Chedorlaomer and his squad went full beast mode, smashing through everyone from the Rephaim to the Amorites. The kings of Sodom and Gomorrah, realizing they were outmatched, tried to make a run for it but ended up either in tar pits or hitting the hills. Meanwhile, Chedorlaomer's crew went on a shopping spree, looting everything, including Abram's nephew Lot, who had been living in Sodom at the time. When Abram got wind that Lot was in trouble, he didn't call the cops; he rallied his 318 home-trained soldiers. They went all commando by night, rescuing Lot and taking back all the loot, including the people. After the rescue, Abram was rolling back with the goods when he was met by the king of Sodom in what's now the VIP section of the valley. But then, out came Melchizedek, king of Salem, with a bread and wine meet-and-greet. He was like, "Abram, you're the man, blessed by the top boss, God Most High." And Abram, feeling generous, tipped him with a tenth of everything. The king of Sodom tried to strike a deal with Abram, "Give me the folks, and you can keep the loot." But Abram was all, "I swore on the high heavens, I wouldn't take as much as a shoelace from you. Don't want you going around saying you made Abram rich." He was only taking the food his crew had eaten, but for his allies, Aner, Eshcol, and Mamre, he was like, "You guys pick your share."

After some heavy drama, God hit Abram up in a vision like, "Don't sweat it, I've got your back and the rewards are gonna be huge." But Abram's there like, "Cool, cool, but how about a little legacy? 'Cause right now, it's looking like my butler's gonna inherit everything." God, not missing a beat, was like, "Nah, your own kid will be your heir," and took Abram outside for a little star-gazing session to show him just how big his family would get. Abram bought into God's plan, hook, line, and sinker, and that faith got him some serious divine brownie points. God promised him land, but Abram, ever the skeptic, asked, "And how's that gonna happen?" God's answer? "Bring me a zoo, and we'll make it official." So Abram did just that, but as he was prepping this divine petting zoo, some scavenger birds tried to crash the party. Abram shooed them away like they were bad vibes at a festival. As the sun dipped, Abram took a supernatural nap, and God dropped some truth bombs about his descendants having a rough ride for 400 years. But, like any good story, there's a silver lining – they'd come out of it loaded. God then turned a simple BBQ into a cosmic contract, promising Abram's future fam a land grab that would make any real estate mogul jealous.

Switching gears to Sarai and Hagar, Sarai was feeling left out of the baby-making magic, so she pitched Abram the idea of going old school with surrogacy via Hagar, her Egyptian slave. Abram, probably not wanting to sleep on the couch, agreed. Fast forward, and Hagar's expecting, but suddenly there's tension in the air. Sarai's playing the blame game, and Hagar's feeling the heat, so she bounces.

Out in the wilderness, Hagar had a divine meet-cute with an angel who's like, "Go back, and also, surprise, you're gonna have a son named Ishmael because God's got your back." The angel also threw in that Ishmael would be a wild card, but in a "changing the game" kind of way. Hagar, now

feeling seen by the big G, headed back, and before you know it, Ishmael's on the scene. Abram's officially a dad at 86, proving it's never too late to start an epic family saga. When Abram was chilling at 99, God rocked up and was like, "Yo, I'm the real MVP, Almighty God. Stick with me, and you'll be golden." He promised Abram a fanbase bigger than any TikTok star's, but there was a catch—Abram had to go all in on this God deal. So, Abram hit the deck, face down, showing mad respect.

God rolled out the VIP treatment, "You're getting an upgrade, buddy. Abram's old news; you're Abraham now, 'cause you're about to be the daddy of, like, a gazillion nations." God wasn't done. He threw in kings and lands like they were going out of style, making sure Abraham knew this was the real deal forever. Then God dropped the bomb about the whole circumcision deal as the VIP pass to this covenant. Every dude in Abraham's crew had to get on board, from the homegrown to the bought ones, marking them as part of the ultimate squad. God then turned to Sarah, giving her the rebrand treatment too. "Sarai's out; Sarah's in. And guess what? You were gonna have a baby. Nations and kings were gonna call you grandma." Abraham, hitting the floor again, couldn't help but crack up. "A kid, with me being ancient and Sarah way past her baby-making days? You're pulling my leg!" But God was dead serious, "Nah, it's gonna be Isaac, and he's gonna carry this covenant on."

God also had a soft spot for Ishmael, promising Abraham he'd make him big too, but Isaac was where it was at for the long-term promise. After God checked out, Abraham didn't waste any time; he and his whole squad, including Ishmael, got circumcised, making it the most intense bonding experience ever.

Fast forward, Abraham was hanging out by his tent when he spotted three dudes. Not wanting to miss out on the desert hospitality badge, he sprinted over, offered them a foot spa, and whipped up a feast faster than you can say "DoorDash." Sarah got in on the action, baking up a storm, while Abraham served up a calf with some curds and milk, hosting what had to be the divine version of a pop-up gourmet experience under the oaks.

Cut to Lot's drama in Sodom. Two angels showed up, and Lot was like, "Don't hit the square, crash at my pad." But before they could chill, the locals went full beast mode, wanting to crash the party. Lot tried to deal, offering his daughters instead (not cool, Lot), but the angels weren't having it. They pulled Lot back, zapped the mob with blindness, and were like, "This place is toast." They told Lot to grab his fam and bounce before God laid the smackdown. Lot tried to warn his soon-to-be sons-in-law, but they thought he was joking. Come sunrise, the angels were like, "Let's roll!" dragging Lot and his fam out of town. "Don't look back," they warned. But Lot's wife couldn't resist and ended up as the world's saltiest statue. Abraham, up early for his VIP meet-and-greet spot with God, peeped the destruction from afar. Sodom and Gomorrah were lit up worse than a bad barbecue. But God remembered Abraham's buddy pass and saved Lot from the ultimate unfollow.

EXODUS

Back in the day, Jacob's crew rolled deep into Egypt, totaling a solid seventy. Joseph was already chilling in Egypt, setting the scene. Fast forward, Joseph and his bros kicked the bucket, but their squad, the Israelites, went full beast mode in the reproduction department, filling up the land faster than a viral TikTok challenge.

Enter the new Pharaoh, a dude who hadn't heard of Joseph's legendary status. Seeing the Israelites multiplying like bunnies, he got shook, thinking they'd side-swap during a throwdown and bounce from Egypt. His master plan? Work them to the bone building cities, hoping to control their numbers. Spoiler: It backfired. The more he pressed, the more they thrived, seriously freaking out the Egyptians. Pharaoh then tried to get sneaky, telling the Hebrew midwives, Shiphrah and Puah, to play a grim reaper role with the newborn boys. But these ladies had guts and God on their side, so they let the boys live. When Pharaoh got wind of this, he was like, "What's up with that?" The midwives played it cool, saying Hebrew women were just too quick on the delivery. God gave props to the midwives, blessing them with their own families, while Pharaoh doubled down on his dark vibes, ordering all Hebrew baby boys to take a one-way trip to the Nile.

Pharaoh's daughter hit the Nile for a spa day, spotted the basket, and found the crying baby. Her heart melted. Big sis, seizing the moment, offered to find a Hebrew nurse. Plot twist: She brought back the baby's real mom. Pharaoh's daughter was like, "Nurse him for me, and I'll pay you." So, mom got her baby back, plus some cash. When the kid got older, he was officially adopted by Pharaoh's daughter and named Moses, meaning "pulled out of the water," because, well, that's exactly what happened. After Moses hit his glow-up, he decided to check out how his peeps were doing. He caught an Egyptian getting rough with a Hebrew – one of his own squad. Looking around and seeing the coast was clear, Moses decided to go full ninja, taking out the Egyptian and giving him a sandy burial. The next day, Moses was out and about when he spotted two Hebrews throwing hands. He stepped in like, "Yo, why you hitting your bro?" But one of them was like, "Who died and made you boss? You gonna off me like you did that Egyptian?" That's when Moses got the chills, realizing his secret mission wasn't so secret. Word got to Pharaoh, and he wasn't about to let Moses slide, so Moses had to dip out fast to Midian, where he hit pause by a well.In Midian, Moses ran into seven sisters at the well, doing the daily water run for their dad's flock. Some local shepherds tried to crash the party, but Moses wasn't having it. He helped the sisters out, then took care of the flock's thirst. When they got back, their dad, Reuel, was like, "You're back early. What's up?" They told him about the Egyptian hero who saved the day.

Reuel was curious, "And you just left this guy out there? Bring him over for some grub!" Moses ended up crashing with Reuel, who even hooked him up with his daughter Zipporah. They had a kid, Gershom, with Moses saying, "Guess I'm an outsider wherever I go." Time flew, and Egypt's king kicked the bucket. Meanwhile, the Israelites were still breaking their backs working. They were so over it, they cried out for help, and their SOS went straight up to God. God heard their cries, remembered His promise to Abraham, Isaac, and Jacob, had a good look at the Israelites' situation, and yup, He was in the know.

Moses was out there in the boondocks, tending to Jethro's sheep—yeah, that's his father-in-law, the big cheese priest of Midian. He took the flock way out west to Horeb, AKA God's mountain. That's when things got lit, literally. Moses spots this bush blazing up, but it wasn't turning to ash. He's like, "Gotta peep this. Why's that bush not toast?" God caught Moses rubbernecking and hollered from the bush, "Moses, Moses!" And Moses was like, "Yup, that's me." God's like, "Hold up, don't come any closer. Kick off those sandals, you're on holy ground." He then hits Moses with, "I'm the God of your dad, the VIP of Abraham, Isaac, and Jacob." Moses practically facepalmed, too shook to look. God spills, "I've seen my peeps suffering in Egypt, heard them begging for help, and I'm feeling their pain. So, I'm about to swoop in, save them from the Egyptians, and relocate them to a primo spot— milk, honey, and the whole shebang, where the Canaanites and their crew hang out. The Israelites' SOS got to me, and I've noticed how rough the Egyptians are on them. So, here's the game plan: You're gonna spring my people from Egypt."

Moses was like, "Me? Hit up Pharaoh and get the Israelites out? You for real?" God reassured him, "I got you. And here's how you'll know I sent you: After you've done the deed, you'll all throw a big worship party right here on this mountain."

Moses, playing it cautious, asked, "So, when I tell the Israelites 'The God of your ancestors sent me,' and they're like, 'What's his name?' what do I say?" God went all mysterious, "I AM WHO I AM. Just tell them, 'I AM sent me over.'" He also told Moses to drop His name, saying, "The Lord, the God of your ancestors... that's my handle forever, and it's how I want to be remembered generation after generation. "Hit up the Israelite elders and lay it down: 'The Lord, the God of our forefathers, has got our backs and is ready to haul us out of Egypt misery to a place dripping with milk and honey.' They'll be on board. Then you all need to bounce up to Pharaoh and be like, 'The Lord needs us to take a three-day wilderness break to do our thing and sacrifice.' But I know Pharaoh's gonna be stubborn until I show him my power moves. Then, he'll have no choice but to let you go. And guess what? You're gonna leave with more than you came with. You'll get the Egyptians to hand over their bling and threads, and you'll deck out your kids. Basically, you'll clean up Egypt."

Moses was getting the jitters, "But what if they call BS on me and say, 'Nah, the Lord never showed up'?" The Lord was like, "Yo, what's that in your grip?" "Just a staff," Moses said. "Chuck it on the ground," God directed. Moses did, and boom, it turned into a snake, and Moses noped out of there. God was like, "Come on, grab its tail." Moses did, and just like that, it was a staff again. God's like, "This is proof so they'll buy that the God of their OGs— Abraham, Isaac, and Jacob—has hit you up." God wasn't done. "Shove your hand in your coat." Moses did and pulled it out looking all leprous, like snow. "Tuck it back in," God said. Moses did, and his hand was back to normal. God's like, "If sign one doesn't convince them, sign two should do the trick. Still no? Scoop Nile water, and on the dry land, it'll turn to blood." Moses was stalling, "Look, talking ain't my thing. I'm all thumbs with words." God clapped back, "Who made mouths? Who decides who can or can't see, or speak, or hear? That's on me. Now hit the road; I'll be your speech coach." Moses played his last card, "Lord, can't you send someone else?" That got God heated, "Isn't Aaron your bro? He's got the gift of gab. He's actually on his way to you. Tell him what's up; I'll guide you both on what to say. He'll be your hype man. You? You'll be like a god to him. Don't forget your staff; that's your magic wand for the signs."

Moses bounced back to his father-in-law Jethro and was like, "Yo, I gotta check on my fam in Egypt, see if they're still kicking." Jethro was chill about it, "Peace out, Moses." Then, God hit up Moses in Midian, "Time to head back to Egypt, dude. Those who had beef with you? Toast. They're gone." So, Moses packed up his fam, hopped them on a donkey, and headed to Egypt with God's magic staff in hand. God was like, "When you hit up Egypt again, show Pharaoh all those sick tricks I taught you. But FYI, I'm gonna make his heart as hard as a rock; dude won't let the peeps go. You'll tell him, 'Listen up, Pharaoh, Israel's my firstborn. Let my kid worship me. No? Okay, your firstborn's gonna have a real bad time.'" En route, at a campsite, things got real tense when the Lord came for Moses, but Zipporah, quick on her feet, did a quick snip-snip on her son, threw the foreskin at Moses's feet, and was like, "You're totally a blood-groom to me now." That cooled things down. "Blood-groom," she said, eyeing the circumcision. God told Aaron, "Go hit up Moses in the desert." So, Aaron did, found Moses at God's mountain, and they had a bro hug. Moses spilled everything God said and the signs he was supposed to pull off. They got all the Israelite VIPs together, Aaron laid down the whole spiel from God, did the signs, and the peeps were all in. Hearing God was on their side, they were super psyched, threw down a worship session. Then, Moses and Aaron rolled up to Pharaoh, "God's memo: 'Let my people go for a desert rave in my honor.'" Pharaoh was like, "'Lord' who? Never heard of him. Plus, no way I'm letting Israel take a break." They're like, "Seriously, God wants us to party in the desert, or things might get ugly with plagues or swords." Pharaoh wasn't having any of it, "Moses, Aaron, quit distracting everyone from work. Get back on it!" He was all, "Look at all these folks, and you want them to just chill? Nah." Pharaoh hit the Israelites with a new rule outta nowhere, "Yo, no more free straw for your bricks, find your own!" He demanded the same brick quota, though, calling them lazybones for wanting to dip out and worship. Pharaoh was like, "Pile on more work; keep 'em too busy for lies."

The taskmasters and foremen spread Pharaoh's new rule,

making life extra crispy for the Israelites, hunting down straw while still hitting those brick quotas. The Israelite foremen got a taste of the whip for not keeping up, making them wonder why they even bothered clocking in.

So, they shot over to Pharaoh, totally frazzled, "Why you gotta do us dirty like this? No straw but all the bricks? You're setting us up to fail!" Pharaoh clapped back, "Lazy, that's what you are! Just looking for excuses to slack off!" The foremen realized they were stuck between a rock and a hard place, especially after getting dissed by Pharaoh. They stumbled upon Moses and Aaron and unloaded, "Thanks a lot, guys! You've made us smell worse than leftovers in Pharaoh's eyes. Now he's got even more reason to wipe us out!"

Moses, feeling all sorts of stressed, shot a prayer up to God, "Yo, God, why'd you even send me? Since I started talking to Pharaoh, it's been nothing but trouble for the peeps, and you haven't done squat to save them!". God was like, "Chill, Moses. You're about to see what I've got up my sleeve. Pharaoh's gonna get a taste of my strong hand, and he'll practically shove you guys out of Egypt." Then, God laid it down for Moses,

"I'm the OG Lord. Told Abe, Ike, and Jake I'd hook them up with Canaan, and I haven't forgotten. Heard my peeps groaning under Egyptian whips and I'm on it. I'll bust you out of slavery, flex my muscles with some epic smackdowns, and make you my VIPs. You'll see, I'm the real deal, the one getting you out of Egypt's grind. I'll hand over Canaan on a silver platter, just like I promised your ancestors."

But when Moses relayed God's pep talk, the Israelites were too beat down and spirit-broken to catch the vibe. God then tagged Moses, "Roll up to Pharaoh and tell him it's time to let my crew go." But Moses was doubting, "Man, if my own homies won't listen, why would Pharaoh, especially with my stutter?" God kept pushing Moses and Aaron, setting them up for the ultimate showdown with Egypt's big boss. Moses hit up Pharaoh with a divine message, but was all, "Yo, my speech game is weak, why would Pharaoh even listen?" The Big G was like, "Check it, Mo, you're gonna be like a superhero to Pharaoh, and your bro Aaron is your hype man." God laid down the plan: "You'll tell Aaron what to spit, and he'll lay it down so Pharaoh gets the memo to free your crew. But, imma make Pharaoh play hard to get by toughening up his heart.

Then, I'll show off some next-level miracles in Egypt." God made it crystal: "Egypt's gonna know who's boss when I flex on them, and the Israelites will walk out like they own the place." Moses and Aaron did their thing, just like God directed. Moses was rocking 80 years, and Aaron was at 83 when they rolled up to Pharaoh. God's game plan involved a magic trick showdown. He told Moses, "When Pharaoh's craving some magic, get Aaron to throw down his staff. It's gonna turn into a snake." And boom, Aaron's staff snake chomped down on the magician's snake staffs, showing who's the real MVP. But Pharaoh's heart was icy; he wasn't feeling it, just like God predicted.

Then came the waterworks – literally. God was like, "Moses, catch Pharaoh at his morning Nile stroll and hit him with, 'God's got a message: Let my people dip so they can throw me a desert party. But you're playing deaf. Watch this – Nile's gonna turn to blood.'" And just like that, Moses and Aaron turned the Nile into a no-go drink zone, with fish belly-up and Egyptians gagging. But Pharaoh's magicians pulled the same party trick, so Pharaoh shrugged it off and kept his heart locked tight.

After a week of blood-water drama, Egypt was thirstier than ever, and Pharaoh was still not budging. The stage was set for God to up the ante, and Moses and Aaron were just getting started on the most epic freedom quest in history.

Moses was tasked with another mission, heading straight to Pharaoh's crib to lay it down: "Listen up, Pharaoh, God's got a message for ya: 'Let my crew go hit up a worship sesh in the desert.'" But Pharaoh was playing tough, so God decided to spice things up with a frog invasion. Imagine, frogs everywhere – in your bed, your oven, even in your mixing bowls. Total frogocalypse. God told Moses to give Aaron the nod, and with a swing of his staff over Egypt's waters, bam, frogs galore. Even the Egyptian magicians tried to pull the same stunt with their magic tricks but ended up adding more frogs to the mix. Pharaoh, now knee-deep in frogs, was desperate. He begged Moses and Aaron, "Pray to your God to take these frogs away, and I'll let your people go." Moses, feeling a bit generous, gave Pharaoh the choice of "when," and Pharaoh was like, "Do it tomorrow." Moses agreed, showing Pharaoh that there's no one quite like their God.

After Moses hit up God, the frogs got the memo and clocked out, leaving Egypt stinking worse than a week-old gym locker. But Pharaoh, seeing some relief, decided to ghost Moses and Aaron, keeping his heart as stiff as a board.

God wasn't done yet. He told Moses to have Aaron turn Egypt's dust into gnats, and just like that, people and animals were covered in these pesky critters. The Egyptian magicians tried to compete but fell short, admitting, "This is God's doing." Yet, Pharaoh's heart remained uncracked, ignoring the clear signs laid out before him. God hit up Moses for another early morning meet-up with Pharaoh. "Yo, Moses, catch Pharaoh by the river and drop this: 'God's saying let my squad go worship, or else He's gonna unleash a flypocalypse on you, your peeps, and your pads. But Goshen, where the homies live, will be chill, no flies there. That's how you'll know God's the real MVP here.'"

Just like that, Egypt turned into a no-fly zone, except it was all flies, everywhere but in Goshen. Pharaoh, feeling the pressure, hit up Moses and Aaron, "Alright, go do your God thing, but keep it in Egypt, okay?" But Moses was like, "Nah, that ain't gonna work. We gotta go off-grid for three days. Doing it here would totally rub the Egyptians the wrong way." Pharaoh, trying to play it cool, was like, "Fine, dip out to the desert, but don't ghost me. And pray for me, yeah?" Moses agreed but warned, "Don't try to play us again, alright?" After Moses prayed, God called off the flies, making Egypt a no-buzz zone again. Yet, Pharaoh's heart was still as stiff as a stale baguette, and he kept the Israelites on lockdown. Next up, God was like, "Moses, round two. Tell Pharaoh, 'Let my people go worship. If not, your animals are gonna have a bad time.'" God was clear: Israel's pets would be fine, but Egypt's would be dropping like flies. Sure enough, the next day, Egyptian livestock was hitting the ground, but the Israelites' animals were just chilling. Pharaoh checked it out, saw it was legit, but still kept his heart on ice, refusing to let the people go.

God was like, "Moses, Aaron, grab some soot from the furnace. Moses, when you toss it up in front of Pharaoh, it's gonna turn into a nasty case of boils all over Egypt." So, they did just that, and boom, everyone, including Pharaoh's magicians, was breaking out in boils. Pharaoh, though, kept his heart as hard as a rock, ignoring them just as God predicted. Next up, God had Moses hit up Pharaoh again with a wake-up call, "God's about to show you His mixtape of plagues, and you're not gonna like this next track. Let my people hit up a festival to worship me, or Egypt's about to get the worst hailstorm playlist ever." God was ready to drop this epic hail to prove there's no DJ like Him on Earth. He even gave Pharaoh a heads-up to save his livestock, but Pharaoh kept playing games. As ordered, Moses cranked the volume on this hailstorm so severe it was like nothing Egypt had ever seen before. It was an all-out blitz on everything outside, except in Goshen; that place was chill because that's where the homies lived. After his place got trashed, Pharaoh hit up Moses and Aaron, all, "My bad, I've sinned. God's the real deal, and I messed up. Make the hail stop, and I'll let your people go." Moses was like, "Aight, I'll ask God to dial it back once I'm out of the city. But I know you and your crew still don't get it." Sure enough, as soon as the weather cleared, Pharaoh was back to his old tricks, heart locked up tighter than before, still not letting the Israelites dip. Just like God said, Pharaoh wasn't about to change his tune. God hit up Moses, "Yo, head over to Pharaoh. I've got

his heart and his crew's hearts on lockdown so I can flex with my signs. You'll have some wild stories to tell your kids and grandkids about how I showed Egypt who's boss." Moses and Aaron bounced into Pharaoh's spot, laying it down, "God's like, 'How long you gonna act too cool for school? Let my peeps go worship me. If not, brace yourself 'cause I'm about to unleash a locust squad tomorrow. They'll be everywhere, eating up everything you got left after the hailstorm hit and making Egypt a snack bar.'" Pharaoh's advisors were freaking out, "Yo, how long we gonna let this dude mess with us? Let's cut them loose before Egypt's a total goner." So, Pharaoh's like, "Alright, Moses, Aaron, get back here. You can dip to worship your God, but who's rolling with you?". Moses shot back, "Everybody's coming. We're talking kids, grannies, goats, and cows. It's a full-on festival for God.". Pharaoh snarked, "Yeah right, as if I'd let everyone go. Just the guys, and don't get any funny ideas." Then he basically kicked them out. God told Moses, "Wave your staff over Egypt, and watch my locust crew drop in." Moses did just that, and boom, locusts everywhere! They devoured everything green. Egypt was like a scene from a disaster flick.

Pharaoh was quick to hit up Moses and Aaron, "My bad, I messed up big time against your God and you. Hook me up with one more favor, pray this death away." Moses was like, "Cool, I got you," and asked God to chill. God flipped the wind, sweeping all the locusts into the Red Sea. Not one locust left chilling in Egypt. But God wasn't done playing. He kept Pharaoh's heart on ice, and the freedom tour was still on hold.

God gave Moses the next move: "Throw your hand up to the sky, and let's hit Egypt with a blackout like they've never seen." Moses did just that, and bam, Egypt was blanketed in darkness so thick you could feel it. For three whole days, nobody could see a thing. Meanwhile, the Israelites were chilling in the light. Pharaoh was like, "Fine, go worship God, but leave your animals." Moses clapped back, "Nah, we're taking our animals too. We gotta have everything ready for God when we get there". God wasn't having any of Pharaoh's stubbornness, so Pharaoh's heart stayed on lockdown. Pharaoh got all up in Moses' face, "Get out and don't let me catch you slipping; next time you do, it's game over for you.". Moses was like, "Cool, cool, we're done here". Then it was time for the grand finale. God told Moses, "One more

plague and Pharaoh will practically kick you out himself. Tell everyone to borrow some bling from their Egyptian neighbors." The Egyptians were actually feeling the Israelites, and Moses was a bit of a celeb in Egypt. Moses dropped the bomb: "At midnight, God's hitting Egypt hard. Every firstborn is going down, from Pharaoh's kid to the servant's daughter, even the animals. Egypt's gonna be wailing like never before. But the Israelites? They won't even hear a dog bark. It's gonna be clear who God's got a soft spot for." He warned Pharaoh's crew would be begging them to dip, and after dropping that mic, Moses stormed out, boiling mad. God was straight up with Moses, "Pharaoh's not gonna budge, so I'm about to show Egypt my full power." Despite all the signs Moses and Aaron threw down, Pharaoh kept his heart as hard as old gum, refusing to let the Israelites bounce. God hit up Moses and Aaron in Egypt with a new plan: "This month's gonna kick off your calendar. On the tenth, everyone's gotta pick a lamb or a kid for their crew, perfect and young. If your squad's too small to eat a whole one, team up with your neighbors. Keep it until the fourteenth, then, as the sun sets, the whole community's gotta do a cookout." "Here's the deal," God continued, "Slap some of that lamb's blood on your doorframes. That night, chow down on the lamb, roasted, not raw or boiled, with some flatbread and bitter greens. Rock your kicks, your cloak, and your walking stick. Eat up quick; it's God's Passover."

God laid it out: "I'm rolling through Egypt tonight, hitting every firstborn. But when I see the blood on your door, I'll skip your house. No bad vibes for you. This is gonna be a night to remember forever, a big-time festival for me. For seven days, you'll eat unleavened bread. Day one, clean house—no yeast allowed. First and last day, you're throwing holy parties, and don't even think about working, except for making food." "This is non-negotiable, for now and forever. From the 14th at sundown to the 21st, it's flatbread only. If anyone even thinks about eating yeast, they're out, whether they're visiting or from around here. Seriously, no leavened stuff. Keep it flat." Moses rallied the elders: "Pick out your Passover lamb, get that blood on your doorposts. That's our sign for God to pass over us when the smackdown hits Egypt." He added, "This is a forever thing. When we get to the promised land, we keep this up. When your kids ask 'What's up with Passover?' you'll say, 'It's all about how God got us out of Egypt and saved our homes when he was laying down the law on the Egyptians.'" The Israelites did as they were told, just like Moses and Aaron laid out.

MOSES' QUEST FOR FREEDOM

So, at the stroke of midnight, God pulled off the ultimate power move and hit every firstborn in Egypt, from Pharaoh's numero uno to the dude in the dungeon, and even the firstborn animals weren't spared. Pharaoh, in his PJs, and all the Egyptians woke up to a nightmare, with every house mourning someone.

Pharaoh hit up Moses and Aaron in the middle of the night like, "Yo, bounce out of Egypt with your crew and go do your God thing. Take your sheep, goats, whatever, and don't forget to leave me a good review". The Egyptians were basically shoving the Israelites out the door, fearing they'd all be ghosted next. The Israelites, in a rush, grabbed their dough before it could even get its rise on, wrapping up their baking gear and booking it.

Following Moses' pro tip, they scored some serious bling from the Egyptians—silver, gold, you name it—basically making a fortune overnight. So, they dipped out from Rameses to Succoth, a massive squad of about 600,000 dudes, not counting the fam and a wild mix of others tagging along, plus a ton of animals. They cooked up the dough they brought from Egypt into flatbread since they had to jet so fast they couldn't even wait for bread to rise. They had been chilling in Egypt for exactly 430 years, and right on cue, at the end of those years, they made the grand exit. That night was lit, a special watch night for God, marking the epic move from Egypt. This was the night they kept watch, a tradition kept alive by the Israelites, generation after generation. God hit up Moses and Aaron with the ultimate Passover how-to: "Listen up, this feast is VIP only. If you've bought someone, they're in after a little snip-snip. But if you're just crashing or getting paid, you're on the outside looking in. This party's indoors—no doggy bags, and keep the bones intact. It's an all-Israelite rave, but if a foreign buddy wants to join, they gotta commit—every guy gets a ticket via circumcision. Then, they're practically family. Same rules for everyone, locals and newbies."

The Israelites were all in, following God's playbook to the letter, as relayed by Moses and Aaron. That very day, God kick-started their epic exit from Egypt, soldiers in formation. Then God's like, "Every firstborn? They're mine now, from humans to fluffy ones." Moses to the crew: "Circle this day—it's when you ghosted Egypt and left slavery on read, thanks to God's epic flex. This month is now your calendar's headliner. And when you hit that deluxe spot flowing with milk and honey—props to your forefathers—you'll throw this bash annually. A solid week of unleavened bread feasting, wrapping up with a huge finale for God. Yeast is basically Voldemort here; not even a speck allowed. This feast is your storytime for the kiddos—it's a biggie, a tangible 'don't forget' note, so the epic saga of our Egyptian jailbreak always stays fresh.

Once you're chilling in the land of milk and honey, keep the party tradition alive, dedicating every firstborn male to God. Got an animal firstborn? Either swap it out or it's curtains. And your sons? Gotta buy them back. And when your little one hits you with a 'Why are we doing this?' drop this wisdom: 'God went full beast mode to spring us from Egypt, the ultimate lockdown. Pharaoh was playing tough, so God hit where it hurt, taking out every firstborn. That's why we throw God a barbecue but keep our boys in the clear. It's our forever reminder, literally hands-on and front-of-mind, of how God led the ultimate breakout from Egypt for us.

When Pharaoh finally hit the road and let the squad go, God didn't take them on the express route through Philistine territory, even though it was the fast track. God was like, "Nah, they might see some action and decide to U-turn back to Egypt." So, He took them on a scenic route towards the Red Sea, through the wilderness, all lined up like they were heading into battle. Moses, being the history buff he was, didn't forget to pack Joseph's bones because Joseph had been adamant like, "When God shows up to help you out, don't forget to take my bones out of here". They bounced from Succoth and made camp at Etham, right on the edge of nowhere. God was leading the way like a true MVP, with a cloud pillar by day to guide them and a fire pillar by night to light up their path. This wasn't a one-night thing; it was all day, every day, without fail. Then, God was like, "Moses, let's shake things up. Tell everyone to camp by Pi-hahiroth between Migdol and the sea. It'll look like they're lost in the desert maze." God planned to make Pharaoh think the Israelites were just wandering around cluelessly so he would chase after them. And, boy, did Pharaoh fall for it! As soon as Pharaoh heard they dipped, he was like, "What did we just do, letting our free labor walk out?" So, he rallied his chariot squad, picked his 600 finest rides plus all the other chariots in Egypt, and went after the Israelites, full throttle. God made Pharaoh stubborn again, and he chased the Israelites down, catching them camping by the sea. The Israelites saw the Egyptians coming and were scared out of their minds, calling out to God and throwing shade at Moses, "Were there no graves in Egypt? You dragged us out here to die in the wilderness!"

But Moses was chill, telling them, "Don't sweat it. Just watch how God's gonna save us today. Those Egyptians tailing us? You won't even see them by tomorrow. God's got this fight; you just keep it down and watch. God was like, "Moses, why the waterworks? Tell the crew to pack up. You, with your staff, give the sea a little wave and let's make a road of dry land through it. The Egyptians? Oh, they'll follow, but it's showtime for me. I'm gonna snag some serious glory from Pharaoh and his speed squad."

So, the guardian angel and the cloud posse got a new gig—blocking duty. They moved to the back, throwing shade and light, making sure the Egyptians and the Israelites didn't mix for a whole night. Moses did a grand gesture over the sea, and just like that, with a blast from God's wind machine, the sea got walls, turning into a dry runway for the Israelites to strut through. Meanwhile, the Egyptians thought it was a good idea to take the same path. Big mistake.

In the wee hours, God turned his divine spotlight on the Egyptians and cranked up the chaos dial. He made their chariot wheels wobble like they were in a bumper car arena, and they were like, "Let's bounce, the Lord's playing for Team Israel.". God told Moses, "Wave goodbye," and as he did, the sea snapped back like a giant rubber band, swallowing up the entire Egyptian fan club—chariots, horsemen, the lot. Not a single one made it out for a sequel. The Israelites? They walked through the sea with an oceanic high-five on either side, landing safely on the other side. Witnessing the Egyptian navy turned submarine, they were all kinds of impressed with God's might, gaining a newfound respect for Moses and

a fresh playlist of songs praising God's name. Moses and the Israelites dropped a hot track for the Lord, a real sea-shanty hit. They were all, "Let's sing to the Lord, 'cause he just dropped the beat on Pharaoh's squad in the sea." The Lord turned into their hype man, their melody of victory. Moses was like, "This is my jam, and I'll praise my God, the OG, and lift Him higher than my Wi-Fi signal." "The Lord's in warrior mode; just check His battle tag," they sang. He turned Pharaoh's ride and his posse into an underwater spectacle, elite troops and all sinking faster than a bad tweet. "God's right hand? Straight-up fire, smashing the enemy like a bug," they continued. "He rolled out the red carpet of wrath, and they got burnt to a crisp."

Then they hit the chorus about the sea going all Moses on command, walls of water turning solid just because God sneezed at them. The enemy was all, "Imma catch up, loot, and flex on 'em," but God just exhaled, and boom, deep-sea diving without the gear. Sunk like the Titanic, no survivors. "Who's like You, God? Out here flexing in holiness, collecting praise like it's vintage vinyl, and doing the impossible?" the song went. God's fans, Israel, got VIP backstage passes, leading them to His exclusive after-party location. "Nations will hear and get the shivers, Philistines will freak, and Moab's tough guys will melt. Canaan's gonna need a chill pill," they sang about their tour. With God's arm flexed, enemies turned into statues, waiting for God's chosen to drop the mic as they passed through. "You're setting us up in your divine penthouse, Lord. You've got the place decked out and ready." And they closed with a promise of God's eternal headlining, "The Lord's gonna reign, not just for a season but forever and ever!"

After the main event, Miriam, with her girl gang, grabbed tambourines, starting the after-party. "Sing to the Lord, for He's sky-high exalted; horse and rider got a sea burial," Miriam led, echoing her bro's hit single. So Moses and crew hit up the Wilderness of Shur, doing their desert marathon without a water station in sight for three whole days. They finally stumbled upon Marah, but plot twist – the water was straight-up nasty, hence the name Marah, which means "Bitter"; talk about on-the-nose branding. The crew was not vibing with the hydration situation, hitting up Moses with a collective, "So, any plans for a drink, or are we just gonna stand here parched?" Moses, in a classic "I got this" move, hit up the Lord, who pointed out a tree. Moses chucked it into the water, and bam, it turned into a 5-star beverage.

Skipping ahead, they found themselves at Elim, where it's basically an oasis with twelve springs and seventy palm trees – talk about a desert deluxe package. Now, enter the Wilderness of Sin (not what it sounds like, folks). The Israelites were on the struggle bus by day 15, post-Egypt escape. The fam was hangry, throwing shade at Moses and Aaron, fantasizing about the Egyptian buffet they left behind. The Lord, in a move of divine room service, was like, "Imma rain bread from heaven." He set up a divine test of obedience involving daily bread pickup, with a double portion pre-Sabbath to cover their day off. Moses and Aaron gave the squad a pep talk about the evening meal and morning bread menu, courtesy of the Lord, because He was over their grumbling directed at Him. Come evening, quail covered the camp like a feathery blanket, and by morning, the ground was sporting a layer of desert frosties, aka manna. The Israelites were like, "What's this?" Moses schooled them, "It's heavenly grub, folks. Gather as per appetite, no more, no less." Some tried hoarding, but their stash turned into a wormy, stinky mess by sunrise, proving Moses right, again. They collected this manna every day, except on Sabbath, when they chilled, because God insisted on a day off. This manna scene went on for forty years until they hit Canaan. They kept a manna sample in a jar for the 'Gram, or, you know, as a testament for future squads, showing God's OG food delivery system. And that's how they rolled, with God's cloud and fire GPS leading the way, and manna on tap till they reached civilization.

THE TEN COMMANDMENTS

1 "Only vibe with me. No other gods."
2 "Don't create fake idols. I'm all you need."
3 "Respect my name. Don't throw it around lightly."
4 "Sundays (or whichever day) are for resting, not for stress. Chill out"
5" Shoutout to your parents. Give them the respect they deserve."
6 "Life is precious. Don't take it."
7 "Stay loyal to your partner."
8 "If it's not yours, don't take it."
9 "Keep your stories straight - no spreading fake news about your squad"

10 "Be content. Don't crave what others have."

When the Israelites caught the epic display – thunder booming like the bass at a concert, lightning flashing like a strobe light, and a mountain smoking like it was prepping for a grand entrance, their knees were knocking. They huddled up and were like, "Moses, bro, you chat with us, but keep the Almighty on silent mode, yeah? Direct convos with Him sound like a one-way ticket to the afterlife." Moses, trying to calm the squad, was like, "Ease up, folks. This whole supernatural show is just God laying down a vibe check. He's not here to spook you; He's making sure you respect the game and don't step out of line." But still, the crowd kept their distance, watching as Moses walked into what looked like the heart of a shadow realm where God was setting the scene. Then the Almighty slid into the DMs with some divine instructions for Moses, "Alright, here's the drill for my chosen crew: You've all seen me turn up the volume from the heavens. Now, listen up. Don't go flexing with silver or gold idols. That's playing with fire, and not the kind we roast s'mores on.

"Instead, throw together a humble dirt altar. That's where

you'll bring your BBQ offerings and your peace offerings – whether it's from your herd of sheep or your lineup of cattle. I'll swing by and drop blessings on every spot that echoes my name. But if you're thinking about getting fancy with a carved stone altar, put those tools away. We're keeping it organic, untouched by human hands. And forget about building stairs; we're not trying to turn this into a peep show. Keep it respectful, keep it holy.

"Let's get something straight," God continued, laying out the blueprint for righteousness. "This isn't just about following orders; it's about setting a standard, a way of life that's all about respect, reverence, and rolling with the divine flow."

PSALMS

Psalm 1

1 Big ups to the one who doesn't roll with the shady crowd, Doesn't post up in the hangout spot with the wrong crew, Or vibe in the squad that thrives on throwing shade!

2 Instead, this dude's all about vibing with the Lord's texts, DM'ing His wisdom day and night.

3 He's like that influencer tree planted right by the hydration station, Dropping fresh fruit right on schedule, leaves all lush, Everything he touches just blooms.

4 But the shady bunch? Nah, they're like last season's trends, Gone with the first gust of wind.

5 So, when the ultimate squad meets up, The wicked won't even be on the guest list, Nor the sinners in the circle of the chill.

6 'Cause the Lord's got His eyes on the squad of the straight-up, But the path of the shady? It's a one-way ticket to Ghost Town.

Psalm 14

1 Picture this: A total face-palm moment when someone's like, "God? LOL, nope." They're out here messing up, doing the most with their bad vibes playlist. No playlist trackers found doing a solid good deed. Zero.

2 Up in the cloud, the Lord's scrolling through humanity's feed, Hoping to spot someone wise, someone swiping right on God.

3 But nah, everyone's ghosted; it's like a mass "left on read" situation. All got caught in the wrong chat; not a single soul passing the vibe check.

4 Do these troublemakers ever hit pause, or nah? They're out here treating my crew like we're just another snack. No shoutouts to the Lord, like ever.

5 But watch them get shook, 'cause God's not ghosting the squad.

6 You've got those making life tough for the low-key heroes, But peep this: the Lord's their epic safe zone.

7 Dreaming of that glow-up for Israel, straight outta Zion! When the Lord flips the script for his crew, Jacob's gonna throw down a dance party, Israel's gonna be all heart-eyes.

Psalm 16

1 Those holy folks down here? They're the cream of the crop, my kind of crowd.

2 Chasing after other 'gods' just racks up the drama; count me out from that mess.

3 Lord, You're my big win, filling my cup; You've got my future locked down.

4 Got me living in the sweet spot; life's looking pretty lush from here.

5 Hats off to the Lord, giving me the night-time pep talks, sorting my thoughts.

6 With the Lord as my guide, I'm steady as a rock, not budging an inch.
7 So my heart's jumping for joy, and I'm totally at ease, body and soul.

8 You're not about to leave me hanging, Lord; not gonna let me fade to nothing.

9 You show me the way to real living, with a joy overload in Your presence, endless party at Your right hand.

Psalm 18

1 Yo, big love to the Lord, my muscle and might,

2 He's my solid ground, my safe house, my hero in flight, My God, my rock where I hide, My shield, my victory song, my tower high.

3 Hit up the Lord, 'cause he's worth all the hype,

Saved me from foes, those vibe killers of life.
4 Death's ropes were cinching tight, fear's flood rising high,

5 Death's noose and Sheol's grip had me eyeing my demise.

6 In my panic, I hollered to the Lord, yelled for my God's aid. He tuned into my frequency, my SOS he swayed.

7 Earth rocked and rolled, mountains shuddered, scared stiff, Anger-fired smoke billowing from Him, making rifts.

8 He breathed out fire, a blaze from his lips did fly,

9 Bent the heavens, came down, dark storm clouds riding by.
10 On a cherub he surfed, on wind wings, he did glide,

11 Darkness his secret spot, storm clouds his hide.

12 His brightness broke through, with hail and coals in his wake,

13 Thundering from heaven, his voice made everything shake.

14 His arrows scattered enemies, lightning made them freak,

15 Ocean beds bared, earth's bones laid bare for all to peek, At your fierce rebuke, Lord, at your nostrils' fiery leak.

16 From on high, he reached, grabbed me from deep water's clutch,

17 Saved me from foes, strong haters, too much.

18 They jumped me in my down day, but the Lord held me up.

19 He set me in wide-open spaces; his love didn't let up.

20 Rewarded for my right living, cleaned hands got me a fresh start,

21 Kept to the Lord's path, didn't let evil take heart.

22 His rules were my road map, didn't stray or depart,

23 Kept clean, steered clear of my own sinful art.

24 So the Lord hooked me up, saw my hands were clean,

25 To the faithful, you show yourself loyal, make the crooked scene seen.

26 You save humble folks but give the proud their due,

27 Light up my life; my God turns my darkness into something new.

28 With you, barriers break, God-powered, I can leap,

29 Your way's perfect, Lord, your word's a promise to keep,

A shield for all who duck for cover, into your safety leap.

30 Who's God but our Lord? Who's a rock but our God?

31 He wraps me in power, makes my path not odd.

32 Deer's feet he gives, sets me up on the heights,

33 Trains me for battle, my arms ready for fights.

34 Your saving help's my shield; your right hand holds me tight,

Your help makes me great, sets my steps just right.

35 You cleared a wide path, no twisting my ankle in flight,

36 I chased my enemies down, didn't quit till they took flight.

37 I smashed them so they couldn't stand, floored by my might,

38 You armed me strong for battle, made my opponents a sorry sight.

39 You made my enemies turn their backs, in defeat, they take flight,

40 You silenced those who hate me, made them fade out of sight.

41 They screamed for help, but no one saved; to the Lord, but he stayed quiet,

42 I ground them to dust, threw them out, street dirt, no riot.

43 You freed me from people's fights; you set me on top, a sight,

44 Foreigners obey me at a word, hearing me, they submit, no fight.

45 Foreigners fade, leave their forts shaking in fright,

46 The Lord lives! Bless my rock! My salvation's God lifts me high.

47 The God who avenges me, puts nations under my sway,

48 Saves me from enemies, you lift me over those who betray.

49 So, I'll thank you among the nations, Lord, sing praises to your name,

50 Great victories for his king, shows unfailing love, forever the same, To David and his line, forever under your fame.

Psalm 19
1 The sky's literally shouting out God's majesty, and that big blue dome is spilling the tea on what He's done.

2 Day to day, it's like they're dropping beats of wisdom; night after night, they're streaming knowledge without a pause.

3 They don't even need words; no sound has to be heard.

4 But their vibe? It's universal, reaching every corner of the globe, giving a shoutout to the sun in its celestial crib.

5 The sun's like a groom bouncing out to his wedding, or an athlete pumped to crush the track.

6 From east to west, it's on a non-stop tour, and there's not a spot that doesn't feel its vibe.

7 God's guidebook is on point, flipping lives around; His truths are solid, giving the clueless a clue.

8 His rules are a total mood lift, His commands are like sunshine for the eyes.

9 Respect for God is clean, lasting forever; His decisions are legit and totally fair.

10 More precious than stacks of gold, even the pure stuff; sweeter than the drip from the honeycomb.

11 They're also a heads-up for His peeps, stick to them and the rewards are epic.

12 But who can spot their own slip-ups? Yo, clear out my hidden mess.

13 And keep me from thinking I know better, don't let those vibes take the wheel. Then I'm all clear, no drama.

14 Let the chat from my lips and the vibe of my heart be cool with You, Lord, my solid ground and my rescuer.

Psalm 29

1 When things get tough, may the Big Boss upstairs hit you up with some backup; let the OG of Jacob be your shield.

2 Hoping He slides into your DMs with some divine support from His holy crib, keeping you boosted from Zion HQ.

3 Fingers crossed He remembers all the cool stuff you've done and gives a thumbs up to your offerings. Pause for effect.

4 Wishing He hooks you up with what you're vibing for and makes all your plans smash.

5 Let's go wild celebrating your wins, waving our team's flag high 'cause of our God. Praying He checks off your wishlist.

6 Now, it's crystal clear the Lord's got His faves; He shouts out from the heavens, flexing His power moves.

7 Some might flex with their fancy rides or their fast horses, but we're all about name-dropping the Lord our God.

8 While they're hitting the dirt and eating dust, we're popping up and holding strong.

9 Yo, Lord, make our leader a legend! Hook us up with a win when we hit You up.

Psalm 23

1 The Lord's my spotlight and my hero— who's gonna scare me?

2 The Lord's the fortress of my life— who's gonna freak me out?

3 When the bad vibes crew tried to take me down, my opposers and haters just tripped and face-planted.

4 Even if I'm like, surrounded by a squad, my heart's chill; even if it feels like battle royale mode,

5 I'm still vibing. There's just one thing I'm hitting up the Lord for, it's my top wishlist item: to crash at the Lord's place for all my days, catching the Lord's aesthetic and chilling in His chill zone.

6 'Cause He's got this secret hideout for me when things get wild;

7 He tucks me under the shadow of His tent; He's got me standing tall on a solid rock.

8 That's when I'll be like, head and shoulders above the drama around me;

9 I'll throw a party in His tent, with all the hype. I'll belt out tunes and drop beats for the Lord.

10 Yo, Lord, listen up when I holler; throw some kindness my way and holla back.

11 My heart's all, "You gotta seek His vibe."

12 Lord, I'm all in on seeking your vibe.

13 Don't go ghost on me; don't get salty and bounce.

14 You've been my squad; don't ghost me or ditch me, O God, my hero.

15 Even if my folks bail on me, the Lord's got my back.

16 With all these challengers, break it down for me, Lord, and guide me on the smooth track.

17 Don't let me fall into my haters' trap, 'cause there are plenty talking trash, spewing hate.

18 I'm holding onto the hope of catching the Lord's vibe in the here and now.

19 Hang tight for the Lord; amp up, keep your heart pumped. Just wait for the Lord.

Psalm 29

1 Give it up for the Lord, you cosmic crew, shout out to the Lord for His epic power and might.

2 Show the Lord the props He deserves; vibe with the Lord in the glow of His awesomeness.

3 The Lord's voice? It's over the oceans, booming with majesty— the Lord, over the endless waters,

4 the Lord's voice, dropping power, the Lord's voice, dazzling with beauty.

5 The Lord's voice can snap cedars like twigs;

6 He's got the cedars of Lebanon doing the breakdance.

7 He makes Lebanon jump like a young calf, Sirion bounces like a wild ox in a rave.

8 The Lord's voice flashes with firework sparks.

9 The Lord's voice rocks the wilds; He's got the wilderness of Kadesh feeling the vibe.

10 The Lord's voice brings life and peels back the forest layers.

11 In His temple, everyone's shouting, "Glory!"

12 The Lord's got His throne above the flood;

13 He's kinging it forever. the Lord hooks His people up with power;

14 He showers His people with chill vibes and peace

Psalm 30

1 Gonna hype you up, Lord, coz you hoisted me up and didn't let my haters have the last laugh over me.

2 Yo, Lord my God, I hit you up for help, and boom, you patched me up.

3 Lord, you pulled me out from the gloom; kept me from being a goner, heading to the shadows.

4 Belt it out for the Lord, all you loyal folks, and big up His sacred name.

5 His stormy mood? Just a hot sec, but His thumbs up? Lifetime warranty.

6 Tears might crash the sleepover, but come sunrise, it's all smiles. Felt all snug, I was like,

7 "Ain't nothing gonna knock me down." Lord, when you were all about that blessing, you had me solid as a mountain; but the sec you looked away, boy, did I freak.

8 Lord, I shot you a message; was all about seeking your good vibes: "What's the win in my checkout, if I dip to the shadows?

9 Can dust throw you a rave? Can it shout out your real talk? Lord, tune in and throw me some mercy; Lord, be my sidekick."

10 You flipped my weep-fest into a dance-off; ditched my grunge gear for party threads, so I can jam out to you and not clam up.

11 Lord my God, I'll shout your praises non-stop.

Psalm 34

1 Gonna big up the Lord non-stop; His hype track's gonna be on loop in my playlist.

2 Bragging rights go to the Lord; the low-key crew will hear it and get all kinds of happy.

3 Let's get loud about how awesome the Lord is; join the fan club and let's lift His name on high, together-style.

4 Shot Him a DM, and He hit me back, pulled me out of the mess I was in.
Eyes on Him? You'll glow up, no facepalms here, only pride.

5 This dude, right here, called out, and the Lord was all ears, scooped him up from the drama.

6 Angel squad of the Lord camps out around those giving Him respect, and bam – safe and sound.

7 Go on, give Him a try and see He's the real deal. Mega joy for those who chill in His shadow!

8 All you set-apart folks, show the Lord some respect, coz those who do, they don't miss out.

9 Even the fierce ones hit a rough patch, but seek the Lord, and you're set – no good thing will you miss.

10 Yo, kiddos, gather 'round; I've got some wisdom to drop about living that Lord-fearing life. Who's keen on loving life, craving more years to soak up the good vibes?

11 Zip it on the evil talk, keep the lies off your lips.

12 Switch up from bad to good, hunt for peace and make it your mission.

13 The Lord's got His eyes on the do-gooders, His ears are all about their SOS.

14 But those troublemakers? He's giving them the cold shoulder, gonna erase them from the memory card.

15 The good guys shout out, and the Lord's all over it, saving them from their hot mess.

16 Close to those feeling the crunch; He's there for the heart-shattered gang.

17 Life throws curveballs at the good ones, but the Lord's their backup every time.

18 He's got them covered, every bone intact; not a single one hits the break.

19 Bad choices spell game over for the baddies, and haters of the good crew? They'll get their due.

21 The Lord's all about saving His crew's life; those who run to Him won't face the music.

Psalm 37

1 Don't stress about those doing wrong, don't be all jelly of folks messing up.

2 They're like fast-fading Snapchat stories, gone like that last piece of pizza.
3 Put your trust in the Big Guy upstairs, do the right thing; chill in your space, you'll be all good.

4 Find your happy in the Lord, and boom, He's got your back, dreams and all.

5 Slide your life into His DMs; trust Him, and watch Him work His magic,

6 Making your good vibes shine bright like daylight, your right moves pop like high noon.

7 Keep it cool before the Lord, wait on Him; don't get all worked up over someone else's highlight reel.

8 Let go of that anger, drop the rage; getting heated only leads to a hot mess.

9 Bad vibes crew? They're on their way out, but those hoping in the Lord, they've got the golden ticket.

10 Fast forward a bit, and the troublemaker's like, "Who?" Search all you want, he's just not there.

11 But the chill folks, they're inheriting the earth, living it up in peace and plenty.

12 Bad guys plot against the good ones, showing their teeth like some bad movie villain.

13 But the Lord's just LOLing at them, 'cause He knows their time's almost up.

14 The baddies have their weapons ready, thinking they can take down the kind-hearted.

15 Spoiler alert: their own schemes backfire, and their weapons? Yeah, they're gonna snap.

16 A little something in the pocket of the good guys beats the overflowing vaults of the naughty.

17 The baddies' strength? It's gonna crack, but the Lord's got the backs of the goodies.

18 The Lord's got His eyes on the legit ones, their legacy's solid, forever.

19 Tough times won't break them, they'll be all set, even when the fridge looks empty.
20 But the wicked? They'll vanish like fog on a sunny day, poof—gone without a trace.

21 The mean ones take without giving back, but the good-hearted are all about sharing the love.

22 Those getting thumbs up from the Lord, they're getting the good land, but the cursed ones? Total shutdown.

23 The Lord's choreographing the steps of a man, finding joy in his journey.

24 Even if he trips, he won't faceplant, 'cause the Lord's holding him up.

25 Been young, now I'm not, but here's the real talk: never seen the good left hanging, nor their kids panhandling.

26 Always open-handed, spreading the love, their kids are like walking heart emojis.

27 Skip the evil, do the good, and you're set for life.

28 'Cause the Lord's all about that justice, He's not ghosting His peeps. 29 They're secure, forever on the guest list, but the baddies' kids? Nowhere to be found.

30 The goodies? They're inheriting the earth, setting up camp there for good.

31 Wisdom's the language of the good, justice is what they're tweeting.

32 God's playbook is their go-to, their steps are all choreographed.

33 The wicked are lurking, eyeing the good, plotting their downfall.

34 But the Lord won't let His homies down, won't let them get a guilty verdict.

35 Hang tight for the Lord, walk His path, He'll lift you up, giving you the earth as a front-row seat to watch the downfall of the wicked.

36 Seen a baddie looking all established, like a luxe tree in Beverly Hills.

37 Came back later, and poof, he was history, went to look him up, and he was just a ghost.

38 Keep an eye on the legit, watch the upright, 'cause peace lovers? They've got a bright future.

39 But the rule-breakers? They're getting wiped out, the wicked's future? Canceled.

40 Rescue ops for the goodies come from the Lord, He's their safe space when things get rough.

41 He's the help and the hero, pulling them from trouble, saving them 'cause they've made Him their go-to hideout.

Psalm 46

1 God's our rock-solid refuge and strength, always there when things go sideways.

2 So, we won't freak out when the Earth gets its shake on, or when mountains decide to take a dive into the ocean's deep blue.

3 Even if the sea throws a tantrum, and mountains start shaking their peaks, we're keeping our cool.

4 There's this river, right? Its streams are pure chill vibes for God's city, the sacred hangout of the Most High.

5 God's in the midst of her; she won't get knocked down. God's got her back when dawn breaks.

6 Nations throw fits, kingdoms crumble; He speaks, and the Earth melts.

7 The Lord Almighty rides with us; the God of Jacob is our safe space. Take that in.

8 Come see the wonders God's cooked up, making the Earth a no-drama zone.

9 He puts an end to wars across the planet, breaking bows, snapping spears, torching tanks.

10 "Drop the weapons," He says, "recognize I'm God, exalted far and wide, boss of the Earth."

11 The Lord Almighty is on our side; the God of Jacob is our safe space.

Psalm 51

1 Yo, God, show me some love, with that kindness of yours that never quits. Wipe my slate clean from all the mess

2 Give my guilt a total scrub down, and get me back to my sin-free self.

3 I'm totally aware of where I've messed up, and my slip-ups are front and center, 24/7.

4 It's like, against You and only You, I've dropped the ball, doing stuff that's way out of line right in Your view. So when You call it like it is, You're totally on point; You're spotless in Your verdict.

5 For real, I've been off track from the get-go;

a troublemaker straight outta the womb.

6 But what You're really after is truth deep down inside, dropping wisdom bombs right in the heart.

7 Hit me with that hyssop, and I'll come out sparkling; wash me, and I'll be brighter than a snow day.

8 Let me catch those vibes of joy and gladness;
make these broken parts of me dance again.

9 Look away from my slip-ups, and delete all traces of my mess-ups.

10 Create a fresh start in me, God, and reboot my spirit to stay the course.

11 Don't cut me off from Your VIP list, or yank Your VIP pass from me.

12 Bring back the thrill of being saved by You;
prop me up with a spirit that's ready to roll.

13 I'll school the wayward in Your ways, and the lost will find their way back to You.

14 Rescue me from this guilt-trip, God, You're my way out—

and my voice will belt out all about Your goodness.

15 God, give me the mic, and I'll drop bars about how awesome You are.

16 You're not about those ritual checklists, or I'd totally do it; You're not after show-off offerings.

17 What gets You is a heart that's all in, cracked wide open and real. You wouldn't turn away from that, God.

18 Make Zion thrive; give it Your stamp of approval; fix up Jerusalem's broken walls.

19 Then You'll get a kick out of the right kind of offerings, the full-on, no-holds-barred kind; then we're talking bulls on Your altar, no kidding.

Psalm 55

1 God, hit me up with a listen, don't ghost me when I'm reaching out.

2 Tune in to my vibe and hit me back. I'm all over the place with my stress,
3 thanks to the hater's talk and the baddies' pressure. They're dumping chaos on me and beefing big time.

4 My heart's doing the cha-cha of fear; death's shadows are doing the tango around me.

5 Panic and shakes have got me booked; horror's got me on its VIP list.

6 I'm like, "Wish I had dove wings! I'd peace out and find my chill zone.

7 I'd yeet myself to the boonies; find my quiet spot in the desert.

8 Sprint to my hideout, away from this gale and hurricane."

9 Lord, throw their words into a blender, 'cause I'm seeing nothing but drama and squabbles in the streets;

10 they're on patrol, making rounds on the city walls. Inside, it's a hot mess of crime and grief;

11 the market's a hotbed for shadiness; deceit doesn't take a day off.

12 It's not some random trolling me— I could handle that; not some enemy flexing— I could just ghost them.

13 But it's you, my equal, my ride-or-die, my bro!

14 We were tight, shared secrets; hit up God's house with the crowd.

15 Surprise them with a one-way ticket down; let them hit up Sheol with all their secrets, 'cause their places are rigged with bad vibes.

16 But I'm dialing up God, and I know He's got my back.

17 Morning, noon, and night, I lay it all out, and He catches every word.

18 Even when it feels like it's me against the world, He's got me walking out scratch-free.

19 God's been boss since forever, and He'll put them in their place, Selah 'cause they're stuck on repeat, no respect for God.

20 My so-called "friend" switched up, broke peace like it was nothing; broke the bro code.

21 His words were like butter, but daggers were up his sleeve. Smooth talker, but his mind's on battle mode.

22 Toss your cares His way, and He'll keep you standing tall; He's not about letting the good ones fall.

23 But those backstabbers? He's got a special place for them; Bloodthirsty and deceitful don't get a full run. Me? I'm sticking with God.

Psalm 62

1 Yo, I'm all chill 'cause God's got me; He's where my help's at.

2 Only He's got my back for real, my rock, my rescue, my safe spot; I'm solid, no wobbling.

3 How long y'all gonna bully someone? You all gang up like he's some shaky wall or a fence about to crash?

4 Their game? Knock him off his high spot. Loving lies, they talk sweet but diss in secret.

5 Just vibe in God's peace, my soul, 'cause He's where my hope's from.

6 Only He's my rock and my saving grace, my fortress; I'm not budging.

7 My rescue and my honor roll on God, my mighty rock. My safe haven is God.

8 Spill your hearts to Him anytime, peeps; He's our hideout.

9 Regular folks are like a breath; VIPs, just a facade. On the scale, they're lighter than air.

10 Don't bank on bullying, or put your bets on stolen goods. Even if your bank account blooms,
don't get hooked on it.

11 God dropped this truth bomb once; I heard it loud and clear twice: Power's all His,

12 And so is loyal love, O Lord. You pay back everyone just desserts.

Psalm 84

1 How epic is your crib, Lord of the Squads?

2 I'm legit craving the vibes of the Lord's place;
my whole being's got FOMO for the living God.

3 Even the tiniest bird scores a cozy spot, and the swift finds a pad for her chicks— right by your epic altars, Boss of the Armies, my Supreme and my God.

4 Blessed are the homies who chill in your space,
singing your praises on repeat. Selah

5 Those folks are winning whose power-up comes from you, with hearts GPS'd on the journey to you.

6 Rolling through life's tough patches, they turn them into spring break destinations; even the dry spells get filled with good vibes.

7 They level up, one victory lap after another; every one of them gets face time with God in Zion.

8 Lord, Commander of the Cosmic Forces, lend me your ear; tune in, God of Jacob.

9 Scope out our defender, God; peep the mug of your MVP.

10 Just one day parking it in your spot beats thousands elsewhere. I'd rather be a doorkeeper in God's house than kick it in the VIP section of the naughty.

11 'Cause the Lord God's like sunlight mixed with a safety net. He dishes out blessings and respect; doesn't hold back the good stuff from those walking the straight line.

12 Big ups to the one betting everything on you, Lord of the Cosmic Crew!

Psalm 88

1 Yo, Lifesaver Supreme, I've been hitting up your line day and night.

2 Let my SOS fly into your DMs; tune into my meltdown.

3 'Cause, for real, I'm up to my neck in troubles, hovering way too close to the edge.

4 I'm basically ghosted among those headed down to the underworld. Feel like a zombie, zero energy left,

5 dumped off with the forgotten dead. I'm like those chill vibes you don't vibe with anymore, snipped from your circle.

6 You've stashed me in the basement of the abyss, in the no-light zone, in the deep end.

7 Your anger's like a ton of bricks on me;
you've got me drowning under your tsunami waves.

8 My squad's ghosting me 'cause of you; I'm like a text left on read. Boxed in, no escape.

9 My eyes are basically raisins from all the tears.
Yo, Lord, I'm waving my hands at you all day;
I'm reaching out for a high-five.

10 You pulling off miracles for the ghost gang?
Do spirits get hyped about you?

11 Is your ride-or-die love talked about in ghost town, your loyalty in the land of forget-me-nots?

12 Your epic moments, do they light up the dark? Your good deeds, do they make headlines in the void?

13 But here I am, shouting for backup, Lord;
my morning memo's heading your way.

14 Lord, why you giving me the cold shoulder?
Why's your face in incognito mode towards me?

15 Been on struggle street since my teen scene,
I've seen your nightmares up close; I'm hanging by a thread.

16 Your fury's got me in a spin; your scare tactics have me wrecked.

17 They're all up in my space 24/7, ganging up on me from all sides.

18 You've hit "unfriend" on my fam and my mates; now, darkness is my plus-one.

Psalm 91
1 So here's the deal, I'm all in with the Lord, my chill zone and my boss level, my God who I'm totally vibing with in trust.

2 He's gonna snatch you away from those sneaky traps and from all that chaos that wants to wreck you.

3 He'll wrap you up in his cozy feathers, and under his wings, you're totally safe. His loyalty? That's your epic shield and armor.

4 No need to freak out about the creepies at night or those arrows zipping by in daylight,

5Not even the darkness that lurks or the midday disasters.

6 Even if it's like a movie scene with thousands dropping left and right, it's all good, you're untouchable.

7 Just grab some popcorn, watch from the sidelines, and see the wrongdoers get what's coming.

8 Because you chose the Lord, the VIP section, as your home base,

9 No drama's gonna hit you, no bad vibes coming near your spot.

10 He's got his angels on speed dial just for you, to keep you on track without a single faceplant.

11 They're like your personal bodyguards, making sure you're cruising without any slip-ups. Lions, snakes? You're walking all over them, the king of the jungle and slithering foes are just your playground.

12 "He's got me on his favorites list," says the Lord, "so I'm pulling him out of trouble. He knows my handle, so he's under my wing."

13 Hit me up, and I'm there, right in the thick of it, to pull you out and make you shine.

14 A lifetime pass to the good stuff, that's what I'm handing him, a front-row seat to witness my win.

Psalm 117
1 Peepin' at the mountains and wonderin', "Where's my backup gonna come from?"

2 Well, my backup's coming straight from the Lord, the Top G creator of sky and dirt.

3 He's not gonna let you trip; Your Guardian's always got one eye open.

4 For real, the Guardian of Israel is never hitting snooze.

5 The Lord's got your back; He's like your personal shade right where you stand.

6 Not even the sun's gonna burn you by day, nor the moon do you dirty by night.

7 The Lord's gonna shield you from all the bad vibes; He's safeguarding your life.

8 The Lord's watching over your ins and outs, keeping tabs on you from this moment to forever.

Psalm 136

1 Throw all the gratitude up to the Lord, 'cause honestly, He's the ultimate good. His love? It's like that forever playlist that never gets old.

2 Big thanks to the supreme God of all gods. His kind of love just keeps on playing, no end in sight.

3 Major props to the ultimate Lord of lords. His brand of love is the kind that sticks around, no expiry date.

4 He's the solo artist behind those mind-blowing wonders. Yeah, His love is the kind of hit that lasts through the ages.

5 Masterfully crafted the heavens with skills that are off the charts.

His love? It's as enduring as the vast sky above.

6 Spread the earth over the waters with the ease of a pro. His love runs deeper than the deepest oceans.

7 Lit up the big lights, the sun for the day, and the moon and stars for the night, because His love shines brighter than the brightest star.

8 The sun taking the day shift, ruling the sky, all thanks to His never-ending, always shining love.
The moon and stars taking over when the sun clocks out, keeping the love light glowing through the darkest nights.

9 Struck down the firstborn of Egypt, showcasing His power, yet His love remained steadfast and unshaken.
10 Led Israel out from their chains, turning their story from captivity to freedom. His love was their guiding light.

11 With a mighty hand and an outstretched arm, He made His love known, a fortress of protection and power.

12 Parted the Red Sea, making a way where there seemed to be none. His love paved the path to salvation.

13 Guided His people through the divided sea, a testament to His guiding light of love that never fails.

14 Sent Pharaoh and his army into the depths, a fierce display of justice, while His love stood victorious and unchallenged.

15 Led His people through the wilderness, showing that even in the unknown, His love is a constant presence.

16 Knocked down great kings, a showcase of His unmatched power, but it was His love that was the true victor.

17 Defeated the famous kings Sihon and Og, making His name known across lands, His love the banner under which He fought.

18 Gave their lands as an inheritance to His people, a gift that spoke volumes of His enduring love and faithfulness.
19 Remembered us in our lowly state, lifting us from our foes. His love, a relentless force for our rescue.

20 Feeds every creature, a provider who ensures that His love is known through sustenance and care.

21 So, give it up for the God of heaven, 'cause His faithful love? Yeah, it's forever.

Psalm 138
1 I'm throwing all my thanks your way, Blasting praises like a playlist for the cosmos.

2 Gonna hit the deck toward your sacred spot,
Shouting "big ups" for your love and real talk. You've put your name and your word Above the whole game.

3 Hit you up, and like a true MVP, you answered;
Pumped up my spirit like a beast mode session.

4 Every ruler out there, They'll catch wind of your promises and thank you.

5 They'll vibe to the ways of the Lord, 'cause your fame is as high as the sky.

6 Even though you're chilling up high, You spot the low-key with a nod; but those full of themselves, you see them coming a mile off.

7 Walk into trouble's den, you're there, shielding me from haters' fire.Your fist ready to do the talking, Your strong arm's gonna pull me through.

8 You're gonna see me through, no doubt. Yo, Lord, your love's the forever type; Don't ghost the masterpiece that's me.

Psalm 139

1 Oh Lord, you've totally scoped me out, understanding my every action, whether I'm lounging or on the move. You grasp my thoughts from a universe away.
2 Whether I'm kicking back or standing tall, you're in tune with every vibe I throw out there, catching my every thought before it even forms.

3 You track my wanderings and my downtime; you're clued into my life's rhythm like the ultimate insider.

4 Before I even form a word, Lord, you know its full story, inside and out, understanding my silence just as clearly as my spoken words.

5 You've got me surrounded, your presence is a constant touch, a reassuring hand on my shoulder in every moment of my life.

6 This kind of knowledge is just too incredible, too high—I can't grasp it, like trying to catch the wind or touch the edge of the universe.

7 Thinking of dodging your Spirit or fleeing from your sight? As if there's a spot in the cosmos where I could hide from your all-seeing eyes.

8 Climb to the heavens, you're there; dive into the depths, and you're still with me. Your presence is a constant, inescapable reality.

9 If I catch the first light to the east or settle on the western frontier, even there your hand guides me, and your strength secures me.

10 Thinking darkness might cloak me from your sight? But for you, night shines as bright as day. Darkness and light are the same in your eyes.
11 You're the master artist who formed me, knitting me together in the cozy workshop of my mother's womb.

12 I'm in awe of how marvelously you've made me; your work is nothing short of breathtaking. My very being resonates with the work of your hands.

13 Hidden away, I was already in your sights; in the secret depths, your eyes saw my unformed substance.

14 Every moment of my life was laid out before a single day had passed, every chapter written in your book, a story crafted by your hand.

15 Your thoughts, oh God, are treasures, a vast expanse of priceless gems. Their depth is beyond measure, an ocean of wisdom and wonder.

16 Attempting to count them would be like trying to tally the sands of the sea; waking up, I find myself still enveloped in your presence.

17 How I wish you'd silence the wicked, those who misuse your name for their deceitful games.

18 They wear a facade of loyalty, yet their hearts are far from you, using your name in vain.

19 Yes, those who oppose you ignite my anger, those who rebel against you are marked as my foes.

20 My disdain for them is total, categorizing them as adversaries in my heart.

21 Dive deep into my heart, God, and unveil what lies within. Put my anxious thoughts to the test.

22 Identify any way in me that strays from your path, and lead me along the eternal highway.

PROVERBS

Steer Clear of Trouble

Kiddo, tune into the wisdom your old man's laying down, and don't brush off what your mom's preaching. Their words? They're like the sickest snapback and chains combo you could rock. Listen up, if the crew's plotting a shady move, trying to drag you in with that "Yo, let's jump some innocent dude just for kicks" or "Let's ghost 'em and swipe their stuff to deck out our digs" - nah, fam, don't even. If they're like "Join our squad, we'll split the swag," just bounce. Don't hit that path with them, 'cause they sprint straight to the bad stuff, quick to start trouble. It's like setting up a trap right where the birds can peep it – pointless, right? But here's the twist: they're actually setting up their own fall. That's the dead-end for anyone hustling dirty money; it's a one-way ticket to ghost town for them.

Wisdom's Shout-Out

Hey, everyone, Wisdom isn't whispering; she's out loud and clear in the streets, raising her voice in the squares. She's over the noise, speaking up at the city gates: "How long, you rookies, will you love being clueless? Mockers soaking in mockery, fools allergic to knowledge?" Heads up—if you tune into my heads-up, I'll pour out my spirit to you, share my insights. But nope, I called, you ignored; offered my help, and you all just looked the other way. You dodged all my solid advice, wouldn't hear a word of my feedback. So, guess what? I'll laugh when panic grips you, mock when disaster whirlwinds through your life. When chaos storms in and stress bulldozes you. That's when you'll call, but I'll hit mute; you'll look for me, but I'll be off the grid. Because you brushed off knowledge, gave the cold shoulder to the fear of the Lord, yawned through my advice, and snubbed all my corrections, you'll feast on the consequences of your choices and binge on your own schemes. For the downfall of the clueless will be their own doing, and the complacency of fools will ruin them.
But anyone who listens to me will live in peace, without fear of trouble knocking.

It's Cool to be Wise

If you're down to soak up my words and stash my commands like hidden treasures inside you, tuning in for real wisdom and setting your heart on getting it; and hey, if you shout out for insight like it's calling dibs and raise your voice for understanding, hunt for it like it's the most epic loot and dig for it like buried gold, then, and only then, will you get what fearing the Lord is all about and find the secret sauce to God's knowledge. 'Cause the Lord is the OG of wisdom; straight from his lips come knowledge and smarts. He's got success on lock for the straight shooters, a defender of those who roll with integrity, keeping watch over justice and covering the backs of his loyal crew. Then you'll get the picture—what's right, just, and fair, and every good path will light up. Wisdom's gonna slide into your heart, and knowledge will be your new jam. Smart thinking will keep an eye on you, understanding will keep you safe, saving you from the wrong crowd—those who talk twisted, ditch what's right for the thrill of the dark, get their kicks from being bad, and are all about the crooked life. It'll also save you from that smooth-talking someone, who left her first love in the dust and ditched her divine promise. Her place leads straight to the graveyard, her tracks head to the ghost town. No one who visits comes back, or catches the road to real living.

So, stick with the good guys, keep on the path of the stand-up folks. 'Cause only the straight-up will chill in the land, the ones with their act together will stick around; but the wicked will get the boot, and the backstabbers will be torn away from it.

Total Trust Vibes

Don't let my life hacks slip from your memory, but keep your heart dialed into my commandments; 'cause they're gonna hook you up with a bunch of extra days, a life full to the brim, and total chill vibes. Make sure loyalty and faithfulness are always your plus-ones. Rock them like your fave necklace; etch them into the core of who you are. Then, watch yourself rack up mad respect and good standing with both the Big Guy upstairs and the peeps down here. Go all in with your trust in the Lord, and don't bank on just your brainpower; in everything you're about, acknowledge Him, and He's got your back, making your road smooth and straight. Don't get all puffed up thinking you know best; keep it real with respect for the Lord and steer clear from the shady stuff. That's like a wellness retreat for your bod and a power-up for your bones. Show some love to the Lord by sharing your stuff and the first fruits of all your grind;

then watch as your storage hits max capacity, and your wine barrels start spilling over with the fresh stuff. Don't get salty over the Lord's coaching, my dude, and don't get all bent out of shape over His tough love; 'cause the Lord throws down discipline on the ones He's got a soft spot for, just like a dad does with his kid who makes him proud.

Unlocking the Chill Life

Check it, peeps: landing wisdom is like hitting the jackpot, and snagging understanding? Even sweeter than scoring viral fame. We're talking bigger returns than the hottest crypto, more bling than your fave influencer's haul. Wisdom's the real treasure, nothing on your wish list even comes close. Holding onto her? You're looking at a life so long, you'll need extra candles for your cake; and let's not forget the riches and clout she's packing. Cruising down her lane is all about those good vibes, and every path she takes you on is as chill as a Sunday morning. She's like that life-giving avocado tree in your feed, everyone hugging her ends up straight-up blessed.

Yo, it was wisdom that laid down the earth's foundation and hung up the sky like the ultimate art installation. Thanks to her, the ocean's got its groove, and the clouds are out here making it rain on the regular. Keep wisdom and insight close—like your phone and headphones. They're your life's playlist and your style's signature accessory. With them, you're walking sure-footed, no facepalms here. Hitting the hay brings zero stress; you'll be out like a light, dreaming sweet. No need to side-eye sudden scares or the downfall of those playing the game dirty. The Lord's got your back, making sure you sidestep all those life traps.

Play it Cool with the Others

When you've got the power to do someone a solid, don't sit on it. If you can help out now, don't hit them with a "Catch you later!" especially when you've got what they need right in your pocket. Plotting against your next-door buddy? That's a major no-go. They trust you, so don't break that vibe. And throwing shade or pointing fingers without a good reason? Save the drama, especially if they haven't crossed you. Chasing after someone who's all about that rough life? Hard pass. Their path? Not a look the universe is vibing with. But if you're walking straight, you're in good company—the Universe's, to be exact. Bad vibes tend to bounce back to the crib of those cooking up trouble, but the chill zones? They're getting all the good stuff. And if you're out there playing the mimic game, expect the Universe to throw some shade right back at ya. But stay humble, and you're golden, catching all those good graces. Endgame? The smart cookies score the respect, while the ones fumbling in the dark? Well, let's just say they get a front-row seat to the shade show.

Dad's Life Hacks

Yo, listen up, kiddos, to the old man's guide on how not to bungle your way through life. Lock in 'cause I'm dropping some solid gold advice here. Don't ghost on my teachings, alright? Back in the day, when I was just a mini-me to my pops, the apple of my mom's eye, my dad was like, "Son, glue your heart to my words. Live by the playbook I'm giving you." He was all about the wisdom life hack, telling me, "Score wisdom, score understanding. Don't let them slip or slide away from what I'm saying. Stick with wisdom—she's your BFF, gonna keep you sharp. Show her some love, and she's got your back."Wisdom's the MVP, no doubt. So make that your goal— grab wisdom. And hey, while you're at it, bag some understanding too.

Treat her right, and she'll lift you up; give her a hug, and she's throwing honors your way. She'll deck you out with a victory chain, crown you with some swaggy bling.

Life Hacks vs Life Wrecks

Yo, kiddo, lean in for the real talk. Scoop up my words, and you're setting yourself up for the long haul. I'm laying down the wisdom track, leading you straight through no-mess lanes. Stride on this path, and you're glitch-free; sprint, and you won't trip up. Clutch onto wisdom like it's your life's login; don't drop it for anything. Dodge the dodgy routes of the no-goods; don't even peek down the road of wrongs. Skip it, swerve it, and keep on stepping. These folks can't hit the hay without cooking up chaos; their Zs are zilch unless they've tripped someone up. They're munching on mischief for breakfast, sipping on strife like it's their morning brew. But you, my dude, you're walking on the sunrise strip, getting brighter by the second. Meanwhile, the baddies are stumbling in the pitch-black, clueless about what trips them up. Heads up, part two: Tune into my vibes, keep my chat close. Don't let them slip; they're life to those who catch them, total body boost. Heart guard, team captain—because that's where life kicks off. Don't let your chat slide into shady, keep your gaze on the prize, straight up. Map your moves, and you're set. No veering into the sketch zone. Now, onto the no-fly zone: Listen tight to my insight, so you dodge the decoys. She might taste like the sweet stuff, talk slicker than oil, but the aftertaste? Pure bitter, sharp as a two-timer's blade. Her steps are a one-way ticket down; she's clueless about the life lane. So, here's the deal: steer clear, don't even hang by her haunt. Or you're donating your best years to the heartbreak hotel, your grind to grifters. Picture this: you're at rock bottom, body spent, going, "Why did I ghost on guidance, side-eye straight talk?" Ignored the coaches, tuned out the mentors. Now, I'm a hot mess, public facepalm. Keep it 100, follow the straight-up path, and don't let the sweet talk trip you.

Vibing Solo vs. Tangled Ties

Yo, here's the thing: Sip from your own vibe, like water from your personal well. Why let your streams become street art, shared with every passerby? Nah, keep that flow exclusive, not for the eyes and thirst of outsiders. Bless your own source, find joy in your day-one babe, the love of your youth. Think of her as your heart's deer, graceful and all. Let her charm be what you vibe with always, getting lost in love that's legit and all yours. Why wander, my dude, into the arms of someone off-limits, or vibe with someone who's all about the wrong turns? Every step you take, every move you make, the Lord's got it on His feed, checking out your path. The wrong moves trap a dude; he gets caught in his own web of mess-ups. Without a guide, he's heading for a crash, lost to his own epic fails.Now, flip the script: If you've gone and locked yourself in by vouching for your buddy, or you've shaken hands with someone you barely know, here's your out. You've talked yourself into a corner, but it's time to unplug and set yourself free.

Hit up your neighbor, lower your pride, and get that freedom talk going. Don't let sleep hit your eyes until you've danced your way out of that snare. Be slick, be quick—like a gazelle dodging the hunt, like a bird winging away from the trap.

The Ultimate Guide to Not Being a Couch Potato

Hey, you champion of chillaxing, ever checked out how ants roll? They're like mini moguls, no boss needed, just doing their thing. Summer hits, and they're all about stocking up, like preppers for the winter apocalypse. So, what's your deal? Gonna make that bed your forever home? When's the snooze fest gonna end? A bit more snoozing, a touch of lounging, and bam—poverty's gonna crash your party like an uninvited guest, neediness tagging along like its annoying plus one.

The Guide to Spotting a Shady Characte

Check this: there's this dude, right? Totally not cool, walking around, spitting lies like it's his job. He's all about those sly winks, sneaky foot taps, and secret finger signals. This guy's heart? A dark web of evil plans and chaos recipes. He's practically a walking disaster movie, loving every second of stirring the pot. But here's the twist—karma hits like a blockbuster finale. Boom! Disaster strikes him outta nowhere, shattering his world like a dropped smartphone screen. No coming back from that, nope.

Stuff the Lord Just Can't Stand

So, there's this list of stuff that really gets under the Lord's skin, right? We're talking about a solid seven things that are a major no-go for Him. First off, those folks who walk around all high and mighty with their noses up in the air? Yeah, that's a hard pass. Then, there are the smooth talkers who couldn't tell the truth if their lives depended on it. And don't even get me started on the people out there causing harm to the innocents. Total deal-breaker. Next up, we've got the masterminds behind all the shady plans, thinking they're being slick but really just playing themselves. And those who can't wait to dive into the next bad idea? Big yikes. Not to mention, the ones who stand up in court and swear to tell the whole truth but end up spinning a web of lies instead. And the cherry on top? The troublemakers who love nothing more than to stir the pot and watch the drama unfold among friends and family. So, yeah, that's the lowdown on the stuff that's sure to land you on the Lord's naughty list. Best to steer clear if you're looking to keep things cool between you and the man upstairs.

Heads Up on Dodging Heartbreak

Yo, listen up! Keep your dad's rules close to heart, and don't even think about dissing your mom's advice. Like, literally wear their words like your fave necklace. Wherever you're headed, these gems will be your GPS; hitting the hay or waking up, they're like your personal Siri. 'Cause, you know, commands are like that cool night light, and teachings? They're your daylight. These wisdom nuggets? They're your personal bodyguards against any heartbreaker with a smooth talk. Don't let her looks or sweet nothings under those lashes hoodwink you. Falling for a hook-up might cost you no more than a sandwich, but messing with someone else's boo? That's like playing hot potato with your life. You think cuddling up with fire and staying chill is possible? Try walking on hot coals and staying frosty. It's the same deal with dipping into another dude's honey pot; you're bound to get stung. People might not side-eye a hungry thief, but get caught, and it's payback time—sevenfold, ripping your wallet big time. Being with someone else's partner is a one-way ticket to Loserville. It's like signing up for a world of hurt, public shame that sticks like a bad tattoo. And trust me, a raging partner won't be calmed by sorrys or pricey "I messed up" gifts. So, my advice? Keep wisdom close, like that no-fail wingman. She's the one who'll steer you clear from anyone batting their lashes with trouble in mind. Stick to these words, and you're golden.

Wisdom's Mic Drop

Yo, peeps, Wisdom's stepping up to the mic! She's got her spot up high, scoping the scene at the crossroads, ready to drop some truth bombs. Right by the city gates, where everyone's rolling in, she's not just whispering – she's hollering: "Hey, humanity! This one's for you. Newbies, time to level up your game; fools, time to wise up. Listen up – I'm only spitting straight facts here, no lies or twisted words coming from me. Everything I say is legit, crystal clear for those who get it, straight-up for those in the know. Opt for my insights over silver, my know-how over the shiniest gold. 'Cause, let's be real – I'm more precious than any bling, nothing else even comes close. I'm Wisdom, and I'm roomies with Cleverness, rolling deep with Insight and Common Sense. Respect the Lord? Then you gotta hate evil – pride, bad moves, and twisted talk, they're not in my crew. I'm the one behind sound advice and solid wisdom, bringing understanding and power to the table. Kings and rulers, they rule by me; leaders and justices, they're all about my guidance. Got love for me? I'm all about that love right back, making sure those who seek me score big time. Riches, honor, enduring wealth, and justice – that's what I'm dealing out. My rewards? Better than the biggest gold haul, sweeter than the purest silver. I'm all about that righteous path, dishing out wealth to my fans, making sure their vaults are stacked. Way back, before the universe was even a thing, the Lord and I were already tight. Before oceans, mountains, or the first clumps of dirt, I was there, crafting the cosmos alongside. From setting the sky up high to laying the ocean's foundation, I was in on it, having a blast, finding joy in humanity's whole vibe.

So, my dudes, tune in; happiness is all about sticking with me. Wisdom's not just old-school; it's about catching life itself, snagging some divine favor. Miss out on me? You're only playing yourself, 'cause ignoring me is basically flirting with disaster

Wisdom's Crib and Folly's Trap House

Wisdom's crib is lit, decked out with seven pillars like a boss. She's got the spread ready, meat and wine on fleek, and the table's set for a feast. Her squad is out, spreading the word from the city's VIP spots: "Yo, newbies, come vibe with me!" She's like, "Get in here and grub up on my bread and sip this fine wine. Leave that clueless vibe behind, and you'll thrive on understanding. But watch out, dissing a hater just brings more drama. Only drop knowledge on the wise; they'll respect you for it. Wise peeps get wiser with each lesson, and the righteous level up big time. Real talk, the fear of the Lord? That's step one to wisdom, and knowing the Holy One? That's when you really get it. Rock wisdom's game, and you'll stack up those years. But if you clown around, you're on your own, bro." Now, Folly? She's wild, clueless, and straight-up reckless. She's posted up at her trap house, calling out to anyone who's passing by, tempting them with stolen treats: "Yo, newbies, come through here! Stolen snacks taste the sweetest, and sneaky eats hit different!" But what they don't know? Her place is a one-way ticket to the underworld, where the vibe's all dark and the guests are ghosts.

MATTHEW'S GOSPEL

Okay, here's the deal: Jesus Christ (aka J.C.) isn't just a big deal because of the miracles and teachings. His family tree is like the ultimate "Where's Who" of ancient VIPs, stretching back to Abraham and David. Think of it as the celestial version of your fave influencer's backstory, but with more plot twists and epic lineage flexes. Abraham kicked things off, not just as a trendsetter in faith but as the founding father of this whole saga. Fast forward through Isaac and Jacob, and you've got a mixtape of ancestors who were part legend, part drama kings. Enter stage left: some unexpected plot twists with Tamar, Rahab, and Ruth—these ladies weren't just footnotes; they were headline acts in their own right, breaking barriers and setting the stage for what was to come. Then you hit the era of kings—like, literal kings, with David leading the pack. His story was a rollercoaster of hits and misses, but it set the tone for a lineage of rulers who had as much drama as your favorite reality TV stars. Then there's this whole Babylonian exile season—think of it as a mid-season plot twist where everything goes off-script, only to set up the biggest comeback story ever. And here's where it gets real: post-exile, the buildup continues until we hit the season finale with Joseph and Mary. Imagine, after all that build-up, the star of the show, Jesus, makes his entrance, flipping the script on everything you thought you knew about heroes.

We're talking 14 generations of history-making, trend-setting ancestors from Abraham to David, another 14 from David to the Babylonian Spotify playlist shuffle, and then 14 more leading up to the season premiere of "Jesus Christ: The Savior." This isn't just a list of names; it's the ultimate throwback playlist leading up to the world's biggest redemption arc, all wrapped up in a narrative that's been binge-watched through the ages. And Jesus? He's not just a character in a book; he's the main event, the influencer of influencers, coming in hot with a message that would turn the world on its head. So when you're scrolling through the genealogy of Jesus, remember: it's more than a list. It's a divine thread connecting generations, a story of promise, and a lineage of epic proportions, culminating in the ultimate plot twist: a savior who's all about flipping scripts and breaking the mold.

The Great Drop: Jesus Christ Hits the Scene

So, here's how the ultimate influencer, J.C. made his debut. Picture this: Mary and Joseph are set to be the next power couple, but then, plot twist—Mary's expecting, and it's all thanks to the Holy Spirit. Joseph, being the stand-up guy he is, thinks, "No drama, we'll keep it on the down-low," planning a quiet split because public breakups are so not his style. But then, dream DMs from an angel change the game. The angel's like, "Joseph, bro, don't stress. Mary's baby is celeb status, straight from the Holy Spirit. He's gonna be named Jesus because he's about to flip the script on sin." And get this: This whole scenario was already in the spoilers from way back, fulfilling the "A virgin will have a baby boy named Immanuel, which means 'God's crashing at our place.'" Joseph wakes up, hits follow on the angel's advice, and makes it official with Mary, but they keep it PG until baby Jesus makes his entrance, and Joseph's like, "Cool, Jesus it is."

Starstruck: The Original Fanboys Make Their Move

Fast forward a bit, and Jesus is chilling in Bethlehem when these astro-influencers from the East hit up Jerusalem. They're on a quest, asking, "Where's the newborn king of the Jews? We saw his birth announcement in the stars and are here to throw him the ultimate welcome party." King Herod catches wind of this and it totally kills his vibe. He pulls together a brainstorm session with the religious elites, asking, "Where's the party at?" "Bethlehem, in Judea," they're all saying, "It's literally been in the tweets for ages." So, Herod, playing it cool, slides into the wise men's DMs and is like, "Do me a solid, find this kid so I can join the fan club too." The wise men catch the star on tour again, and it leads them straight to Jesus. When they see it, they lose it—total joy overload. They roll up, see Jesus with Mary, and it's instant worship mode. They break out the top-tier gifts: gold, influencer frankincense, and VIP myrrh. But then, another dream DM warns them, "Herod's double-tapping is fake," so they ghost him and take the scenic route home.

Epic Escape to Egypt

So, after the wise men dipped, leaving Herod on read, an angel slides into Joseph's dreams again with some urgent news: "Yo,

Joseph, you gotta bounce—like, now. Herod's on a mission to swipe left on Jesus. Egypt's your hideout. Stay put till I hit you up." Joseph didn't waste a second. He grabbed Mary and Jesus for a midnight ghosting session to Egypt, staying under the radar until Herod was out of the picture. This whole detour? It was all part of the bigger plot, fulfilling the "Called my Son out of Egypt" prophecy.

Herod's Meltdown: The Bethlehem Blockbuster

Meanwhile, back at the palace, Herod's losing it, realizing the wise men gave him the slip. In a total power trip move, he orders a heartless swipe at all the toddler boys in Bethlehem, trying to catch Jesus in his net. This dark episode was already predicted by Jeremiah, painting a picture of deep sorrow in Ramah, with moms like Rachel in inconsolable grief because their lights were brutally snuffed out.

The Chill Return to Nazareth

Fast forward, Herod's reign ends, and it's safe for the holy family to head back. Cue angelic DM: "Joseph, it's go time. Herod's crew is done. Pack up for Israel." But the plot thickens when Joseph hears Archelaus is the new boss in Judea. Another dream warning (Joseph's inbox is divine-led 24/7) diverts them to Galilee, landing in a low-key spot called Nazareth. This move wasn't random; it was all about setting the stage for Jesus to be known as the Nazarene, ticking off another prophecy box.

John the Baptist: The Hype Man

Back in the day, John the Baptist hit the scene like the original wilderness influencer, rocking camel-hair fits and a diet that would make any vegan foodie pause—locusts and wild honey. He wasn't just about that desert life; he had a message that went viral: "Hit the reset button, fam, 'cause heaven's kingdom is dropping soon!" John was the real deal, fulfilling the old-school tweet from Isaiah: "Listen up, someone's yelling in the desert, 'Get the road ready for the Lord; make it a straight shot!'" So, everyone from downtown Jerusalem to the 'burbs of Judea was lining up to get baptized in the Jordan River, spilling their tea, confessing their sins, and getting that fresh start. But when the Pharisees and Sadducees rolled up, trying to sneak into the baptism like VIPs at a club, John was having none of it. He called them out, "Y'all are like a snake pit! Who tipped you off to escape the upcoming fire sale? Show some real change, not just talk. And don't pull the 'We're related to Abraham' card. God can turn these stones into Abraham's fam if He wants. Every tree not bringing the good vibes and fruit is getting axed and turned into firewood." John then laid it down: "I'm here splashing you with water as a sign you're ready to turn things around, but the one coming next? He's on another level. I'm not even on the guest list to handle his sandals. He's going to immerse you in the Holy Spirit and fire. He's got the winnowing fork ready to sort the wheat from the chaff—keeping the good stuff, but the rest? It's a bonfire that doesn't quit."

The Ultimate Collab: Jesus Gets Baptized

So, J.C. hits up John at the Jordan, looking to get baptized. John's like, "Wait, what? Bro, I should be getting baptized by you, and you're coming to me?" But Jesus is all, "Chill, let's do this. It's all part of the plan to keep things 100." John's convinced, and boom, the baptism happens. Right after Jesus comes up from the water, it's like the sky cracks open for a VIP reveal, and the Spirit of God descends like a super chill dove, lighting up Jesus. Then,

outta nowhere, a voice from the sky drops, "This is my son, the real MVP, and yeah, I'm all about it."

Jesus vs. The Great Challenge

Post-baptism, Jesus heads into the desert, Spirit-led, to face off with the devil. After a 40-day fast that left Him super hungry, the devil slides in with a challenge, "Yo, if you're really the Son of God, turn these stones into a bread buffet." Jesus claps back, "Nah, life's not just about the snacks. It's all about vibing on God's words." Next, the devil whisks Jesus to the holy city, gets Him to the highest point of the temple, and is like, "If you're really the Son of God, jump off. The scriptures say angels got your back." But Jesus isn't playing, "Scriptures also say, 'Don't put God to the test.'" Not giving up, the devil shows Jesus all the world's bling and offers it up, "All this can be yours if you just hit the deck and worship me." Jesus is firm, "Get lost, Satan! It's all about worshiping God, and Him alone." With that, the devil bounces, and angels roll up to take care of Jesus, like the celestial crew they are.

Galilee Gets Lit

So, when Jesus caught wind that John had been thrown behind

bars (major bummer), he was like, "Time to bounce." He packs up from Nazareth and heads to Capernaum, seaside living in the areas of Zebulun and Naphtali. Why there? Because Isaiah, the ancient prophet-slash-spoiler-giver, was all, "This place is gonna shine." Basically, Jesus was about to turn their darkness into an epic light show, proving even back then, location was everything. With his new base set up, Jesus starts dropping truth bombs left and right: "Yo, it's time to hit the reset button, 'cause heaven is closer than your next TikTok scroll."

The OG Squad Formation

Strolling along the Sea of Galilee, Jesus spots Simon (Peter for short) and his bro Andrew. They're just there, casting nets, living that fisherman life. Jesus, in pure boss mode, hits them with an offer they can't refuse: "How 'bout you fish for people instead?" They look at each other, shrug, and are like, "Sure, beats working weekends." Nets dropped. Following commenced. But wait, there's more. Jesus, on a recruitment spree, finds James and John, Zebedee's boys, in the middle of a net-fixing sesh. He calls them out, and faster than you can say "ghosted," they ditch their boat, their dad (sorry,

Zebs), and their fishy biz to join the Jesus start-up.

Galilee's Viral Sensation: J.C.

Jesus started touring Galilee like a headliner, hitting up synagogues, dropping sermons like hot tracks, and basically turning into the go-to guy for anyone feeling less than their best. He wasn't just talking the talk; he was walking it, healing every kind of illness and bad vibe that came his way. Word about him spread faster than a meme in Syria. People started bringing the sick, those vibing on a totally different (and not fun) spiritual level, folks with pain that just wouldn't quit, individuals caught in a body glitch (like seizures), and those who couldn't move. Jesus, in his chill mode, healed them all.

The result? J.C. started pulling crowds like he was the main event at Coachella. Folks from Galilee, the Decapolis (which is like the ancient version of a multi-city tour), Jerusalem, Judea, and even places beyond the Jordan were showing up. Everyone wanted a piece of that miraculous action, proving Jesus was the ultimate influencer before influencers were even a thing.

The Sermon on the Mount: Jesus Drops the Mic

So, Jesus peeps the crowd, sizes it up, and decides it's time for a hilltop TED talk. He finds a comfy spot on the mountain, sits down, and his crew gathers around. Then, he starts laying down some serious wisdom:

The Beatitude Beat Drops

1 "Big ups to the spirit-broke squad, 'cause heaven's VIP list has got your names all over it.

2 Shoutout to the heartbroken crew; comfort's on its way like a DM slide from the universe.

3 Props to the humble homies; you're gonna inherit the earth like it's your personal playlist.

4 High-fives to those who are starving for what's right; you'll be full like your phone on max charge.

5 Hats off to the mercy givers; you'll get that mercy back like an echo in a canyon.

6 Cheers to the pure-hearted; you're gonna see God like He's on your IG live.

Salute to the peacemakers; you're the real MVPs, sons of God.

7 Big respect to those getting shade thrown for doing right; heaven's got a spot reserved for you.

And when the haters come at you with insults, persecution, and straight-up lies 'cause of me? Throw a party, 'cause your heaven score is off the charts. Remember, that's the OG prophets' vibe check too.

Jesus basically flips the script on what it means to be blessed, serving up a fresh perspective that's all about the underdog, the overlooked, and the straight-up genuine hearts. It's a masterclass in spiritual street cred, pointing out that the real wins aren't always where you'd expect.

OG Believers

Jesus gets real and goes, "Y'all are the salt of the earth. But, no cap, if salt loses its vibe, how do you even salt? At that point, it's just dirt seasoning. Nobody's here for that." Then He flips the script, "You're also the light of the world. A city on a hill is basically the original influencer; you can't miss it. And who lights a lamp just to hide it? Nah, you put that on blast so everyone gets lit up. Let your light flex in front of everyone, so they're like, 'Wow, must shout out to the Big Guy upstairs for these epic deeds.'"

Jesus: Not Here to Cancel, But to Complete

"Don't get it twisted—I'm not here to ghost the Law or the Prophets. I'm here to complete the story. For real, not even the tiniest emoji or the smallest swipe will disappear from the law until everything's done and dusted. If anyone plays fast and loose with even the low-key commands and tells others to do the same, they're gonna be the least hyped in heaven. But stick to the script and teach it? You're heaven's MVP.

"You gotta level up your righteousness game beyond the scribes and Pharisees, or you're not making the cut for heaven's guest list."

Heart Vibes Matter

"You've all heard the old-school rule, 'No murking each other.' But I'm saying, if you're even throwing shade or getting salty with someone, you're in the hot seat. Throw around insults, and you're looking at court time. Call someone a fool? You're practically booking a one-way ticket to the burn zone. "So, if you're about to drop your offering and remember someone's got beef with you, hit pause. Go sort it out first, then come back and make your offering. Got drama with someone? Squash that beef fast, or it's gonna escalate, and you might just end up in the clink, paying up every last dime."

Swiping Right with Integrity

Jesus lays it down, "You've all seen the command 'No swiping on someone else's boo.' But let's keep it 100—if you're scrolling and you pause a little too long on someone's pic with that '👀' emoji vibe, you're already in the danger zone in your heart. And if part of you—like, say, your right eye—is making you double-tap on trouble, it's time to hit 'block' on that impulse. Better to lose one follower than have your whole vibe canceled. As for that 'it's complicated' relationship status? Back in the day, you'd send a 'we're done' DM. But I'm telling you now, ending things without a solid reason is like tagging them in a drama without cause. And clicking 'interested' on someone freshly single? Yeah, that's not the move."

(Soo… Jesus isn't just talking about the old-school rules; he was about getting to the heart of matters, ensuring that your internal vibe matches your external actions. It's all about keeping your heart and intentions pure, making sure your actions on the outside don't lead you or anyone else down a sketchy path.)

Keeping It Real 101 with J.C.

Jesus is like, "You've all been told, 'Don't flake on your promises,' especially to the Big Guy upstairs. But let's get real—ditch the whole swear-on-anything vibe. Swearing by heaven? That's God's crib. Earth? His footrest. Jerusalem? His city. And don't even get started on your own head—you can't even control your hair color without some help. So, here's the deal: When you say 'yes,' make sure it's a solid 'yes.' 'No'? It better mean 'no.' Anything extra is just playing into the drama king downstairs."

Extra Mile Mode: Activated

And about that old 'eye for an eye' business? Jesus flips the script: "If someone's coming at you sideways, don't clap back. Instead, hit them with the unexpected—offer the other cheek. Someone's trying to take your threads? Give them your hoodie too. Got someone making you do the most, like carrying their stuff? Don't just go one mile; hit them with two. And if someone's hitting you up for a favor or a loan, don't ghost them."

Swipe Right on Your Enemies

Jesus drops this wisdom, "You've heard the old school 'Like your buddy, block your hater.' But I'm flipping the script: Heart-react your enemies and hit up the group chat praying for those who throw shade your way. This is how you level up to VIP status as children of your Father in heaven. He's out here giving sunrise and rain checks to both the ghosters and the followers. If you're only nice to your squad, what kind of clout is that? Even the tax collectors—who are basically the trolls of society—do that much. And if you're just saying 'hey' to your inner circle, how are you doing anything extra? Everyone does that. Aim high—like, heavenly Father high."

Stealth Mode Generosity

Moving on to giving, Jesus is all, "Don't flex your good deeds for the 'Gram. If you're helping someone out, don't blast it with a trumpet like those clout chasers in synagogues or on Main Street looking for likes. For real, they're getting exactly what they're after—empty likes. But when you help out, keep it on the down-low. No need for the left hand to catch what the right hand is throwing. Do it so low-key that even you forget about it. Your Father, who's all about that incognito life, will hit you back with the real rewards."

(In a nutshell, Jesus is teaching us the art of genuine love and kindness—not for the views or the likes, but because it's the right playlist for life, where the secret to being cool is being kind, especially when no one's watching.)

DMs to the Divine: The Prayer Protocol

Jesus is like, "When you hit up the divine DMs, don't be that person who makes a public spectacle of it. You know the type—always praying in full view to snag likes and followers. Yeah, they get their 'reward,' but it's all for show. Instead, when you want to chat with the Big Guy, find your chill spot, close the door, and keep it just between you two. Your Father's got that incognito mode on lock and sees what's up in secret. He'll hook you up for keeping it real.

And when you're sending up those prayers, don't spam with words like you're trying to hit a word count. Some folks think they'll be heard for their marathon texts. Nah, your Dad's ahead of the game; He knows what you need before you even hit send."

The Blueprint for Sliding into Heavenly DMs

"So, here's the deal on how to craft that prayer DM:

"Our Father chilling in heaven, Let your name be kept sacred. Your kingdom come, your vibe be all over, On earth just like it's popping in heaven. Slide us the daily bread we need. And cancel our debts, just like we cancel the ones who owe us. Keep us clear of temptations, And save us from the clout chaser."

If you're all about forgiving those who trip you up, your heavenly Father's got your back and will clear your slate too. But if you're holding grudges, don't expect to get your own slip-ups wiped."

No Shade Zone

J.C. is like, "Hold up on the judgment, fam. The way you're throwing shade is exactly how it'll come back to you. You're out here using the zoom lens on your bro's tiny mess-up while you're walking around with a whole mess of your own. Imagine trying to help your friend pick out a speck from his eye when you've got the equivalent of a 2x4 in yours. Talk about a reality check—clear your own vision before you try to fix someone else's."

Don't Waste Your Vibes

"And for real, don't waste your gems on those who won't appreciate them. It's like giving your playlist to someone who only listens to noise. They won't get it, and they might even come at you for it."

DM the Universe: You've Got Mail

"Here's a life hack: Hit up the universe with your requests. Ask, and you'll get a response. Seek, and you'll find what you're looking for. Knock, and you're in. It's like everyone who slides into the DMs gets a reply, finds what they're searching for, or gets the door opened.

Think about it—if your kid asks for a snack, you're not going to prank them with a rock or a snake. Even if we're all a bit off

track, we still know how to hook up our kids with the good stuff. Imagine how much more your cosmic parent is ready to drop blessings on those who hit Him up."

Golden Rule Alert

"And here's the mic drop: Treat others like you want to be treated. It's that simple. This isn't new—it's the golden rule, the foundation of all the teachings. So, before you go off on someone, think about if you'd like that kind of feedback loop aimed at you."

VIP Pass to the Ultimate Party

Jesus is like, "Yo, if you're aiming for that exclusive afterparty in heaven, you gotta find the VIP entrance. There's this massive gate with a super wide road that everyone seems to be crashing, but it's a one-way ticket to nowhere good. The real deal? It's this low-key, narrow gate with a tricky path that leads to the real deal—life. But heads up, it's not everyone's go-to since finding it is like spotting a decent avocado at the grocery store—rare.

Watch Out for the Fakes

And about those peeps who look all cozy and cute like sheep but are actually on the prowl like wolves on the inside? Stay woke. You'll spot them by the vibes they're putting out. I mean, you don't get fresh grapes from a bramble bush or Insta-worthy figs from thistles, right? Same way, a legit person spreads good vibes, but a faker? Only bad news bears. A good vibe can't come from a bad vibe factory, and vice versa. Every vibe that's not bringing the good is gonna get cleared out.

Real Recognizes Real

Not everyone dropping my name with a 'Lord, Lord' is getting into the big bash. It's all about who's living out those heavenly vibes my Dad's all about. On the big day, a bunch of name-droppers will be like, 'Didn't we do all this cool stuff in your name?' And I'll be straight-up, 'Who even are you? You missed the whole point. Bye!'

(Jesus is laying down the essentials: the way to live that's in sync with the heavenly vibes isn't about the show you put on but the realness of your actions. It's about walking that talk, avoiding the easy path that everyone else is taking, and staying sharp to the real from the fake.)

Build It Like a Boss

Jesus lays it down, "If you're tuning into my vibes and actually doing the thing, you're like the ultimate DIY guru who builds his crib on bedrock. When life throws its worst—torrential downpours, flood-level rivers, hurricane-force winds—your place stands solid because it's anchored. But hit the snooze button on my words, and you're the dude who thinks building a beach house on a dune is a killer idea. Sure, it looks Insta-ready, but then nature hits 'unleash chaos' mode, and suddenly, it's a disaster movie starring your house. It doesn't just fall apart; it's a blockbuster collapse."

Crowd Goes Wild

When J.C. wraps up, everyone's mind is blown. His teaching style? It's got that 'straight from the source' authority vibe, not like the scribes who always seem to be reading the instruction manual out loud.

Detox Mode: Activated

Post-mountain chill session, Jesus is back with the crowd when a dude with leprosy steps up, hits the kneel button, and is like, "Boss, if you're game, you can sort me out." Jesus, being all about that action, reaches out, touches him, and is like, "Bet. You're clean." And just like that, the leprosy checks out. Then Jesus is all, "Mum's the word on this, yeah? But go show yourself to the priest, do the thing Moses said to do. It's solid proof for them."

Centurion's Epic Faith Drop

So, Jesus rolls into Capernaum, and this centurion dude comes up, all urgent-like, "Yo, Lord, my guy at home is stuck in bed, totally paralyzed and in major pain."

Jesus, being Jesus, is like, "You want me to swing by and handle it?" But the centurion hits him with, "Nah, I'm not on that level for you to come over. Just hit the airwaves with your healing vibes, and I know he'll be all good. I get how authority works—I've got soldiers who do what I say, and even my crew at home jumps when I say jump." Jesus is shook. He turns to the crowd and is like, "For real, I haven't seen this kind of trust vibes anywhere in Israel. Watch, folks from all over are gonna rock up to the heavenly party with the OGs Abraham, Isaac, and Jacob, while the hometown crowd might just miss the invite." Then to the centurion, "You got it, dude. Your faith just made it happen." And just like that, his servant's back to 100% at home.

House Calls in Capernaum

Next up, Jesus pops into Peter's place and finds his mother-in-law down with a fever. A simple touch, and bam, fever's gone. She's up and about, probably fixing snacks or something. As the sun dips, everyone starts bringing their possessed friends and family. Jesus, with just a word, is sending those demons packing and patching up the sick left and right, all fulfilling the throwback prophecy from Isaiah: "He's out here carrying our frailties and brushing off our illnesses like it's nothing."

The Real Price Tag of the Follow Train

Seeing the crowd getting hype, Jesus is like, "Let's bounce to the other side." Just then, a scribe rolls up, all starry-eyed, "Teacher, I'm down for whatever, wherever." Jesus hits him with the reality check, "Look, foxes got their Airbnb, birds are set with treehouse vibes, but the Son of Man? No fixed address."

Then, another dude's like, "Yo, Lord, hit pause—I gotta go handle some family business first." But Jesus is straight-up, "Roll with me now. The world's got its own cycles; let's focus on what's alive."

Chill Mode in the Storm

So, they're all in the boat when outta nowhere, this mega storm decides to crash their float. The boat's getting all Titanic, and Jesus is in the back catching Zs. His crew's freaking out, waking him up like, "Boss, we're about to be fish food!" Jesus peeps their panic and is like, "Why you all scared? Where's that faith at?" Then he stands up, gives the storm a stern talking-to, and boom—ocean's as chill as a spa day. The squad's jaws hit the deck, "Who even is this guy? Even the storm's playing follow the leader with him!"

Epic Demon-Pig Swap

When Jesus hit up the Gadarenes, he was greeted not by a welcome committee but by two dudes with some serious bad vibes—like, 'stay away' level because of the demon situation. They were straight out of a horror scene, chilling in tombs and scaring off anyone daring to take a shortcut. They start yelling at J.C., "Yo, Son of God! You here to start the party early and kick us out before it's time?" Spotting a pig squad munching away in the distance, the demons shoot their shot, "If you're gonna evict us, at least let us crash with those pigs." Jesus, probably with just a flick of his wrist, is like, "Bet. Go on." Next thing you know, the demons bail from the dudes and the pigs go full action-movie, diving off a cliff into the sea. RIP, pig squad. The pig herders are shook, sprinting to town to spill the tea on the demon exorcism gone wild. The whole town comes out, sees Jesus, and instead of asking for autographs, they're like, "Um, could you not hang around here?"

Bedridden Buddy Lifted

Back in his hometown, Jesus is met with a squad carrying their friend on a stretcher, hoping for a miracle. Jesus, catching the faith vibes, hits the paralytic with, "Be brave, kiddo, your sins are on me now." Cue the scribes in the back, thinking, "He can't just say that, can he?" Jesus, reading minds like tweets, is like, "Why you gotta be so negative? What's easier, saying 'sins are gone' or 'get up and walk'? Watch this." He turns to the stretcher guy, "Time to bounce. Grab your bed and head home." And just like that, the guy's up and out, leaving the crowd completely gobsmacked, throwing up praise and wondering when God started handing out such epic skills to humans.

Matthew Hits the Follow Button

So, Jesus is just strolling along when he spots Matthew chilling at the toll booth, probably swiping through some scrolls. Jesus hits him with a simple, "Yo, follow me." No hashtags, no filters. And Matthew? He just logs out of his toll booth account and hits follow IRL. Next thing you know, Jesus is at a dinner, and it's like the who's who of the not-so-righteous. Tax collectors, sinners—the kind of crowd that would make the 'holier-than-thou' squad clutch their pearls. The Pharisees, always on the lookout for some gossip, are like, "Why's your guy dining with the downtown crew?" Jesus overhears and drops this truth bomb, "Healthy folks don't need a doc. I'm here for the ones who know they're not on the A-list. Mercy over metrics, folks. I'm not scouting for saints; I'm calling out to the real, raw, and ready."

Fasting? Mmhhhh…

Then, John's crew rolls up with a fasting FAQ, "How come we're on this spiritual detox and your guys are all feast mode?" Jesus lays it down, "Look, you don't mope at a wedding while the main man's still partying. But sure, when he dips, then it's time to fast. And let's be real—you don't slap a fresh patch on your vintage denim, and you definitely don't store the latest vintage in an old-school flask. New vibes need new spaces. It's all about keeping it fresh and fitting."

Epic Comebacks

While Jesus was dropping knowledge, a local VIP shows up, slides to his knees, and is like, "My daughter just hit game over, but I know you've got the cheat codes for life. Just touch her, and she'll respawn." Jesus, up for the challenge, heads over with his squad. En route, this lady who's been dealing with a never-ending health glitch for twelve years thinks, "If I can just snag a piece of his hoodie, I'll be all good." She makes the stealthiest move and taps his cloak. Jesus, feeling the power-up, spins around and spots her. "Yo, braveheart, your trust level just unlocked your healing." Boom, she's back to full health, just like that. Arriving at the

VIP's crib, the place is like a sad scene from a music video—flute players, crying, the works. Jesus, in pure chill mode, is like, "Everyone, out. She's just hitting snooze." They laugh, thinking he's trolling. Crowd gets yeeted outside, Jesus strolls in, offers the girl a hand, and she's up and about, probably wondering why there's a crowd in her living room. Word gets out, and Jesus's follower count skyrockets.

Seeing is Believing

Next up, Jesus encounters two blind guys who've been tailing him, shouting, "Yo, Son of David, throw us some mercy!" Jesus, in a private chat, is like, "You guys think I can fix this?"

"100%, Lord."

A touch, a "Believe it and see it," and their world goes from audio to 4K Ultra HD. Jesus hits them with a "Keep this on the DL," but they're like the original influencers, spreading his @handle across the region.

Mic Drop Moment with a Mute Man

As Jesus and crew are about to dip, they're met by a guy who's been on mute because of a demon cramping his style. Jesus,

doing his thing, evicts the demon, and suddenly, the guy's chatting up a storm. The crowd's mind? Blown. They're tweeting, "Never seen anything like this in Israel!" But the Pharisees, ever the party poopers, are like, "He's basically using demon magic to kick demons out. #Conspiracy."

#CompassionGoals and the Harvest Hype

Jesus, on his never-ending tour of good vibes, hits every town and village, dropping knowledge in synagogues, spreading the good news, and fixing up everyone's ailments. Seeing the crowds looking all lost and down, he's hit with a wave of feels—like seeing puppies without an IG account. He turns to his squad, "Look at all these peeps needing a vibe check. The harvest is popping, but we're short on farmers. Hit up the Harvest Boss for some extra hands."

Squad Goals: The Holy Dozen

Then J.C. gathers his core twelve, giving them the go-ahead to ghost demons and patch up peeps. Here's the roster: Peter (the rock), Andrew (his bro), the Zebedee boys (James and John), Philip, Bartholomew (aka Nate), Thomas (the question guy),

Matthew (ex-money collector), James Jr., Thaddaeus (low-key legend), Simon (the intense one), and, oh, Judas (spoiler: not the MVP). Jesus is like, "Alright, listen up. Stick to the home turf—Israel's lost sheep. Your message? 'Heaven's knocking.' Heal, resurrect, clean up, and kick out demons. And keep it light—no gold, no extra kicks, just the essentials. You're living off the land, crew. Hospitality's key, but if they're not vibing with you, peace out and dust off." "Remember, Sodom and Gomorrah will look like a timeout compared to what's in store for the no-welcome wagon towns."

Heads Up: It's About to Get Real

J.C. hits them with the real talk: "I'm sending you out like noobs in a pro gamer lobby. So, you gotta be slick as a TikTok trend and pure as your fresh playlist. Watch out, 'cause they're gonna drag you into the drama, making you the main act in their cancel culture courtrooms and whip you up in their clout-chasing synagogues. You'll even find yourselves in the spotlight, facing off with the bigwigs and influencers, all because you're part of my crew. But when they try to put you on the spot, don't sweat the script. The right words will download straight from the Spirit, no Wi-Fi needed. Brace yourselves; it's gonna be like a family feud on steroids, with betrayals left and right. Being **#TeamJesus** will put you on everyone's hit list, but stick it out till the final season, and you're golden. If they start ghosting you in one place, swipe left, and hit up the next. You'll be on this roadshow till I'm back for the sequel. Remember, a student isn't above the master. If they've been throwing shade at me, you better believe you're gonna get some too."

No Fear, Just Vibe

"But don't let them shake you. Everything in the DMs is gonna go public, and every secret will drop like a hot track. The stuff I'm laying down after hours? Blast it from the rooftops come sunrise. Scared of those who can only mess with your body? Nah. Keep your eyes on the One who's got the full admin rights over body and soul. Think about it: a couple of sparrows are basically loose change, but even they don't hit the ground without God's say-so. And you? He's got your back down to the last hair—numbered and noted. So, keep your head up. You're worth way more than a bunch of sparrows to the Big Guy upstairs."

Team Jesus: The Ultimate Shoutout

Jesus lays it out, "If you rep me in your Insta stories and TikToks, consider it mutual. I'll give you a shoutout in the most exclusive place—my Dad's heavenly feed. But if you act like you don't know me when it counts, I'll have to hit 'unfollow' when it comes to vouching for you upstairs.

And don't get it twisted—I didn't come to sprinkle fairy dust and make everything chill. I'm here to mix it up, big time. I'm talking family group chats turning into battlegrounds, with loyalty tests that make reality TV look tame. If you're more about pleasing fam than standing by me, it's a no from me. And if you're not down to shoulder the struggles like a daily vlog challenge, you're not on my team. Finding your vibe in life? Cool, but if you lose yourself for my sake, you're unlocking the ultimate level.

Hydration Nation Gets Heavenly Props

When it comes to the welcome wagon, rolling out the red carpet for my squad is like rolling it out for me, and that's like rolling it out for the Big Boss who sent me. Show some love to a prophet or a righteous dude, and you're banking their level of rewards. Even if it's just sliding a DM or offering a cup of cold water to a newbie because they're part of the crew, that's it—you're securing your spot in the rewards program. Trust, it's a loyalty card that never expires."

J.C.'s Reality Check from Behind Bars

After setting his squad with the latest mission updates, Jesus hits up other towns to spread the vibe. Meanwhile, John's catching up on the celestial buzz from his cell and shoots a text via his followers, "Yo, are you the main event we've been waiting for, or is there another drop coming?" Jesus texts back, "Roll the highlight reel back to John: blind folks are seeing TikToks, the lame are hitting up dance challenges, leprosy's getting ghosted, the deaf are streaming playlists, the dead are hitting the restart button, and the broke are getting the best news. Plus, bonus points for not getting salty about what I'm about." As John's crew heads out, Jesus turns to the crowd for a little Q&A sesh about John: "What were you expecting to find in the desert? A dude getting swayed by every trend? Or maybe someone in hypebeast gear? Nah, luxury loungewear is for palace life. So, a prophet? Absolutely, and he's dropping more than just fire tweets. John's the VIP the script talked about, setting the stage for the main act. J.C. lays it down, "For real, no one's topped John in the human charts, but even the underdog in heaven's lineup is on another level. Since John stepped onto the scene, it's been non-stop action, with everyone trying to cop a piece of the kingdom like it's a limited drop. He's basically the finale of the 'prophet and law' season, and if you're clued in, he's the comeback special—Elijah 2.0. Tune in if you're catching what I'm laying down."

Swipe Left on This Generation

J.C. hits them with a zinger, "What's this generation like? Imagine kids chilling in the marketplace, hitting up their friends with a beat drop, expecting them to dance, or laying down a sad track, waiting for the tears. But nope, everyone's just scrolling past. John pulled a full detox, and they're like, 'He's got some demons.' I come in, ready to party, and suddenly I'm the bad guy, too cozy with the tax crew and the sinners squad. But hey, real talk, actions speak louder than any tweet."

The Miracle Ghosters

Then, Jesus goes full-on "Woe to you" mode on the towns that ghosted his miracle vibes. "Chorazin, Bethsaida, you guys saw the magic and still scrolled on by. Tyre and Sidon would've been all over a repentance trend if they saw half of what you did. And Capernaum? Thinking you're on a VIP list to heaven? More like heading to a major downfall. Sodom would've been standing strong today if they caught my tour."

Chill Vibes and Heavy Truths

But then, Jesus flips the script, "Big shoutout to you, Dad, for keeping the insiders guessing and making the little ones your faves. It's all in the family plan, right? Everything's on my plate now, and knowing the fam comes down to an invite from me.

Feeling weighed down? I've got you. My way of life is the real deal—humble and chill, and you'll find your stride. My path? It's the scenic route, no heavy lifting required."

Sabbath Game Strong

Cruising through some grain fields on the Sabbath, the disciples start snacking. Some

Pharisees slide into the DMs with a "Gotcha," but Jesus is ready, "Ever read about David's munchies run, or how the temple crew breaks Sabbath rules but still gets a pass? Spoiler: I'm bigger than the temple. If you really got the memo on mercy over rituals, we wouldn't be having this chat. By the way, I'm running the Sabbath show now.

(Jesus isn't just about bending rules; he's rewriting the playbook on what it means to live, love, and let go in a way that's real, raw, and totally radical. It's less about the performance, more about the heart—and always about keeping it merciful.)

Handy Healing on the Sabbath

So Jesus rolls up in the synagogue and spots a guy with a hand that's not playing ball—it's all shriveled up. The Pharisees, always looking for a gotcha moment, throw a curveball question about the legality of miracle work on rest days. Jesus, ever the king of clapbacks, hits them with, "Say one of you has a sheep and it decides to take a dive into a pit on the Sabbath. You gonna leave it there? Nah, you'd haul it out because even you know a sheep's worth the effort. Now, if we're valuing sheep over peeps, we got our priorities messed up. Helping out is always in season, even on the Sabbath." Then, to the guy with the wonky hand, "Yo, stretch out your hand." Dude does it, and bam, it's like new, fully operational. The Pharisees, though? Not celebrating. They storm off to cook up some sinister plot against Jesus.

Low-Key… Legend

Aware that he's now on their hit list, Jesus dips but still ends up with a crowd. He goes on a healing spree, but he's all about keeping it on the DL, fulfilling what Isaiah said about him being the chill servant who's here to bring justice without causing a scene. He's not about the drama or the loud protests in the streets. He's gentle with those who are barely hanging on, fanning the tiny flames of hope and faith until justice scores the win. And in his name, folks from all over are finding something to believe in, a reason to hope.

When Demons Get the Boot

So, a dude shows up in front of Jesus, can't see or talk because of a demon cramping his style. J.C., being the ultimate fixer, sends the demon packing, and suddenly the guy's chatting and spotting things like he's got

20/20 vision. The crowd's jaw drops, buzzing, "Is this the Son of David making moves?" But the Pharisees, ever the vibe killers, start spreading their usual fake news, "He's only kicking demons out because he's got the demon boss on speed dial." Jesus, catching their shady thoughts, hits them with logic, "Listen, if a squad's fighting itself, it's basically hitting the self-destruct button. If I'm teaming up with the demon boss, how's his empire supposed to last? And if your own crew is doing exorcisms, who are they teaming up with? Checkmate. If I'm booting out demons with God's own swipe, then guess what? God's kingdom just dropped right on your doorstep."

It's All About the Squad Goals

He goes on, "You can't just waltz into a strong dude's house and snag his sneakers without tying him up first, right? Same deal with demons. If you're not rolling with me, you're rolling out. And if you're not helping me gather, you're basically scattering." Then, dropping a truth bomb, "Every mistake and slip-up can be wiped clean, but dissing the Holy Spirit? That's the one line you don't cross. Trash talk me, and it's cool, but smack talk the Spirit, and it's game over, now and forever."

Fruit Check: Real Talk Edition

"Look, it's simple—good trees, good fruit; bad trees, bad fruit. You can't expect apple emojis from a cactus. And you, Pharisees, acting all snakey, how can you expect to say anything legit when you're running on E? Your mouth spills what your heart's filled with. The good ones pull out good vibes like they're hosting a giveaway, and the bad ones? It's trash talk city. Come Judgment Day, you're gonna have to explain every single 'lol' and 'omg' you threw around. Your own chat history is either your ticket in or your downfall.

Demanding the Ultimate TikTok Challenge

So, the scribes and Pharisees, always on the hunt for some drama, roll up to Jesus and are like, "Hey, Teacher, hit us with a sign that'll trend." Jesus, not one to play into their games, claps back, "This generation's always scrolling for signs, but the only DM you're gonna get is the Jonah alert. Just like Jonah was the original content creator in that fish's belly for a three-night binge, I'm about to drop a three-day ghosting act in the heart of the earth. And guess what? The folks from Nineveh and the Queen of the South got their act together way faster than you lot, and they didn't even have the spoilers. They'll be the first to hit 'unfollow' on this generation come judgment day because they recognized game when they saw it, and here I am, next level, and you're still not convinced."

Ghosting 101

"Let's talk hauntings. When a sketchy spirit decides its human crib isn't vibing anymore, it goes on a quest through the desert snap stories looking for chill spots but ends up with nada. So, it thinks, 'Let's check out my old digs.' Finds it all Marie Kondo-ed, totally empty. What does it do? It slides into the DMs of seven other spirits sketchier than itself, throws a house party in the person it left, making the comeback way worse than the original exit. That's pretty much this gen in a nutshell—always ending up in a bigger mess."

Who's My Fam, Really?

While Jesus is deep in convo with the crowd, his fam—mom and bros—are on the outside trying to get a word. Someone's like, "Psst, your squad's outside trying to chat." Jesus flips the script, "Who are we calling family here?" Then, with a dramatic hand gesture towards his disciples, "Boom, here's my real fam. Anyone who's on board with my Dad's master plan, we're talking brothers, sisters, even moms."

Storytime with Jesus: The Sower's Saga

Fast forward, and Jesus hits the beach, drawing such a massive crowd he has to kick back in a boat while everyone else camps out on the sand. He launches into story mode: "Peep this—a farmer's out here throwing seeds. Some seeds pull a faceplant on the path, and birds swoop in like it's a free buffet. Some seeds land on the rock concert ground, shoot up fast 'cause the dirt's shallow, but then the sun's like, 'Not today,' and they're toast 'cause they got no roots. Then you've got seeds rolling into thornville, where they get all choked up and can't even. But here's the win—some seeds hit the jackpot, land in the good stuff, and boom—they're popping off fruit like nobody's business, multiplying what was sown by up to a hundred times. Tune in if you're picking up what I'm putting down.

Parables: Jesus' Secret Sauce

The disciples, puzzled, slide up to Jesus, "Yo, why you always hitting them with these cryptic stories?" Jesus leans in, "Here's the scoop: The VIP pass to Kingdom secrets is all yours, but for the crowd, it's a bit more like a riddle. It's like, the more you 'get it,' the more you'll get. And if you're not catching on, even the little you have got going might slip through your fingers. It's all about seeing without seeing, and hearing without really listening—that's the vibe for many. It's like Isaiah was talking right about them: 'You can keep on listening, but you won't get it; keep on looking, but you won't really see.' Their hearts? Too tough. Ears? Might as well be on mute. Eyes? Practically closed. If they weren't, they might actually get the picture, make a U-turn, and I'd patch them right up." "Peep this—you're the lucky ones. Your eyes and ears are on the inside track. Prophets and all the righteous peeps from way back would've done anything to catch a glimpse or hear a bit of what you're privy to."

Breaking Down the Sower's Story

"So, about that sower story: When someone catches wind of the Kingdom vibe but it doesn't click, it's like the dark side swoops in and deletes the message before it even lands. That's the path scenario. The rocky ground? That's someone vibing with the message at first—like, 'Yes, let's go!' But it's a flash in the pan. No roots, so when the going gets tough, they're out. Thorny ground folks? They hear it, sure, but then life's stresses and the chase for cash clutter everything up, and the message gets ghosted. But good soil? That's the one who really listens, gets it, and goes full bloom—producing mad results, way more than what was initially dropped."

The Epic of Wheat vs. Weeds

Jesus drops another story: "Picture this: Heaven's vibe is like a dude who plants top-tier seeds in his field. But then, under the cover of night, some sneaky hater sprinkles in a bunch of weed seeds and bails. Fast forward, and both the premium wheat and the party-crasher weeds are popping up together. The field crew hits up the boss, 'Boss, didn't you plant the good stuff? Where'd this riffraff come from?' He's like, 'That's the work of a rival, no doubt.' They're all, 'Want us to dive in and weed 'em out?' 'Nah,' the boss man says. 'You might yank out the good with the bad. Let's just chill till harvest. Then, we'll sort the keepers from the burners.'

Mustard Seed and Yeast: Tiny but Mighty

Next, Jesus spins another one: "The heaven kingdom is like a mustard seed. Looks like nothing in your palm, right? But plant that bad boy, and bam—it's the tree where all the birds wanna hang. And then there's the yeast tale. A woman works some yeast into like fifty pounds of dough. Sounds like a workout, but it gets the whole batch rising."

(In these parables, Jesus is schooling us on the kingdom's unexpected growth and mixed bag of good and bad, showing that patience and perspective can reveal the true nature of things. And just like a tiny seed or a bit of yeast can change the game, small beginnings and hidden actions have a way of transforming the big picture.)

Parable Drop: Secret Codes Unlocked

So Jesus is out here, spinning tales left and right, not dropping a single truth bomb without wrapping it in a parable. It's like he's fulfilling that old-school prophecy vibe: "I'm gonna spill the cosmic tea in stories; reveal the mysteries that have been on the down-low since day one."

Deep Dive into the Wheat and Weeds Saga

Post-storytime, Jesus and the squad hit up a private session. The crew's like, "Break down that wheat-weeds drama for us." Jesus lays it out: "Alright, the one planting the premium seeds, that's me—the Son of Man. The field? That's the big wide world. The top-shelf seeds are kingdom kids, while the weeds? They're team trouble, courtesy of the bad guy, the devil. Fast forward to the finale—the harvest's when we wrap this age up, and the harvest crew? Angels. When it's go-time, I'll send my angel squad to clean house, pulling all the troublemakers and rule-breakers. They're headed straight for the fire pit—cue the waterworks and teeth-grinding. But the legit ones? They'll be lighting up the kingdom like the sun at high noon. If you're tuned in, don't miss this beat."

(Jesus isn't just telling stories for the 'gram; he's unpacking the kingdom's reality, showing the ultimate showdown between good and evil, with a clear line on who's who and what's what. It's all about staying on the right side of the story, where the end game is shining bright in the good vibes of the Father's realm.)

Epic Finds and Divine Investments

Jesus hits them with another one: "Imagine this: The kingdom of heaven is like stumbling upon a hidden Fortnite loot chest in a field. A dude finds it, sneakily buries it again, then Yeets out to liquidate his entire inventory to buy the field. Talk about all in. Switching gears, "Also, the kingdom vibe is like a hypebeast hunting for the ultimate limited-edition pearl. When he finally tracks down the Supreme drop of pearls, he goes full beast mode, sells his entire sneaker collection, and cops it.

Fishing for the Future

And again, "Think of the kingdom of heaven like dropping a massive Battle Royale net in the ocean, scooping up all kinds of players. Once the lobby's full, it's time to sort out the pros from the noobs. The keepers get VIP access, while the rest get booted from the game. So, when the final season drops, the angels will squad up, sorting the trolls from the team players, and tossing the griefers into the lava pit. That's where you'll catch

the sound of major salt and the grind of teeth."

Unlocking the Wisdom Loot Box

After laying down some heavy parable content, Jesus checks in with the squad, "Y'all tracking with all this?" They're like, "Yeah, we got you." "So here's the deal," Jesus explains, "every OG scripture teacher who gets with the kingdom program is like that one friend who's got an epic collection of both vintage and latest drop sneakers. They know just when to flex each pair."

Homecoming Flop

Post-parable drop, Jesus hits up his old stomping grounds, throwing down wisdom and wonders in the local hangout spot. But instead of getting props, the hometown crowd's throwing shade, "Isn't this the local handyman's kid? Mary's son? And don't we know his siblings? How's he pulling off these tricks?" They can't wrap their heads around it, and Jesus is like, "A prophet's only dissed in his hometown and his own crib." Due to the vibe check fail, he kept the miracles on the low there, all because of their swipe left on belief.

Drama at the Royal Court

Meanwhile, King Herod's catching wind of Jesus and starts having a major throwback moment, thinking Jesus is John the Baptist back from his grave, hence the power surge. Backstory: Herod had John locked up because John wasn't about Herod's sketchy marriage moves. Herod was tempted to go full Game of Thrones on John but knew the people would riot because they were all in on John being a legit prophet. At Herod's birthday bash, Herodias's daughter puts on a show, and Herod, probably a bit too turnt, vows to grant her any wish. Mom whispers, "Yo, ask for John's head on a plate." Despite major regrets, Herod's stuck by his word and his rep in front of the squad, so he orders the hit. John's head ends up a grim centerpiece, delivered to mom by her daughter. John's crew takes care of the aftermath, then heads to Jesus with the news.

(In these scenes, Jesus lays out the reality of wisdom's value, faces rejection among the familiar, and a grim tale unfolds at Herod's court, highlighting the cost of truth-telling and the impact of not fitting the expected mold.)

Epic Buffet and Water Stunts

When Jesus caught wind of the drama, he hit the water for some solo time. But the crowd wasn't having it; they tracked him down like he was dropping concert tickets. Landing on shore, Jesus, seeing the massive fanbase, goes full-on healer mode out of sheer compassion.

Come dinner time, the disciples were like, "Yo, Jesus, it's late and we're out in the sticks. Let's wrap and send everyone to hit up the drive-thru."

Jesus flips it, "Nah, you're up. Feed them."

The squad's baffled, "We've got a snack pack here—five loaves, two fish. That's it." "Bring them over," Jesus says. After getting everyone seated, he does a heavenly shoutout, breaks the bread like he's starting a trend, and hands it off to the disciples to distribute. Boom—everyone's feasting, and they even bag up twelve baskets of foodie leftovers. Headcount? A solid 5k men, not counting the women and kids tagging along.

Surf's Up with J.C.

Post-meal, Jesus hustles the disciples into a boat for the next spot while he clears out the crowd. Then, it's mountain retreat time for some one-on-one with the big guy upstairs. Meanwhile, the disciples are in this nautical nightmare, waves slapping the boat around because the wind's throwing a tantrum. Out of nowhere, Jesus decides to take a moonlit walk—on the water, no less. The crew's spooked, "Ghost alert!" They're freaking out big time. J.C. calls out, "Chill, it's me. No fear." Peter, caught up in the moment, is like, "If it's really you, let me hit that water walk." "Come on," Jesus says. Peter's out the boat, pulling off this water walk move, but then gets cold feet because, wind. He starts sinking, shouting, "Jesus, bro, save me!" Jesus, ever the lifesaver, grabs him, "Faith, dude, where'd it go?" Back in the boat, the wind's like, "I'm out." The disciples are mind-blown, "For real, you're the Son of God."

#ElderlyTraditions

Pharisees and scribes roll up on Jesus, launching a hygiene inquisition, "Yo, why do your crew ignore elder traditions and not bother with a pre-snack handwash?" Jesus claps back, "And why do you ditch God's rules for your own remixes? God's like, 'Respect your folks or it's game over,' but you're out here saying, 'Nah, if I label my stuff as a temple donation, I'm excused from family duties.' That's how you're playing God's commands on mute with your tradition." Then, dropping a truth bomb from Isaiah, "You're all talk, no heart—doing a lip-sync battle with devotion but missing the beat."

It's What's Inside That Counts

Gathering the crowd for a teachable moment, Jesus goes, "Heads up, it's not the snack that taints you; it's the trash talk and heart spam that does." Disciples give a heads-up, "You know the Pharisees are throwing a fit over this, right?" Jesus, unfazed, "Any trend God didn't start is getting axed. Ignore them; they're like blind TikTok dancers leading each other into faceplants." Peter's scratching his head, "Run that by us again?" Jesus, a tad exasperated, "Still not getting it? Whatever you eat just hits the digestive track and exits, stage left. But the venom you spit? That's heart-sourced. Evil plots, violence, cheating, low-key thefts, fake news, and trash talk—that's the crud that truly wrecks a person, not ditching the hand sanitizer."

Epic Faith from an Unexpected Fan

As Jesus hits up the Tyre and Sidon scene, a Canaanite mom crashes the party, launching into a plea, "Mercy, Lord, Son of David! My girl's caught up in some serious demon drama." Jesus plays it cool, radio silence. The disciples, feeling the secondhand stress, are like, "Can you maybe... not ignore her? She's turning this into a whole thing."

Jesus drops a line, "I'm here for the Israel crew, not the global tour yet." But this mom isn't about to hit 'unfollow.' She goes full prostration, "Lord, seriously, I need a win here." J.C., testing the waters, is like, "You know, it's not cool to snag the kids' snacks and toss them to the pups." She claps back with the ultimate comeback, "True, true, but even the pups snag crumbs under the table." Jesus, impressed by her quick wit and unwavering faith, "You got it, your faith's on fire. Your wish is granted." Boom—her daughter's back in the normal life, demon-free.

Healing Spree by the Sea

Next up, Jesus takes a chill session by the Sea of Galilee, hitting up a mountainside spot.

Crowds flock in—lame, blind, mute, all sorts. They're laid out at Jesus' feet like he's running a divine M.A.S.H. unit. He goes to work, and the transformations are jaw-dropping. Mutes are chatting, the lame are doing parkour, the blind are catching sunsets, and the crowd goes wild, throwing up praises to the God of Israel.

Snack Time Sequel: The 4K Feast

J.C., feeling for the crowd after a three-day binge of wisdom and wonder, tells his disciples, "These peeps are running on E, and I can't have them fainting on the trek back." Disciples are scratching their heads, "How are we supposed to cater this desert rave with zero DoorDash options?" Jesus, ever the problem-solver, "What's in the pantry?" "Seven loaves and a couple of fish sticks," they report. After getting everyone cozy on the ground, Jesus does his thing—blesses the grub, breaks it down, and the disciples start the biggest picnic spread. Everyone's chowing down and, believe it or not, they're packing up seven Coachella-sized baskets of leftovers. The headcount? A solid 4K, not counting the fam and kids tagging along. Post-meal, Jesus hits the waters towards Magadan, probably in need of a quiet cruise.

Forecasting Fails & Faith Facts

Queue the Pharisees and Sadducees, looking for some celestial magic trick to validate Jesus. He claps back, "You're all weathermen when it's about sunsets and storm clouds but can't decode the era we're in. Looking for a show? The only sneak peek you're getting is the Jonah reboot." Mic drop, Jesus exits stage left. Meanwhile, the disciples are on the boat, facepalming for leaving the bread behind. Jesus, seizing the teachable moment, "Watch out for the Pharisees and Sadducees' brand of yeast." The squad's lost in the sauce, thinking it's about their bread blunder. Jesus, doing a facepalm of his own, "Do you not recall the 5K dinner or this latest 4K snacking miracle? How are we still on the topic of bread? I'm talking about the Pharisees and Sadducees' mixtape of miss-the-point teachings." Lightbulb moment for the disciples as they finally get the memo

Peter Drops the Mic

In the chill vibes of Caesarea Philippi, Jesus hits his crew with a pop quiz, "What's the word on the street about the Son of Man?" The squad's like, "Well, some are vibing with you as John the Bap 2.0, others are throwing back to Elijah or Jeremiah vibes, or maybe another prophet from the greatest hits." Jesus gets personal, "Cool, cool, but who do *you* guys think I am?" Simon Peter, stepping up, "You're the real deal—the Messiah, the Son of the living God." Jesus gives Peter the nod, "Big ups, Simon son of Jonah! This wasn't a hot take you just stumbled on—it's straight-up divine intel. And you, Peter? You're the bedrock I'm building my squad on, and not even the darkest corners are breaking through. I'm handing you the master key to heaven's gates. Whatever you lock down here, consider it locked up there, and vice versa." Then, plot twist, Jesus is like, "Zip it on the Messiah talk for now."

Spoiler Alert: The Rough Road Ahead

Next, J.C. starts laying down some serious future tracks, "Heads up, we're heading to Jerusalem, where things are gonna get messy with the top brass, leading to me checking out but also making the ultimate comeback on day three." Peter, in full panic mode, pulls Jesus aside, "Hard pass, Lord. That's not on your playlist." Jesus, spinning around, "Ease up, 'Satan'! You're barking up the wrong tree, thinking way too small."

Following Jesus: The Final Challenge

Jesus then turns the table, "Wanna ride with me? Time to ghost your ego, pick up that struggle, and hit follow. Trying to clinch onto your life as you know it? You're gonna lose it. But if you're down to lose it for my sake, you're gonna find the real deal. What's the point of winning the 'gram but losing yourself? And trust, when I roll back in with my crew, we're keeping score and handing out props based on the real plays." And just to drop their jaws, "Some of you here are gonna catch a live preview of the kingdom before you hit your expiration data."

The Ultimate Glow-Up on the Mountain

Jesus decides it's time for a private show with Peter, James, and John, so they hit up a high mountain for some alone time. Up there, Jesus pulls off the ultimate glow-up: His face is blasting sunshine, and his fit turns pure white. Then, out of nowhere, Moses and Elijah crash the party, having a deep chat with Jesus.

Peter, ever the hype man, is like, "Lord, this spot is lit. Let's set up some VIP tents— one for you, one for Moses, and one for Elijah." Mid-sentence, a cloud with the brightness of a thousand notifications envelops them, and God's voice drops from the cloud, "This is my beloved Son, hitting all the right notes. Tune into him!" This divine shoutout scares the bejeezus out of the disciples, faceplanting in awe. Jesus, being the bro he is, helps them up, "Chill, no need for panic attacks." They peek up, and it's just Jesus in his usual form.

Don't Drop the Spoilers

On the trek down, Jesus is like, "Zip it on this mountain top remix until I've made my big comeback from the dead." The disciples, now in a Q&A mood, "But what's the deal with Elijah's pre-game show?" Jesus breaks it down, "Elijah's set to make things right. But spoiler: He already dropped by, and everyone just did him dirty, same as they're gonna do to the Son of Man." Lightbulb moment for the disciples—it's John the Baptist they're talking about.

Demon-Busting Downhill

Back with the crowd, a desperate dad kneels before Jesus, "Lord, my kid's caught in a nightmare loop of seizures, diving into fires and water. Your crew couldn't cut it." Jesus, a tad frustrated with the faithless vibes, "Bring the kid over." With just a word, Jesus kicks the demon to the curb, and the boy's back to normal, just like that. The disciples, in private, "So, why did we strike out on that one?" Jesus, laying down some real talk, "It's your faith—or the lack of it. Even with a faith no bigger than a mustard seed, you could've pulled off some major moves. Nothing's off-limits then."

Round Two

While chilling in Galilee, Jesus hits his crew with a sequel spoiler: "So, the Son of Man's about to get double-crossed and handed over. They're gonna end him, but plot twist—three days later, he's back." This news got them all in their feels, majorly distressed.

Tax Season Plot Twist

Back in Capernaum, the tax collectors come sniffing around Peter, "Your guy pays the temple tax, right?" Peter's like, "Yeah, sure." Before Peter can even bring it up, Jesus is already on it, "Simon, who do you think gets taxed, the king's kids or the randoms?" "Randoms," Peter figures. "So, technically, we're exempt," Jesus says. "But let's keep it chill and not stir the pot. Hit up the lake, catch a fish, and you'll find enough coin in its mouth to clear our tax bill—for both of us."

Who's Top Dog in Heaven?

The disciples, now curious about the celestial leaderboard, ask Jesus, "Who's king of the hill in heaven?" Jesus, calling over a kiddo, drops this truth bomb, "Unless you hit the reset button and get on this child's level, you're not even getting through the gate. Whoever's got this kid's chill vibes is top of the charts in heaven. And rolling out the welcome mat for one kid is like rolling it out for me." "But if anyone trips up one of these believers, they'd be better off with cement shoes in the deep end. World's a trip mine of temptations—inevitable, but mega oof for the one who sets them off. If your hand or foot gets you in trouble, chop it off. Better to be handicapped in life than fully equipped for a dive into the eternal bonfire. Same goes if your eye's your downfall

—scoop it out. One-eyed living beats a two-eyed roast."

VIP Angels and The One That Got Away

Jesus starts off with a heartwarmer, "Don't sleep on these kids because their guardian angels have VIP access to my Dad upstairs. Picture this: A shepherd's got 100 sheep, but one decides to do a runner. Won't he leave the 99 on the chill slopes to hunt for the wanderer? And when he finds it, it's party time for that one sheep, way more than for the 99 that stayed put. Same vibes from my Dad—he's not about losing even one of these little legends.

Bro Code: Restoration Edition

Moving on, Jesus lays down the bro code for squashing beef. "If your bro messes up with you, hit him up one-on-one to clear the air. If he gets the message, you've both won. If not, bring in a couple more to keep it 100, making sure every side of the story gets a fair hearing. Still a no-go? Then it's time to bring in the whole crew. And if he's still acting up, then you gotta treat him like he's outside the circle, like a total stranger or that guy always dodging his taxes."

"And here's the real talk—what you decide on earth, consider it cosigned by heaven. Plus, when even just two or three of you are synced up in my name, I'm right there in the mix."

The Saga of the Petty Servant

Peter's like, "Yo, Jesus, how many times do I gotta forgive someone? Seven times good?" Jesus hits back, "Try seventy times seven. Let me break it down: Heaven's kingdom is like a CEO ready to balance the books. He's got this guy who owes him more cash than a billionaire's shopping spree. Dude can't pay up, so CEO's like, 'Sell everything. We're clearing this debt.' The guy's in full panic, face down, 'Give me a sec, and I'll sort everything.' CEO feels the vibes, cancels the debt, and lets him walk. But then, this guy finds someone who owes him lunch money, grabs him like he's in a WWE match, 'Cough up the cash!' The debtor pleads for time, but no dice—our guy throws him in the clink over pocket change. The office is shook, tells the CEO everything, and he drags Mr. Unforgiving back, 'I let you off the hook, and you couldn't do the same for someone else?' Mad as hell, CEO hands him over to the muscle until he pays up. Moral of the story? If you're not about that forgiveness life, expect the same treatment from the big guy upstairs."

Divorce Debate Goes 0-100

Next scene, Jesus rolls into Judea, crowds in tow, still doing his healing thing. Pharisees pop up, trying to trip him up on divorce laws, "Can a guy divorce for, like, any reason?" Jesus, schooling them with Genesis, "Didn't you read the OG relationship goals? 'Male and female,' and 'two become one.' What God glued together, let's not rip apart." "But Moses said we could hand out divorce papers!" they challenge. Jesus claps back, "Moses threw you that 'cause your hearts were as tough as old boots. But from the start, it wasn't supposed to be that way. Ditch your wife for another, and it's straight-up adultery, except for, you know, cheating." Disciples are mind-blown, "Sounds like marriage is hardcore." Jesus lays it out, "Not everyone's cut out for this. Some are single for the kingdom's sake. If you can handle that, do it."

VIP Passes for the Kiddos

So, kids were being brought to Jesus for some divine high-fives and prayers, right? But the disciples were acting like bouncers at a VIP event, trying to turn them away. Jesus was like, "Chill, let the kids through. Heaven's guest list is basically made for them." After giving them the blessing, he rolled out.

The Saga of the Loaded Questioner

Next up, this rich young dude rolls up to Jesus, popping the million-dollar question, "Yo, Teacher, what's the cheat code for eternal life?" Jesus throws it back, "Why hit me up about what's good? Only God's got the goods. But if you're game, just follow the rules." The guy's like, "Which ones, specifically?" Jesus lists off the usual: no killing, no cheating, no stealing, no lying, respect your folks, and love your neighbor like your latest binge-watch. The young ruler claims, "Done all that. What's missing?" Jesus, sensing a teachable moment, "Wanna level up? Liquidate your assets, help out the poor, and you'll have VIP access in heaven. Then, hit follow on me." Hearing this, the guy's mood dropped faster than a bad connection. Owning too much stuff, he couldn't hit that unfollow on his lifestyle.

The Camel Challenge

Jesus turns to the squad, "Honestly, it's tougher for a rich dude to enter heaven than for a camel to squeeze through a needle's eye." The disciples' jaws hit the floor, "Then who's got a shot at this?" Jesus, with that hope in his eyes, "On your own, it's a no-go. But with God, everything's on the table." Peter, always looking for the angle, "We've ditched it all to follow you. What's in it for us?" Jesus lays it out, "When it's time for the big reset, and I'm chilling on my throne, you'll be right there with me, calling the shots for Israel. And anyone who's given up the fam or the farm for me gets it back a hundredfold, plus a ticket to eternal life. But here's the twist: the first in line might just end up at the back, and the underdogs might lead the pack."

The Ultimate Workday Plot Twist

Imagine the kingdom of heaven as this chill vineyard owner who's up at dawn to recruit some help. He finds a crew, agrees to pay them a fair day's wage, and sends them to get their hands dirty.

But this owner's on a hiring spree—heads out again at brunch time, then mid-afternoon, and even hits up the late crowd at happy hour. Each time, he finds people just hanging out and he's like, "Why waste the day? Jump in, I'll pay

you right." Come quitting time, he flips the script and tells his manager to settle up, starting with the last-minute joiners. Plot twist: everyone gets the same payday, sparking some major side-eye from the sunrise squad. They're all, "Hold up, we slaved all day, and you're paying us the same as these one-hour wonders?" The owner's like, "Mate, we shook on a deal, right? Take your cash and head out. I'm feeling generous today—why's that got you salty?" So here's the kicker: "The last will be first, and the first, last."

Spoiler Alert 3.0: The Jerusalem Journey

On their way to Jerusalem, Jesus pulls his closest twelve for a sneak peek of what's next: "We're heading to the big city, and it's about to get real. I'll be handed over, sentenced to death by the top dogs, then tossed to the outsiders for a round of mockery, a whip session, and finally, they'll pin me up. But plot twist—three days later, I'm hitting the reset button."

Reality Check

Zebedee's squad's mom hits Jesus up, aiming high: "Can my boys sit right next to you in your kingdom?" Jesus, keeping it real, challenges them, "Ready to face what I'm about to? It's not all glitz." They claim they are, not fully grasping the depth. Jesus lays down the truth, "You'll share my struggles, but the top spots? That's for Dad to decide."

Disciple Drama and Jesus' Masterclass in Greatness

Hearing about the request, the crew gets salty. Jesus calls a huddle, flipping the script on power and greatness. "Real leaders serve," he says, "Look at me—I'm here to serve, not to be served."

Miracle Encore for the Faithful Fans

Exiting Jericho, two blind fans call out to Jesus. Despite the crowd's shushing, they shout louder. Jesus, moved, asks, "What do you want?" "To see," they reply. A touch from Jesus, and their sight's restored. Instantly, they're on team Jesus.

The King's Humble Entry

Approaching Jerusalem, Jesus sends two disciples on a unique mission: fetch a donkey. It's all to fulfill a prophecy, showcasing a king who enters not with pomp but with humility. Jesus rides in, the crowd goes wild,

paving his path with clothes and branches, shouting "Hosanna!" Jerusalem buzzes with curiosity, "Who's this?" The crowd proudly claims, "It's Jesus, the prophet from Nazareth."

Temple Cleanup Gone Viral

Jesus rolls up in the temple, finds it turned into a shopping mall, and goes full beast mode— flipping tables and bench-pressing dove cages. He's like, "This spot's supposed to be for DMs with the Big Guy, not your shady deals!"

Kid's Choir Backs Jesus

While he's at it, the blind and lame show up, and Jesus hooks them up with instant heals. But then, the kid fan club starts their "Hosanna" flash mob, and the temple bigwigs are not vibing. They're all, "You hearing this?" Jesus claps back with, "Ever read the part where kids spit the truth? Yeah, thought so."

Fig Tree Gets Ghosted

Next day, Jesus is on a snack run, spots a fig tree slacking on the job, and basically curses it into becoming a tree jerky. Disciples are shook, "How'd the tree tap out so fast?" Jesus is like, "Faith's the key. Believe hard enough, and you could yeet a mountain into the ocean."

Who Gave You the Keys?

Back in the temple, the religious suits corner Jesus with, "Who let you run this show?" Jesus, ever the riddle master, hits them with a counter-question about John's creds. They huddle up, afraid to pick a side because either answer's got them losing face. Playing it safe, they go with, "No clue," and Jesus is like, "Then, no tea for you either." Through these episodes, Jesus isn't just flipping tables and cursing trees; he's challenging norms, questioning authority, and illustrating faith's real-world impact, all while keeping his cool in the face of haters and skeptics, proving actions (and faith) speak louder than words.

The Tale of the Flip-Flop Brothers

So, there's this dad with two sons. He hits up the first one, like, "Yo, hit the vineyard, we got work." The kid's all, "Nah, not feeling it," but then does a 180 and actually goes. The dad asks son number two the same, and this one's all, "Sure thing," but ends up binging shows instead. Jesus drops the mic, asking, "Who's the real MVP here?" Everyone's like, "The first

dude." And Jesus is like, "Exactly, and here's the kicker: the outcasts you diss are getting into heaven's VIP lounge way before you."

Epic Vineyard Drama

Next parable's got a plot twist vibe. A landowner sets up this awesome vineyard and then dips out. Come harvest, he sends his crew to collect, but the renters go full-on villain mode—beating, offing, and stoning his messengers. Not cool. The landowner sends more messengers, and it's the same deal. Then he sends his son, thinking they'll respect him, but they're like, "Lol, no," and kill him to snatch his inheritance. Jesus hits them with the real talk: "What do you think the vineyard owner will do?" They're all, "He's gonna go 'Terminator' on them and hand the vineyard to folks who actually deliver." Jesus then throws some Scripture shade, reminding them about the rejected stone turning VIP. He's basically saying, "Heads up, the kingdom's getting a new crew, one that gets the job done." The religious big shots realize Jesus is spilling tea about them. They want to grab him, but they chicken out because the crowd's eating up his every word, treating him like the latest trendsetter prophet.

Wedding Banquet Goes Viral

Imagine God's kingdom as this lit wedding party a king threw for his son. He hits up his guest list, but they're all, "Nah, got better plans." So, he sends a Snapchat: "Party's poppin', food's on point, come thru." But nah, they ghost him, some even rough up his messengers. King goes zero to a hundred real quick, serves up some justice, and then decides to make it an open invite. His crew hits the streets, filling the venue with a mixtape of good and bad peeps. But yo, there's this one dude chilling without his party fit. King's like, "Bro, how'd you even?" Dude's speechless. Gets booted to the shadow realm— total mood killer. Jesus wraps it up, "Invite's out, but not everyone's making the cut."

#TaxSeason Drama

Pharisees, looking to start something, roll up with the Herodians. Playing sweet, they're like, "Yo, Jesus, is dodging taxes chill or nah?" Jesus, seeing through the fake news, pulls out a coin. "Who's this dude?" "Caesar," they say. Jesus drops wisdom, "Pay up to Caesar, but don't forget what's due to God." Minds. Blown.

Sadducees Get Schooled

Same day, Sadducees slide in, trying to trip Jesus up with some soap opera scenario about a widow and seven brothers. "So, in heaven, who's she married to?" they ask. Jesus, not missing a beat, is like, "Y'all don't get it. Heaven's not an episode of 'The Bachelor.' It's more like an angelic hangout. And about the dead being alive? God's not the God of the dead, but of the living." Crowd's jaw = dropped.

Top-Tier Commands Drop

After Jesus put the Sadducees on mute, the Pharisees huddled up for round two. One law pro steps up with a quiz: "Yo, Jesus, hit us with the greatest command." Jesus lays it down smooth: "Love God with everything you've got—heart, soul, brain. That's the top track. And the next one's a banger too: Love your peeps like you love yourself. These two are the playlist all the other rules jam to."

Messiah Mic Drop

Then Jesus flips the script, "What's the 411 on the Messiah? Whose fam is he from?" Easy, they say, "David's crew." But Jesus spins it, "Then why's David calling him 'boss' in the hits? If David's giving him props, how's he just a descendant?" Crickets. They got nothing. That day, the question game was officially retired.

Calling Out the Flexers Guide

So, Jesus drops this truth bomb on the crowd and his squad: "Yo, the scribes and Pharisees are chilling in Moses' hot seat. Do what they say but don't copy their moves. They're all talk, no action. Heavy lifting? Not their jam. They're all about that look-at-me life, making their swag loud and their titles longer. "Don't get caught up in their title game. You've got one MVP, and you're all on the same team. And forget calling anyone 'father' like they're your OG, 'cause you've got the Big Guy upstairs. And instructors? Pfft, you've got one Teacher, and that's the Messiah. Wanna be top dog? Then be the team's water boy. Tryna climb that social ladder will only get you a reality check. "Man, those Pharisees and scribes are straight-up ghosting heaven's door, not stepping in or letting others. They're globe-trotting, flipping people into twice the hell-raiser they are. And don't get me started on their 'oath logic'— temple vs. temple gold, altar vs. gift on it. Like, hello? What's got more cred, the bling or the place that makes the bling sacred? "Big

oof to them for majoring in herb tithing while ghosting on the biggies like justice, mercy, and loyalty. It's like, you'd fish out a fly from your drink but then chug a camel smoothie. And oh, polishing the outside while the inside's a hot mess? That's like being a glam zombie tomb— pretty outside, dead inside. "They're all, 'If we were back in the day, we wouldn't mess with the prophets.' Right. They're basically signing their ancestors' sin receipt. Viper squad! How you gonna dodge the express to hell? Heads up, I'm sending in the real deal—prophets, wise peeps, and scholars. Some you'll off, some you'll whip, and some you'll chase city to city. So yeah, every drop of righteous blood spilled, from Abel to Zechariah, that's on you. Spoiler: it's all gonna hit the fan this gen."

Jerusalem's Drama and End-Times Tea

Jerusalem, oh Jerusalem, the city that's got a rep for ghosting prophets and treating messengers like dodgeball targets. How I've wanted to pull you close, like a mama hen with her chicks, but nah, you weren't feeling it. So, here's the tea: your place is gonna be ghost town vibes. And don't expect to see me until you're all about that

"Blessed is he who comes in the vibe of the Lord" energy.

End-Times Spoilers

Chillin' on Mount Olives, the crew slides into Jesus' DMs asking, "Spill the tea—when's all this going down, and what's the sign you're about to drop the final season?" Jesus is like, "Peep this—don't let anyone catfish you. A bunch of posers will rock up claiming, 'I'm the Messiah,' leading loads to play the fool. You'll hear about beefs and battle royales, but keep your cool; it's just the trailer, not the main feature. Nations will throw shade, and natural disasters will be on the daily. But hey, that's just the universe warming up.

It Gets Intense

You'll be thrown under the bus, some of you will get the axe, and you'll be on everyone's hit list because of team Jesus. Friendships will go south, trust issues will be the norm, and the fake news will be everywhere. With chaos as the new trend, people's hearts will frost over. But the real MVPs are the ones who stick it out to the final credits. And this gospel? It's going global, a shoutout to every corner of the world, then it's showtime—the finale."

The Ultimate Finale

Okay, vibe check: when you spot the "no-chill abomination" that Daniel the OG prophet talked about doing a TikTok dance in the holy zone (y'all, get the hint), it's time to yeet outta Judea and hit the mountains. If you're chilling on your roof, don't even think about diving into your house for that forgotten phone charger. And if you're out in the fields, forget the jacket—just run! Shoutout to the preggers and nursing moms, yikes, those days are gonna be tough. Send up a quick prayer that your sprint isn't in winter or—major oof—on a Sabbath. 'Cause what's coming is the ultimate stress test, the kind of chaos that's never been seen and never will again. If those days weren't put on fast-forward, nobody would survive. But for the squad's sake, there's gonna be a mercy cut. If anyone slides into your DMs with, "Yo, Messiah's just dropped at this spot," or "Quick, he's hiding in the storage unit," don't fall for it. Fake messiahs and wannabe prophets are gonna pop up, pulling off insane stunts to trick even the VIPs. But hey, I've given you the heads up. Don't chase after them. The real deal will be as obvious as lightning stretching from Snapchat to TikTok. Wherever the drama is, that's where you'll find the action.

Son of Man's Grand Entrance

Right after the world hits peak meltdown, the sun's gonna ghost us, the moon will bail on its glow-up, stars will literally drop out of the sky, and the whole universe will hit a snag. Then, boom, the Son of Man's big reveal lights up the sky, and everyone's gonna be straight-up mourning. He'll rock up with clouds like it's his personal Uber, flexing power and mad glory. Angel squad rolls out with the cosmic trumpet blast, rounding up the chosen peeps from every corner of the globe.

Life Hack From the Fig Tree

Peep this trick from the fig tree: when its twigs get soft and it starts flexing leaves, you know summer's just around the corner. Same goes for these prophecies—when you see them unfolding, know that it's go-time, like, right at the doorstep. Bet on it, this generation won't peace out until all this drama unfolds. Heaven and earth might hit the reset button, but my words? They're sticking around forever.

The Ultimate Drop Date: To Be Announced

Alright, let's get this straight: nobody's got the inside scoop on the grand finale—not even heaven's VIPs or the Son himself—just the Big Boss up top. It's gonna be like the OG days of Noah. People were just living their best life, swiping right, throwing wedding hashtags around until Noah hit up the ark and the flood did a major plot twist. That's how it's gonna go down when the Son of Man makes His comeback. Imagine, two dudes will be chilling in a field, one gets picked for the VIP list, the other's left on read. Two ladies will be grinding it out at work, and suddenly, one gets the golden ticket, the other's ghosted. So, keep those notifications on, 'cause you've got no clue when the Boss is gonna drop in. If you knew the exact time the heist was going down, you'd be on watch. So, stay woke! The comeback could be at the most random hour.

How to Be MVP in the Waiting Game

Who's the real MVP? The one who's got the keys to the house and dishes out the snacks on time. Mega props to the one caught actually doing their thing when the Boss rolls up. That's the one getting the whole empire. But if you've got that shady servant vibing, thinking, "Eh, the Boss is on a long one," and starts going all WWE on his mates and crashing with the party crowd, surprise! The Boss is gonna show up when least expected, going full-on ninja, leaving Mr. Shady in a world of regret.

The RSVP Challenge

Now picture this: the kingdom of heaven is like ten influencers gearing up for the wedding of the century. Five are playing it smart, five are just not on the ball. The smart crew packed extra juice for their lamps, but the others? Nah. Then, plot twist, the groom's running on rapper time. While everyone's catching Z's, bam, "He's here! Party's this way!"

All ten wake up, trying to get their glow on. The not-so-ready squad's like, "Yo, pass some juice, we're fading here!" But the prepped squad's all, "Nuh-uh, go hit up the 24/7 store." Plot twist again: while the unprepared are out shopping, the groom arrives, and the party starts without them. They finally show up, tapping on the door, "Hey, let us in!" But the groom's like, "Who dis?" Moral of the story: Stay sharp, 'cause no one's dropping hints about when the party starts.

The Final Talent Showdown

So, here's the scoop, fam: Picture a dude about to hit the road, right? He lines up his squad and dishes out his stash: one bro gets five big ones, another scores two, and the last dude gets a single talent—yeah, based on what they can handle. Off the boss goes. The guy with five talents? He's on fire, doubles his money. The dude with two? Same deal, doubles up. But the guy with just one? He goes all ninja, buries it in the ground— like, "Catch you later, boss's money." Time flies, the boss rolls back and it's reckoning time. Mr. Five Talents steps up, drops another five on the table. Boss is all, "Epic win, my dude! You crushed it with a little, now you're heading up the big leagues. Party on in my VIP lounge." Two Talent guy gets the same high-fives, same VIP pass. But here comes One Talent bro, all, "Boss, you're kinda intense, reaping where you haven't sown and all that jazz. Got me shook, so I buried your cash to keep it safe. Ta-da, exactly what you gave me." Boss is not vibing, goes, "Bro, you lazy, no-good servant! You knew my rep, should've at least banked my cash for some interest. Nah, give your talent to Mr. Ten Talents. More gets more, that's the rule. And you? You're cut. Off to the shadow realm you go, where the vibe is majorly down."

Team Sheep vs Team Goat

Fast forward, when the Son of Man hits up in full bling, angels in tow, throne shining like a diamond. Humanity's gonna line up, and it's sorting time, sheep on the right, goats on the left. To the sheep, the King's like, "Squad, you're in. Welcome to the kingdom VIP zone, been waiting for you since day one. "Here's why: you hooked me up when I was hitting rock bottom—fed me, watered me, welcomed me, clothed me, looked after me when I was sick, hit me up even in the slammer." Righteous crew's gonna be like, "Wait, when did we ever do that for you?" And the King's gonna drop, "Legit, every time you were there for someone struggling, you were there for me." Then, turning to the goats, it's gonna be, "You lot, out. You left me hanging—hungry, thirsty, a total stranger, naked, sick, and all alone." They'll be like, "When did we ghost you?" And he's gonna hit back, "For real, whenever you scrolled past someone in need, you scrolled past me." And just like that, the goats are on a one-way trip to nope city, but the righteous? They're living it up, forever style.

Betrayal at Dinner Party

Alright, peeps, storytime: After dropping some truth bombs, Jesus hits his squad with a calendar check: "Yo, Passover's dropping in two days, and spoiler alert, they're gonna pin me up for the big sleep." Cut to the bigwigs—the head honchos of the priest squad and the old-school crew chilling in Caiaphas' crib, cooking up a scheme to snatch Jesus without causing a scene. "Let's keep it on the down-low during the fest," they whispered, "don't wanna spark a riot." Now, flashback to Bethany, Jesus is kicking it at Simon the ex-leper's pad. In walks a lady with some next-level pricey perfume, pouring it all over J's head. The disciples are flipping their lids, "What's with the splurge? Could've cashed that in for the poor!" But J's like, "Chill, she's doing me solid. You've got forever to help the poor, but I'm on a timer. She's just prepping me for what's coming. Mark my words, her story's going global." Enter Judas, the squad's own sneak, who dips to the priests with an offer they can't refuse: "What's in it for me if I deliver?" Boom, thirty silver coins in the pocket. And so, the hunt begins.

Fast forward to Passover prep time. The crew's like, "Boss, where we setting up?" Jesus sends them downtown: "Tell my guy, 'Teacher's rolling through to kick off Passover with the squad.'" They get it all set, and by nightfall, they're all lounging at the table. Mid-munch, Jesus drops a bomb: "One of you's gonna stab me in the back." Cue the drama, everyone's all, "Me? No way, Lord!" But Jesus points the finger: "The dude double-dipping with me, that's my backstabber. Sure, it's all in the script, but man, rough times for that guy." Judas plays it cool: "Rabbi, you don't mean me?" Jesus, with the mic drop: "You said it, not me." Then Jesus gets all ceremonial, breaking bread: "Munch on this, it's me." Sips wine, "Drink up, it's my deal-sealing blood for the big forgive. Let's not get tipsy till the next level in Dad's place." After a singalong, they bounce to the Mount of Olives.

The Scheme Against Jesus

After Jesus dropped all those truth bombs, he huddled up with his squad and was like, "Yo, you all know that big event, Passover, is just around the corner, right? Stuff's gonna get real – they're gonna hand me over to be nailed." Meanwhile, the top dog priest and the old-school leaders were vibing in the high priest Caiaphas's backyard. They were plotting to sneakily grab Jesus and take him out. But they were like, "Let's keep it chill during the festival. We don't want everyone losing their minds."

The VIP Treatment

So, Jesus was chilling in Bethany at Simon the leper's pad, right? This woman rolls up with a jar of super boujee perfume and just goes for it—dumps it on Jesus' head while he's maxing out at the table. The disciples see this and they're like, "Bruh, why you gotta waste it like that?" They're thinking, "That could've been sold for mad cash and given to the less fortunate." But Jesus, catching the vibe, is like, "Yo, why you gotta hassle her? She's doing something epic for me. You've always got the poor folks around, but I won't always be kicking it with you. She's actually hooking me up for what's coming next." And Jesus drops this: "For real, wherever this story gets told around the globe, what she did will be shouted out in her honor." Then Judas Iscariot, one of the squad, sneaks off to the chief priests and is all, "So, what's in it for me if I spill the beans on Jesus?" They count out thirty silver coins for him. From then on, he's on the lookout for the perfect chance to do the dirty.

The Setup at the Passover

When Passover prep time rolls around, the disciples hit up Jesus, "Hey, where you want us to get the Passover dinner ready?" Jesus is like, "Hit up the city, find this dude and tell him, 'The Teacher's got plans to celebrate Passover at your spot with the crew.'" So, they get everything set up just like Jesus said. Come dinner time, Jesus and the twelve are lounging at the table. Mid-bite, Jesus says, "Heads up, one of you is gonna stab me in the back." They're all shook, throwing around, "It's not me, right, Lord?" Jesus lays it down, "The one who's dipping bread with me is the one. Yeah, things are going down as they gotta, but man, it's rough for the dude who betrays me. Better if he'd never been born." Judas, playing it cool, is like, "It's not me, Rabbi, right?" Jesus looks him in the eye, "You said it."

The Ultimate Dinner Party

So, they're all munching away, right? Jesus grabs some bread, hits it with a blessing, breaks it, and hands it out like, "Yo, dig in, this is my body." Then he's like, "Hold up, got something else." Takes a cup, gives a shoutout of thanks, passes it around, and goes, "Everyone, get a sip. This? It's my blood, sealing the deal for a huge forgiveness drop. It's for the squad." He adds, "But check it, I'm hitting pause on the wine until we can toast in my Dad's epic kingdom." After belting out a hymn, they bounced to the Mount of Olives.

Peter's Fail Predicted

Jesus then drops a truth bomb: "Peeps, tonight's the night you're gonna ghost me. It's like that old tune: hit the shepherd, and the flock's gonna scatter." But he's like, "After I'm back, catch you in Galilee." Peter's feeling all hype, "Even if everyone else bails, I'm not ditching." Jesus looks at him, "Bro, before the rooster's morning jam, you're gonna act like you don't know me. Thrice." Peter's all in, "Nah, I'd ride or die with you." And the rest are nodding along.

Chill Session Turns Intense in the Garden

They roll up to Gethsemane. Jesus tells the crew, "Park it here. I'm off to chat with the man upstairs." He takes Peter and the Zebedee bros, feeling all kinds of heavy, and spills, "Guys, my heart's kinda breaking. Stick with me, yeah?" He steps away, faceplants, and prays, "Dad, if there's any way to skip this cup, I'm down. But, it's your call, not mine." Comes back to find his homies snoozing. "Peter, you couldn't stay woke for one hour?" He's like, "Keep it 100, pray you don't bail when it gets real. Spirit's willing, but the body's not." Goes off to pray round two, "If this cup's gotta be drained, I'll do it. Your plan, not mine." Finds them asleep again—they just couldn't. After his third chat with God, he's back, finds them still catching Zs, and is like, "Still sleeping? Time's up. We've got company—the dude selling me out is almost here. Let's roll."

The Great Betrayal

Just as Jesus was laying down some truths, Judas rolls up, part of the OG twelve, but not solo—he brought a whole flash mob armed to the teeth, thanks to a tip-off from the religious bigwigs. The signal was a kiss: "The dude I smooch, that's your guy. Grab him." So, Judas goes straight for Jesus, "Hey, Teacher!" and lands the kiss of doom. Jesus, cool as ever, goes, "Buddy, what's this about?" Right on cue, the mob swoops in and cuffs him. In the heat of the moment, one of Jesus's crew gets all action-hero, swings his sword, and offs a servant's ear. Jesus is like, "Chill with the swords, guys. Anyone who lives by that vibe will crash by it. You think I can't hit up my Dad and get an angel army on speed dial? But then, how would we play out the script written ages ago?" He turns to the crowd, "Really? Rolling up like I'm some prime-time villain? I was right there in the temple, easy pickings, but no dice. Anyway, this is all going down to tick all the prophecy boxes." And just like that, his squad bails, ghosting him.

The High-Stakes Face-off

So, the Jesus entourage drags him to Caiaphas, where the religious elite are all huddled up. Peter's tailing from a safe distance, ending up kicking it with the help, trying to catch how it'll all go down. The chief priests and their crew were on a mission for some dirt on Jesus to get him the death penalty, but no dice. Even with a lineup of liars, the charges weren't sticking. Finally, a couple step up, "This guy said he could DIY the temple in three days." The high priest is on his feet, pressing Jesus, "You gonna stand there silent? What do you say to these charges?" Jesus plays it cool, silent. The high priest goes all in, "I'm putting you on oath—tell us if you're the Messiah, God's own." Jesus hits back, "You said it. Plus, you'll see me next, chilling at God's right hand, cruising in on cloud nine." The high priest loses it, "Blasphemy! We don't need more from the peanut gallery. You heard it!" The verdict? "He's got to go." Then it gets ugly—they're spitting, hitting, mocking, "Hey, Messiah, who clocked you?"

Peter's Epic Fail

Meanwhile, Peter's out in the yard, trying to blend in, when a servant girl sidles up, "You were rolling with Jesus, the Galilean, weren't you?" Peter's like, "No clue what you're on about."

Barely out to the entrance, another lady spots him, tells everyone, "This dude was with Jesus!" Again, Peter's all, "I swear, never met the guy."

Not long after, some bystanders corner Peter, "Come on, your accent's a dead giveaway. You're one of them." Peter loses it, cursing, "I told you, I don't know him!" Cue rooster crowing, and it hits Peter—Jesus called it. He'd deny him thrice before the rooster announced dawn. Peter's crushed, stepping out into the night, tears streaming.

Judas Hits Undo

Judas, who totally snitched on Jesus, was hit with major regret vibes after seeing Jesus was about to get the ultimate penalty. He tried to bounce back the betrayal coins to the chief priests and elders, confessing, "Big oof—I betrayed the real one." They hit him with a cold, "Sounds like a you problem." So, he yeeted the silver in the temple and dipped out, ending his story in the saddest way. The chief priests, now stuck with this guilt cash, decided it was too cursed to mix with the temple funds. They went shopping instead, picking up a field for outsiders' final chill spot, hence the name "Blood Field," ticking off a prophecy as Jeremiah had once spilled.

Jesus' Chill Session with Pilate

Jesus is now face-to-face with Pilate, who's like, "You're the King of the Jews, huh?" Jesus throws back, "You said it, not me." Even as the religious crew threw shade, Jesus kept it silent, leaving Pilate totally bamboozled by his calm.

Choose Your Fighter: Jesus or Barabbas

Pilate's fest tradition was to let the people swipe right on freeing a prisoner. On the roster was Barabbas, public enemy number one, or Jesus, Mr. Christ himself. Pilate, sensing some major jealousy, put the ball in the crowd's court, low-key hoping they'd pick Jesus. But then, Pilate's wife slides into his DMs, "Babe, leave that innocent guy alone. Had the worst dream about him." Yet, the religious influencers and their fanbase were hyping up Team Barabbas, pushing for Jesus to take the L. When Pilate tried to clear his conscience, the crowd went full send on "Crucify him!" Pilate, seeing no way out and not wanting to catch heat, did the whole "I'm washing my hands of this" routine in front of everyone, "This ain't on me." So, Pilate let Barabbas ghost and handed Jesus over for a savage pre-crucifixion glow-down.

Savage Mode: Engaged

The soldiers pulled Jesus into Pilate's HQ, turning their cruelty up to 100. They switched his fit for a scarlet joke, topped him with a thorn crown, and handed him a scepter, just to kneel and mock, "Big up, King of the Jews!" They weren't done though; they spat on him, took turns hitting him, then swapped his fit back and led him off to be crucified.

The Ultimate Showdown at Skull Place

As they were heading out, they snagged a guy named Simon from Cyrene to lug Jesus's cross. When they hit Golgotha, which is basically "Skull Central," they tried to get Jesus to sip on some bitter wine, but he wasn't having it. After pinning him up, they gambled for his threads and just chilled there, keeping an eye on him. They slapped a sign over his head: "This Is Jesus, the King of the Jews," making it IG official. Next up, Jesus got two criminals as his cross neighbors, one on each side, turning the scene into the most tragic collab. Passersby threw shade, hurling insults and head shakes, like, "Hey, Mr. 'I'll rebuild the temple in three days,' how 'bout you save yourself? Or if you're really God's kid, just bounce off that cross!" The religious elite were no better, tossing out taunts like, "He saved others, but can't save himself? LOL. Come down now, and we'll hit follow." Even the criminals hanging with him were throwing disses his way.

Lights Out and Curtain Call

From high noon till three, the whole land was like a phone on

Do Not Disturb: total darkness. Around the 3 p.m. mark, Jesus shouted, "Elí, Elí, lemáh sabachtháni?" which is "My God, my God, why'd you ghost me?" Some thought he was calling out for Elijah to slide into his DMs. One guy made a quick move, soaked a sponge in some sour wine, and offered it up on a stick for Jesus to drink. Meanwhile, others were like, "Pause, let's see if Elijah shows up for a dramatic rescue." But then, Jesus let out one more loud call and checked out. Right then, the temple curtain ripped down the middle like a bad movie sequel, the earth shook, rocks split, and tombs popped open, setting up the scene for the saints' epic comeback tour after Jesus rose, making appearances all over the holy city. The centurion and his crew, witnessing this whole earth-shattering event, were shook, "No cap, this dude was legit the Son of God." A bunch of loyal women followers, who'd been with Jesus from the get-go, were there too, keeping watch from a safe TikTok distance. Among them were Mary Magdalene, Mary, mother of James and Joseph, and the Zebedee boys' mom.

The Afterparty in a Rock Star's Tomb

Come evening, Joseph of Arimathea, a low-key but wealthy Jesus fan, hit up Pilate for Jesus's body. Pilate said "Yeet," and handed it over. Joseph wrapped Jesus in some fresh linens and laid him in his own rock-hewn VIP suite, sealing it with a massive stone.Mary Magdalene and the other Mary were there, just sitting and facing the tomb, probably in disbelief and heartache.

The next day, the religious heads and Pharisees had a pow-wow with Pilate, "Yo, remember how that 'deceiver' said he'd be back in three days? Let's lock down that tomb tight, so his crew can't pull a fast one and start rumors he's back." Pilate was like, "You've got your squad, make it Fort Knox." So, they went full Mission Impossible on the tomb, sealing the stone and posting guards to prevent any spoiler alerts.

Epic Comeback Morning

After the chill vibes of Sabbath, as Sunday was just starting to light up, Mary Magdalene and the other Mary were on a mission to check out Jesus' final drop spot. But then—boom—a wild earthquake hit because an angel straight from heaven's VIP section came down, pushed the stone aside like it was nothing, and perched on it like a boss. This angel was glowing like a lightning bolt, decked out in threads whiter than snow. The guards? They were so scared they might as well have been playing the mannequin challenge. The angel was like, "No stress, ladies. I know you're here for Jesus, the one they nailed. Guess what? He's not here. He pulled the ultimate 'I'm out' move, just like he said he would. Pop in, check his former chill spot. Then, hit up his crew and tell them, 'He's back from the dead, and btw, he's gonna beat you to Galilee. Catch him there.' Got it? Good." So, the Marys dipped out from there, a mix of scared and hyped, and sprinted to break the news to the disciples. And who pops up? Jesus himself, going, "Hey!" They dropped, hugged his feet, and totally fan-girled. Jesus was all, "Chill, no fear. Go tell the bros to head to Galilee. They'll see me there."

Guard Drama and Fake News

While this was going down, some of the guard squad hit up downtown to spill to the chief priests all the supernatural tea. The priests and the elders brainstormed and threw a stack of cash at the soldiers, like, "Spin this tale: 'His fan club pulled a fast one and ghosted him while we caught Z's.'" And they're like, "Don't sweat the governor. We'll smooth talk him. You're in the clear." So, the guards took the bribe and spread that fake news, which is still getting likes and shares to this day.

The Ultimate Challenge

The eleven disciples made the trek to Galilee, hitting up the mountain Jesus had tagged for them. When they caught sight of him, they were all in—well, almost all; a couple were hitting the pause button. Jesus strolled up and dropped this: "I've got all the power—upstairs and downstairs. Here's your mission: Make followers out of everyone, everywhere. Dunk them in the name of the Father, the Son, and the Holy Spirit. Teach them to keep all the rules I've laid down. And don't you forget, I'm with you, every step, every day, till the end of the show."

MARK'S GOSPEL

The Intro to Jesus' Mixtape

Kickoff time: we're diving into the story of J.C., the Big Guy upstairs' Son. Right off the bat, Isaiah, the ancient hype man, laid down some tracks: "Heads up, I'm sending my lead guy to get the stage ready for you. He's the one yelling in the desert, 'Clear the path, make it smooth for the Boss.'" Enter stage left: John, rocking that desert chic with camel-hair threads and a leather belt, snacking on locusts and wild honey because why not? He's out there in the wild, hosting the ultimate baptism bash—splash zone for sin washing. People from all over were trekking to him, confessing their mess-ups and diving into the Jordan for a fresh start. John's message was clear: "The main act is yet to come, and I'm just the warm-up. I might be dipping you in water, but He's going to upgrade you with the Holy Spirit."

J.C. Hits the Scene

Fast-forward, and Jesus from Nazareth makes his grand entrance, getting baptized in John's pop-up river event. The moment he's up from the water, the sky splits wide open like a season finale cliffhanger, and the Spirit swoops down like a serene dove. Then, out of nowhere, a voice booms from the heavens, "This is my son, killing it as always."

Desert Bootcamp

Right after, the Spirit's like, "Let's take this to the desert," and Jesus is out there for a solid 40-day survival challenge, facing down Satan's tricks, chilling with wild beasts, and angelic beings are on handout duty.

Galilee's New Headliner

Post John's arrest, Jesus hits Galilee with his debut single: "Times are changing, God's kingdom is VIP access now. Turn it around and tune into this good news."

Recruiting the Squad

While strolling by Galilee Lake, he spots Simon and Andrew mid-cast in their fishing grind. Jesus throws out, "Swap those fish for a human catch." Instantly, they're all in, ghosting their nets. Further down, James and John are in the family boat doing some net maintenance. A call from Jesus, and they're hitting eject on the family business, leaving Zebedee with the crew in a plot twist.

Capernaum Crowd Goes Wild

In Capernaum, Jesus crashes the synagogue scene, dropping knowledge like a boss. His words had the crowd's minds blown—this wasn't your regular scribe's talk. Mid-lecture, a demon-possessed heckler tries to throw shade, "Yo, Jesus, you here to wreck us? I know your game—you're God's chosen!" Jesus, cool as ever, is like, "Mute button, hit the road." Demon's out with a mic drop, leaving the guy chill. The crowd's buzzing, "What's this? New authority in town! Even the shadow crew listens." Word of Jesus spread like wildfire across Galilee.

Capernaum's Pop-Up Clinic

So, they bounced from the synagogue and crashed at Simon and Andrew's place, rolling deep with James and John. Simon's mother-in-law was KO'd in bed, burning up. They hit up Jesus ASAP. Jesus strolled in, gave her a hand, and just like that, she's up and at 'em, whipping up snacks like nothing happened. As the sun dipped, it turned into a full-on healing fest outside their door. The whole town turned up, making it the spot.

Jesus was on fire, fixing up all sorts of sick vibes and giving demons the boot, no autographs allowed.

Dawn Patrol and Road Trip

Crack of dawn, while it was still pitch black outside, Jesus snuck off for some solo time to recharge with some prayer. But Simon and the squad were on a mission, tracking him down. They're like, "Dude, everyone's on the lookout for you." J.C. was all, "Let's roll out to the next spots. Got to spread the good word, that's the game plan."

Galilee Gets the Good News

Jesus went full tour mode in Galilee, hitting every synagogue and sending demons packing. Then this guy with leprosy slides up, all serious, like, "If you're down, you can totally clear this up." Jesus, feeling it, reaches out, zaps him clean, and is like, "You're set, but keep it on the DL. Just do the right thing and show the priests, make it official." But this dude? Couldn't keep it quiet. Went full influencer, blasting his story everywhere, turning Jesus into an off-the-grid celeb. Now Jesus had to keep it low-key in the wilds, but that didn't stop the crowds from tracking him down from all over.

Healing Season

Back in Capernaum, Jesus turned his spot into the hottest venue in town. The place was so packed, you couldn't even slide into the DMs, let alone the door. He was dropping wisdom bombs left and right when suddenly, it turned into an episode of "Extreme Home Makeovers." Four dudes showed up, carrying their buddy who couldn't move his legs, but they couldn't get through the crowd. So, they went full ninja, climbed the roof, and literally dropped in, lowering their friend right in front of Jesus. Seeing how far they went, Jesus was impressed. He looks at the guy on the mat and is like, "Bro, your sins are canceled." Meanwhile, some scribes in the back are sipping their haterade, thinking, "Who does this guy think he is? Only God can delete sins like that." Jesus, catching their vibe instantly, hits them with, "Why you guys always gotta be so negative? What's easier to say? 'Your sins are gone,' or 'Get up and walk'? But just so you know I'm legit," he tells the paralyzed dude, "Rise up, grab your mat, and head home." And just like that, the guy pops up, grabs his mat, and struts out like it's a catwalk, leaving everyone shook. They're all tweeting, "OMG, did that just happen? #blessed"

Levi's Big Move

Next up, Jesus is strolling by the sea, still gathering crowds like he's dropping exclusive merch. He spots Levi, the tax collector, in his booth, probably scrolling through receipts or whatever tax collectors do. Jesus hits him with a simple, "Yo, follow me." Levi's like, "Say less," drops everything, and joins the crew. Then they're at Levi's place, throwing down with a bunch of tax collectors and the so-called "sinners." Basically, a "sinners' supper" with Jesus guest-starring. The Pharisees, always on the prowl for some drama, start whispering to his disciples, "He's really gonna dine with these types?" Jesus overhears and lays down the truth, "Look, the healthy don't need a doc. I'm here for the ones who know they're messed up. I'm not trying to call up the goody two-shoes; I'm here for the lost cause club."

Why Aren't Your Crew Fasting?

So, word got around that Jesus and his squad weren't into the fasting scene like John's crew and the Pharisees. People were curious, hitting up Jesus with, "Why are your guys all about that feast life when everyone else is on the spiritual cleanse?" Jesus breaks it down: "Look, you don't expect party guests to skip the cake while the guest of honor's around, right? But hey, there'll come a time when the party's over, and then, yeah, they'll hit the fasting app hard. Also, mixing old school with new vibes? That's a recipe for disaster. It's like expecting your vintage jeans to handle a fresh patch or pouring the latest craft brew into an ancient flask. Spoiler: it doesn't end well."

Sabbath Showdown

Cruising through some grainfields on the Sabbath, J.C.'s crew started snacking. The Pharisees popped up, itching for a gotcha moment, "Hey, why are they breaking Sabbath rules?" J.C. hits them with a history lesson about David doing what it takes to feed his crew, ending with, "Sabbath's supposed to work for us, not the other way around. And FYI, I'm the boss of the Sabbath."

Healing on the DL

Next, in the synagogue, there's this guy with a hand that's all out of whack. The Pharisees are lurking, hoping Jesus slips up and heals on the Sabbath. Jesus, seeing right through them, puts the man on the spot and throws a challenge: "What's the Sabbath

for? Helping or hurting? Saving or destroying?"

…Silence…

With a mix of anger and sadness, Jesus tells the guy, "Stretch out your hand." Boom. Hand's back to normal. Pharisees storm out, plotting with the Herodians on how to cancel Jesus.

Crowd Control

Jesus heads to the beach, but the fanbase has grown – everyone from everywhere is showing up. Jesus, needing some personal space, gets a boat ready. Sick people are pressing in, trying to get a touch, while demons are drama queens, shouting, "You're the Son of God!" Jesus is all about keeping it on the down-low, though.

Assembling the Squad

Jesus does a mountain retreat, handpicks twelve for his inner circle – giving them the go-ahead to preach and demon-bust. Simon gets a rebrand as Peter; James and John are dubbed "Sons of Thunder" – talk about squad goals.

Drama at Home Base

Back at the house, it's so packed, snacking is off the table. Jesus' fam thinks he's lost it and stages an intervention. Meanwhile, scribes are throwing shade, claiming Jesus is teaming up with Beelzebul. Jesus calls a family meeting, dropping parables like, "Satan can't be ousting himself – that's just bad for business. And you can't rob a place without dealing with the security first." He lays down the ultimate truth bomb: "You can be forgiven for just about anything, but dissing the Holy Spirit? That's the one-way ticket to Nopeville." They were accusing him of being a demon's BFF, which, honestly, was way off base.

Finding Your True Squad

So, Jesus is there, chilling with the crowd, when his fam sends him a text from outside, "Hey, your mom and your siblings are here looking for you." The crowd's like, "FYI, your family's waiting." Jesus throws a curveball, "Who even are my mom and my brothers?" Scanning the room, he drops, "Look, these peeps? They're my real fam. Anyone who's down with God's plan is my brother, sister, and yes, even my mom."

The Story of the Ultimate Influencer

Next, Jesus hits the beach, and it's like he's launching a new line—crowds flocking, so he hops on a boat for a floating TED Talk. He kicks off with this story: "Check out this farmer throwing seeds everywhere. Some seeds are like ghost followers; birds just snatch them up. Others land on the 'seen-zoned' rocky spots, they pop up fast but can't handle the heat. Then there's the drama seeds, getting all tangled up in thornville, totally choked out. But some seeds? They find the prime real estate, thriving and blowing up big time." He wraps with, "If you've got ears, you better listen." Later, when it's just the crew, they're like, "What's with the cryptic stories?" Jesus leans in, "You get the VIP pass to the kingdom secrets, but for the outsiders, it's all riddles. It's like they see but don't get the picture, hear but miss the track—keeps them from flipping a U-turn and getting the clear."

Deep Dive into the Influencer Parable

"Still not getting it?" Jesus says, "Alright, let's break it down. The farmer's dropping truth bombs. Some folks are like concrete—truth lands, but before it can click, bam, it's gone. Then you've got the hype crowd, all about that instant gratification, but bail at the first sign of a storm. And don't get me started on the worrywarts and the bling chasers—truth gets strangled out before it can hit their feed. But then, there are those good soil souls, they soak up the truth, and it transforms them, producing mad growth."

Lit Up Your Light

J.C. hit them with a real talk: "You wouldn't snag a lamp just to stash it under a basket or a bed, right? It's all about putting it on a stand for the whole room to get lit. Everything that's been on the DL is gonna hit everyone's feed eventually. If you've got the ears for it, you better listen up." He went on, "Be careful how you tune in. The vibe you throw out there is gonna boomerang back to you— plus some. For the crew that's got their game on, they're gonna level up. But for those who haven't even started? Even their starter pack is gonna disappear."

The Sneaky Seed Saga

Diving deeper, Jesus was like, "The Kingdom's kinda like a dude who plants seeds and then hits the hay. Night and day, he's off the clock, but those seeds?

They're grinding away underground, sprouting and growing, and he's clueless about how. It's all automatic—from sprout to full-on grain. And the moment it's showtime, he's out there with the sickle because it's harvest o'clock."

The Epic of the Mustard Seed

And Jesus wasn't done. "How can we even describe God's Kingdom? It's like the mustard seed. Tiny dude of the seed world, but once it's in the ground, it goes beast mode— bigger than all the garden celebs, throwing shade with its branches so all the bird influencers are nesting in it."

Parable Drop

He kept on feeding them truths with a side of parables, tailored to what they could vibe with. Publicly, it was all in metaphors, but behind the scenes, he decoded everything for his day-ones. When the day was wrapping up, Jesus was like, "Let's hit the other side of the lake." They dipped out, leaving the fan club behind, Jesus already onboard catching Zs. Suddenly, a wild storm pops off, waves throwing a rave on the boat. Jesus is out there snoozing on a pillow while everyone's freaking out, "Yo, Teacher, you sleeping through our Titanic moment?" Jesus wakes up, gives the wind and the sea a "Chill, bro," and everything goes silent, like the storm just got ghosted. Turning to the squad, he's like, "What's with the panic? Where's your chill?" They're all shook, whispering, "Who even is this guy? Even the wind and the waves are hitting pause for him."

Epic Demon Clearance Sale

So, Jesus and his squad hit up the Gerasenes, and right off the boat, this dude who's been living the cave life, 'cause he's too wild for society, comes charging. No chains could hold him down; he was breaking free like a supernatural escape artist, always screaming and doing the most. Spotting Jesus, he slides in like, "Yo, Jesus, High God's MVP, chill with the torment, yeah?" Jesus, already on it, was like, "Out you go, spooky spirit!" Jesus hits him with the "Who are you?" and the reply was, "Call me Legion, 'cause we're a whole squad." These spirits are now begging Jesus not to ghost them out of town but instead send them into some local pigs. Jesus gives the thumbs up, and next thing, these demons pull a lemming move with about two thousand pigs, making a splash dive into the sea. The pig herders booked it, spreading the

tea all over town. People came, saw the once-possessed guy chilling and dressed (big change), and got freaked out. After getting the lowdown, they're like, "Jesus, maybe take your roadshow elsewhere?" As Jesus was dipping out, the ex-demon dude wanted to join the entourage, but Jesus was like, "Nah, go flex your testimony at home." So, he did, turning into a one-man hype machine across ten cities.

Healing Hits and Miraculous Comebacks

Back on the homefront, Jesus attracts a mob by the sea. Jairus, a big shot at the synagogue, throws himself at Jesus' kicks, "My kid's on the brink. Throw some of that healing magic her way." Jesus, being Jesus, is down for it. Meanwhile, this woman who's been bleeding out for twelve years, and basically a VIP at the doctor's office with no luck, sneaks up and snags a piece of Jesus' cloak. Instantly, she's feeling top-notch. Jesus spins around, "Who snagged my power?" The woman, all kinds of nervous, owns up. Jesus is all, "Your trust in me sorted you out. Peace out and be well." As they're chatting, Jairus gets word his daughter's checked out. Jesus overhears and tells him, "Don't hit panic mode. Just believe."

Only the inner circle gets to roll with Him to Jairus' place, where there's a full-blown drama scene. Jesus is like, "Chill, she's just napping." Everyone's LOLing until Jesus makes them bounce, grabs the girl's hand, and is like, "Hey, up and at 'em." And just like that, she's walking around, leaving everyone shook. Jesus caps it off with a classic, "Mum's the word, but maybe get her a snack."

Hometown Haters

So Jesus rolls back to Nazareth, his old stomping grounds, with his crew in tow. Sabbath hits, and he starts dropping wisdom in the synagogue, leaving everyone shook. "Who's this guy?" they whisper. "How's he pulling off these epic moves? Ain't this the local handyman, Mary's kid?" They couldn't handle it, throwing shade instead of respect. Jesus hits them with a truth bomb: "A prophet's got cred everywhere but his own zip code, with his kin and in his own crib." Basically, Nazareth was a no-miracle zone, except for a few low-key healings, all thanks to their vibe check fail.

Squad Goals: Mission Time

Next up, Jesus huddles the Twelve and pairs them off for some away games, handing them the keys to the demon-banishing kingdom. Packing list? Super minimalist: just a stick—no snacks, no bag, no cash. "Rock sandals, but leave the spare tee," he says. "Crash at the first crib that lets you in, and stay put till you bounce. If any spot gives you the cold shoulder, peace out and dust off those sandals as you go. Makes a statement." Off they went, preaching the turnaround life, kicking demons out, and doing the whole healing tour.

Drama Alert: John's Curtain Call

King Herod catches wind of Jesus and starts piecing things together, "That's gotta be John, back from the dead, showing off those power moves." The rumor mill was wild—some guessed Elijah, others a throwback prophet. Here's the tea: Herod had John locked up because he wasn't cool with Herod marrying his bro's wife, Herodias. And boy, did she hold a grudge. Herod kinda dug John's talks, though, found him fascinating yet confusing. Then, at Herod's big birthday bash, Herodias's daughter puts on a show, and Herod's so hyped he offers her anything—up to half the kingdom. Mom whispers, "Go for John's head," and just like that, the party takes a dark turn. Despite being bummed, Herod can't back down in front of his squad, so he sends the executioner. Head on a platter, delivered to the girl, then to mom. John's crew later picks up the pieces, literally.

The Ultimate Picnic

So, the apostles roll up to Jesus, buzzing about all the epic stuff they've been up to. Jesus, seeing they're all running on empty, is like, "Let's ghost this scene and hit up a chill spot to recharge." They tried to sneak off, but their fans were on them like they were dropping concert tickets, racing ahead to catch them on the other side. Landing, Jesus peeps the massive crowd and his heart just melts—seeing them all wandering without a clue, he jumps into teach mode. As the day starts to wrap, the squad's like, "Yo, Jesus, it's getting late and this place is a ghost town. Maybe send the crowd to grab some grub?" But Jesus flips the script, "Nah, you feed them." The disciples are bugging, "What, are we supposed to drop a fortune on bread for this flash mob?" Jesus, ever the problem solver, asks, "What's in the pantry?" They scrounge up five loaves and two fish. Jesus gets everyone cozy on the grass, takes the food, hits it with a heavenly shoutout, and starts the biggest share-a-thon. Loaves and fish going viral, and everyone's stuffed. They even had leftovers—twelve baskets full. And get this, the headcount was 5k guys, not even counting the rest of the crowd.

Surf's Up, J.C. Style

Post-dinner, Jesus nudges the disciples to hit the water without him while he plays crowd control. Later, he peaces out to hit up a mountain solo for some prayer time. Meanwhile, the disciples are in the middle of the lake, battling a beast of a headwind. Cue Jesus, casual as you like, taking a midnight stroll ON the water. The squad spots him and straight-up thinks it's ghost time. Panic. Jesus calls out, "Chill, it's just me. No fear." He hops in the boat, and bam, wind's like, "I'm out." The disciples are mind-blown, especially since the whole bread-and-fish remix went right over their heads.

Healing Tour, Non-Stop

Landing at Gennesaret, Jesus is instantly mobbed. News spreads like wildfire, and it's sick people city, everyone hoping for a touch of his cloak. And guess what? Touch and heal was 100% effective—total health reboot for all.

When Traditions Get a Reality Check

Jesus rolls back into town, and the Pharisees and some scribe types who were major fans of traditions from way back when are already on his case. They're like, "Yo, why are your guys eating with dirty hands? Didn't they get the memo on elder-approved handwashing rituals?" Jesus, not missing a beat, throws some ancient tweets their way, "Isaiah called you out big time: 'These peeps honor me with their lips, but their hearts are out in the next zip code. They're all about those human-made rules.'" Basically, Jesus tells them they're so into their old school rulebook, they're missing the whole point of what God actually said.

Heart Matters 101

Dragging everyone in for a quick lesson, Jesus is like, "Listen up, it's not the outside stuff that messes you up; it's the junk that comes out of you that does." Later, in a private Q&A, he breaks it down Barney-style for his crew, "Guys, really? Food doesn't hit your soul, just your stomach, then it's out." And yeah, Jesus just called everything on the menu fair game. But here's the kicker: it's the nasty stuff like greed, lies, and all sorts of bad vibes brewing in the heart that really mess things up. That's the real trash that needs taking out.

Faith Without Borders

Switching scenes, Jesus tries to keep it low-key in Tyre, but a mom with a daughter on the struggle bus finds him. She's not even a local, but she's desperate. Jesus tests her with, "Should we really be giving your slice to the pups?" But she claps back with, "Even pups catch crumbs." Jesus, impressed by her comeback and faith, is like, "You're good to go. Your kid's free from trouble." Boom, demon eviction notice served.

Leveling Up

Next up, Jesus hits the Decapolis, where they bring him a dude who's got a no-entry sign on sound and a locked-up tongue. Jesus takes him aside for some one-on-one, does a bit of a ritual with fingers, spit, and a heavenward look, then hits him with an "Ephphatha!"—that's "Open up!" for the non-Aramaic speakers. Instantly, the guy's tuning in and chatting up a storm. Despite Jesus playing the "Keep it on the DL" card, word spreads like wildfire. People are mind-blown, "He's got everything dialed in—got the deaf hearing and the silent speaking."

Miracle Meal Pt. 2

So, Jesus is chilling with a huge crowd again, and guess what? Everyone's tummies were rumbling 'cause the snack stash was empty. Jesus, being the ultimate host, is like, "Man, I can't send these peeps home hungry; they'll faint on their way back, and some of them are from way outta town." The disciples are scratching their heads, "Um, how are we supposed to whip up a feast in the middle of nowhere?" Jesus does a quick inventory check, "What snacks we got?" "Seven loaves," they report. With that, Jesus gets everyone seated, does his blessing thing, breaks the bread, and—bam!—food for all. Even had a few small fish to round out the meal. Everyone's stuffed, and they even bagged up seven baskets of leftovers. Headcount? A cool 4k. After the feast, Jesus and the gang jet off to Dalmanutha.

Bread Drama and Pharisee Yeast

No chill, the Pharisees pop up, trying to press Jesus for some sky-high miracle to prove himself. Jesus, totally over it, lets out a deep sigh, "Why you always need a sign?" Spoiler: He wasn't giving them the satisfaction. Back in the boat, the disciples realize they're low on bread. Jesus throws out a warning about the "yeast of the Pharisees and Herod," but they're all hung up on the bread situation. Jesus facepalms, "Guys, seriously? Remember the 5k and the 4k picnics? How much leftovers did we have?" They get it, finally.

Blind Man Gets Visual Upgrade

Next stop, Bethsaida. A blind man gets the VIP Jesus treatment—out of the village, a little spit-and-pray action, and suddenly, the guy's mixing up people and trees. Jesus goes in for round two, and boom, the man's got HD vision. "Don't hit up the village," Jesus says, sending him off with a clear view.

Who's the Man?

On a walk to Caesarea Philippi, Jesus hits his crew with a pop quiz, "Who do folks say I am?" They throw around some names—John the B, Elijah, some old-school prophet. But then Jesus gets personal, "What about you guys? Who am I to you?" Peter steps up, "You're the real deal, the Messiah." Jesus is like, "Keep it on the DL, though."

On their low-key tour through Galilee, Jesus pulls his crew aside for a sequel no one saw coming. He's like, "Listen up, I'm gonna get double-crossed and taken out. But plot twist—I'll be back in three days." The disciples are all kinds of confused but too shook to ask for deets.

The Greatness Debate

Back in Capernaum, Jesus, playing the chill host, hits them with, "So, what was the tea on the road?" Silence. They'd been caught in a classic "Who's the GOAT?" debate. Jesus, ever the peacekeeper, gathers them for a sit-down: "Wanna be the MVP? Then you gotta play support, be everyone's hype man." He pulls a kid into the circle and is like, "Welcoming this little dude is like welcoming me, and that's basically rolling out the red carpet for the Big Boss who sent me."

Freelance Exorcist Gets a Pass

John, trying to shift gears, is like, "Yo, we saw this rando casting out demons with your brand,

and we tried to shut it down 'cause he wasn't in our squad." Jesus is all, "Chill, if he's not throwing shade, he's in the clear. Doing good in my name? That's the team spirit. And hey, even a splash of water for the crew earns big props."

Jesus Lays Down the Real Talk

Getting serious, Jesus drops some heavy truth: "Leading one of these kiddos astray? That's a one-way ticket to the worst kind of splashdown. And if something about you is causing a faceplant into sin? It's better to cut ties and live half-equipped than to be fully kitted out on a fast-track to the hot seat." He wraps it with, "Life's gonna test you—make sure you keep your flavor, stay seasoned. Keep the peace in the squad."

Swipe Left on Divorce Drama

So, Jesus hits Judea, instantly becomes the center of a pop-up seminar. The Pharisees slide in, hoping to catch Jesus on the hot topic: divorce. They're like, "So, can a guy get a 'thank u, next' with his wife or what?" Jesus, flipping the script back to OG guidelines, is like, "What did Moses DM you?" They're all, "Moses was cool with the breakup texts." But Jesus is like,

"Yeah, 'cause y'all were hard-hearted. But real talk, from day one, it was all about sticking together. What God's matched, don't let anyone mess with." Later, indoors, the disciples want the tea on this, and Jesus lays it down: bounce on your spouse for another, and it's a major foul.

#BlessedKids

Next up, people are queueing to get Jesus' autograph for their kids, but the disciples are acting like bouncers. Jesus, not having it, tells them to let the kiddos through. "Kingdom of God's VIP list? It's kids-first. Gotta welcome it with a child-like 'gram follow to get in." Then, it's full-on cuddle time as He blesses them.

Rich Kid Blues

Enter stage left: a loaded young dude kneels before Jesus, "Hey, what's the cheat code for eternal life?" Jesus, keeping it 100, is like, "Why call me good? Only the Big Boss upstairs qualifies. But you know the drill: no killing, cheating, stealing, lying, or dishonoring the 'rents." Dude's confident, "Been there, done that since my diaper days." Jesus, with a look of love, drops the bomb, "One thing's missing. Garage sale everything, donate to the 'gram worthy causes, then we can roll." But rich boy can't even, leaves all in his feels 'cause his wallet's too thicc.

Camel Through a Needle?

Jesus then vibes with His crew, "Rich folks entering God's kingdom? Tougher than threading a camel through a needle's eye." Disciples are mind-blown, "So, who's getting in then?" Jesus, with that hope sparkle, goes, "With peeps, it's a no-go, but God's got the hacks, all things are doable." Peter's like, "Yo, we're all-in, left everything." Jesus promises, "Stick with me, and the payback's epic—not just stuff and fam but with a side of challenges, yet scoring eternal life when the game ends. The leaderboard's gonna flip—first will be last, last grabbing the gold."

Spoiler Alert 3.0: The Final Season Trailer

So, they're road-tripping to Jerusalem, and Jesus is setting the pace upfront. The disciples are all hyped, but the fan club's getting the jitters. Jesus pulls his inner circle for a sneak peek: "Heads up, we're hitting Jerusalem, and it's gonna be intense. I'm gonna get passed around like a hot potato—chief priests, scribes, you name it—

ending with a major plot twist: death, then a three-day later comeback."

When Ambition Gets a Reality Check

Meanwhile, James and John, the Zebedee bros, slide up to Jesus with a big ask, "Yo, Jesus, hook us up with VIP seats in your kingdom." Jesus, eyebrow raised, is like, "You sure you're ready for what I'm signed up for?" They're all, "Totally." But Jesus breaks it to them, "The VIP seats? That's not my call. It's already on someone else's guest list." The rest of the squad gets wind of this and starts throwing shade at the bros. Jesus gathers everyone for a quick life lesson, "Look, the world's big shots love to flex their power, but we're flipping the script. Wanna be the GOAT? Be everyone's go-to. I'm here setting the pace—not to chill and be served, but to serve and go all-in for everyone."

#BlessedBeTheEyes

Next stop, Jericho. As they're dipping out, Bartimaeus, a blind beggar, starts shouting for Jesus. The crowd's trying to mute him, but he's got no chill, "Yo, Jesus, help a brother out!" Jesus, hearing the commotion, is like, "Bring him here." The crowd's tone changes, "You're up, he's

asking for you!" Bartimaeus, ditching his coat like it's last season's fashion, hops up and makes his way to Jesus. Jesus, playing it cool, asks, "What's on your wishlist?" Bartimaeus shoots his shot, "I wanna see the world, teacher." Jesus, with a nod, "You got it. Your trust has got you the VIP pass." Boom— Bartimaeus's sight is restored, and he's now part of the Jesus roadshow.

J.C.'s Epic Entrance

So, Jesus and the squad are about to make their grand entrance into Jerusalem, and He's like, "Yo, peeps, scoot over to that village and you'll find a colt that's basically a zero-mile ride. Snag it for me. If anyone's got beef, just tell 'em I need it for a hot sec." The disciples find the ride exactly where Jesus said, and when the locals are like, "Umm, excuse me, what are you doing?" they drop the "Jesus needs it" card, and it's all good. They deck out the colt in their best threads, and Jesus makes his grand entry. The crowd's losing it, rolling out the red carpet with their cloaks and tree branches, hyping up Jesus with some serious "Hosanna" chants. It's like the original palm Sunday Funday. After checking out the temple scene and finding it not to his liking (because, spoiler, it was late), Jesus and the crew hit up Bethany to crash.

The Fig Tree Gets a Time-Out

Next morning, Jesus is on the hunt for some breakfast, spots a fig tree, but it's all leaves and no eats. Jesus, not here for the false advertising, hits it with a "No snacks for you, ever again!" Disciples are all ears.

Temple Flip or Flop

Back in Jerusalem, Jesus walks into the temple and finds a whole marketplace vibe. Not pleased, he starts flipping tables like it's a clearance sale, saying, "This place is supposed to be a chill spot for prayer, not your personal Etsy shop." The temple bigwigs catch wind of this and start plotting Jesus' one-star review because everyone else is totally here for his teachings.

The Fig Tree's No Good, Very Bad Day

Strolling by the next day, the crew notices the fig tree's now a crispy critter from the roots up. Peter's like, "Whoa, check it out! That tree you dissed is totally toasted."

Jesus turns it into a teachable moment: "Y'all need to trust in God. Seriously, you could tell a mountain to go skinny-dipping and, believing it'll happen, it will. Keep your prayers bold, believe you've already snagged what you've asked for, and don't forget to hit the forgive button so you're on good terms upstairs."

Jesus Gets Quizzed on His Authority

Back in Jerusalem, Jesus is taking his daily temple stroll when the top dogs of the religious scene roll up, all like, "Hey, who gave you the VIP pass to do all this cool stuff?" Jesus, ever the master of clapbacks, is like, "I'll hit you with a quick Q, you give me an A, and I'll spill the tea on my creds. Was John's splash zone event heaven-endorsed or just a human hype thing?" They huddle up, sweating, 'cause either answer's a trap. Admitting John was legit means they're busted for not backing him, but dissing him means facing the crowd's wrath—they're all John fans. So, they pull the "IDK" card. Jesus, with a smirk, is like, "Guess you don't get to know where my authority's from either."

The Savage Vineyard Saga

Then Jesus drops a parable that's basically a thriller. This guy sets up a prime vineyard, leases it out, and heads off. Come harvest, he sends a buddy to collect his share, but the renters are feeling extra villainous, giving the messenger a beatdown. The owner keeps sending friends, who get either the beat-em-up or the RIP treatment. Finally, he sends his son, thinking they'll respect him, but they're like, "Nah, let's off him and inherit this place." Spoiler alert: The owner's coming to bring the hammer down on these guys and hand over the vineyard to folks who actually get how to share. The religious bigwigs realize Jesus is throwing shade at them with this story and peace out to plot their next move.

The Taxing Question

Next up, team Pharisee and some Herod fanboys try to catch Jesus slipping on taxes. They butter him up, "You're all about the truth, no playing favorites. So, what's the word—do we pay Caesar or what?" Jesus, seeing through the flattery, is like, "Why you playing? Show me a denarius." They whip out the coin, and Jesus hits them with, "Who's got his selfie on this? Caesar, right? So, give Caesar what's his, and don't forget to give God what's God's." Minds. Blown. Jesus isn't just dodging traps; he's schooling everyone on what's up in the kingdom of God. From calling out the leaders' lack of faith to highlighting the importance of doing right by God and not just getting tangled in worldly matters, He's making it clear: it's about where your heart's at, not just what you say or do. And when it comes to authority, His comes straight from the top.

Resurrection Riddle Meets Mic Drop

So the Sadducees, who are totally not on board with the whole resurrection vibe, decide to test Jesus with a brain teaser: a woman ends up marrying seven brothers (one after the other because #NoSurvivors), and they're like, "In the zombie apocalypse (a.k.a. resurrection), whose bae is she?" Jesus, probably internally rolling his eyes, schools them: "Y'all are missing the whole point. Post-resurrection, it's not about swiping right or left; we're all vibing like angels." Then drops the truth bomb that God's not the God of the dead, but of the living, basically telling them they're barking up the wrong afterlife tree.

Top of the Charts: Commandment Edition

A scribe cruises up, legit impressed by Jesus' answers, and is like, "What's the number one commandment on God's Top 40?" Jesus hits him with the classics: "Love God with everything you've got, and your neighbor like your own selfie." The scribe is all, "Spot on, Teacher. Doing that beats any playlist of sacrifices and offerings." Jesus gives him a nod of respect, "You're almost sliding into the kingdom's DMs."

Who's Your Daddy, Messiah?

While chilling in the temple, Jesus throws a curveball, "Why do the scribes say the Messiah is David's son when even David calls him 'Lord' in the charts? How does that work?" The crowd's eating it up, loving the tea being spilled.

Fashion Police: Scribe Edition

Jesus then goes on a bit of a rant about the scribes loving their influencer lifestyle—long robes, VIP greetings, front row seats, and all that clout chasing, all while exploiting widows. He's like, "The unfollow button is coming for them."

Widow's Mite: True Giving Goals

Chilling by the treasury, Jesus is people-watching as they drop their cash. The rich are making it rain, but then this widow comes by and drops two tiny coins, basically her last drop of cloud storage. Jesus gathers his crew, "This lady, right here, just out-gave everyone. They gave from their excess emojis, but she hit send on her whole heart." As they're bouncing from the temple, a disciple's all, "Whoa, look at these sick builds!" Jesus, ready to drop the final track of the day, is like, "Enjoy the view, 'cause it's all getting demo'd. Not one stone's gonna stay in the friend zone."

Apocalypse 101

Chillin' on the Mount of Olives, Peter, James, John, and Andrew hit Jesus with a DM: "Spill the tea, when's the world gonna hit the reset button, and what's the sign it's all going down?" Jesus, turning into the ultimate truth influencer, is like, "Peep this—don't let anyone slide into your DMs claiming they're the real deal. A bunch of posers will try it, saying 'It's me, fam,' leading peeps astray. You'll hear about World War Z and rumors that'll make you wanna check your bunker, but keep your chill—it's just the pre-show."

Spoiler Alert: It Gets Bumpy

"Brace yourselves," Jesus continues, "You're gonna get dragged into court, get a reality check in the synagogues, and even do some time on live feed in front of the bigwigs, all for the 'gram. But it's all good—every corner of the globe needs to catch the live broadcast of the gospel. And when they try to cancel you, just hit 'em with whatever the Spirit drops in your chat."

"Family drama's gonna hit max levels—trust issues 101. Stick it out, though; last one standing gets the crown."

Disaster Movie Special Effect

"When you peep the ultimate nope situation chilling where it shouldn't be, it's time to ghost Judea like you're in a parkour run. Don't even slide back in for your jacket or TikTok-worthy vids. And if you're expecting or got mini-you's, yikes—double tap on those prayers it's not in frostbite season. It's gonna be a hot mess, on a scale never seen before or ever again. But for the squad, the Director's gonna yell 'cut' early." "See someone flexing

as Messiah or dropping miracle clips? Hard pass. The fakes are gonna be out in full force, trying to finesse even the VIP list. Keep those eyes peeled; I've DM'd you all the deets."

Epic Season Finale

"After the worst season ever, the sky's going dark mode, stars dropping like bad reviews, and cosmic chaos. But then, boom, Son of Man's coming in HD, full glory, making that grand entrance. Angel squad's gonna be on the worldwide collect call, rounding up the fam."

Fig Tree Drops a Truth Bomb

"Here's a quick life hack from the fig tree: When it hits that glow-up and pops leaves, you know it's almost vacay season. Same vibes when you see all these spoilers happening—it means I'm just around the corner, ready to knock." "This gen's got front row seats until the credits roll. Heaven and earth are on a timer, but My playlist? Eternal."

"When's It Gonna Happen?" Guide

Jesus hits them with the real talk: "'Bout that end-of-the-world party? Not even the squad upstairs or yours truly has the deets—only the Big Boss knows the drop date. So, keep those eyes peeled, fam, 'cause it's gonna pop off when you least expect."

Imagine you're the homie left in charge while the main man's on vacay. He's like, "Keep the place lit and don't get caught snoozin'." That's the vibe—stay woke, 'cause surprise visits are kinda His thing. And yeah, this goes for everyone—stay sharp!

Undercover Operation: Jesus Edition

Fast forward, and it's almost Passover. The head honchos and the brain trust are scheming to catch Jesus on the low, hoping to avoid making the crowd go wild.

VIP Spa Treatment in Bethany

Over in Bethany, Jesus is kicking it at Simon the once-leper's crib when this lady crashes with some next-level expensive perfume, giving Jesus the royal treatment. The squad's not having it, all, "Could've cashed that in for the poor!" But Jesus is all about the gesture, "Chill, she's prepping me for what's coming.

This act? It's going down in history."

And then there's Judas, plotting a clout chase with the chief priests, eyeing that cash reward for a Jesus spoiler.

Passover Prep: Mission Impossible

Jesus sends his duo on a covert op: "Hit up downtown, look for the dude with the water jar—yeah, it'll stick out, trust—and he'll show you to our top-secret dinner spot." They find the place just as Jesus had DM'd, and they set up the squad's last supper.

Dinner Drama: Betrayal Edition

At dinner, Jesus drops a bombshell, "One of you is gonna ghost me." The crew's shook, hitting Him with the "It's not me, right?" one by one. Jesus narrows it down, "It's the one double-dipping with me. Dude's about to make a mega oof. Would've been better if he'd never hit 'accept' on the friend request."

Jesus' Ultimate Squad Dinner

So, Jesus and the gang were vibing at dinner when He grabbed some bread, did a quick bless up, broke it, and was like, "Yo, this bread is me. Take a bite." Then He snagged a cup, gave it a thankful shoutout, and passed it around, saying, "Sip on this—it's my squad pact juice, pouring out for everyone. BTW, I'm hitting pause on the vine vibes until we reunite in the ultimate kingdom bash." Post-jam session, they bounced to the Mount of Olives. Jesus then hit them with a reality check, "Y'all gonna ghost me soon, 'cause the script says so." Peter was all, "Nah, not me." Jesus side-eyed him, "Bruh, before the rooster's second solo, you'll act like you don't know me—thrice." Peter and the crew were hardcore denying, but Jesus knew the drill.

Nightmare Mode in Gethsemane

They rolled up to Gethsemane, and Jesus was feeling all the feels, super stressed. He took his inner circle—Peter, James, and John—deeper in and was like, "My soul's in deep dark mode. Keep watch." Jesus needed some alone time, dropped to the ground, and hit up God, "Pops, if there's any way to skip this level, let's do it. But yeah, your call, not mine." Came back to find the squad snoozing, called out Peter for crashing, and went for round two of praying, only to find them KO'd again.

Betrayal Level: Judas

Mid-heart-to-heart with God, Judas showed up, rolling deep with a mob geared up for trouble, courtesy of the religious big shots. Judas went straight for Jesus with a "Rabbi!" and the traitor's kiss. Bam, Jesus got grabbed. One of the squad went all ninja, slicing off a servant's ear, but Jesus was like, "Seriously, we doing this now? I've been chilling at the temple, and y'all pull up like I'm the bad guy?" Then, classic, everyone bailed, including some random dude who noped out so fast he left his threads behind and sprinted off in his birthday suit.

Drama in the Courtyard: Jesus vs. The Squad

So, they dragged Jesus to the high priest's VIP lounge, where all the top-tier religious influencers were gathered. Meanwhile, Peter was low-key lurking in the background, trying to stay warm without drawing attention. The big wigs were on a mission to cancel Jesus for good, but their stories weren't syncing up. They were throwing around fake news like, "We heard Him say He'd DIY a temple rebuild in three days without even hitting up Home Depot." Spoiler: their group chat was a mess. The high priest, looking for that gotcha moment, was all, "Yo, Jesus, you got a rebuttal to this mess?" Jesus played it cool, stayed mum. Round two: "Come on, spill – you the VIP they've been tweeting about?" Jesus, finally chiming in: "You said it, not me. And yeah, you'll see me kicking it with the big boss soon enough." The high priest went full drama queen, ripping his designer robe, "OMG, did you hear that? Cancel him!" They went low, spitting and roughing up Jesus, trying to make Him do party tricks. "Who hit you? Guess!" Style was not their strong suit.

Peter's Epic Fail

Cut to Peter, trying to blend in when a server girl was like, "Aren't you part of that Jesus crew?" Peter's all, "New phone, who dis?" Denial level: Expert. But then, another sighting, and the same line, "Nah, must be a glitch." Crew members started to clock him, "Bro, you totally have that Galilean accent." Peter lost it, "Swear I don't know this Jesus!" Cue the rooster's remix, and it all hit Peter like a bad TikTok challenge. Jesus called it – Peter bawled his eyes out.

Jesus Stands Before Pilate

As soon as the sun was up, after the bigwigs—the elders, scribes, and the whole Sanhedrin—had their pow-wow, the chief priests got Jesus all tied up, marched him over, and handed him off to Pilate. Pilate hit him with the question, "So, you're the King of the Jews?" Jesus shot back, "You said it, not me." The chief priests were piling on the accusations, thick and fast. Pilate pressed him again, "You hearing this? They're throwing a lot at you." But Jesus, he kept his cool, didn't say a word, leaving Pilate totally baffled.

The Choice Between Jesus and Barabbas

Festival time had Pilate usually playing the crowd pleaser, releasing a prisoner they picked. Barabbas was the name on everyone's lips, a rebel locked up for murder during an uprising. The crowd, whipped into a frenzy by the chief priests, pushed for Barabbas' release. Pilate, trying to get a handle on the situation, asked, "What am I supposed to do with your so-called King of the Jews?" "Crucify him!" they roared back. Pilate, seeking some sense, asked, "What for? What's he done?" But "Crucify him!" was all they shouted, louder and louder. Pilate, aiming to calm the storm, let Barabbas loose and handed Jesus over for a brutal whipping, then to be crucified.

The Soldiers Mock Jesus

The soldiers dragged Jesus into the governor's digs, rallying the entire squad. They decked him out in a purple mockery of a robe, twisted up a crown of thorns, and jammed it on his head. Then the salute, "Hail, King of the Jews!" accompanied by a hailstorm of hits to the head and spit. They knelt mockingly before him. After their cruel charade, they stripped the purple robe off and put his own clothes back on him.

Nailed Up with a Couple of Rule-Breakers

So they took Jesus to get crucified, right? On the way, they snag Simon from Cyrene (this dude just walking by, dad to Alexander and Rufus), and they're like, "Here, carry this cross." They end up at this place called Golgotha, which pretty much means Skull Town. They offer Jesus some wine mixed with myrrh, but Jesus is like, "Nah, I'm good." They nail Him up, and then they start rolling dice to divvy up His clothes, seeing who gets what. It's around 9 AM when they get Jesus up on the cross, with a sign saying "The King of the Jews." And yeah, they crucify two other guys with Him, one on each side. People walking by are tossing insults, shaking their heads like, "Look at You! Said You'd rebuild the temple in three days, and look at You now! Come down from there if You're so powerful!" Even the religious bigwigs are joining in the trash talk, "Saved others, but can't save Himself? Messiah, right? King of Israel? Prove it—come down from that cross!" And the guys hanging next to Him? They're giving Him grief too.

Jesus Final Moments

Around noon, the whole place goes dark for like three hours. At three, Jesus shouts, "Eloi, Eloi, lemá sabachtháni?" which means "My God, my God, why have You ghosted me?" Some folks standing there think He's calling for Elijah. One guy runs to get a sponge soaked in sour wine, sticks it on a stick, and offers it to Jesus, like, "Wait up, let's see if Elijah pops by to help." Then Jesus cries out loud one last time and that's it. The curtain in the temple rips right down the middle. The centurion standing right in front of Jesus sees how He dies and is like, "For real, this man was God's Son." Off at a distance, a bunch of women are watching, including Mary Magdalene, Mary the mom of James the younger and Joses, and Salome. These women had been following Him in Galilee, taking care of Him, along with many other women who came up to Jerusalem with Him.

Jesus's Burial

Evening's coming on, right before the Sabbath, and Joseph of Arimathea, this well-respected council member who was also waiting for God's kingdom, decides it's go-time. He goes boldly to Pilate and asks for Jesus's body. Pilate's shocked Jesus is already dead, checks with the centurion, and then gives the go-ahead to Joseph. Joseph grabs some linen, takes Jesus down, wraps Him up, and places Him in a tomb cut out of rock, then rolls a stone in front of it. Mary Magdalene and Mary, Joses's mom, are there watching where He's laid.

Resurrection Morning Got Lit

So, after the whole Sabbath vibe, Mary Magdalene, Mary the mom of James, and Salome were like, "Let's spice things up," planning to go jazz up Jesus' resting spot. Early Sunday morning, they hit the road at dawn, wondering, "Who's gonna help us yeet this massive stone away from the tomb's door?" Bam! They look up and see the stone's already been yeeted aside. Walking into the tomb, they spot this young dude chilling in a white robe, and they're totally spooked. He's like, "Chill, ladies. You're looking for Jesus of Nazareth, the one who got crucified, right? Plot twist: He's not here. He's pulled a total comeback. Check out his VIP spot. But yo, go tell his squad and Peter, 'He's hitting up Galilee, and you're gonna catch up with him there, just like he said.'" They booked it out of there, totally shook and not dropping a word to anyone because they were scared out of their minds.

Easter Sunday's Surprise Drops

[Now, get this: early on Sunday, Jesus decides to make his first epic comeback appearance to Mary Magdalene, who had been like his personal demon bouncer, kicking out seven of them. She runs to tell the mourning crew, but they're like, "Nah, can't be true," totally not buying it. Later, Jesus pulls another surprise appearance, this time looking all incognito, to two buddies taking a stroll in the countryside. They rush back to spill the tea to the others, but again, no one's believing their story either.]

Epic Squad Goals Unlocked

So, Jesus crashes the dinner party of the Eleven, throwing

some major shade for not believing the comeback stories. He's like, "Seriously, squad? Time for a reality check." Then, he hits them with the ultimate challenge: "Hit up the entire world and spread the good news to every creature out there. 16 Those who are down and get dunked will be cool, but those giving the cold shoulder will be on the outs. 17 And yo, check this—believers will be on some next-level vibes: booting out demons, chatting in fresh lingo, 18 snake handling without drama, sipping poison like it's nothing, and playing the healing game on the sick, making them bounce back."

Jesus Hits the Cosmic Elevator

After dropping this truth bomb, Jesus gets beamed up to the VIP lounge in heaven, snagging the best seat right next to God. 20 Meanwhile, the squad hit the ground running, spreading the word far and wide, with Jesus backing them up from the sidelines, making sure those miraculous signs followed through, sealing the deal on his words.

LUKE'S GOSPEL

To Theophilus, the OG Seeker

Yo Theophilus, big man, a
bunch of peeps have tried to lay
down the story of the dope stuff
that went down among us, just
like the OG witnesses and word-
spreaders passed it to us. I did a
deep dive, went full detective
mode from the get-go, and
decided to hit you up with the
deets, top to bottom, so you can
be all in on the truth of what
you've been schooled on.

John's Epic Intro

Back in King Herod's reign in
Judea, there was this priest,
Zechariah, part of the Abijah
squad, and his partner Elizabeth,
straight out of Aaron's crew.
Both were tight with God,
walking the line, blameless by
God's standards. But yo, they
had no little ones because
Elizabeth was hitting a block,
and they were both getting on in
years, like way up there.
Zechariah's crew was on temple
duty, and he scored the incense
gig by lot, which was a big deal
back then. So, while he was up in
God's grill, laying down the

Boom! Angel of the Lord pops
up next to the incense spot, and
Zechariah is shook, straight-up
terrified. But the angel's like,
"Chill, Z, your prayers have been
heard. Liz is gonna drop a son,
and you'll call him John. It's
gonna be lit; he'll be a big deal
before God, never hitting the
sauce, Holy Spirit-filled from the
womb. He's gonna flip the script
for many in Israel, rolling out in
Elijah's vibe, turning hearts,
prepping peeps for the Lord."
Zechariah's like, "How am I
supposed to buy that? I'm old,
and Liz isn't exactly in her spring
chicken years." Gabriel claps
back, "I'm Gabriel, God's right-
hand messenger, here to bring
you the good news. But since
you're playing the doubt game,
you're gonna be on mute until all
this goes down, 'cause you
weren't vibing with my word."
Meanwhile, folks outside are
wondering why Z's taking
forever. When he finally steps
out and can't spit a word, they
get it—he's had a divine meet-
up. He's home-signing his story
but stays silent. After his shift,
he hits home, Liz catches a baby
vibe, and after five months she's
like, "Big up to the Lord for
scrubbing my shame and
hooking me up in front of the

squad." Keep it 100, Theophilus. This is how it all kicked off.

The Dedication to Theophilus

Yo, so a bunch of peeps have tried to line up the story of the stuff that went down among us, just like those first-hand homies and message carriers passed onto us. I thought, "Why not?" After doing my homework from the get-go, I decided to drop you a DM, Theophilus, so you're totally clued in on the deets you've been taught.

Gabriel Drops News on John's Debut

Back in King Herod's era in Judea, there was this priest, Zechariah, part of Abijah's crew, and his wife, Elizabeth, from Aaron's fam. Both were tight with God, living by the book without a single fault. But, bummer, they couldn't have kids, and they were getting on in years. Zechariah's squad was on temple duty, and his turn came to hit up the sanctuary of the Lord and burn some incense. The place was packed, everyone praying outside while Zechariah was doing his thing inside. Then, bam! Angel Gabriel shows up on the right side of the altar. Zechariah freaked out, but Gabriel was like, "Chill, Zechariah, your prayer's been answered. Liz is gonna have a boy, and you'll name him John. It's gonna be lit because he'll be great and live clean, filled with the Holy Spirit even before his debut. He's gonna turn many peeps back to God. Running ahead of the Lord with Elijah's vibe, he'll get hearts aligned — kids to parents, and the no-goes to the wisdom of the just, prepping everyone for the Lord." Zechariah's like, "How can I be sure of this? I'm old, and my wife's no spring chicken." Gabriel's all, "I'm Gabriel, dude, I stand in God's presence. I was sent to spill this good news. But since you're doubting, you'll be on mute until this all goes down." Meanwhile, everyone's wondering, "What's taking Zechariah so long?" When he finally comes out and can't talk, they're like, "He must've seen something wild in there." After his temple gig, he heads home, and soon after, Elizabeth's expecting. She's over the moon, "God's taken away my shame!"

Mary's Fire Mixtape

Mary steps up: "My soul's blasting the Lord's epic beats, and my spirit's poppin' in God, my hype man, 'cause He's thrown a spotlight on His low-key girl. And yo, everyone's gonna say I got mad blessings, 'cause the Big Boss did some next-level stuff for me, and His tag is all kinds of holy. His fam gets that mercy flow, from one gen to the next, He flexed His arm and scattered the too-proud, playing 4D chess with their minds; knocked rulers off their high horses and bigged up the underdogs. Filled the hungry with top-tier snacks and told the rich to skate on an empty stomach. He's got Israel's back, keeping it 100, remembering to be all merciful to Abe and his crew forever, just like He promised." Mary chilled with Liz for about three months before heading back.

The Birth and Naming of John the VIP

Time's up, and Liz pops out a boy. The neighborhood and the fam are hyped 'cause the Lord dished out mega mercy. On circumcision day, everyone thought he'd be Little Zechariah, but his mom's like, "Nah, he's gonna be John." "But no one's named that in your fam!" they argued. They start signing to Zechariah, who asks for a tablet and writes, "His name is John," leaving everyone shook. Suddenly, Zechariah's chatting away, blessing God. The word spread, and everyone in Judea's hills was talking about it, wondering, "What's this kid gonna turn out to be?" 'Cause clearly, the Lord's favor was all over him.

Zechariah's Prophecy

Then Zechariah, filled with the Holy Spirit, lays down some prophecy: "Blessed be the Lord, God of Israel, 'cause He visited us, dropping salvation in our laps, raising a mighty savior from David's fam, just like He promised through His ancient VIP messengers —salvation from our haters and all who got beef with us. He's shown our ancestors mad love, remembering His holy contract with Abe, giving us the green light to serve Him fear-free, in holiness and righteousness, right in His presence, all our days. And you, my little dude, will be known.

The Big Debut of Jesus

So, Caesar Augustus was like, "I wanna count everyone in the empire," sparking the first-ever empire-wide roll call. This was happening while Quirinius was the big boss in Syria. Everyone bounced to their hometown to sign up. Joseph hit the road from Nazareth in Galilee to Bethlehem in Judea, David's old stomping grounds, because that's where his family tree rooted. He took Mary with him, who was pretty much his fiancée and expecting a baby. Right when they got there, it was go-time for Mary, and she gave birth to her first kiddo. She swaddled him all cozy and popped him in a manger since every inn was like, "No vacancy."

Shepherds and Angel Squad

Meanwhile, some shepherds were chilling with their sheep at night when, boom, an angel lit up the sky, and they were shook. But the angel was like, "Chill, I've got epic news of mega joy for everyone: Today in Bethlehem, your savior, the VIP, the Lord, just made his grand entrance. You'll find the baby swaddled up and crashing in a manger." Suddenly, the sky was packed with angels, throwing a huge praise party for God: "Big ups to God up high, and peace on earth to the cool people!" After the angel crew bounced back to heaven, the shepherds were like, "Let's roll to Bethlehem and check out this scoop the Lord clued us into." They zipped over and found Mary, Joseph, and the baby in the manger. Post-visit, they spread the word, blowing everyone's minds with the news about the kiddo. Mary kept all these moments, turning them over in her heart. The shepherds went back, hyping up and thanking God for everything they'd seen and heard, just like it was told to them.

Jesus Gets His Name and His Blessings

Eight days later, it was time for the baby's circumcision, and they named him Jesus, the name the angel dropped before he was even conceived. After Mary and Joseph did everything required by Moses' law, they brought Jesus to Jerusalem to introduce him to the Lord, as per the playbook: "Every firstborn dude is dedicated to the Lord." They also brought the standard offering, a pair of turtledoves or two young pigeons, keeping it by the book.

Simeon's Lit Review

So, in Jerusalem, there was this chill guy named Simeon. Super righteous and devout, always on the lookout for the big comfort move for Israel, and he was all in with the Holy Spirit. The Holy Spirit had slid into his DMs to promise he wouldn't kick the bucket before he caught a glimpse of the Lord's MVP, the Messiah. Led by the vibe, he hit up the temple. When Jesus' folks showed up to do the usual law stuff, Simeon scooped Jesus into his arms and was like, "Okay, Big Boss, I'm good to peace out now, just like You tweeted. My own eyes have peeped Your epic save, ready to drop jaws in front of everyone: a beacon for the nations and major clout for Your peeps, Israel." Jesus' mom and dad were mind-blown by the props Simeon was giving. Then Simeon, doubling down on blessings, hit Mary with some real talk: "This kiddo's gonna be a game-changer — lifting some, tripping others. He's a walking hot take, guaranteed to spark debate — a heart-check for many. And yeah, Mary, it's gonna sting like you're on the business end of a sword."

Anna's Hot Take

And don't sleep on Anna, the prophetess, from the Asher squad. She'd been around the block, married seven years, then solo for eighty-four. She wasn't about that leaving-the-temple life, vibing with God through all-night prayer and fasting sessions. She rolled up right at this holy moment, started bigging up God, and didn't miss a chance to chat about the child to anyone in Jerusalem holding out for the big turnaround.

Chillin' in the Temple

Every year, Jesus' fam hit up Jerusalem for the ultimate Passover rave. When Jesus hit the big one-two, they made their annual trip, festival style. Post-fest, as the fam squad started their trek back, Jesus pulled a sneaky one and stayed back in Jerusalem. His folks, clueless, assumed he was mingling in the caravan somewhere. A whole day later, they're like, "Wait, where's Jesus?" Panic mode: they high-tail it back to Jerusalem. Three days of frantic searching later, they find him in the temple, just casually dropping knowledge bombs on the teachers, who were all kinds of impressed. Mary and Joseph were shook. Mary's like, "Kid, you had us worried sick!" And Jesus hits them with, "Why were you stressing? Didn't you figure I'd be at my Dad's place?" That flew right over their heads. So, Jesus moseys on back to Nazareth with them and sticks to the rules. Mary's keeping all these wild stories to ponder on. Meanwhile, Jesus is leveling up in wisdom, gaining XP with God and everyone else.

Desert DJ Drops Truth Tracks

Fast forward to Tiberius Caesar's reign, with Pontius Pilate and Herod running different parts of the show. John, Zechariah's kid, is out in the wilds getting direct downloads from God. He's all over the Jordan hood, shouting about turning a new leaf for a fresh start with God. Isaiah's mixtape had this track: "Yo, make way for the Lord, straighten up!" John's remix was about flattening life's rough patches so everyone could catch the God show. Crowds flocked for a spiritual cleanse, and John's like, "Y'all better shape up and show real change. Don't just name-drop Abraham as your get-out-of-judgment-free card." He's all, "Produce some goodness or it's tree-chopping time." The crowd's like, "What do we do?" John's practical: "Got two shirts? Share one. Got snacks? Ditto." Tax collectors and soldiers slide in, asking for life hacks. John's advice: "Keep it honest, and don't be bullies." Everyone's buzzing, wondering if John's the main event. But he's clear, "I'm just the warm-up act. The headliner's on his way, and he's next level—Holy Spirit and fire kind of vibes." John kept dishing out truth, even calling out Herod for his shady moves, which got him a VIP pass to prison.

Ghostbuster in Capernaum

So Jesus cruises down to Capernaum, hitting up the Sabbath scene with teachings that pack a punch. Mid-sermon, this dude with a demon vibe interrupts, screaming, "Yo, Jesus! Chill! You here to wreck us? I'm onto you, you're that holy VIP!" Jesus, unfazed, is like, "Zip it, and bounce!" And just like that, the demon does a dramatic exit, leaving the guy unscathed. Crowd's mind = blown. They're all, "Whoa, what's up with His words? Even the unholy squad listens!" And bam, Jesus' fame skyrockets.

Capernaum's Healin' Hotspot

Post-synagogue, Jesus drops by Simon's and finds his mother-in-law down with fever heat. A stern look and a word from Jesus, and she's up serving snacks like nothing happened. Sunset hits, and it's like a divine clinic at Simon's door. Jesus is hands-on, healing everyone. Demons out here outing Him as the Son of God, but He's shushing them, "No spoilers!"

Dawn of the Squad

Next day, Jesus hits Lake Gennesaret. Spots Simon's empty boat and turns it into His floating pulpit. Post-sermon, He's like, "Simon, deep end, nets down, fish party." Simon's skeptical, "Bruh, been at it all night. Zero. But aight, your call." Boom, net-breaking, boat-sinking loads of fish. Simon's shook, hits the deck, "I'm too messed up for this miracle gig." But Jesus, with a grin, "Fear not, you're in the people-fishing biz now." And just like that, they ditched it all to follow Him.

Detox Squad Rollout

In some town, there was this dude covered in leprosy. Spots him, dives face-first, and is like, "Yo, Chief, hit me up with that cleanse if you're down." Jesus, being a bro, reaches out, zaps him with the clean vibe, "Totally willing. Be clean, bro." And just like that, leprosy ghosted. Jesus is all, "Mum's the word, but hit up the priest, do the Moses thing as proof you're all clear." Of course, Jesus goes viral, crowds swarm for some of that healing magic. Jesus, needing some me-time, dips out to chat with the sky.

Epic Heal & Forgive Session

On a teaching day, Jesus is dropping wisdom bombs, with Pharisees and teach squad from everywhere parked there. The vibe? Healing. Enter stage left, squad carrying their buddy on a mat cause he's all paralyzed. No entry? No problem. Rooftop express it is, right down to Jesus. Jesus sees this, "Bro, your sins are cancelled." Cue the religious keyboard warriors, "Blasphemy!" Jesus, catching their vibe,

"What's easier? 'Sins are nixed' or 'Get up and walk'? Watch this." Paralyzed dude walks out like it's nothing, crowd loses it, "We just witnessed next-level stuff!"

Levi's Lit Leave

Jesus strolls, spots Levi minting coins at the tax booth, "Yo, roll with me." Levi's like, "Peace out, tax life," and throws a massive feast for Jesus, aka J.C. the Lord. Tax collectors? Check. Other peeps? Double check. Pharisees? Party poopers, "Why you brunching with the sin squad?" Jesus, "Healthy folks don't need a doc. I'm here for the sick, not the selfie-righteous."

Fasting? Nah, We Feasting

They quiz Jesus, "Why do your squad feast while everyone else is on a fasting vibe?" Jesus, "Can't have the squad on a hunger strike while I'm here, can you? Wait till I bounce, then they can hit the fast button." And then Jesus drops this gem, "You don't patch old threads with new fabric. You don't store fresh vino in old skins. And let's be real, nobody after the old wine wants the new, 'cause they're all about that vintage life."

Sabbath Snack Attack

So, Jesus and his squad were strolling through some grain fields on a chill Sabbath, doing a bit of a snack-and-stroll, much to the Pharisees' dismay. "Yo, isn't this kinda sketch on the Sabbath?" they grilled Him. Jesus hits back with, "Ever heard of the time David hit up the holy snack bar? Yeah, he wasn't supposed to, but did anyway. Moral of the story? I'm the boss of the Sabbath."

Sabbath Heal & Deal

Next up, Jesus is teaching in the synagogue, spots a dude with a not-so-funky fresh hand. The Pharisees were lurking, hoping Jesus would pull a heal so they could start some drama. Jesus, catching their vibe, is like, "Step up, my man," to the guy. Then, to the Pharisees, "What's the Sabbath for? Doing solid or shady stuff?" Boom, he heals the guy's hand, leaving the Pharisees in a huff, plotting their next move.

Squad Goals

Jesus hits up a mountain for some one-on-one time with the Big Guy, then calls up his crew at daybreak. He picks out twelve VIPs, dubbing them apostles: we got the brothers Peter and Andrew, the dynamic duo James and John, plus Philip, Bartholomew, Matthew, Thomas, another James, Simon the Rebel, Judas son of James, and, oh, Judas Iscariot (spoiler: not the MVP)

Jesus then rolls down with his posse to a flat spot, drawing crowds from everywhere – Judea, Jerusalem, even Tyre and Sidon folks showed up for some healing and wisdom. Everyone's trying to get a piece of that healing energy Jesus was dishing out.

Blessed Be the Squad

Jesus, eyeing his disciples, drops some blessings:

1 "Shoutout to the broke - Kingdom's all yours.
2 Big ups to the hungry - you'll be chowing down soon.
3 Props to the weepers - get ready to crack up laughing.

And when folks diss you, push you out, and trash your name all for the squad leader? Dance it out, 'cause you're scoring big in heaven. Remember, that's how they played the OG truth-tellers."

Yikes for the High-Rollers

Heads up, you rich folks living your best life now, you've got your comfy vibes already. To you chowing down 'til you're stuffed, get ready for the munchies.

Laughing now? Brace yourselves for the ugly cry later. And if everyone's hyping you up, watch out - that's how they rolled with the fake prophets back in the day.

How to Be Chill with Your Haters

Alright, listen up if you're actually paying attention: Show some love to your haters, be cool to those who can't stand you,
Bless the ones throwing shade, send good vibes to those dissing you.
Someone slaps you? Turn the other cheek. Takes your jacket? Offer your hoodie too. Someone's asking for a favor? Just do it. And if they ghost you with your stuff, don't sweat asking back.
Treat people like you wanna be treated, simple as that. Loving your fan club? No biggie, everyone does that. And if you're nice only to get something back, that's basic – even the shady folks do that. But here's the deal: love your enemies, be the good guy, and expect zilch in return. You'll be totally rocking it, and you'll be like VIPs in heaven's squad. 'Cause the big guy upstairs, he's all about giving chances to the thankless and the troublemakers. Stay kind, just like your cosmic dad is kind.

Judgment Free Zone

Don't be throwing shade, and you won't get shaded. Don't cancel others, and you won't be canceled. Forgive, and you'll get the pass too. Give it away, and watch it come back like a boomerang – a nice, full, overflowing measure will spill right into your lap. 'Cause the universe has this boomerang policy: what you send out comes back at ya.

Blind Leading the Blind??

Here's a fun one: Can a blind person guide another blind? Expect a faceplant, both of you. A student doesn't outsmart the teacher, but a pro student becomes like the teacher. Why obsess over a speck in your buddy's eye when you've got a whole plank in yours? Playing the 'holier-than-thou' card? Please. Sort your own mess first; then you can help clear up your friend's minor glitches.

Fruit Vibes Only

Good vibes only, folks: A legit tree doesn't grow whack fruit. You can tell a tree by its fruit – you're not picking berries from a cactus, are ya? A good-hearted person dishes out goodness 'cause they've got goodness on tap. The opposite for the not-so-good. It's like your mouth spills what your heart's filled with.

House Party: Rock vs. Sand Edition

Why call me the boss if you're not down with my playbook? Here's the deal: Rock with me and my words, and you're like a DJ building a house on a solid beat. Storm hits, and your party doesn't stop. But ignore my tracks? It's like setting up your turntables on the sand. Good luck with that – first sign of trouble, and it's game over, party crashed.

Faith of a Centurion (Boss Level)

So Jesus had just finished dropping some wisdom and heads into Capernaum. There's this centurion with a top-tier servant hitting red on the health bar, about to check out. The centurion, catching wind of Jesus, sends the town VIPs to get Jesus on board to save his servant. They hit Jesus with, "This dude's legit, he's got love for our crew and even bankrolled our prayer spot." As Jesus rolled up, the centurion sent his squad with a message: "Yo, Lord, don't sweat coming all the way. I'm not on your level to host you. Just hit the heal button from there, and we're cool. I get the whole chain of command thing; I've got soldiers who jump when I say jump." Jesus was shook. He turns to the crowd and is like, "Not even in Israel have I seen this kind of epic faith." And boom, servant's back to 100%.

Next up, Jesus heads to Nain. As he's about to enter, a funeral procession's happening. It's a widow's only son, and she's heartbroken. Jesus sees her, hits her with, "Don't cry." Walks up, touches the coffin, and is like, "Yo, young blood, time to wake up!" Dead dude sits up, starts chatting, and Jesus reunites him with his mom. The crowd's mind = blown. They're all, "A prophet's among us, and God's definitely checking in on His peeps." News went viral in no time.

Bigging Up John the B

John the B, chilling in prison, hears about Jesus' latest drops and sends his crew to ask, "You the one or we waiting for another?"

Jesus, after a healing spree, is like, "Go tell John the playlist: blind folks seeing, lame walking, lepers all clear, deaf hearing tunes, dead are up for round two, and the broke are getting some good news. Blessed if you're vibing and not tripping over me." After sending them back, Jesus turns to the crowd for a John the B appreciation moment. "What, you thought John was a weather vane? Or maybe you expected him in designer gear? Nah, those types chill in palaces. John's the real deal, the hype man Isaiah rapped about. Honestly, no one tops John, but even the newbie in God's kingdom is playing on a whole new level."

The crowd, especially the tax collectors, were nodding along, digging the righteousness vibe since they were team John from the start. But the Pharisees and the law experts, skipping John's baptism like it was a bad track, totally missed the beat.

This Gen's Vibe Check

So, what's the deal with this gen? It's like when you drop the sickest beats and nobody vibes, or you serve deep tracks and no one sheds a tear. John the B hits the scene, fasting, and y'all are like, "He's got a demon!" The Son of Man shows up, feasting, and suddenly it's "Look at him, a foodie and wino, buddy-buddy with the tax crew and sin squad!" But you know, wisdom's got her own fanbase.

Dinner Drama with a Side of Grace

Now, picture this: Jesus gets a dinner invite from a Pharisee, rolls up, and lounges at the table. In walks this notorious woman from town with her luxury perfume. She's behind Jesus, crying waterfalls, gives his feet a shower with her tears, dries them with her hair, lands kisses, and goes full spa treatment with her perfume. The host's thinking, "If this Jesus was legit, he'd know she's bad news." Jesus, catching the vibe, hits Simon with, "Yo, Simon, story time." Goes like, "Imagine two peeps owe cash—one owes a fortune, the other peanuts. Both debts get cleared. Who's throwing more love?" Simon's like, "The big spender, I guess." Jesus nods, "Bingo." Then, flipping the script, Jesus tells Simon, "See this lady? You skipped the welcome kit—no water, no welcome smooch, no oil. But she's out here, giving me the VIP treatment. Her love's off the charts because she got a major debt drop. Little forgiveness, little love." And to the woman, "Your sins? Canceled. Peace out."

Girl Squad Goals

Next, Jesus is on tour, hitting up towns with the good news. The Twelve are tagging along, plus a squad of ladies who've been through the wringer but came out strong—like Mary Magdalene, who ditched seven demons, Joanna with the VIP pass, Susanna, and a bunch of others funding the mission from their stash.

Story Time with the Sower

So, Jesus pulls this crowd, right? Like everyone's rolling up from every corner to catch what he's laying down. He launches into this story: "Check it, there's this dude tossing seeds everywhere. Some seeds got yeeted onto a path, got stomped on, and then bird squad swooped in for a snack. Some landed on rocky vibes, sprouted, but then ghosted 'cause they were thirsty. Others got tangled up with thorns and got straight-up choked. But some hit the jackpot, landed in the good stuff, and boom—harvest city, like a hundredfold." He drops the mic with, "If you've got ears, you better be listening."

Behind the Scenes with Parables

His crew's all puzzled, like, "Bro, what's with the riddle?" Jesus goes, "Alright, squad, you get the VIP pass to the kingdom secrets, but for everyone else, it's like riddles so they can look and not see, listen and not get it."

Seed Story Unpacked

Here's the scoop: The seed's the word. The sidewalk seeds? That's when peeps hear it, but then life's buzzkills swoop in and yoink it before it sticks. The rocky ground crew? They're all hype at first, but bail when it gets tough 'cause they're not rooted. Thorns? That's when life's bling, stress, and fun times choke out the word, so it's a no-go on the fruit. But the good soil gang? They're legit, hearing the word, holding it tight, and going the distance to make things happen.

ùLamp Under a Basket? As If!

J.C. is like, "Who lights up a lamp and then hides it? Nah, you put it out there so everyone can get in on the glow. Everything that's under wraps is gonna get uncovered, and all the secret stuff will hit the spotlight. So, listen up good—what you've got, you'll get more of. But if you're empty-handed, even the little you think you've got is gonna disappear."

Who's My Crew?

When Jesus' fam tried to get through the mob to see him, someone's like, "Yo, your fam's outside, waiting." Jesus hits back, "Nah, my real fam? They're the ones tuning in and doing the thing with God's word."

So, Jesus and his squad hit the lake in a boat, right? Jesus decides it's naptime, but then a wild storm decides to crash their cruise. The disciples freak, waking Jesus up like, "Bro, we're literally about to become fish food!" Jesus, cool as a cucumber, tells the storm to sit down and chill. Boom, instant zen mode. The crew's jaws drop, and they're like, "Who even is this guy? Even the weather's listening to him!"

Epic Demon Eviction Party

Next up, they hit Gerasene's shores, and this wild dude with a demon-posse rolls up from the graveyards. Dude's been living there rent-free, no clothes, no chill. He sees Jesus and throws himself down like, "Yo, Jesus, chill! What do you want with me?" Jesus, in his demon-busting mood, is like, "Name, please?" "Legion," says the dude, 'cause he's got a whole squad in there. The demons negotiate a transfer to a bunch of pigs, and Jesus is like, "Sure, why not?" Next thing, those pigs take a nosedive into the lake. The pig herders bolt, spreading the news like wildfire. Everyone's freaking out, and the once-possessed dude is now fanboying over Jesus, all cleaned up and sane. Jesus hits him with, "Go home, tell your peeps the good news." And the guy becomes Jesus' hype man in town.

Back in town, Jesus is mobbed by fans. Enter Jairus, a big-deal synagogue boss, begging Jesus to save his dying daughter. En route, a woman with a never-ending bleed sneaks a touch of Jesus' cloak and gets instant healing. Jesus is like, "Who tapped me?" After some back and forth, the lady fesses up, and Jesus is all, "Your faith is your backstage pass to health. Peace out." Meanwhile, Jairus gets the worst DM ever: "Your daughter's dead, leave the teacher alone." Jesus overhears and is like, "Fear's cancelled, just believe." At Jairus' house, he's met with a funeral vibe but switches it up, saying, "Chill, she's just napping." Laughter turns to shock when he wakes her up like it's Sunday morning. He's like, "Get this girl a snack!" and everyone's minds are blown, but Jesus is all about keeping it on the down-low.

Squad Goals: The Twelve Get Superpowers

So, Jesus rounds up his crew of twelve and basically gives them the ultimate power-up: authority over all the demons and some mad healing skills. He's like, "Alright, squad, it's showtime. Spread the good vibes of God's kingdom and fix up the sick." But catch this: "Pack light, fam—no extra kicks, no snack stash, no cash. Just roll with what you got." If a spot doesn't roll out the welcome mat, they're to dust off their sneakers in protest and bounce. Off they zoomed, village to village, dropping truth bombs and health buffs everywhere.

Herod's Major FOMO

Meanwhile, Herod's scratching his head big time. He's hearing all these wild rumors about Jesus—like, is John the Bap back from his headless state? Is Elijah dropping in for a comeback tour? Herod's like, "Didn't I already deal with John? Who's this Jesus dude?" Major FOMO hitting him; he's dying to meet Jesus.

Epic Bread-n-Fish Remix

The apostles regroup with Jesus, spilling the tea on their adventures. Jesus takes them for some chill time in Bethsaida, but the crowd's like a magnet. Jesus, ever the host, heals and teaches. Come dinner, the disciples are all, "Jesus, bro, we can't feed this massive TikTok meetup." Jesus is like, "Hold my sandals." With just a boy-band amount of food, he throws the ultimate feast, and bam, everyone's stuffed, with leftovers to boot. In a private pow-wow, Jesus hits them with, "So, who's the buzz about me?" Disciples throw around names like they're on Celebrity Prophet. But Peter, going for the win, drops, "You're the real MVP, God's Messiah." But Jesus, keeping it on the DL, is like, "Listen up, don't tweet this yet. I gotta go through some heavy stuff, get ghosted by the VIPs, take a major L, but then hit 'em with the biggest comeback of all time."

Then he lays it down: "Wanna ride with me? Get ready to leave that ego, carry your own struggles, and stick close. 'Cause chasing clout? That's a dead end. Real talk: If you're not down with me now, don't expect to be rolling with me when I'm shining with the big G and the angel squad. But hey, some of you here? You're gonna peep the kingdom before you drop the mic for good."

Mountain Top Glow-Up with Jesus & Co.

About a week after dropping some truth bombs, Jesus takes his OG trio—Peter, John, and James—for a little mountain retreat. Mid-prayer, Jesus starts glowing different, like his clothes hit the ultimate bleach cycle. Then, outta nowhere, Moses and Elijah pop up for a celestial TED talk about Jesus' upcoming big move in Jerusalem. While the trio is catching Zs, they wake up to find Jesus in full divine swag mode with Moses and Elijah ghosting. Peter, totally missing the room's vibe, offers to build some VIP tents. Talk about not reading the room! Then, as if the scene wasn't extra enough, a cloud rolls in, and God's voice booms out, "This is my Son, the

MVP—listen up!" Post-voice bomb, it's just Jesus standing there. The trio zip it, not spilling the tea to anyone.

J.C. Schools a Demon (and the Disciples)

Next day, back to reality, and a crowd's waiting. A desperate dad shouts about his son being demon-hassled. The disciples flunked demon-busting 101, and Jesus is all, "This generation's got me facepalming. Bring the kid here." Jesus, being the boss he is, tells the demon to take a hike and hands the boy back, demon-free. Crowd's mind = blown.

Spoiler Alert: Jesus' Encore

In the midst of the wow-fest, Jesus huddles the crew and hits them with a reality check: "Brace yourselves, I'm about to be handed over." But it's like he's speaking ancient Martian—total confusion, but they're too shook to ask.

The Greatness Debate Gets a Reality Check

Then, out of nowhere, a "who's the GOAT" debate breaks out among them. Jesus, reading their thought bubbles, pulls a kid into the mix and is like, "You wanna be big? Welcome the little guys. That's real greatness."

Road Trip to Jerusalem Gets Rocky

J.C. sets his GPS for Jerusalem, but the Samaritan Airbnb falls through big time—no welcome mat. James and John, ready to go full 'Elijah: Fire Remix,' get a stern "chill" from Jesus. So, it's on to Plan B: next village.

Chasing the Dream with Jesus

While hitting the road, some dude's like, "Yo, Jesus, I'm down to follow you to the ends of the earth." Jesus hits back, "Cool, but just FYI, foxes have their chill spots, birds have their hangouts, but I'm basically couch-surfing without a couch." Another guy's like, "Hold up, let me hit pause and bury my dad first." Jesus is straight-up, "Let the ghost followers handle their own. You're with me now—time to broadcast the kingdom vibes." Then, another hopeful follower's like, "BRB, gotta drop a goodbye TikTok with the fam." Jesus lays it down, "Once you're in this, looking back is a no-go. We're moving forward only, no rewinds."

Epic Send-Off for the Seventy-Two

Next up, Jesus lines up a squad of seventy-two and sends them on a sneak preview tour—pairing them up for some buddy-cop kingdom spreading. "The vibe is ripe for the picking," he says, "but the crew is thin. Hit up the big guy to drop more helpers." Heading out, Jesus is like, "Travel light—no bags, no extra kicks, and skip the small talk. When you crash at a place, bless it. If they're cool, your peace sticks. If not, take back your good vibes and hit the road." In towns that roll out the red carpet, heal up the sick and drop the "Kingdom's knocking" line. But for the towns giving you the cold shoulder? Dust off those Yeezys as a parting gift and peace out with a warning that even Sodom had it easier. Jesus then throws shade at Chorazin and Bethsaida for sleeping on his miracles. "Tyre and Sidon would've turned their life around for less, but you? Nah." And Capernaum, aiming high but ending up in the basement.

Seventy-Two's Victory Lap

The seventy-two bounce back, hyped, "Boss, even the demons are hitting the deck in your name!" Jesus, with a proud mentor vibe, "Saw Satan get the boot from the VIP lounge. And yeah, you've got that demon-stomping pass. But keep the real win in mind—your names are VIP-listed in heaven."

Exclusive Reveal Party

J.C., feeling the spirit, throws some love upstairs, "Big shoutout to you, Dad, for keeping the know-it-alls guessing while the newbies get the inside scoop." To his crew, "Y'all are catching sights and sounds prophets and kings would've killed for. Consider yourselves blessed."

Road Trip with a Twist: The Good Samaritan Story

So, this law pro was trying to catch Jesus in a quiz. He's like, "Yo, what's the cheat code for eternal life?" Jesus flips it back, "You're the expert. You tell me." Dude answers with the classic, "Love God with everything you've got and your neighbor like your selfie game." Jesus nods, "Spot on. Do that and you're golden." But the guy, wanting to sound extra smart, goes, "And who exactly is my 'neighbor'?" Jesus spins this tale: "So, a guy's on his way down from Jerusalem to Jericho, ends up in a

beatdown so bad he's half a meme. A priest walks by, sees him, but just ghosts him. Same with a Levite—total ignore. But then, this Samaritan dude rolls up, hearts in his eyes, goes full first aid on him, even shacks him up in a B&B on his own dime, promising to cover the sequel."Jesus mic drops, "So, who's the real MVP to the beat-up guy?" The expert's like, "The one who went all 'Care Bear' on him." Jesus is like, "Bingo. Now go and be that guy."

Martha vs. Mary: The Ultimate Sibling Showdown

Next scene, Jesus crashes at Martha and Mary's pad. Mary's all Zen at Jesus' feet, soaking up the wisdom. Martha's running a one-woman show in the kitchen, eventually hitting her breaking point. She's like, "Lord, hello? Little help here?" Jesus tells her, "Martha, Martha, you're stressing over the small stuff. Mary's got the right idea—she's scored the VIP pass, and it's a no-take-backs situation." Later, after Jesus finishes a prayer sesh, a disciple's like, "Teach us to slide into DMs with the Big Guy upstairs." Jesus is like, "When you hit up Heaven, start with 'Hey Dad, keep it holy. Let's get your kingdom on. Drop us our daily grub. Pardon our oopsies, as we're cool with those who mess up with us. And keep us clear of the temptation trap.'"

Midnight Snack Crisis

Imagine this: You hit up your buddy at midnight, like, "Yo, I've got a friend crashing at my place and zero snacks. Hook me up with some bread?" And your friend's all, "Dude, seriously? We're all in bed. The door's locked. Can't help." But because you're totally shameless and keep bugging, he'll eventually roll out of bed and give you whatever you need just to get some peace. So, here's the deal: Keep asking, and you'll get it. Keep looking, and you'll find it. Keep knocking, and you'll get in. It's like, if you keep texting, eventually you'll get a reply. If any kid asked their dad for a fish, would he hand over a snake? Or ask for an egg and get a scorpion? Even if you're not parent of the year, you still know how to not totally fail at giving. Imagine how much cooler stuff your cosmic dad will drop in your lap if you just ask!

Jesus was kicking out a silent demon, and when the dude could finally talk, everyone was shook. But some haters were like, "He's teaming up with the head demon to kick these guys out." Others wanted some cosmic fireworks as proof. Jesus was like, "If I'm on demon dude's team, how are we winning? Think about it. If I'm kicking demons out with God's own finger, then, surprise, God's VIP lounge has arrived. It's like if a burglar tries to break into a house guarded by The Rock. Good luck with that. If you're not in my crew, you're out. Simple."

Ghost's Revenge

J.C. gets real spooky and says, "When a ghost gets evicted, it wanders around looking for a new haunt. Finding nowhere, it decides to check back into its old haunt. Finding the place all nice and tidy, it invites a whole squad of even nastier friends, and they throw a wilder party. End of the day, you're way worse off than before."

Real #Blessed Vibes

While Jesus was dropping wisdom bombs, a lady in the crowd was like, "Blessed is the mom who got to have you!" But Jesus was like, "Nah, the real MVPs are the ones who tune into God's podcast and actually follow through."

The Jonah Mic Drop

So, Jesus peeps the growing crowd and drops the truth bomb: "Y'all are chasing after miracles like they're the latest trend, but the only teaser you're getting is the 'Jonah Was Here' trailer. Just like Jonah was a wakeup call for Nineveh, I'm the wake-up call for you guys. And guess what? The queen from way down south and the Nineveh crew will be shaking their heads at you come judgment day because they knew how to recognize real wisdom and change their ways. And here I am, outclassing Solomon and Jonah, and you're still sleeping on it."

Body Lightbulb Moment

"Nobody lights up a lamp to hide it in the basement. You put it out there so it lights up the room. Your eyes are like the lamp for your body. If your outlook is bright, you're all lit up. If it's not, you're walking around in the dark. Make sure that inner light isn't on the fritz. If you're shining bright inside out, you're like a room bathed in sunlight."

Calling Out the Fakes

At a Pharisee's dinner invite, Jesus skips the hand wash, and the host is shook. Jesus claps back, "You guys are all about that surface clean but inside you're hoarding greed like it's limited edition. How about you declutter that heart and actually help the needy? That's the real cleanse."

"Big oof to you Pharisees, fixating on spice tithes but skimming over the hefty stuff like fairness and God-love. You're all about those VIP seats and social media shoutouts. "And you! You're like those stealth graves people walk over without a clue. An expert in the law tries to get offended, and Jesus doesn't hold back: "You're laying out impossible standards and not lifting a finger to help. You honor the prophets your ancestors ghosted. You're basically signing off on what they did by keeping up appearances. "Massive woe to you, law geeks! You've locked the door to understanding and swallowed the key. You're not getting in, and you're blocking the entrance for everyone else." After dipping out, the legal squad and the Pharisees turn up the heat, throwing hard questions, waiting to catch him in a hot take.

Spotting the Fakes 101

So, Jesus sees this mega crowd and kicks off with, "Yo, disciples, watch out for Pharisee-brand yeast. It's all about that fake life. Nothing's staying secret for long; what's whispered in the DMs will be shouted from the rooftops.

Keeping It 100

"Give me a shout-out down here, and you'll get one in the celestial VIP lounge. Ghost me, and you're ghosted there too. Blaspheme against the Holy Spirit, though? That's the ultimate party foul – no coming back from that.

Story Time: Greed Alert!

A dude's like, "Yo, Jesus, make my bro share the inheritance." Jesus is like, "Man, who made me Judge Judy?" Then hits them with a story: "Rich guy hoards his wealth, plans to retire early, but God's like, 'Game over, dude. Who's gonna spend your stash now?'" Moral of the story? Hoarding treasure for yourself doesn't make you rich in God's eyes.

Chill, Don't Sweat the Small Stuff

Jesus then turns to His crew, "Why you stressing about food and clothes? Look at the birds and flowers, living their best life without a care. God's got their back. You're definitely on His radar. King Solomon in all his drip wasn't as fly as them.

Trust Fund in Heaven

"Keep your eyes on the real prize – God's kingdom. All the essentials will fall into place. Fear not, my peeps, God's psyched to hook you up with the kingdom. Liquidate those assets, help out the needy. Your heavenly bank account is fraud-proof.

Be On Your Toes

"Stay woke, lamps on. Be like those peeps ready to open up the moment the boss is back from the rave. Those who are ready? Major props – the boss will serve up a midnight snack. Even if he rolls in at dawn and finds you ready, you're blessed. Always be on your game; you never know when I'm dropping by."

Who's the Real MVP?

Peter's like, "Yo, Jesus, you droppin' this wisdom bomb for

us or everyone out here?" Jesus fires back, "Who's the MVP manager who gets the boss's thumbs-up to run the show? The one caught hustling hard when the boss rolls up. That dude gets the keys to the kingdom. No cap, he's gonna be living large. But if he's chilling, thinking, 'Ah, the boss is probs stuck in traffic,' starts throwing wild parties, surprise! The boss shows up when least expected, and let's just say, it won't end well for Mr. Party Animal. The know-it-all not walking the talk gets the mega beatdown, while the clueless one gets off easier. Got a lot? Expect a pop quiz.

Not Chillin', But Grillin'

J.C. is like, "I'm here to spark a fire, and I'm all jittery till it's lit! Got my own dunk tank to deal with, and it's no pool party." Thinking I'm all about peace? Nah, I'm mixing it up big time. It's gonna be family feud style, with everyone picking sides.

Jesus then hits the crowd with, "You're all weather whizzes. Cloudy west? 'Rain's a'coming!' South wind? 'Heatwave alert!' Yet, y'all can't read the room when it comes to what's up nowadays? Seriously, folks?

Sort It Before Court

"Why not use your big brain to avoid drama? If you're beefing with someone, squash it before it goes Judge Judy on you. Otherwise, it's from the courtroom to the big house, and you're not walking out till your wallet's empty.

The Parable of the Barren Fig Tree

So, this guy's got a fig tree chilling in his vineyard, right? He's hunting for some figgy snacks but finds zilch. Tells his gardener, "Yo, I've been eyeing this tree for three years hoping for a fig feast, and nada. Ax it! Why let it hog the dirt?" Gardener's like, "Whoa, chief, let's vibe with it one more year. I'll pamper it with some spa treatment – dig around, toss in some gourmet compost. If it's still a dud, then sure, we chop."

Healing a Daughter of Abraham

On a chill Sabbath in the synagogue, Jesus spots this lady who's been all bent out of shape for eighteen years because of a nasty spirit. Jesus, being the legend he is, tells her, "Girl, you're hitting the reset button on your back." Lays hands on her, and bam! She's straight-up glorifying God. But the synagogue's head honcho gets salty, "We've got six days to hustle. Heal on those days, not on our chill day." Jesus claps back, "You all untie your donkeys on the Sabbath, but you're tripping about setting free a daughter of Abraham from Satan's no-good grip after eighteen long years? C'mon, get your priorities straight!" Crowd's going wild, cheering for Jesus, while the haters were left looking like they sucked on a lemon.

Mustard Seed and Yeast Vibes

Jesus then drops two truth bombs. "Kingdom of God? It's like a mustard seed. Tiny, but grows into a chill spot for birds. And it's like yeast that a lady mixed into a mega batch of flour until the whole thing was vibing."

The Exclusive VIP Door

As Jesus is touring around, someone's like, "Jesus, is the guest list for heaven super exclusive or what?" Jesus goes, "Aim for the VIP entrance. It's narrow, and not everyone's getting the bouncer's nod. Once the main event starts, it's no use name-dropping or

saying we hung out. If you're not on the list, it's a no-go. The real tear-jerker? Seeing the OG VIPs inside while you're left in the cold."

Jesus Throws Shade at Herod

Some Pharisees try to scare Jesus, "Herod's out for your head!" Jesus is all, "Run and tell that sly fox, 'I'm booked — casting out demons and fixing folks up. Got a tight schedule, but hey, catch me if you can.'" Adds, "It's wild, but a prophet's got no business dying outside of Jerusalem."

Jerusalem, the Heartbreaker

Jesus gets real soft for a sec, "Jerusalem, you're breaking my heart, ditching those who come with peace. I wanted to hug it out like a hen with her chicks, but you weren't feeling it. Well, brace yourself for a ghost town vibe until you're ready to welcome the real peace dealer."

Sabbath Drama at a Pharisee's Crib

So, Jesus rocks up to a Pharisee's pad for some grub on the Sabbath, right? And there's this guy looking like a water balloon. Jesus, eyeballing the room, is like, "Yo, is it chill to fix someone up on the Sabbath or what?" Crickets. He heals the dude and sends him on his merry way. Then drops a truth bomb, "If your kid or your cow took a nosedive into a well on the Sabbath, you wouldn't just leave them hanging, would ya?" Mic drop. Silence from the peanut gallery.

How to Not Be a Seat Hog

At this shindig, Jesus peeps how everyone's scrambling for the VIP seats. He spins this tale, "Imagine you're at a wedding and you snag the top spot. Then the host is like, 'Uh, this seat's for someone else.' Boom, you're trotting to the back, red-faced. Instead, aim low from the get-go, so when the host spots you, you get the upgrade. Remember, trying to be all that gets you nowhere, but keeping it real gets you places." To the host, Jesus says, "Next time you throw a bash, skip the usual suspects. Hit up the down-and-outs, the broke, the hobblers, and the blind. You'll be the real MVP because they can't hit you back with an invite. Your karma's gonna cash in big time when things get real at the endgame."

Epic Banquet Fail

Some dude, getting all dreamy, is like, "Man, being in God's crib must be lit." Jesus rolls with it, "So, this guy throws a mega feast and hits up a bunch of peeps. When it's go-time, everyone's bailing with lame excuses. One's gotta check out his new dirt patch, another's gotta test drive his oxen, and another's just tied the knot. The host is steamed and tells his crew, 'Hit the streets and the back lanes. Drag in the broke, the busted, and the blind.' Even after the place is popping, there's room for more. So, the host is like, 'Scour the sticks and the ditches, make 'em come. I want a full house!' Heads up, the original guest list? Yeah, they're gonna miss out big time."

VIP Pass to Discipleship Ain't Easy

So, Jesus is rolling deep with a massive crowd when he spins around and drops this bomb: "If you're not ready to ghost your fam and even your own selfie game, you can't roll with me. And yo, if you're not up for hauling your own struggle bus, forget about being my homie. Think about it, would you start building a sky-high tower without checking your bank account first? Or what general would march into battle without sliding into the strategy DMs first? Same way, if you're clinging to your stuff more than your

TikTok followers, you ain't ready for this squad."

Sheep Gone Wild and Other Tales

Jesus then flips the script with some stories 'cause the tax collectors and the 'sinners' are all up in his grill, and the keyboard warriors and rule sticklers are throwing shade. He's like, "Imagine one of your squad dips, wouldn't you hit up every spot to find them? And when you do, it's party time, right? Heaven throws down harder for one turn-around soul than for a bunch of goody two-shoes who think they're too cool for school." Then he's all, "Ladies, you know when you drop one of your bling rings and turn your place upside down to find it? And when you do, it's all over your Snap? That's how it goes down when someone gets their act together – angels throw a rave." Next, Jesus tells them about a dude with two sons. The younger one is like, "Pops, cash me out. I'm outta here." He blows all his dough and hits rock bottom, chilling with the pigs. Finally, he's like, "Wait, even the interns at my dad's place live better than this." So he heads back, rehearsing his 'I'm sorry' speech. But his dad, seeing him from a mile away, sprints and tackles him with a bear hug and

smooches. He's like, "Yo, get this man a designer robe, the family ring, some fresh kicks, and fire up the grill – my boy's back!" Meanwhile, the older bro's out in the fields, comes back, hears the bass dropping, and he's salty. "All these years I've been the good son and you never threw me a pizza party!" Dad's like, "Son, you're always with me, all I've got is yours. But we gotta pop bottles 'cause your bro was basically dead to us, and now he's back. He was lost, now he's found." And there you have it – whether you're lost or just not vibing, there's always a way back to the squad, and the welcome back party? Legendary.

The Story of the Slick Manager

So, J.C. is schooling his crew and goes, "Picture this: a big-shot's got a manager who's basically throwing his cash around like confetti. The big-shot's like, 'Bruh, the internet's buzzing with memes about you tanking my empire. Pack up your desk, you're done.' The manager's freaking out, thinking, 'What's my next move? I can't hack manual labor and Tinder bio saying 'professional beggar' is a no-go. Got it! I'll slide into everyone's DMs so they'll hit me up with couch offers when I'm jobless.'" He hits up the big-shot's clients. To the first, he's like, "Yo, you owe my boss a lake of olive oil. Let's make it a pond." To another, "You owe a mountain of wheat, right? Let's call it a hill."

The big-shot ends up clapping for the manager's slick moves because he played it smarter than a cat with a laser pointer. Jesus is like, "For real, the peeps of today are sharper in their squad than the light kids. Listen up, use that Insta-fame and TikTok treasure to make buds who'll invite you to the VIP section in the afterlife. Trust, being solid in the small stuff means you're gold in the big leagues. If you're sketchy with your Netflix password, who's gonna trust you with the Wi-Fi code?" Then Jesus flips the script, "You can't pledge loyalty to God and your Gucci addiction at the same time." The cash-loving Pharisees start LOLing, but Jesus throws shade, "You guys love a good front row at the temple and VIP tags, but the Big G's got your number. What's lit on Instagram is basically a dumpster fire to God. "The rulebook and the prophets were the talk of the town until John showed up. Now, it's all about crashing the Kingdom of God party. And trust, heaven and earth will ghost us before a single emoji from God's texts gets left on read.

"Ditching your wife to update your relationship status or swiping right on someone else's ex? That's playing dirty in the Kingdom playbook."

The Tale of Gucci Guy and Broke Lazarus

So, there was this dude, decked out in all purple everything and designer gear, living it up with feasts every single day. Meanwhile, Lazarus, this poor guy with a rough life and health to match, was chilling at Mr. High-Roller's gate, dreaming about leftover UberEats. But nah, only the local dogs paid him any mind, giving his wounds some slobbery attention. Eventually, Lazarus peaced out from this world, and angels VIP escorted him to chill with Abraham. The rich dude also checked out but found himself in the VIP lounge of Hades, feeling the heat. From way downtown, he spots Abraham with Lazarus by his side and shouts, "Yo, Abe, do me a solid? Send Lazarus with some water, 'cause this place is lit, and not in a good way." Abe's like, "Remember how you had it all and Lazarus had nada? Well, tables have turned, bro. Plus, there's this massive gap between us, so no one's doing any cross-visiting." Rich man's like, "Aight,

155

then at least send Lazarus to my fam to drop a truth bomb, so they dodge this hot mess."

But Abe's response? "They've got all the deets they need to turn things around. If they're ghosting Moses and the crew, not even a TikTok from the grave's gonna change their minds." Jesus then flips to his squad, "Listen up, fam, life's gonna throw some shade, but don't be the reason someone else trips up. Better to take a swim with cement shoes than mess with one of the little homies. And keep it 100 - if your bro messes up, call him out. If he hits you with the 'my b,' forgive him. Even if you gotta replay that scene seven times a day."

Faith on Fleek

The squad's like, "Hey, J.C., we need more faith." Jesus hits back, "If you had faith even as tiny as a clout chaser's conscience, you could slide into the DMs of nature, telling a tree to take a dive, and it'd actually do it. Imagine you've got a helper, right? You wouldn't be like, 'Hey, kick back, relax, dinner's on me.' Nah, you'd be like, 'Make sure I'm fed first, then you can crash.' You don't throw thank you parties for them just doing their job. That's the vibe. After you've done all the things, just remember you're just doing your thing. No need for trophies for playing the game."

Skincare Squad and the Solo Shoutout

So Jesus was hitting the road, halfway between Samaria and Galilee, when he stumbled upon a squad of ten dudes with leprosy. They kept their distance but hollered at the top of their lungs, "Yo, Jesus, Master, throw some mercy our way!" Jesus peeped them and was like, "Bet. Go show yourselves to the priests." And just like that, as they hit the road, they got their glow-up. But check it, only one of the crew, realizing he was back to flawless, spun around and came back with a victory yell, giving props to God. He was all in Jesus' grill, face down, super thankful. Oh, and plot twist, the dude was a Samaritan. Jesus was all, "Hold up, weren't there ten of you? Where's the rest of the squad? Only this outsider came back to give God the glory?" Then, to the Samaritan, he's like, "Rise and shine, homie. Your faith's got you covered."

Kingdom Kiki

When the Pharisees got all up in his grill about when the kingdom was gonna drop, Jesus clapped back, "Look, the kingdom of God isn't some red carpet event. Don't wait for the 'It's over here!' or 'It's over there!' Because, FYI, the kingdom of God? It's chilling among you." Then he slid into the DMs of his disciples, "Listen, there'll come a time you'll be thirsting for one of the days of the Son of Man, but it's gonna be a no-show. People will try to lead you on a wild goose chase. Don't fall for it. Just like lightning that lights up the whole sky, that's how it's gonna be. But first, I gotta go through some stuff and get ghosted by this gen. It's gonna be just like the OG binge-watchers in Noah's time and Lot's prime time – life was their reality show until the season finale hit them like a ton of bricks. That's the tea when the Son of Man spills the spotlight. On D-Day, don't be that guy running back into the house for his kicks or that girl in the field looking back. Remember Lot's wifey? Yeah, don't be her. Trying to clutch onto your life? You'll lose it. But if you're down to lose it for me, you're golden. Picture it: one will be chilling, the other taken. It's gonna be a selective RSVP." They're like, "Where's the afterparty, Jesus?" He hits them with, "Just follow the buzzards; they know where the party's at."

The Savage Widow and the Judge

Jesus was all about that prayer life, telling this story: Imagine this judge, right? Dude had zero chill for God or peeps. And there's this widow, keeps badgering him for justice against her hater. The judge is fed up, thinks, "I couldn't care less about God or anyone, but this lady's gonna meme me to death if I don't sort her out." So he does. Jesus is like, "Catch the drift of what Mr. Heart-of-Stone said. If this guy can cave, how much quicker will God sort out his VIPs who spam him day and night? He won't ghost them. But real talk, when I make the comeback, will I catch anyone on fleek with faith?"

The Parable of the Selfie #NoFilter

So Jesus dropped this story for peeps who were totally into their own hype, thinking they're the MVPs of goodness while side-eyeing everyone else. Picture this: Two guys hit up the temple to shoot a prayer. One, a Pharisee, basically does a selfie prayer, "Yo, big shoutout to myself for not being a basic like others—cheaters, wrongdoers, or even like that tax dude over there. I'm on that fasting cleanse twice a week and donate a chunk of my clout."

Meanwhile, the tax collector's chilling in the back, wouldn't even glance skyward, just beating his chest like, "Bro, mercy on me, a legit mess-up." Plot twist: This low-key guy gets the thumbs up from God, not Mr. Hashtag Blessed. 'Cause here's the deal: flex too hard, and you'll get checked; stay humble, and you get the hype.

Viral Kiddo Blessings

Peeps were bringing their tiny tots to J for some holy high-fives, but the squad was like, "Not cool," trying to wave them off. Jesus was all, "Nah, let the munchkins roll through. Heaven's VIP list is basically these little legends. Real talk, if you're not vibing like a kid, you're not making the guest list."

Then this influencer hits up Jesus, "Yo, teach, what's the hack for eternal life?" J flips it, "Why call me good? Only the Boss upstairs is legit. You know the drill: no cheating, no taking lives, no five-finger discounts, keep it real, respect the fam." The guy's like, "Been there, done that since my sandbox days." Jesus checks him, "Cool, but here's the catch: sell your swag, help out the broke, and you'll score treasure in heaven. Then, hit me up." Dude's face dropped. He had more subscriptions than he could count.

#BlessedOrBusted

Jesus sees the mood dip and drops, "Tough for the loaded to enter God's domain. Easier for a camel to squeeze through a piercing needle." The crowd's mind-blown, "Then who's making the cut?" Jesus, "With peeps, it's a no-go; with God, all the likes."

Peter's like, "Yo, we ditched our starter packs for you." Jesus promises, "For real, anyone who's ditched their crew or crib for the kingdom's gonna score big-time now and lock in eternal life." Then he pulls the squad for a spoiler, "We're hitting up Jerusalem, and it's all going down—the whole prophecy playlist. I'm gonna get dragged, dissed, and dissed some more; they'll even drop a diss track, then ghost me. But I'll drop the mic on the third day." Flew right over their heads, though.

Blind Man Sees

Rolling up to Jericho, a blind fan's on the sidelines. Hearing the hype, he's like, "What's the tea?" "Jesus is passing through." So he starts shouting, "Yo, Jesus, Son of D, help a brother out!" Crowd's trying to mute him, but he's just turning up the volume, "Have mercy on me!" Jesus pauses the parade, "Bring him." Up close, "What's your wishlist?" "To see the world in HD." Jesus hits him with, "You're good to go—your faith's your ticket." Boom—vision's 20/20. He starts following Jesus, hyping Him up all the way, with the whole crowd dropping likes and shares.

Zacchaeus: The Original Social Climber

So, Jesus rolls into Jericho, doing His thing, and there's this dude, Zacchaeus. Big shot tax collector, rolling in dough but kinda short. He's trying to catch a glimpse of Jesus but can't see over the crowd. Solution? He books it ahead and scales a sycamore like it's his personal viewing platform. Jesus spots him and is like, "Yo, Zac! Let's crash at your pad today." Zacchaeus nearly falls out of the tree in excitement, hurries down, and throws the ultimate house party for Jesus. Crowd's salty, whispering, "He's hanging with the sinners now?" But Zac's all, "Check it, I'm flipping the script—half my wealth's going to the poor, and if I've scammed anyone, I'm paying back fourfold." Jesus gives him props, "This place is blessed today. Zac's one of the fam now. I'm here to flip the script for the lost, not the found."

The Ten Minas: Make It Rain with Responsibility

Jesus keeps the parables coming because everyone's thinking the kingdom of God's about to drop like a fire album. He's like, "Imagine a noble peacing out to get crowned, leaves his squad with some cash, tells 'em to keep the hustle going. But the locals are throwing shade, not feeling his rule. He comes back, crown on head, checks the books. First guy's investment's booming, gets a city. Second guy, decent returns, gets a smaller gig. The dude who did nada? Loses everything. It's like, make good with what you got, or it's bye-bye."

Entry of the King: Jesus Does Jerusalem

Fast forward, Jesus is hitting up Jerusalem. Sends his bros to snag a ride—a donkey no one's ever ridden. "If anyone's tripping,"

He says, "just tell 'em the Boss needs it." They find the donkey, throw their threads over it for Jesus to ride. People are laying down their clothes on the road like it's the red carpet. As Jesus makes His grand entrance, the crowd's losing it, shouting blessings. Some Pharisees in the mix are not vibing, "Teacher, get your disciples on a leash!" Jesus fires back, "If they zip it, the stones will start shouting."

Cruising up to Jerusalem, Jesus caught sight of the city and just lost it, tears and all. He's like, "Jerusalem, babe, if only you knew what's up. Peace was knocking, and you left it on read. Heads up, though, rough times ahead. Enemies gonna circle you like vultures, leaving nada behind. All 'cause you ghosted when God slid into your DMs."

Temple Clean-Up Crew

Jesus rolls into the temple and starts flipping tables, sending the sales squad packing. He's all, "This place? It's supposed to be a chill spot for prayer, but y'all turned it into a hotbed for hustlers!" Day in, day out, Jesus taught there, snagging everyone's attention while the bigwigs plotted his mic drop moment.

When They Questioned Jesus' Swag

So, Jesus is dropping truth bombs in the temple, and the establishment's like, "Who even let you in the door?" Jesus, ever the riddler, hits back with, "I got a Q for you—if we're playing 'Who's got the creds?' where did John get his splash?" They're in a pickle 'cause either answer's a trap. Admitting John's divine backing puts them in a bind; denying it has them facing a rock concert, old-school stoning style. So, they cop out with, "No clue," and Jesus is like, "Then I'm keeping my secrets to myself."

The Vineyard Drama

Jesus spins this tale: Dude plants a vineyard, hires some farmers, then jets. Come harvest, he sends his crew to collect, but those tenant farmers are playing hardball, roughing up his guys. After two beatdowns, he's like, "I'll send my son; they'll respect him." Spoiler: They didn't. They off him, thinking they'll inherit the goods. Jesus drops the mic, "What do you think the owner's gonna do? Spoiler: It's payback time." The crowd's shook, "No way, Jose!" But Jesus, pointing to scripture, hints he's the plot twist they never saw coming.

The haters try to trip J.C. up with talk of taxes, hoping to snag him with a gotcha question about paying up to Caesar. Jesus, one step ahead, is like, "Yo, toss me a coin." They do, and he's all, "Whose face is this?" "Caesar's," they admit. Jesus schools them, "Then give Caesar his due, and don't forget to hook God up with what's His." Minds blown, they zip it, marveling at his slick comeback.

Sadducees vs. Resurrection: Epic Fail

So the Sadducees roll up, all high and mighty, thinking they're slick with a trick question about the afterlife—'cause they're all "Resurrection? As if!" They're like, "Yo, J.C., peep this: dude dies, leaves a widow, his bro marries her, rinse and repeat till all seven bros are ghosted. So, in Heaven's VIP section, who gets dibs on the lady?" Jesus facepalms, "Y'all, Heaven's not your typical Friday night. Marriage ain't a thing there. We're all about that angelic vibe, living it up as God's kids. Moses even dropped hints about the afterlife being legit. God's not about the dead life. He's the God of the lit, living squad."

Who's Your Daddy, Christ?

Jesus flips the script, "Why's everyone stuck on Christ being David's mini-me? David himself was all, 'Lord said to my Lord, park it here till I put your haters under your sneakers.' If David calls him 'Lord,' how's he just a junior?" Mic drop.

Scribe Burn

While everyone's ears are perked, Jesus goes, "Eyeball the scribes, strutting in their flex robes, soaking up 'Hey's' in town, VIP seating in synagogues, and front-row at feasts. They're all about that show life, praying for clout while they're low-key robbing grannies. The karma bus is gonna hit them hard."

#Blessed: The Widow's Two Cents

Jesus spots the high rollers flaunting their donations but gives props to a widow tossing in two cents, "Real talk, she outdid them all. While they're dropping change from their overflow, she went all in with her life savings."

End Times Sneak Peek

Disciples, all curious, hit up Jesus, "So, when's the big show and what are the sneak peeks?" Jesus is like, "Stay woke. Don't chase after every 'Messiah' wannabe or doomsday teaser. Wars, natural disasters, and some real spooky stuff are just the opening acts. But first, you'll catch some heat for rolling with me. It's all part of the gig. Stick it out, and you're golden."

Jerusalem's Epic Time-Out

When you peep Jerusalem getting all cozy with armies, that's your cue: Desolation's dropping a hot new track. If you're chilling in Judea, yeet to the mountains. City folks, bail out. Country peeps, don't even. It's payback time, fulfilling all that ancient tea. Pregnant and nursing moms, big oof for you. It's gonna be a wild ride with no respawn. Jerusalem's about to get a serious trampling, courtesy of the Gentiles, till their season finale hits.

Son of Man's Grand Entrance

Buckle up, 'cause the universe's gonna throw some cosmic shade with sun, moon, and star drama. Earth's gonna have a major meltdown, with oceans throwing tantrums. Humanity's gonna be shook, with a side of existential dread, 'cause the cosmos is getting a remix. But then, bam! Son of Man's making a cloud entrance, full swag and glory. When you see the pre-party

starting, pop that spine straight and look sharp—your glow-up's knocking.

Fig Tree Spills the Tea

Peep this: Fig tree's popping leaves? Summer's sliding into your DMs. Same vibes when you see all these cosmic shenanigans—God's kingdom is hitting up close. This gen's got front row seats till the curtain call. Heaven and earth are dipping out, but my words? They're eternal.

Stay Woke, Fam

Don't get caught sleeping. Party hard, but don't blackout or get sucked into life's drama, or you'll miss the main event. It's gonna ambush everyone, worldwide. Keep those eyes peeled, prayers on point, so you can dodge the chaos and stand tall in the VIP section with the Son of Man.

Teaching by Day, Chilling by Night

Jesus was all about that temple life by day, spitting wisdom. By night, he was hitting up the Mount of Olives for some R&R. Everyone was up at dawn, thirsty for those temple talks.

The Betrayal Scheme

Passover's rolling up, and the high-key haters, the chief priests and scribes, are plotting a Jesus takedown. Enter Judas, the squad's traitor, making deals and seeking the perfect ghosting moment when the Insta crowd ain't watching.

Passover Prep Goes Spy

Passover's on the horizon, and Jesus sends Peter and John for some undercover grocery shopping. "Look for the dude with the water jug—total giveaway. He'll show you to the VIP lounge upstairs." They find everything just as Jesus had DM'd them, and the feast is set.

OG Lord's Supper

When dinner hour hits, J.C. is all about that table life with the apostles. He's like, "Been dying to have this meal before my big exit. This is the last supper till we hit up God's kingdom." He shares the cup, "Pass this around, 'cause it's the last round with you guys till kingdom come." Breaks bread, "This is me, for you. Don't forget me." Then hits them with, "This cup's the new deal, signed with my blood. But yo, the traitor's hand's on the table." The squad's

buzzing, trying to figure out who's about to drop the ultimate betrayal.

Squad Squabble Over Who's the MVP

So, the squad got into a bit of a tiff over who's the MVP among them. Jesus was like, "Look, in the world of the 'Gram and TikTok, peeps flex and get called 'Big Shots.' But here in our crew, we flip the script. Wanna be the GOAT? Be the newbie. Leading? Serve up the snacks. 'Cause who's really the boss? The one chilling at the table or the one serving up the feast? Plot twist: I'm here handing out the appetizers. You guys stuck with me through the rough patches. So, here's the deal: You're gonna be chilling at my table in the VIP section of my kingdom, calling the shots for the twelve tribes."

Peter's Epic Fail Predicted

"Yo, Simon, buddy, heads up! The dark side wants to shake you up like a Polaroid picture. But I shot a prayer your way, so your vibe won't crash. And when you've bounced back, prop up the bros." Peter's all, "Lord, I'm ride or die, even if it means jail time or the end of the line." Jesus hits him with, "Bro, before the rooster's morning drop, you'll hit unfollow on me three times."

Gear Up for Some Rough Patches

Jesus was like, "Remember the good old days when I sent you backpacking without a dime or kicks, and you were cool?" They're like, "All good, Jesus." He's like, "Well, times are changing. Pack your bags, grab your wallet. No sword? Sell that vintage tee and arm up. It's about to get real, fulfilling the 'He's with the rebels' script." They whip out two swords. Jesus is like, "Cool it, that's plenty."

Late Night Prayer Sesh

Jesus hits up his usual spot, the Mount of Olives, with the crew tagging along. He's like, "Pray hard, so you don't faceplant into temptation." Goes off for some solo time, drops to his knees, and is all, "Dad, if there's a plan B, I'm all ears. But your call, not mine." Angel squad comes down for a pep talk. Jesus is sweating buckets, praying hardcore. Finds the disciples catching Zs, hits them with, "Wakey wakey, keep the prayers going to dodge the temptation bullet."

Judas Goes Full Reality TV Betrayal

In the middle of his heart-to-heart with the sky, here comes Judas leading a flash mob, aiming for a betrayal TikTok challenge. Jesus, seeing the kiss coming, is like, "Really, Judas? A kiss is your Judas move?" The crew's ready to throw down, "Jesus, we going full ninja?" One of them goes samurai on the high priest's crew, ear drops. Jesus is all, "Chill, let's not make this a UFC match," and does a quick ear fixer-upper. Then, to the arrest squad, "You're rolling up like I'm public enemy #1? Been in your faces daily, and now you pull a ninja move in the dark? This is your spotlight, enjoy."

Peter Hits the Unfollow Button

They drag Jesus to the VIP religious club, and Peter's creeping in the background. Fireside, a girl's like, "This dude's part of the Jesus crew." Peter's like, "Never seen the guy." Round two, someone else is like, "You're one of them!" Peter's all, "Wrong guy!" Hour later, another's convinced, "Def a Galilean." Peter's losing it, "No clue what you're on about!" Right then, rooster's like, "Cock-a-doodle-doo!" Jesus locks eyes with Peter. Boom, prophecy fulfilled. Peter's out, crying a river. So, the squad holding Jesus went full troll mode, throwing shade and LOLs his way. They slapped a blindfold on him and turned it into a guessing game, "Hey, Mystic Meg, who just tagged you?" They're throwing out all kinds of salty comments, making the hate comments section look tame.

Sunrise Drama with the Bigwigs

As the sun pops up, the VIPs of the religious club, aka Team Too-Serious, pull Jesus into their circle. They're like, "Spill the tea, you claim to be the MVP?" Jesus is all, "Even if I drop the truth bomb, you'll just hit snooze. And asking questions? You won't play ball. But here's a spoiler: I'm about to snag the best seat beside the Big Boss." They all go wide-eyed, "Hold up, you're saying you're the Son of God?" Jesus, playing it cool, "You said it, not me." And they're like, "No more Insta polls needed, we got the soundbite we wanted straight from the source!"

Jesus Crashes Pilate's Party

Then, they drag Jesus to Pilate's pad, throwing around accusations like, "This dude's messing with the empire, dodging taxes, and claiming he's king of the cool kids." Pilate, checking Jesus out, "So, you're the so-called king?" Jesus gives him the "Your words, buddy." Pilate's verdict to the Twitter mob? "This guy's clean in my book." But the crowd's not having it, "Nah, he's been stirring up all sorts of drama, from way back in Galilee to downtown."

Detour to Herod's Hangout

Hearing "Galilee," Pilate's like, "Oh, that's Herod's turf. Send him over." Herod's psyched to meet Jesus, hoping for some front-row magic tricks. But Jesus keeps it zipped, not giving Herod the viral content he's after. Herod and his crew turn it into a meme fest, decking Jesus out in Insta-worthy fits before sending him back to Pilate. Plot twist: Pilate and Herod become besties over their shared Jesus problem.

The Ultimate Poll: Jesus or Barabbas

Back with Pilate, he's like, "Look, I've done the deep dive, and this guy's clean. Herod agrees. So, a little whip action, and he's free to go." But the crowd's on a different vibe, "Nah, drop Jesus, give us

Barabbas!" (FYI, Barabbas is in the slammer for being the OG rebel and a thriller villain.) Pilate's trying to be the voice of reason, "Seriously, what's this guy done except break your boring rules?" But the mob's hitting caps lock, "NAIL HIM TO THE CROSS!" Their spamming wins. Pilate caves, giving them Barabbas for a peace treaty and letting them have their way with Jesus. So, they're escorting J.C. to the main event, and they draft Simon from Cyrene to carry the backstage gear, aka the cross. A whole fan club's trailing behind, with the ladies doing the ugly cry for Jesus. He's like, "Ladies, save those tears for your own Spotify sad playlists. It's gonna get way worse."

Collab Gone Wrong

Fast forward, they're at Skull HQ, setting up Jesus and two bad boys for the ultimate showdown. Jesus, hanging there, goes all high road, "Dad, they're clueless, forgive them." Meanwhile, they're rolling dice for his fit like it's Black Friday. The peanut gallery's throwing shade, "He's supposed to be the MVP, right? Do some self-saving magic, bro!" And the Roman squad's joining in with the trash talk, all while posting, "King of the Jews" above his head for the 'gram. Cut to the criminal duo: one's throwing major sass at Jesus, while the other's like, "Chill, bro, we're here 'cause we messed up; he's clean." He shoots his shot, "Yo, Jesus, hit me up in your kingdom." Jesus, being a solid bro, "Bet. You're rolling with me to paradise."

The Finale

Now it's hitting midday, and suddenly it's lights out across the board till about snack time, with the sun taking a break. Jesus, in his final mic drop, shouts, "Dad, I'm coming home," and logs out. The centurion's now a believer, "This guy was the real deal." Crowd's heading home, low-key shook, while his squad and the Galilee girl gang are lurking from afar.

Afterparty in a Rock Crib

Enter Joseph of Arimathea, not vibing with the council's drama, scores Jesus's body, and wraps it up MTV Cribs style in a fresh tomb. It's now Sabbath Eve, and the spice girls — the ladies from Galilee — peep where he's laid, then peace out to prep some aromatic goods.

Plot Twist!

Come Sunday morning, the girl squad's rolling up with their spice rack to find the stone's been yeeted away from the tomb. Inside? Ghosted. They're 100% shook until these two glow-up dudes appear, "Why you looking for the alive among the dead? He's not here; he's pulled the greatest escape. Remember he called it back in Galilee?" Memory lane hits them, and they dash to spill the tea to the squad, but the guys are thinking it's all a tall tale. Peter, though, hits the ground running to the tomb, peeks inside, and it's just laundry day with no body. He's wandering off, mind blown by the plot twist.

So the very same day, a duo was hitting up Emmaus, about seven miles off from the Jerusalem buzz. They're deep in convo about all the drama that went down. Mid-debate, Jesus slides in stealth mode and joins their stroll. Plot twist: they're clueless about who he is. Jesus, playing it cool, is like, "So, what's the tea, fam? Why the long faces?" They stop dead in their tracks, looking all kinds of bummed out. Cleopas is shook, "Bro, you must be the only one in Jerusalem who hasn't caught up on the latest. We're talking Jesus of Nazareth, major influencer, did wonders in action and speech, right? Our head honchos handed him a death sentence, and boom, crucifixion. We thought he was the game-changer for Israel. Plot thickens, it's day three since that mess. Then, our girl squad hits us with a ghost story from the tomb, but Jesus? Nowhere to be found." Jesus, probably rolling his eyes, "Y'all slow or what? Didn't you do your homework? The Messiah had to walk through the fire to hit that glory." Then, he goes full professor, breaking down the Scriptures, featuring himself. As they hit Emmaus, Jesus acts like he's going further. But they're like, "No, no, stay with us, it's getting dark." Jesus agrees, and at dinner, goes for the big reveal - breaks bread, and just like that, vanishes. Mind blown, they're like, "Our hearts were doing the Harlem Shake when he talked on the road!"

Ghosting Ghost Rumors

Zooming back to Jerusalem, they crash the disciples' pity party with, "Guess who's back?" Just as they're sharing, Jesus ghost-busts his own rumor by popping in, "Peace, I'm not a ghost!" They're freaking out, but Jesus is like, "Chill, check out the hands and feet. Ghosts don't have muscles." Still in disbelief, they hand over some fish, and he chows down. Jesus caps it off, "Told ya, everything had to go

167

down this way - suffering, comeback, and the big forgiveness tour starting from Jerusalem. You're all part of the squad now." Drops the mic with, "Wait here till you get the heavenly Wi-Fi signal."

Sky-High Goodbye

He escorts them to Bethany's outskirts, hits them with a heavenly bless up, and ascends like he's got a meeting with the clouds. They hit Jerusalem, high on spiritual vibes, turning the temple into their happy dance floor, giving props to God.

JOHN'S GOSPEL

The Great Throwback and Light Vibes

So, back in the day, before anything was a thing, there was the Word. And this Word was chilling with God, and, plot twist, was actually God. From the jump, this Word was with God, crafting everything in existence. Nothing got made without him. He was the life of the party, and this life brought the spotlight to humanity. This light was vibing in the shadows, but the darkness was like, "Nah, can't touch this." Enter stage left, a dude named John, sent by God as the OG hype man for the light. He wasn't the main event but came to drop hints so everyone could catch the real show. The real MVP, the light, was about to make a grand entrance. Though he designed the world, the world was clueless about him. He hit up his own crib, but his fam didn't roll out the welcome mat. But for the squad who did welcome him, he hooked them up with the VIP pass to become God's kids, a status not determined by human clout but by divine choice. The Word then decided to get in on the human experience, moved into the neighborhood, and we got a front-row seat to his majesty, loaded with grace and truth. John was all, "This is the guy I was talking about!" We're talking endless grace, a major upgrade from the old rules handed down by Moses. Grace and truth are Jesus's signature moves. No one's ever laid eyes on God, but Jesus, who's tight with the Father, spilled all the divine tea.

John's Reality Check

When the religious bigwigs from the capital sent their crew to grill John, he was straight up, "I'm not the star of the show." They're like, "Elijah? That prophet guy?" John's all, "Nope, try again." They pressed him for deets for their report back home, and John's like, "I'm just the warm-up act, yelling in the desert, 'Get the road ready for the Lord!'" Quoting the classics, of course. Sent by the skeptic squad, the Pharisees, they're like, "So why the water show?" John's there with his water bucket, "I'm just setting the stage. The headliner's already here, and I'm not even fit to handle his kicks." This all went down in Bethany, across the Jordan, where John was doing his thing in the river.

So, the next day, John spots J.C. heading his way and is like, "Yo, peep this, it's the Lamb of God who's gonna delete the world's sins!" He's like, "This dude is legit; he's the main act I've been hyping up. Didn't know him from Adam, but then I saw the Spirit float down like a dove and stick with him. That's when I knew he's the real deal, the one who's gonna shower us all in the Holy Spirit vibes." John's so shook, he's like, "For real, this guy is God's Son." Next scene, John's chilling with his crew. Sees Jesus stroll by again and can't help but shout, "Lamb of God alert!" His two buds catch the hint and start tailing Jesus. Jesus spins around, "What's up? What you looking for?" They're like, "Rabbi, where you crashing?" Jesus hits them with, "Roll with me and find out." So they did, and it turned into an epic hangout sesh. Andrew, one of the tag-alongs, bolts to find his bro Simon, buzzing with news, "Dude, we found the Messiah!" And when Simon meets Jesus, Jesus is all, "You're Simon? Now you're Peter, which means 'Rock.'"

The Squad Grows

The next day, Jesus is vibing towards Galilee, spots Philip, and is like, "Yo, follow me." Philip, now part of the crew, runs to Nathanael with the scoop, "We hit the jackpot! Found the guy Moses and the prophets were all tweeting about: Jesus from Nazareth." Nathanael's skeptical, "Nazareth? Can anything legit come from there?" Philip's like, "Just come and see, bro." As Nathanael walks up, Jesus nods, "Check this guy, a true-blue Israelite, no fakes." Nathanael's puzzled, "How you know me?" Jesus winks, "Spotted you under that fig tree before Philip even got to you." Nathanael's mind is blown, "Rabbi, you're the top dog, the King of Israel!" Jesus, playing it cool, "You're impressed by the fig tree thing? Hold my drink, you haven't seen anything yet. Heaven's about to throw down some serious cameos."

Water Into Top-Shelf Vino

Flash forward, there's a wedding in Cana, and Jesus' mom is there. Jesus and the disciples crash the party too. Mid-party, they're out of wine. Jesus' mom whispers to him, "They're on empty." Jesus is like, "Chill, mom, my time hasn't hit yet." But she tells the staff, "Whatever he says, just do it." So, Jesus spots six stone jars, tells the staff to fill 'em with H2O. Once filled, he's like, "Scoop some, and take it to the DJ." They do, and the DJ's mind is blown by the taste. He pulls the groom aside, "Everyone else serves the cheap stuff last. You saved the best for the encore!" This party trick in Cana was Jesus' debut miracle, putting his glory on full display and his disciples are all in. After the bash, Jesus hits Capernaum for a family trip, doesn't stay long though.

Temple Tidying Up

So, with Passover on the horizon, Jesus hits up Jerusalem and finds the temple turned into a flea market. He whips up a DIY whip and goes full clean-up mode, yeeting the livestock sellers and the money exchangers, flipping tables like a boss. He's like, "Yo, this is supposed to be a chill prayer spot, not your personal Etsy shop!" The squad recalls a prophecy about Jesus being all fired up for his Father's house. The locals challenge him, "Yo, show us a miracle if you're gonna act all high and mighty." Jesus hits them with, "Tear down this temple, and I'll have it back up in three days." They're baffled, thinking he's talking about the actual building, but he's hinting at his resurrection.

Late-Night Chat with Nicodemus

Enter Nicodemus, a top elite Pharisee, sneaking in after dark to chat with Jesus. He's like,

"Rabbi, your miracle game is strong. God's definitely on your side." Jesus drops a truth bomb, "Listen, you gotta be reborn to see God's kingdom." Nic's confused, "Reborn? Dude, how's an old guy supposed to crawl back into his mom's womb?" J.C. schools him on being reborn of water and spirit, making it clear it's not about a physical do-over but a spiritual transformation. Nicodemus is still scratching his head, and Jesus is surprised, "You're a teacher and you don't get this?"

Epic Throwdown: Light vs. Dark

Jesus keeps it 100, explaining how he's the one-way ticket to heaven and how God's love is so off the charts, he sent his one and only Son to save the world, not to diss it. Believing in him is a free pass from judgement, but ghosting him means you're already on the losing side, loving the darkness more than the light because their deeds are shady.

John's Final Mic Drop

Meanwhile, J.C. and his crew set up a pop-up baptism shop in Judean countryside, low-key competing with John the Baptist. Some of John's fans are salty, telling him, "Your former protégé is stealing your spotlight and everyone's heading his way." John's chill about it, "Look, everything I got is from the big guy upstairs. I was the opening act, now it's his show. He's the main event, I'm just the hype man. He's gotta shine brighter, and I'm cool taking a backseat."

The One from Heaven

So, the dude from upstairs is literally above it all. Earthlings chat about earth stuff, but the Heaven guy? He's on another level. He's out here dropping truth bombs he's seen firsthand, but peeps just aren't picking up what he's putting down. If you're vibing with his vibe, you're acknowledging that God's not playing. The guy God sent is like the ultimate truth speaker, rocking the Holy Spirit unlimited plan. God's all about his Son, handing him the keys to everything. Believing in the Son is your ticket to forever life, but ghosting him? You're basically asking for a storm of divine side-eye.

Jesus and the Samaritan Influencer

Jesus peaces out to Galilee cuz the Pharisees are keeping tabs on his follower count. On the way, he needs to hit up Samaria and ends up at this vintage well around lunchtime. Enter Samaritan woman, stage left, coming to snag some water. Jesus is like, "Yo, hit me up with a drink," which totally throws her because Jews and Samaritans don't usually mix. Jesus goes, "If you knew who's asking, you'd be the one asking me for that top-tier, never-ending water." She's all, "Um, you've got no gear and this well's an OG. You better than Jacob?" Jesus explains, drinking from his well means you'll never thirst again—it's like an eternal life spring. She's sold, "Sign me up for that water so I don't have to keep coming here." Jesus, playing it cool, goes, "Go call your hubby and come back." Plot twist: she's got no hubby. Jesus knows her whole relationship history, leaving her shook, recognizing him as a prophet. They get into a debate about the right spot to worship, and Jesus is like, "It's not about the location. It's all happening in spirit and truth now, and that's the vibe God's looking for." She mentions the Messiah, and Jesus casually drops, "You're looking at him."

The Ripened Harvest

Jesus' squad rolls up, totally shook to see him chatting up a Samaritan lady. But no one's got the guts to ask, "Yo, what's the deal here?" The woman, mind blown, ditches her water jar, books it to town, and is like, "Y'all, this guy knew my whole life story. Is he the real deal?" The whole town's intrigued and heads out to check Jesus. Meanwhile, the disciples are all, "Teacher, you gotta eat." But Jesus is on another level, saying, "I've got the kind of food you don't even know about." The crew's confused, whispering, "Did someone sneak him a snack?" Jesus schools them, "My real food? Doing what the Big Guy upstairs wants and wrapping up his project. You're all, 'Harvest time's ages away,' but I'm telling you, the fields are prime for picking right now."

The Savior of the World

Turns out, the Samaritan influencer did her thing, and a bunch from her town believed in Jesus because of her spill. They invite him over, and he hangs for a couple of days, winning over even more folks. They're like, "Forget the hearsay, we've heard the man ourselves. He's legit the world's savior."

A Galilean Welcome

Fast forward, Jesus heads to Galilee. Despite the saying, "A prophet's got no cred in his hometown," Galilee rolled out the red carpet because they'd seen his vibe at the festival.

The Second Sign: Healing an Official's Son

Back in Cana—yeah, the water-into-wine spot—a bigwig's kid is on the brink. Hearing Jesus is in town, he begs him to save his son. Jesus is like, "Y'all only believe with your eyes, huh?" But upon the official's plea, Jesus assures, "Your boy's gonna make it." The man trusts Jesus' word, heads home, and bam—finds his son healthy. Turns out, Jesus' word was the exact moment the fever peaced out. And just like that, his whole fam is on Team Jesus.

Jesus Crashes the Temple Market

Come Passover, Jesus hits Jerusalem and finds the temple turned into a flea market. Whip in hand, he clears the place out, flipping tables and schooling them, "This is supposed to be a chill spot for prayer, not a shopping spree!" His crew recalls a prophecy about this kind of zeal. The locals demand a miracle as proof. Jesus drops a teaser, "Tear down this temple, and I'll have it back up in three days." They're thinking construction time, but he's hinting at his resurrection. Post-resurrection, his squad connects the dots and believes. In town for Passover, Jesus is doing mind-blowing stuff, and while many are digging it, Jesus keeps his cards close, fully aware of the human heart's capacity for flip-flopping.

Jesus and Nic at Night

Nicodemus, a Pharisee and big deal among the Jews, hits Jesus up after dark. "Rabbi, your miracles are next level. God's gotta be with you." Jesus hits him with, "You wanna see God's kingdom? You've gotta be reborn." Nic's puzzled, "Reborn? How's an old-timer like me supposed to pull that off?" Jesus explains, "It's not about hitting the rewind; it's a birth of water and spirit. It's like catching the wind—you can't see it, but you see its effects." Nic's still scratching his head. Jesus wonders how he's a teacher of Israel and missing the basics. He keeps it 100: "I'm talking heavenly business. And just as Moses lifted up that snake in the desert, so must the Son of Man be lifted to give everyone a shot at forever life. God's love sent me, not to trash the world, but to save it. Embrace this truth, step into the light, and let your life show what God's up to."

Bigging Up Dad and the Bro

So, Jesus hits them with, "Yo, my Dad's always on the grind, and so am I." This got the crowd mega salty. Not only was Jesus doing his thing on rest day, but he was also calling God his Dad, basically saying they're on the same level. Jesus keeps it 100, "I can't just do stuff on my own whim. I'm mirroring my Dad. Whatever epic stuff he does, I'm on it too. Dad's got mad love for me and lets me in on all his cool projects. And trust, he's gonna blow your minds with what we've got lined up. Just like Dad brings folks back to life, I've got that power too. Dad's handed over the judge's gavel to me, so showing me respect is key—if you're dissing me, you're dissing him."

Life's Cheat Codes and Ultimate Judging

Jesus drops another truth bomb, "Hear me out and believe the Big Guy who sent me, and you're set for life—no game over, you're moving straight from the 'dead zone' to 'life unlimited'. An epic moment's coming, actually, it's already knocking. The dead will catch my vibe and live again. Dad's got life in himself and guess what? He's passed that on to me too. And yeah, he's made me the judge 'cause I'm the Son of Man. Don't freak out, but everyone's gonna hear my call. Good vibes? Welcome to life eternal. Bad vibes? Well, it's not looking great. My judgments are on point, 'cause I'm not about my agenda—I'm here to run Dad's play.

Real Talk From Real Peeps

If it were just me bigging myself up, you'd be right to question it. But there's someone else vouching for me, and his creds are solid. You checked in with John, and he was all about that truth life. Not that I need human props, but John was like a lit torch, and you all were down to bask in his glow for a sec.

Epic Snack Time: The Five Thousand Feast

So, Jesus and the squad hit up the Sea of Galilee, aka Tiberias. A massive crowd was tailing them, all hyped up over the sick healing skills Jesus was showcasing. They hit a chill spot on a hill, with Passover vibes in the air. Spotting the crowd rolling in, Jesus hits up Philip with a pop quiz, "Yo, where can we cop some grub for the crew?" He was just messing, though, 'cause he had a plan up his sleeve. Philip's like, "Dude, even a year's salary wouldn't get

everyone a nibble." Then Andrew, Peter's bro, chimes in, "Got this kid here with five barley loaves and a couple of fish, but that's a drop in the ocean for this mob." Jesus is all, "Park it, everyone." They found a nice patch of grass and had everyone take a seat—like 5k dudes, not counting women and kids. Jesus grabs the bread, does a big thank you to the sky, and starts the biggest share-a-thon, same with the fish, everyone's munching away. Post-feast, Jesus is like, "Let's clean up, don't waste a crumb." Boom, they filled twelve baskets with the bread bits left by the eaters. The crowd loses it, "This guy's gotta be the Prophet we've been waiting for." Catching on to their plan to crown him on the spot, Jesus ghosts to the hills solo.

Evening hits, and the squad heads to the sea. They jump in a boat, aiming for Capernaum. It's dark, Jesus hasn't shown, and suddenly, the sea goes wild. They're a few miles out, and bam, Jesus is just strolling on the water towards them. They freak, but Jesus is like, "Chill, it's just me." They're like, "Bet, hop in," and just like that, they hit the shore they were aiming for.

The Five Thousand's Epic Buffet

After Jesus took a mini-cruise across the Sea of Galilee, a massive fanbase followed because they were all about those healing vibes. Hitting up a mountain with his crew, Jesus spotted a festival-sized crowd heading his way.

Passover's Coming Up

With Passover on the horizon, Jesus threw a pop quiz at Philip about feeding the masses. Philip's like, "Even a year's salary wouldn't buy enough mini-snacks for this crowd." Andrew chimes in about a kid with a snack pack of five barley loaves and two fish, adding, "But that's just a drop in the ocean here." J.C. got everyone to hit the deck on the grass. Taking the loaves and fish, he whipped up a miracle meal, everyone ate their fill, and they still packed up twelve baskets of leftovers. The crowd lost it, "This guy's gotta be the Prophet we've been waiting for!"

As night fell, the disciples took a boat out, but Jesus played it solo. Then he decided to walk on water to catch up, totally spooking his crew. But he's like, "Chill, it's me."

The Next Day's Crowd: "Where's J.C.?"

Realizing Jesus and his posse had ghosted, the crowd sailed to Capernaum on a Jesus quest. Finding him, they're like, "Rabbi, when did you sneak over here?" Jesus hit them with truth, "You're here for the miracle munchies, not the signs. Aim for the eternal grub I'm offering, backed by the Big Guy." They're puzzled, "How do we sign up for God's work?" Jesus: "Just believe in the one He's sent." The crowd wanted more proof, reminiscing about their ancestors' desert buffet. Jesus corrected, "Heavenly bread's on me, not Moses. It's the real deal for the world." Everyone's like, "Perma-bread? Count us in."

I Am the Bread of Life

Jesus laid it out, "I'm the bread of life. Stick with me, you won't be hungry or thirsty. But seeing isn't always believing, huh? Anyway, anyone Dad sends my way, I welcome with open arms." The locals were baffled, "Isn't this Joseph's kid? How's he now the bread from heaven?" Jesus urged, "Ease up on the whining. No one can come to me unless it's a divine setup. The prophets said everyone will be taught by God. If you listen and learn, you'll get me." "Trust me, and you snag eternal life. I'm the upgrade from your ancestors' desert diet. My flesh is the real feast for life eternal." This convo went down in the Capernaum synagogue, turning from a teaching moment to a tough pill for many followers. Whispering started, "This is intense. Who can handle it?" Aware of the brewing storm, Jesus challenged, "Does this freak you out? What if you see me heading back up? Spirit's where it's at; flesh doesn't cut it. My words are spirit and life. But hey, some of you aren't on board." Knowing who was who from the get-go, Jesus wasn't surprised when some fans unfollowed. Turning to his VIPs, he asked, "What about you guys, bouncing too?" Peter stepped up, "You've got the words of forever life. We're all in. We've seen enough to know you're the real deal." But Jesus threw a curveball, "I picked you lot, yet one of you's about to ghost me big time." He meant Judas, the ultimate party pooper.

Bro Talk: Jesus Keeps It Low-Key

So Jesus was cruising around Galilee because, let's be real, Judea was a no-go zone with folks out for his hide. With the Jewish Coachella (Festival of Shelters) on the horizon, his bros were like, "Dude, hit up Judea so your fans can catch your latest miracles. You're not gonna trend hiding here. If you've got the goods, go viral with it."

Plot twist: His own squad wasn't buying into his hype. Jesus clapped back, "Chill, my spotlight moment isn't here yet. You guys can hit up the fest anytime; no one's beefing with you. The world's got a bone to pick with me because I'm calling out its shady business. I'm sitting this one out till my cue hits." And with that, he ghosted on the Judea trip.

Jesus Sneaks into Coachella

Post-bro departure, Jesus pulled a stealth move and headed to the fest, blending in like a ninja. The crowd was on high alert, "Where's that guy?" Whispers flew left and right - some stanning him, "He's legit," while others were throwing shade, "He's playing us." Despite the buzz, folks were tight-lipped, scared to drop hot takes in public. Mid-fest, Jesus crashed the temple scene, dropping wisdom bombs. The crowd was shook, "How's this guy schooling us without a diploma?" Jesus schooled them, "This wisdom isn't mine. It's from the HQ upstairs. If you're down with His plan, you'll get where I'm coming from. I'm not here for my own trailer; I'm all about giving props to the One who sent me. Moses handed you the rulebook, yet here you are, plotting my exit." Crowd's like, "You're tripping, who's out to get you?" Jesus, keeping it 100, "Did one heal-and-chill, and you're all losing it. Moses got you on that circumcision routine – not his OG idea, but you roll with it even on rest days. So, why the hate when I hit the refresh button on a dude during Sabbath? Let's not judge the book by its cover; aim for the real deal."

Who's That Guy?

Some peeps in Jerusalem were all, "Isn't this the dude everyone's been wanting to cancel? Yet here he is, all loud and proud, and nobody's making a move. Could the big shots actually think he's the real deal, the MVP, the Messiah?" But then they're like, "Nah, we know this guy's backstory. Everyone knows the Messiah's gonna drop in unannounced." While Jesus was dropping truth bombs in the temple, he goes, "Y'all think you know me and my origins, but I'm here on a mission from the one who's legit. You don't know Him; I do because I'm His direct envoy." Then they got all grabby but couldn't touch him because it wasn't showtime yet. Still, many in the crowd were vibing with him, whispering, "Could the Messiah do more epic stuff than this dude?" The Pharisees caught wind of the fan club and sent their goons to scoop him up. Jesus hit them with, "I'm only here for a hot minute. Then I'm out to the one who sent me. You'll look for me but won't find me because where I'm headed, you can't follow." The locals were baffled, "Where's he gonna bounce that we can't track him? He's not going international on us, is he? What's with the cryptic, 'You will look for me, and you will not find me; and where I am, you cannot come'?"

On the festival's closing night, Jesus stood up and shouted, "If anyone's parched, come to me and drink! Believe in me, and you'll be like a fountain of life-giving water." He was hinting at the Spirit squad that believers were gonna get, but they were still waiting for Jesus to be put in the spotlight.

Team Jesus vs. Team Doubt

The crowd was split. Some were Team Prophet; others were Team Messiah. But then the skeptics piped up, "Messiah from Galilee? Doesn't add up. The good book says he's supposed to roll out from David's hood, Bethlehem." So, the crowd was all over the place. Some were ready to grab him, but Jesus was untouchable.

Guard Squad Flips Script

When the temple bouncers reported back empty-handed, the chief priests and Pharisees were like, "What the heck?" The guards were all, "No one ever dropped the mic like him!" The Pharisees were losing it, "You got played too? Show me one big shot or Pharisee who's on team Jesus. Nah, it's just this law-ignorant mob that's cursed." Nicodemus, trying to be the voice of reason, chimes in, "Hold up, since when do we judge a dude without hearing him out?" They clapped back, "What, you one of those Galilee fanboys? Do your homework; no prophet comes from there."

Drama Alert: Caught in the Act

Bright and early, J.C. hit the temple courts, and everyone rocked up to listen. The scribes and Pharisees dragged in a lady caught in the no-no zone, putting her on blast in front of everyone. "Moses in the rulebook says to stone such women. Your take, Jesus?" They were fishing for something to pin on him. Jesus went all zen, doodling in the dirt. They kept pestering him until he stood tall and dropped, "Alright, whoever here is squeaky clean, you throw the first rock." He got back to his dirt doodling, and one by one, they bailed, the older dudes leading the exit. It was just Jesus and the lady. He looked up, "They all bounce? No one threw shade?" She's like, "Nada, Lord." Jesus: "Cool, I'm not throwing shade either. Go on, but let's not do a repeat performance, yeah?"

Spotlight's on Me, Folks

Jesus hit 'em with a spotlight moment: "Yo, I'm the light of this whole party. Follow me, and you'll never trip in the dark 'cause you'll have the VIP glow." The Pharisees threw shade, "Bro, you're your own hype man. That doesn't count." Jesus clapped back, "Even if I'm soloing this, my rep's legit 'cause I know where I'm from and where I'm headed. You're clueless about my backstory. 15 You're all about that surface level judgment. I'm not here to judge, but if I did, it'd be straight facts 'cause it's not just me; it's me and the big guy upstairs. 17 Your own rulebook says it takes two to tango on the truth. 18 I'm one witness, and my Dad's the other." They're like, "So where's your dad in all this?" Jesus dropped the mic, "You don't know me or my Dad. If you got me, you'd get Him too."

Spoiler Alert: I'm Heading Out

Jesus then hit them with a cryptic, "I'm peacing out, and you'll be on the hunt but stuck in your mess. Where I'm jetting, you can't tag along." The crowd's all, "Is he gonna ghost us? Why's he saying we can't follow?" Jesus got real, "You're stuck in the low-res version of life. I'm HD, from the top. You're all about this world; I'm not. 24 Listen up, if you don't vibe with me, you're staying in the sin bin." They're like, "Who even are you?"

Jesus: "I've been straight with you from day one. 26 I've got loads to say and judge, but the Sender's legit, and I'm just passing along His playlist."

Keeping It 100: Truth Will Set You Free

A bunch of them started believing, and Jesus was like, "Stick with my tracks, and you're legit my crew. 32 You'll hit up the truth, and that truth's gonna cut you loose." They got all high and mighty, "We're Abraham's fan club; we've never been on anyone's leash. What's this 'set free' talk?" Jesus laid it down, "Listen, if you're playing in the sin sandbox, you're not freestyling; you're locked in. 35 A guest doesn't get permanent crib access, but family does. 36 So if I cut you loose, you're truly living that free life."

Throwdown: Who's Your Daddy?

They tried to claim Abraham as their squad leader. Jesus was like, "If Abe was your homeboy, you wouldn't be plotting against me. 40 I'm here dropping truth bombs I got from God, and here you are, trying to cancel me. Abe didn't roll like that. 41 You're on your daddy's mission." "God's our father." Jesus: "If that was true, you'd be my fan 'cause I came from God. 43 You can't even tune into my frequency 'cause you're not about God's life. 44 Your real daddy's the devil, and you're all about his hit list. 45 But because I'm all about the truth, you're not buying it."

Epic Mic Drop: Before Abe, I Am

They tried to label him a Samaritan with some bad vibes. Jesus kept it cool, "I'm here honoring my Father, and you're

180

all about dishonor. 50 I'm not chasing claps; that's His job. 51 And here's the kicker: stick with my words, and you're not facing the end game." They lost it, "Now you're saying you're bigger than Abe and the prophets? Who do you think you are?" Jesus went all-in, "Your approval? Don't need it. It's all about my Father, who you claim as your God but don't really know. 56 Abe was stoked to see my time; he saw it and was hype." They're like, "You're not even a half-century old, and you've hung out with Abraham?" Jesus: "For real, for real, before Abe got his start, I am." That's when they lost their minds and started picking up rocks, but Jesu vanished from the scene.

Spotlight Savior Does it Again

So, Jesus is cruising by and spots a dude who's been blind from the get-go. His squad's like, "Yo, Jesus, who messed up? This guy or his folks?" Jesus is like, "Nah, it's not about who messed up. It's showtime for God's skills. 4 We've gotta hustle with the daylight we got. I'm the world's spotlight." Then he whips up some DIY mud with his spit, slaps it on the guy's eyes, and is like, "Hit up the pool of Siloam and take a wash." Dude does it and bam! Sight restored. Neighbors and onlookers are all,

"Isn't this the same guy who was always hitting us up for change?" Some are convinced; others are like, "Nah, just a look-alike." But the guy's insistent, "For real, it's me." They're like, "So how'd you score the vision upgrade?" He's all, "This Jesus dude worked some mud magic on my eyes, sent me to wash, and now I'm seeing 4K." "Where's he at?" they wanted to know. "Got me," he says.

Blind Guy Goes Viral

They drag him to the Pharisees, 'cause apparently, Jesus chose the Sabbath to play in the mud. Pharisees are split; some are throwing shade at Jesus for breaking the Sabbath, while others are mind-blown, "How's a rule-breaker pulling off miracles?" They grill the guy, "Your take on him?" "Prophet status," he shoots back. But the Jews are on the fence till they pull in his folks, pressing them for the backstory. Parents are playing it safe, "He's an adult, grill him." Round two with the blind-now-seeing dude, Pharisees are trying to get him to throw Jesus under the bus, "C'mon, spill, he's a sinner right?" Dude's like, "Sinner or not, all I know is I was in the dark, now I'm all about that light." They keep badgering him for the deets, and he's getting fed up, "Why the encore? You looking to join his fan club?" They lose it, "You're on Team Jesus. We're old school, Team Moses." He claps back, "You're missing the plot. You don't even know where your lead character's from, yet he's out here giving me a whole new outlook on life. 31 God's not about that sinner life, but here we are. 32 Show me another time in history where someone rebooted a born-blind guy's vision. 33 If this Jesus wasn't God's right-hand man, he couldn't pull off a thing." They're all, "You're schooling us? You were born a hot mess!" And just like that, they kicked him to the curb.

Seeing the Real Deal

When Jesus heard they'd given the blind guy the boot, he tracked him down and hit him with, "You vibin' with the Son of Man?" The guy's like, "Point him out so I can hit that follow button." Jesus is all, "You're looking at him. Surprise!" Dude's mind = blown. Drops to his knees and goes full fan mode, "I believe!" Jesus throws down some wisdom, "I'm here flipping the script so the blind can see and the sighted might just realize they're missing the whole show." Some nearby Pharisees catch this and get all insecure, "We're not blind too, are we?" Jesus claps back, "If you were actually blind, you'd be off the hook. But since you claim you can see, your guilt's sticking around."

Shepherd Vibes Only

Then Jesus drops a truth bomb, "Look, the legit shepherd doesn't sneak in; he walks in like he owns the place. The sheep dig his voice. He's got VIP access. 5 Strangers? Nah, sheep aren't about that life. They'll bolt." Jesus is trying to spell it out, but they're missing the point. So he goes again, "For real, I'm the gate. Anyone who tries to jump the fence is up to no good. I'm the real deal, the VIP entrance to life at its fullest." Jesus keeps it 100, "I'm the top shepherd. I'd take a bullet for my sheep. The rent-a-guard bails at the first sign of trouble, but not me. 14 I'm tight with my sheep, and we're on a first-name basis, just like me and the Big Guy upstairs. And yeah, I've got sheep from all over, not just this pen. They'll hear me out, and we'll all be one big happy family. I'm all in, laying down my life to pick it up again because that's the mission I'm on." This talk split the crowd. Some were like, "He's out of his mind! Don't listen!" While others were picking up what he was putting down, "This ain't crazy talk. Can a madman open the eyes of the blind?"

Winter Festival Drama

Fast forward to winter in Jerusalem at the Festival of Dedication. Jesus is chilling in Solomon's Colonnade when the locals circle up, demanding, "Spill it. Are you the Messiah or what?" Jesus is like, "I've been telling you, but you're not hitting 'subscribe.' My actions scream who I am, but you're not my flock, hence the disconnect." He lays it out, "My sheep get me. They follow because they know my voice equals life forever, and they're safe with me. My Dad, who's the real MVP, has got them, and no one can mess with that. Me and the Father? We're synced." This convo had the crowd at odds, with some ready to write him off as a lunatic, while others couldn't ignore the miracles staring them in the face.

Rock Dodge 2.0

So, the crowd's back at it again, ready to chuck stones at Jesus. Jesus, chill as ever, is like, "For real, guys? Which of my good vibes are you stoning me for?" They're all, "Nah, it's not your good deeds. It's 'cause you're out here acting like you're the main character, claiming to be God." Jesus hits them with a logic bomb, "Hold up, didn't your own rulebook say 'you are gods'? If those old school guys got the godly shoutout for hearing from God, why you tripping when I say I'm the Son of God? Check the receipts — my miracles back me up. If you can't get on board with my words, at least believe the hype from the miracles. They're proof we're tight, me and the Big Guy upstairs." They tried to grab him again, but Jesus was like a ninja, slipped right through.

Across the Jordan Fan Club

Jesus bounces back to where John used to dunk people in water, hanging out and dropping truth bombs. People were showing up like, "John was cool and all, didn't do magic tricks, but everything he said about this dude? Spot on." And boom, belief was spreading.

Lazarus Napping Hard

Cut to Bethany, Lazarus is out cold (and by cold, I mean dead). His sisters, Mary and Martha, hit up Jesus, "Yo, your boy Lazarus is in a bad way." Jesus is like, "Chill, this won't end in a funeral. It's all for the spotlight moment for God, so the Son can shine." Despite being tight with Lazarus and his sisters, Jesus chills for two more days before saying, "Alright, let's roll back to Judea." The disciples are freaking, "Rabbi, they're literally stone-cold fans there waiting to take you out, and you wanna go back?" Jesus, dropping wisdom, talks about making moves while there's light. Then drops, "Lazarus is sleeping, but I'm gonna wake him up." The crew misunderstands, thinking Lazarus is just snoozing. Jesus lays it out, "No, guys, Lazarus is dead. And it's good I wasn't there, 'cause now you'll really believe. Let's hit the road." Thomas, ever the optimist, is like, "Great, let's go get KO'd with him."

Lazarus: The Comeback Kid

Jesus rocks up to find Lazarus has been chilling in the tomb for four days. Bethany's buzzing, lots of peeps have come to console Martha and Mary. Martha hears Jesus is on the approach, runs out to meet him, "Lord, if you were here, my bro would still be partying. But I know even now, God's got you." Jesus promises a Lazarus revival. Martha's like, "Sure, in the zombie apocalypse." Jesus clarifies, "Nah, I'm the life hack here. Believing in me means even death can't touch you. You in?" Martha's all in, "You're the real deal, the Son of God, the one we've been waiting for."

When Martha Slid into Mary's DMs

So Martha hits up Mary on the DL, like, "Psst, Teach is here, and he's asking for you." Mary hears this, springs up like she's on a launchpad, and zooms off to Jesus. Now, Jesus was chillin' outside the village, waiting. The grief squad in the house notices Mary dipping out fast and thinks, "Oh, she's off to the tomb to have a solo cry sesh." But nah, Mary beelines it to Jesus, drops at his kicks, and is all, "Boss, if you had been here, Lazarus would still be chillin' with us." Seeing Mary all teary, and the cry crew joining in, Jesus gets all kinds of shook up.

Jesus Shows He's Got Feels Too

"Where's the dude laid to rest?" Jesus asks. They're like, "Come see." And guess what? Jesus cried. Yep, even the onlookers were like, "Wow, he really dug Lazarus." But of course, there's always a few throwing shade, "Couldn't Mr. Miracle Eyes have done something?"

Lazarus: The Comeback King

Getting to the tomb, which was more of a stone-cold cave with a rock for a door, Jesus is like,

"Yo, move that stone." Martha's like, "Uh, Jesus, it's been four days... it's gonna reek." Jesus is like, "Trust, you're gonna wanna Snapchat this." So they roll away the stone, and Jesus does a quick shoutout to the Big Guy, then yells, "Lazarus, get out here!" And what do you know, Lazarus moonwalks out of the tomb, still wrapped up like a mummy. Jesus is like, "Someone help him out of that getup."

Conspiracy Theories Go Wild

After this epic show, a bunch of the onlookers hit that "believe" button on Jesus. But there's always a few snitches. They run to the Pharisees and spill the tea on Jesus' latest drop. Cue the emergency meeting of the religious bigwigs. They're all, "If we let this dude keep trending, we're gonna be cancelled by the Romans." Caiaphas, the VIP priest of the year, is like, "Y'all missing the point. Better for one dude to take the L than for our whole vibe to get shutdown." Little did he know he was actually dropping a prophecy that Jesus was the one-man rescue plan for the whole crew, not just the home team but all the scattered fam too.

Jesus Goes Incognito

Post-plot, Jesus goes ghost mode, hitting up a lowkey spot called Ephraim with his squad, dodging the Judean paparazzi. With Passover coming up, everyone's buzzing in Jerusalem, doing their ritual thing, but also low-key on the lookout for Jesus, whispering, "You think he'll show at the fest?" The top dogs and Pharisees had the snitch hotline set up, "Yo, if you peep Jesus, drop us a pin so we can scoop him up."

Pre-Passover Vibes with Jesus and Lazarus

Six days before the big Passover bash, Jesus cruises into Bethany where Lazarus, the dude he brought back from the dead-zones, was chilling. They threw a dinner party in Jesus' honor. Martha was playing hostess, Lazarus was kicking it with Jesus at the table, and then Mary went all in. She grabbed a pound of this super boujee nard perfume, gave Jesus' feet a spa treatment, and wiped them down with her hair. The whole place was smelling like a luxury perfume store.

Judas Gets Salty Over Perfume Economics

But Judas Iscariot, who was about to pull the ultimate betrayal move, was like, "Yo, why didn't we eBay this perfume for a hefty sum and donate the cash to the needy?" Spoiler alert: He couldn't care less about the needy; dude had sticky fingers and was eyeing the cash box. J.C. was like, "Chill, she's prepping me for what's coming. The needy are always around, but I'm here for a limited time offer."

Plot Twist: Lazarus on the Hit List

Word got out Jesus was in town, and folks weren't just there for him but also to eyeball Lazarus, the living proof of Jesus' power. The big shots decided Lazarus needed to go too because his walking-talking miracle status was turning too many heads Jesus' way. Next up, Jesus heads to Jerusalem, and the crowd goes wild. They're breaking out palm branches, throwing down a welcome fit for a king, and shouting, "Hosanna! Blessed is the king mode in God's name!" Jesus finds a young donkey, hops on, fulfilling that old-school prophecy about Zion's king cruising in humble style.

Jesus Drops Truth Bombs

Some Greeks showed up wanting a meet-and-greet with Jesus. Jesus, knowing his clock was ticking, was like, "It's go time for the Son of Man to shine. You gotta be like a seed – die to sprout big. Love your life too much, and you'll lose it. Hate it in this crazy world, and you'll keep it forever." Then Jesus gets real deep, talking about how troubled he is but knowing this is the moment everything's been leading up to. Heaven's PA system kicks in, backing Jesus up, while the crowd's trying to figure out if it's thunder or an angel DJing. Jesus clears it up, "That was for you, not me. It's crunch time for the world. The big boss of bad's about to get the boot. And when I get lifted, I'm bringing everyone to my level." The crowd's confused about this whole 'Son of Man getting lifted' business because they thought the Messiah was an eternal gig. Jesus hits them with, "Light's on a timer, folks. Walk in it while you can, so you don't trip in the dark. Stick with the light, become kids of the light." After dropping this mic, Jesus ducks out to lay low.

Isaiah's Spoiler Alert Comes True

Even though Jesus was out here performing sign after sign, folks were still sleeping on him. This was Isaiah's mixtape coming to life – you know, the track where he's all, "Who's vibing to our tunes? Who's catching these miracles?" Straight-up, they couldn't vibe because Isaiah dropped another verse about them getting their eyes and hearts on airplane mode so they wouldn't get the picture and hit up for a heal. Isaiah wasn't just throwing guesses; he saw Jesus' VIP glow-up and was talking about him way back. Yet, some peeps, even the big-wigs, believed in Jesus on the down-low 'cause they didn't want to lose their cool club passes to the synagogue. They were all about that clout from peeps rather than a thumbs up from the big G.

Jesus Drops the Mic on His Mission

Jesus goes full volume, "Yo, hitting the 'believe' button on me is like sending a friend request to the one who sent me. Seeing me is like seeing Him. I'm here to light up the world, so nobody's gotta chill in the dark. I'm not about that judge life; I came for the save. But ghost on me and my words, and those very words will be your judge come finale day. Everything I've said, straight

from the Father – it's all about that eternal life."

The Ultimate Humble Brag: Foot Washing 101

Before the Passover Festival, Jesus knew it was almost time to bounce back to the Father. He loved his crew till the end. Dinner time, and Judas was already plotting his betrayal playlist. Jesus, fully aware he's the main man with everything under control, switches gears from dinner to pedicure mode. He wraps a towel around his waist and starts a foot-washing spree. Peter's like, "You washing my feet? As if!" Jesus hits back, "If I don't, you're not rolling with my squad." Peter, not wanting to miss out, goes, "Then hit me up with a full bath!" Jesus explains it's all about being squeaky clean in spirit; it's not about the dirt. "You're clean, but not everyone," hinting at the betrayal mixtape about to drop.

What the Foot Washing really Means

After getting their feet spa, Jesus, back in his gear, was like, "Catch the lesson? You call me the Boss, and you're right. So if I'm down to wash your feet, you better be ready to do the same. It's all about setting the pace; do as I do. Remember, no crew member is bigger than the captain. Knowing this, you're set if you hit follow. I'm not talking about everyone; I've picked my squad. But gotta fulfill those throwback prophecies: 'Even my homie has ghosted me.'" He's dropping these hints so when the betrayal hits, they'll know he's the real deal. "Mark my words, accepting someone I send is like accepting me, and that's like accepting the One who sent me."

Judas's Epic Fail Alert

After dropping some heavy truth bombs, Jesus got all in his feels and dropped the bombshell, "Yo, one of y'all is gonna ghost me big time." The squad's eyes darted around like, "Who's he talking about?" The fave disciple, chilling next to Jesus, got the signal from Peter to scoop the deets. Leaning back, he's like, "Yo, boss, who's the traitor?" Jesus dishes, "The one who scores this dipped bread." He passes the bread to Judas, and boom, it's like cueing the villain music. Judas takes a bite, and it's like he invited the darkness in. Jesus, knowing the game's up, tells him, "Do your thing, but make it snappy." Everyone else is clueless, thinking Judas is on a late-night snack run or dropping some coins for the needy. Judas

bounces, and yeah, it's all shades of night out there.

The Love Command: Squad Goals

Once Judas exits stage left, Jesus gets real, "Now's my moment, and it's all for the glory." He hits them with, "I'm not sticking around much longer. You can't tag along where I'm headed." Drops the love bomb next: "New rule, folks – love each other like I loved you. That's how you'll rep my squad."

Peter's Oopsie Daisy

Peter, ever the eager beaver, is like, "Where you off to, Jesus?" Jesus lays it down, "You can't follow now, but you'll get there." Peter's all in, "I'd totally take a bullet for you!" Jesus side-eyes, "Oh, really? Before the rooster crows, you'll act like you don't know me. Thrice."

VIP Pass to the Father

Into the heart-to-heart, Jesus goes, "Don't freak out. Trust in God, trust also in me. My Dad's place? Big enough for all. I'm off to prep your VIP spots. I'll come back to pick you up, so you'll be where I am. And you know the road to where I'm heading." Thomas, ever the skeptic, "We

188

don't even know your destination, how we gonna know the way?" Jesus schools him, "I am the Google Maps, the truth, and the life passport. No one gets to the Dad except through me. If you've seen me, you've seen the Big Guy." Philip, wanting more, "Just show us the Father, and we'll be set." Jesus, a bit exasperated, "Philip, bro, we've been hanging out this long, and you still don't get it? Seeing me is seeing the Father. It's all about the teamwork."

Power-Ups in Jesus's Name

Leveling up, Jesus promises, "Stick with me, and you'll do even bigger stuff than I've done, 'cause I'm hitting up the Father. Ask anything in my name, and I'm on it – makes for a great Father-Son collab."

The Ultimate Sidekick: The Spirit

Jesus, getting to the heart of the afterparty plans, "If you're really into me, you'll keep my vibes going. And I'll hook you up with another Helper, the Spirit of Truth. The world can't handle him, but you'll know him – he's gonna be crashing with you and in you."

Squad Goals: The Ultimate Fam

Jesus is like, "Ain't leaving you solo; I'm bouncing back." He drops, "Soon, you'll see me 'cause I'm living, you'll be living. We're all gonna be in this epic fam jam - Me, Pops, and you. It's all about that love life." He answers Judas 2.0, saying, "If someone's really into me, we're moving in. Not feeling it? Then, it's a no from us."

Jesus goes, "I'm leaving you some chill vibes, not the fake peace the world tries to slide into your DMs. Keep your heart chill and fear on mute. You heard me, I'm out but also coming back. If you're really rooting for me, you'd throw a party 'cause I'm heading to Pops, who's kinda a big deal."

Vine & Branches: Staying Connected

Jesus, getting all green-thumbed, is like, "I'm the real deal vine, Pops is the gardener. If you're not vibing with fruit, you're out. Stick with me, and you'll be the fruit ninja. Try going solo, and you're basically kindling. Stick with me, ask what you want, and it's yours. That's how we roll and show we're legit."

189

He's like, "Just as Pops has got my back, I've got yours. Stay in my love loop. Here's the deal: love each other hardcore. No love beats giving it all for your squad. You're not my minions; you're my peeps 'cause I've shared the deets from Pops. You didn't DM me; I slid into yours. You're chosen to go big, bear fruit, and whatever you ask Pops in my tag, you got it. Commandment? Just love each other, no trolls allowed."

When Haters Hate

"Feeling the hate? That's 'cause you're with me. You're not from around here; I handpicked you, so the world's gonna be salty. Remember, they threw shade at me first. They'll come at you 'cause they don't get who sent me. They're clueless about Pops and me, but they've run out of excuses. Hate on me, they're hating on Pops. They've seen the awesomeness and still chose to hate. It's like they're fulfilling their own burn book: 'Hated me for no reason.' Mic drop."

Squad Alert: The Ultimate Truth Squad

Jesus drops, "When the ultimate truth squad member, aka the Holy Ghost, slides into your DMs from Pops, He's gonna spill all about me. And you'll be spilling too 'cause you've been rolling with me from day one."

No More Sugarcoating

He's like, "I've been real with you to keep you from tripping. They're gonna kick you out of the cool clubs, and some might even think they're scoring heaven points by ghosting you. It's all 'cause they're clueless about me and the Big Guy. I've been holding back some deets 'cause you weren't ready. But it's about to get real. I'm peacing out, but it's all good 'cause I'm sending the Holy Ghost. He's gonna school everyone on the real deal about sin, what's right, and who's boss. He's all about that truth life and will keep you updated on the future hits."

From Tears to Cheers

Jesus hits them with, "BRB, but then you'll see me again, and your vibe will go from sad reacts only to pure joy. It's like when the struggle is real, but then you win big. Ask anything using my name, and it's yours. That's how you max out your joy level."

"Been talking in riddles, but soon it's gonna be straight talk from me. You'll get direct access to the Big Guy, no need for middlemen. The Father's got mad love for you 'cause you're on Team Jesus. I came from the Big Guy, did my thing, and now I'm heading back up."

Disciples Level Up

Disciples are all, "Now you're talking our language! No more head-scratchers. We're all in, believing you're straight outta heaven." Jesus is like, "You believe now? Brace yourselves; it's about to get lonely, but we're not really solo 'cause the Father's got us. I've spilled all this so you can find your chill in me. World's gonna bring the drama, but keep your head up. I've got this. Victory's mine."

Epic Squad Chat in the Sky

Jesus hit up the sky chat, going, "Yo, Dad, it's time. Make your boy shine so I can make you look good too. You handed me the VIP pass to give everyone a shot at forever life just by knowing you're the real MVP and I'm your main man."

Squad Goals: Protect and Unite

He's like, "I've let the crew you hooked me up with know who you are. They've been solid, keeping it real with your message. Now, I'm about to bounce back to you, so keep them safe in our secret handshake, so they can be tight like we are. While I was down here, I kept them in our squad, except for that one dude who had to bail, making those old scriptures come true."

#SquadPrayers for Everyone

Jesus wasn't just talking about his day-ones. He's also sending good vibes for anyone down the line who's gonna catch the wave through them. "Let's get everyone on the same squad vibes, like you and me, Dad, so the whole world gets it—you sent me."

Ultimate Showdown in the Garden

Post-heart-to-heart with the sky, Jesus and his crew rolled up to their usual hangout spot. Judas, flipping the script, brought a whole welcome committee—except they were not there to party. They came packing heat. Jesus stepped up, all, "Who you looking for?" They're like, "Jesus of Nazareth." And he's just, "You found him." And boom, they hit the deck. When they tried it again, Jesus was like, "I already told you, it's me. But let my peeps bounce." This was all part of the plan, keeping his squad safe. Then Peter went all ninja mode, but Jesus was like, "Chill, bro, I gotta see this through." So, in a world where doing the right thing might get you side-eye from the crowd, Jesus was setting up the ultimate comeback, all about sticking together and spreading those good vibes.

The Epic Plot Twist and Cold Nights

So, the squad of soldiers, the big boss, and the Jewish VIPs cuffed Jesus and took him on a little tour. First stop was Annas' place, 'cause he's kinda the father-in-law of the year, Caiaphas, who thought one dude taking the fall could save the squad.

Peter's Epic Fails

Meanwhile, Peter and another bro were tailing Jesus. This other dude was tight with the high priest, so he slipped into the VIP area, leaving Peter out in the cold. Literally. When a doorkeeper chick spotted Peter, she was like, "You're one of his homies, aren't you?" And Peter was all, "Nah, you got the wrong guy." There they were, trying to get warm, and Peter's just chilling, denying he knows Jesus.

The Interrogation Lounge

Inside, the high priest was grilling Jesus about his followers and his Ted Talks. Jesus was straight up, "I've been an open book in your fave hangout spots. Why the third degree? Ask the audience; they heard it all." Then, outta nowhere, one official thought Jesus needed a reality check with a slap for his supposed sass to the high priest. Jesus, keeping it cool, was like, "If I'm wrong, prove it. Otherwise, why the slap?"

Peter's Remix of Denials

Back to Peter by the fire, getting grilled harder than a BBQ party. "Surely, you're one of them?" And again, "Nope, not me." Then a cousin of the ear surgery patient from the garden's like, "Yo, weren't you the ninja with him?" And Peter's like, "No way!" And just like that, cue the rooster remix.

Pilate's Early Morning Drama

Fast forward to Jesus being led to Pilate's crib early in the A.M. The accusers wouldn't step inside 'cause they didn't wanna miss out on Passover dinner. Pilate, trying to keep the peace, was like, "So, what's this guy done?" They were all, "Trust us, he's bad news." Pilate, not wanting to get his hands dirty, was like, "Deal with it your way." But they wanted the full drama, "We can't; we need you for the final act."

King or Not?

Pilate and Jesus had a one-on-one. "You the king around here?" Jesus, dropping truth bombs, "My kingdom's not about this life. If it were, my crew would've fought to keep me from being caught. I'm here to speak truth." Pilate, puzzled by the concept, "Truth, what's that?"

Choose Your Fighter: Jesus or Barabbas

Then Pilate, trying to keep up with tradition, was like, "You want me to drop charges and let him join your Passover party?" But the crowd went wild for Barabbas, the OG rebel, leaving Jesus in the lurch. And there you have it, folks. The story of how Jesus went from being the main event to watching the crowd choose the chaos candidate, all while Peter was having his own "I don't know him" marathon and Pilate was philosophizing about truth.

The Great Makeover Gone Wrong

So, Pilate decided to give Jesus a makeover nobody asked for. They whipped him up, slapped on a DIY crown of thorns, and threw on a royal purple robe just for the LOLs. They kept trolling him with, "Yo, King of the Jews!" while giving him the slap-challenge treatment.

Pilate's Reality Check

Pilate was like, "Peeps, I'm gonna show him to you just to prove he's chill." Out comes Jesus, looking like he's about to drop the saddest album of the year, and Pilate's like, "Behold the dude!" But the crowd and the temple squad were all, "Nah, let's just crucify him!" Hearing them play the "Son of God" card, Pilate was shook. He pulled Jesus aside for a private chat, "Where you from, bro?" Jesus kept it mysterious. Pilate tried flexing his power, but Jesus hit him with, "You ain't in charge unless the Big Guy says so." Pilate was low-key trying to free Jesus, but the crowd played the Caesar card, and Pilate caved.

The Final Walk

So, they took Jesus to get crucified. He had to lug his own

cross to Skull Place. There, they nailed him up with a couple of others, setting up Jesus in the center spotlight. Pilate put up a sign, "Jesus of Nazareth, the King of the Jews," which ticked off the chief priests even more. The soldiers turned his clothes into a mini lottery, fulfilling one of those old-school prophecies. Meanwhile, Jesus' squad, including his mom and Mary Magdalene, were there. Jesus, being the ultimate son, made sure his mom was taken care of, passing her off to his fave disciple.

The Grand Finale

Knowing he was about to drop the mic, Jesus called for a drink. Once he got his sip of vintage sour wine, he was like, "It's a wrap." And with that, he checked out, leaving everyone waiting for the encore.

The Mystery of the Missing Boss

Early bird Mary Magdalene hit up the tomb while it was still pitch black outside, only to find the VIP entrance stone rolled away. Freaking out, she sprinted to Simon Peter and the beloved disciple, panting, "Yo, they've yoinked the Lord, and we're clueless where they've stashed him!"

The Tomb Raider Sprint

Peter and the beloved disciple bolted towards the tomb. It turned into a foot race, but the beloved disciple was channeling his inner Usain Bolt and got there first. He peeked inside, saw the linens chilling there, but didn't barge in. Peter, not one to care about breaking and entering, barged in, noticed the linens, and the special head wrapping doing its own solo performance in a corner. The beloved disciple finally entered, saw the setup, and was like, "Oh, snap, it's all coming together." Yet, the plot of him rising from the dead was still not clicking.

Mary and the Heavenly Crew

Back at the tomb, Mary was having her own solo sob fest. When she peeked into the tomb, she spotted two angels in white, chilling like it was just another day in paradise. They hit her with, "Girl, why the waterworks?" She's like, "They've kidnapped my Lord, and it's a mystery where they've dumped him!"

Plot Twist: Gardener or the G.O.A.T?

As she turned, she saw Jesus standing there but mistook him

for the gardener. Jesus, playing it cool, was like, "Why crying? Who you looking for?" Mary, thinking he might be the groundskeeper with insider info, was like, "Buddy, if you've moved him, spill the beans, and I'll handle from there." Jesus dropped the bomb with a simple, "Mary." She whipped around and was all, "Rabboni!" (which is teacher talk for "You're the man!"). Jesus was like, "Ease up on the hug, I've got a reunion in the clouds to attend to. But go tell my bros I'm heading up to the big family reunion."

Ghost Protocol with the Disciples

That evening, while the disciples were holed up playing 'Scared of the Jews', Jesus ghosted in and was like, "Peace out, peeps." He showed them his battle scars, and they went from zero to hero, joy maxed out. Jesus hit them again with, "Peace, dudes. Just like the Big Guy sent me, I'm tagging you in." He then gave them a breath of fresh air, "Catch the Holy Spirit. Forgiveness is in your hands now."

Doubting Thomas Crashes the Party

Thomas was MIA during Jesus's cameo, so when the crew was like, "We've seen the boss!" he was all, "Pics or it didn't happen. Need to feel the scars to believe." Fast forward a week, Jesus crashed their hideout again, doors locked and all, and was straight-up like, "Peace, again." To Thomas, he was like, "CSI time, check the evidence. Stop the doubt, start the belief." Thomas was shook, "My Lord and my God!" Jesus, dropping wisdom, "You believe 'cause you've seen. Bless up to those who believe without the receipts."

Beachside Comeback Tour

Next up, Jesus decided to crash the disciples' fishing trip by the Sea of Tiberias. It was like a surprise encore at their fave spot: Peter, Thomas (aka "Twin"), Nathanael (the Cana guy), the Zebedee bros, and a couple more of the squad were all chilling. Peter was like, "Yo, I'm hitting the waves for some fish." The crew was like, "Count us in." They spent the whole night out there, but their nets were as empty as a concert hall during soundcheck. At dawn, Jesus was chilling on the beach, but they didn't clock it was him.

He shouted, "Yo, any luck catching dinner?" "Nada," they hollered back. Jesus was like, "Try the right side of the boat, and you'll hit the jackpot." Boom! The net almost broke with the amount of fish. The beloved disciple had his lightbulb moment, "It's the Boss!" Peter, hearing it's Jesus, basically does a cannonball into the sea to get to him ASAP. Landing on shore, they found Jesus had started a BBQ, fish grilling, bread ready to serve. "Bring some of those fish you just caught," Jesus said. Peter hauled the net in, packed with 153 big ones, and yet, the net's still not ripped. Jesus was like, "Breakfast's ready!" No one played the "Who are you?" game; they knew it was the Lord. Jesus played chef, serving up bread and fish. This breakfast gig was Jesus' third surprise appearance post-resurrection.

Peter's Comeback

Post-breakfast, Jesus got real with Peter. "Simon, son of John, you into me more than these?" "Yeah, Lord, you know I'm your fan," Peter said. "Look after my lambs," Jesus hit back. He hit repeat twice more on the love question, upgrading to "Take care of my sheep." By the third ask, Peter's feeling the pinch, "Lord, you know everything; you got this, I'm all in." Jesus got deep, hinting at Peter's future with, "When you're old, you'll be led where you'd rather not." It was a sneak peek at how Peter would later rock the stage for God. Wrapping it up, Jesus laid down the challenge, "Follow me."

Squashing the Fake News

So Peter flips around and spots the fave disciple tailing them, the same bro who was chilling close to Jesus at dinner and was like, "Yo, Jesus, who's gonna double-cross you?" Catching sight of him, Peter's like, "Yo, Jesus, what's the deal with him?" Jesus hits back, "If I want him to stick around till I drop back in, what's it to you? You do you and follow me." This sparked a wild rumor among the squad that this disciple wouldn't kick the bucket. But Jesus didn't exactly say he wouldn't bite the dust; he was more like, "If I want him to chill until I make my grand entrance again, how's that your biz?"

ACTS

Chillin' for the Spirit

Jesus was like, "Stick around in Jerusalem, folks. You've heard me talk about the big surprise from Dad. John got you all wet with water, but you're about to get a shower of the Holy Spirit." The crew got curious, "Hey, are you going to make Israel the top dog again now?" Jesus was like, "Hold up, the timing's up to Dad. But here's what's up: You'll get a power boost from the Holy Spirit and spread the word about me from here to the ends of the earth."

Exit Stage Up

After dropping that truth, Jesus took an elevator to the clouds right in front of them. While they were still staring, slack-jawed, into the sky, a couple of heaven's messengers popped up and said, "Why are you all standing around looking at the sky? Jesus will come back just like you saw him go."

Back to Base

So they hit the road back to Jerusalem, gathered in the upper room, with the whole gang, the women, Jesus' mom, and his brothers. Everyone was in sync, constantly hitting up prayer together.

Looking for Judas' Replacement

Peter stood up among the believers (about 120 people were there) and said, "Guys, we saw it coming. Judas left us and went down in history. Now we need someone else to take his spot." They wanted someone who'd been with Jesus all along, from his baptism to his ascension. They nominated two dudes: Joseph (also known as Barsabbas or Justus) and Matthias. After a quick convo with the Almighty, "Lord, you know everyone inside out. Who's the right pick?" They cast lots, and Matthias got the role, joining the apostle squad.

Pentecost Party Goes Viral

When Pentecost hit, the squad was all chilling in one spot. Suddenly, the ultimate soundwave from the sky filled the whole crib, and they spotted what looked like fire emojis landing on each of them. Boom! They were all filled with the Holy Spirit and started chatting in all sorts of languages, as the Spirit hit the play button on them. Now, Jerusalem was hosting a diverse crowd, devout peeps from every corner of the globe. When this heavenly playlist started, a crowd gathered, totally shook because everyone heard their own jams being played. They were like, "Aren't these all local boys? How's every one of us vibing in our mother tongue? Parthians, Medes, you name it - they're all hearing the greatest hits of God in their own lingo." The crowd was all hyped and confused, wondering, "What's up with this?" While a few party poopers were like, "They're just wasted."

Peter Grabs the Mic

Peter, rolling deep with the Eleven, stood up, amplified his voice, and was like, "Listen up, peeps of Jerusalem, lend me your ears. These folks aren't wasted; it's barely breakfast time! Nah, this is straight out of the prophet Joel's mixtape:

1 'In the endgame days, God says, I'll stream my Spirit on everyone; your kids will drop truth bombs, your youngins will see beyond, and your oldies will dream big. I'll even have my servants, guys and gals, broadcasting live with prophecies.
2 The sky will turn into a special effects show, and down here will be lit with miracles: blood, fire, smoke signals.

3 The sun will hit snooze, and the moon will turn bloodshot before the ultimate day of the Lord crashes the scene.
4 And everyone who hits up the Lord's hotline will be saved.'

Listen here, folks: Jesus from Nazareth, God's own endorsement with blockbuster miracles and wonders, you all know the drill. Even though you handed him over on a silver platter to be taken out, according to the grand script and God's preview, God hit the rewind on his death, 'cause death couldn't pin him down. David even dropped some bars about him:

1 I always see the Lord in my corner, so I'm steady.
2 That's why I'm all joy, and I'm resting easy,
3 'Cause you won't ghost me down under, nor let your VIP see decay.
4 You've shown me the path to life; your presence is my VIP pass to joy.'

So, fam, David's still resting in his grave to this day, but he saw the future and prophesied about the resurrection of the Messiah - that he wouldn't be ghosted in Hades nor his body hit decay. God has lifted Jesus up - we're all eyewitnesses. He's now the VIP at God's right hand, dropping the Holy Spirit hit tracks you're all experiencing. David wasn't talking about hitting the skies; he said, 'God told my Lord to chill at His right hand until the beat drops on his enemies.'

So, let it be known all over Israel that God has crowned this Jesus, whom you nailed, as both Lord and the ultimate DJ."

Time to Hit the Reset Button

When the crowd caught wind of Peter's mic drop, they felt a gut punch and were like, "Yo, bros, what's our next move?" Peter was all, "It's time for a fresh start! Get baptized, every single one of you, in the vibe of Jesus Christ for a clean slate, and snag that Holy Spirit bonus. This dope offer isn't just for you, but for your squad and even those peeps way out there, as many as the Big Boss calls."

Peter kept at it, laying down some serious truth, urging them, "Dodge this busted generation!" And just like that, about three thou joined the fam that very day.

#SquadGoals: Early Church Edition

They were all about that apostle's teaching, hanging out, breaking bread, and vibing in prayer. Awe was the daily mood because the apostles were pulling off legit wonders left and right. The believers were tight, sharing everything. They'd sell stuff and spread the wealth, making sure nobody was left wanting. Daily meet-ups in the temple, home-cooked meals with pure joy and legit hearts, all while giving props to God. And guess what? Their circle kept getting bigger every single day with peeps getting saved.

Epic Comeback of a Lame Dude

Peter and John were temple-bound for prayer time when they bumped into a guy who'd been benched since birth. Parked daily at the temple's MVP entrance for some spare change, he hit up Peter and John for some cash. Peter was like, "Eyeballs here, buddy." Expecting some coin, the guy got the shock of his life when Peter dropped, "I'm broke, but here's what I got: In the name of Jesus Christ the Nazarene, take a hike!" Grabbing his hand, Peter got him on his feet, and boom! The guy's legs went from zero to hero.

He was jumping, stepping, and shouting God's praises, turning the temple entrance into his personal hype zone. Everyone recognized him as the usual beggar and were mind-blown by his glow-up.

Street Preaching Hits Different

Clinging to Peter and John, the man became the center of a massive flash mob in Solomon's Colonnade. Peter seized the moment: "Folks, why the dropped jaws? You think we got special powers? Nah. It's all God, who jazzed up Jesus, the one you dissed and handed over. You chose a killer over the Life Giver, but God wasn't having it and brought Jesus back. This dude standing before you is living proof, all thanks to faith in Jesus' name." "Look, I get it. You and your leaders were clueless. But God turned your mess into His masterpiece, just as He promised. Time to turn things around, wipe the slate clean, and get ready for the ultimate refresh, waiting for Jesus to hit the scene again. Moses, all the prophets, they all hinted at this. You're the heirs of those promises made to Abraham. Jesus came first to you guys to turn your lives from cursed to blessed."

Wrap-Up and Call to Action

This call to action is your invite to join the epic story unfolding since day one. The vibe check here is clear: It's about transformation, unity, and stepping into a new day with the squad, ready to change the world, one act of kindness and bold move of faith at a time.

The Unplanned Sleepover

So, Peter and John were vibing with the crowd, dropping truth bombs about Jesus and the whole living-again gig. This ruffled some feathers among the temple bigwigs and the Sadducee squad, who weren't fans of the resurrection talk. They decided to crash the party, scooping up Peter and John for an impromptu sleepover in the slammer. It was already past curfew, anyway. But plot twist: their words already planted seeds, and the believer count hit a whopping five thousand dudes.

Facing the Music: Peter and John vs. The Big Shots

The next scene opens with Jerusalem's who's who - rulers, elders, you name it - all gathered, starring Annas the VIP priest, Caiaphas, and the family. They put Peter and John center stage for a pop quiz: "How'd you pull off that miracle, huh? Whose crew are you repping?" Fueled by some Holy Spirit energy, Peter goes, "Listen up, leaders and elders! If we're on trial for a good deed, let's get one thing straight: it's all because of Jesus

Christ from Nazareth. Yep, the one you benched and God MVP'ed. He's the real game-changer, the cornerstone you missed. And guess what? He's the only ticket to salvation. No one else on the roster."

Mic Drop Moments

The council couldn't believe their ears. Peter and John, just regular dudes, were schooling them with confidence straight out of a Jesus seminar. And with the healed guy as their Exhibit A, the big shots were speechless. They hit the pause button, stepping into their huddle zone, whispering, "Now what? This miracle's no secret; it's Jerusalem's latest buzz. We can't pretend it didn't happen." Their genius plan? A stern "Don't you dare" talk about Jesus. But Peter and John were like, "We'll let you decide what's right in God's eyes—to listen to you or Him. But for us, there's no mute button on what we've seen and heard.". After a bit more huffing and puffing, they let them go, cornered by public opinion praising God for the mind-blowing miracle on a dude over forty.

Rally Cry for Courage

Back with their crew, Peter and John spilled everything. The squad's response? A power-up prayer to the Big Boss: "Lord, Creator of all, You called the shots through David, hinting at this showdown. You've got Herod, Pilate, and everyone else playing their part in Your epic plot. Now, with threats looming, crank up our boldness dial. Unleash healing, signs, and wonders in Jesus' name, would You?"

Prayer so powerful, their meeting spot shook. They were all supercharged with the Holy Spirit, ready to preach with zero chill.

Sharing is Caring Squad Goals

The whole crew of believers was vibing on the same wavelength, not even tripping about who owned what. They were all about that communal life, sharing everything. The apostles were out there, flexing their God-powered muscles, giving shoutouts to Jesus' comeback story, and everybody was feeling the love. Nobody was hitting up the group chat asking for help 'cause everyone was looking out for each other. Big props to Barnabas, the hype man, who sold his field and dropped the cash at the apostles' kicks as a major move.

Ghosted by Greed: Ananias and Sapphira's Epic Fail

Then there's this duo, Ananias and Sapphira, who thought they could play it slick by holding back some cash after selling their spot. Peter's like, "Bro, why you gotta play the Holy Spirit like that?" Spoiler: Ananias hits the floor, dead. Hours later, Sapphira walks in, clueless, and doubles down on the lie. Peter's basically, "Did you really think you could pull a fast one on God?" Boom, she's down for the count too. Talk about a reality check that had everyone shook.

Apostles Dropping Miracles Like It's Hot

The apostles were out there in Solomon's Colonnade, making waves with all kinds of miraculous mic drops. Even though not everyone dared to join their squad, folks couldn't help but respect their game. The believer count was skyrocketing, with peeps bringing the sick to just catch Peter's shadow. And it wasn't just locals; peeps were rolling in from the burbs, all getting their heal on.

Jailbreak: Angel Edition

Just when the apostles were hitting their stride, the high priest and his Sadducee friends got all jelly and threw them in the slammer. But plot twist: an angel pops the cell doors at night and is all like, "Hit the temple, keep the truth bombs coming." So, they're back at it by dawn, unfazed.

Round Two: Apostles vs. The Man

The high priest is all, "Round up the apostles," but when the squad hits the jail, it's a ghost scene. Then, plot twist: they're found chilling in the temple, teaching. Brought back without a fuss (because let's be real, nobody wanted that stoning drama), they're standing trial again. High priest goes, "Didn't we hit the mute button on you guys?" And Peter's like, "Sorry, not sorry, we answer to a higher call." They drop the mic saying Jesus is the real MVP, and they, along with the Holy Spirit, are here to spill that tea.

Gamaliel Drops Some Wisdom

When the squad heard the apostles' comeback, they were ready to throw hands, real talk. But then Gamaliel, this OG Pharisee and law professor everyone respected, was like, "Yo, timeout!" After sending the apostles out, he schooled everyone, "Fellas, let's chill for a sec. Remember Theudas? Dude thought he was the bomb, but got KO'd and his crew fizzled. And that Judas guy? Same story. Here's the thing—if these apostle dudes are just blowing smoke, they'll crash and burn on their own. But if they're on a God-level mission, we're basically trying to punch the sky. Bad idea." They took his advice, whipped the apostles (literally), told them to zip it about Jesus, and let them go. The apostles left high-fiving, proud to get dissed for the Big J. They kept on spreading the Jesus vibe, non-stop, everywhere.

The Magnificent Seven

As the follower count was blowing up, the Greek-speaking bros were beefing with the Hebrew crew 'cause their widows were getting the cold shoulder at mealtime. The Twelve were like, "We can't be all up in the kitchen and miss out on dropping truth bombs. Let's get seven stand-up guys, loaded with spirit and smarts, to handle the grind." Everyone was down with that. They picked Stephen and the gang, had a little prayer and hand-laying ceremony, and bam, problem solved. This leveled up the word-spreading game big time, even got a bunch of priests on board.

Stephen, the Powerhouse

Then there's Stephen, dude was lit with grace and power, doing mind-blowing stuff left and right. But some synagogue guys got all salty and tried to throw down in a debate. Spoiler: They got wrecked. Not ones to take an L gracefully, they went full soap opera, hiring some guys to trash talk Stephen, saying he dissed Moses and God. They got the crowd and the big shots riled up, dragged Stephen to court, and even brought in some fake news crew to say Stephen was talking smack about the temple and Moses. Everyone in court couldn't help but notice Stephen's face was glowing like he just swiped right on an angel.

"Yo, top dog," Stephen started, "lemme lay it down. The God of all the bling appeared to Abraham back in the day, telling him to hit the road to a VIP zone He'd show off later. Fast forward, Abraham's fam got the short end in Egypt, but God's plan was cooking. He turned Joseph from a bros' bazaar bargain into Egypt's big boss. Famine hit, and Jacob's squad ran to Egypt, setting the stage for the next episode.

The fam drama hit peak soap opera when Joseph's bros, green

with envy, sold him off. But plot twist: God was with him, flipping the script from pit to palace. Joseph, now Pharaoh's right-hand man, saved the day during a gnarly famine, reuniting with his fam in a tear-jerker reveal. They all moved to Egypt, turning a family reunion into an epic saga ending in Shechem.

When the Egyptian sequel started, Moses entered the scene, a total heart-stealer since birth. Raised in Pharaoh's crib, he was all set for an Egyptian Cribs episode. But at 40, Moses had his 'who am I?' moment, defending his kin and bouncing to Midian as a fugitive dad. Fast forward another 40, and God's like, 'Moses, you're up!' with a burning bush cameo, sending him to lead the ultimate escape.

Desert Deeds and Divine Deliverance

Moses, once ghosted by his own, became the comeback kid with God's backing, showcasing plagues and parting seas, all while rocking the wilderness for 40 years. So, Stephen's like, 'You see the pattern? Big G's always rolling out the red carpet in unexpected ways, and yet folks keep missing the premiere.'" Stephen's sermon wasn't just history 101; it was a wake-up call, reminding them that the divine plot twists in their story were far from over, and they were on the verge of missing the latest reveal.

When Israel Ghosted God

"So, this Moses dude was like, 'Yo, peeps, God's gonna drop a prophet like me among you.' But our squad was playing hard to get, dissing Moses and getting all nostalgic for Egypt. They went full arts and crafts, whipping up a golden calf and throwing a party for something they made. God was like, 'Fine, you wanna star gaze and party with Moloch? Pack your bags for Babylon.'

God's OG Tent Meeting

"Our peeps had this lit tabernacle, per God's DIY manual to Moses. It was all mobile until David was like, 'Let's settle down.' Solomon built a crib for God, but God's like, 'I'm too big for your tiny houses. I made the universe, remember?'

"Y'all, why you always gotta be so stubborn? You're like that one friend who won't listen. Your ancestors were pro at giving prophets a hard time, even offing the ones hinting about the MVP, Jesus. And here you are, standing on their not-so-holy ground.

Stephen Drops the Mic

"While Stephen's dropping truth bombs, the crowd's losing it, grinding their teeth like they skipped dental day. But Stephen, catching a heavenly vision, is all, 'Guys, check it out! Jesus is chilling at God's right hand!' Total mic drop, but instead of applause, he gets an all-access pass to Rock City.

Saul, the Party Crasher

"Enter Saul, giving thumbs up to Stephen's stoning. It kicked off a mega purge against the church crew, scattering them like confetti. Saul turned into the church's nightmare, playing hide and seek with believers, except the losers got a one-way ticket to prison.

Philip Turns Samaria Into Party Central

"While the church folks were getting the boot, Philip hit up Samaria, turning water into wine with his preachin' and miracle mixin'. Demons were hitting high notes as they bailed, and the lame were breaking into dance moves. Samaria was popping, all thanks to Philip's Jesus jams."

Simon's Epic Fail and the Holy Hustle

Simon was vibin' hard when he saw the Holy Spirit's guest list was VIP only through the apostles' squad. So, he tried to slide some silver their way, thinking he could buy his way into the spiritual elite club. Peter was like, "Bro, keep your cash; you can't Venmo your way to God's gifts. Heart check time – you're off-key and tangled in some bad vibes." Simon, all panicked, was like, "Yo, hit me up with a prayer so I don't end up cursed."
After droppin' truth bombs and spreading the good news all the way back to J-town, they were giving shoutouts to God through Samaritan streets.

Desert Road Vibes and the Ethiopian Trendsetter

Then there's Philip getting a divine DM: "Hit the desert highway." He bumps into this Ethiopian finance guru – a queen's right-hand man, binge-reading Isaiah while cruisin'. Philip hustles over and is like, "Getting anything from that read?" The official's like, "How can I? It's like decoding my ex's texts without the emojis."
They're rolling and hit this spot where there's water. The official's like, "Hold up, why not get baptized right here?" No sooner said than done, they're

both in the water faster than you can say "splash." Post-baptism, Philip pulls a Houdini, and the official keeps cruising, probably blasting his victory playlist.

Philip then pops up in Azotus, still on his mission, spreading the Jesus vibe from town to town.

Saul's Wild Ride to Team Jesus

So Saul was on his way, all fired up to drag some Jesus fans back to the big city, when BAM! God's spotlight hits him hard. Down he goes, and he's like, "Who's calling me out?" Boom, it's Jesus on the line, telling him he's playing for the wrong team. Saul's shook, blind, and on a forced fast for three days.

Ananias Dials Down the Drama

God pings Ananias, like, "Yo, I've got a mission for you." Ananias is all, "Wait, THAT Saul?" But God's got plans. Ananias hits up Saul, gives him the world's most epic eye-opening, and bam, Saul's baptized, munching on some grub, and ready to roll. Saul's now hanging with the disciples, flipping his script big time. He's out there, "Jesus is the real deal," and everyone's mind is blown. They're like, "Isn't this the guy?" But Saul's got his debate game on point, proving Jesus is the MVP.

Dorcas Gets a Second Season

In Joppa, there's this disciple, Tabitha, aka Dorcas, who's basically a charity superstar. But plot twist, she checks out. The crew, in tears, shows Peter all the Etsy-level crafts she made. Peter, solo in the room, hits her with a "Wakey wakey," and bam, she's back! News spreads like wildfire, and Peter's crashing with Simon, the leather king.

Cornelius's Holy DM

Over in Caesarea, Cornelius, a big-deal Roman officer with a heart of gold, gets a divine DM: "Hey, Cornelius, your good vibes have reached HQ. Fetch Peter from Joppa." Cornelius, being the go-getter he is, sends his squad to Joppa (yeah, Joppa). Meanwhile, Peter's rooftop chilling, gets the munchies, and bam, falls into a foodie fever dream. God's like, "Eat up, Pete!" Peter's all, "Nah, that's not on my diet plan, God." God's reply: "What I've cleaned, you can't call dirty." This goes down three times, just to make sure Peter gets the memo.

Peter and Cornelius: The Collab

Peter, now clued in by the Spirit, meets Cornelius's welcoming committee. They hit the road, and Cornelius rolls out the red carpet, ready to fanboy over Peter. Peter, keeping it real, is like, "Chill, man, I'm human just like you." He steps in, sees a packed house, and drops, "God's opened my eyes. No one's off-limits now."

Cornelius Spills the Tea

Cornelius is all, "I was just chilling, praying, when this shiny dude shows up saying, 'God's got your back.' Told me to hit you up, Peter." Peter's like, "Cool, cool, cool. God's message is for everyone. Let's hear it." And that sets the stage for one epic meetup, breaking all the old-school rules.

Breaking News: God's VIP List is Open to Everyone

Peter steps up and drops this truth bomb: "Listen up, peeps, God isn't playing favorites. It doesn't matter where you're from; if you're about that respect and doing good, you're in. God's peace deal? It's through Jesus Christ, who's boss of all. You've heard the stories, how Jesus went superhero mode in Judea, sprinkling that Holy Spirit spice and power, doing good, and ghostbusting because God had his back. Despite his heroics, some folks played the ultimate villain and hung him up to dry. But plot twist: God's like 'Not today' and brings him back on day three. We had dinner with resurrected Jesus; we're not kidding. He told us to hit the streets and spill the tea that he's the real deal, the judge of living and dead, and everyone who's into him gets a sin clean-up."

Gentiles Get the Holy Spirit Mic Drop

While Peter's still mic-dropping truths, the Holy Spirit crashes the party on the Gentiles, leaving the Jewish believers shook because the Holy Spirit playlist is now playing on Gentile Spotify too. Peter's like, "Any reason these folks can't take the plunge and get baptized? They're as Holy Spirit remix as we are." Boom, water everywhere, and they're baptized in Jesus' name. Sleepover invitations were handed out right after.

Peter's Food Fight Vision Gets Real

Back in Jerusalem, Peter's catching heat for crashing Gentile parties. He's all, "Let me walk you through my vision quest: I'm hangry in Joppa, and God's like, 'Eat up, Pete.' I'm like, 'No way, God, I'm a clean eater.' God hits back, 'Don't @ me with that impure talk.' This goes down three times. Then these three Caesarea dudes show up, Holy Spirit's like, 'Go with the flow, Pete.' So, we roll up to Cornelius's crib, and he's like, 'An angel told me you'd drop some salvation truth bombs.' The second I start talking, the Holy Spirit shows up like it's Pentecost 2.0. Remember how Jesus said we'd get the Holy Spirit shower? That's what went down, and who am I to ghost God's invite?" Silence, then applause. Everyone hits mute, processes the info, and then it's all applause in heaven's direction. They're like, "Wow, God's handing out life passes to the Gentiles too."

Antioch's Lit Mixtape Drop

So, after Stephen's epic exit, his squad got scattered all the way to Phoenicia, Cyprus, and Antioch, sticking to their Jewish roots until some brave souls from Cyprus and Cyrene hit up Antioch. They started spitting bars about Lord Jesus to the Greeks, and it was straight fire! The Lord's vibe was so strong that a massive crowd turned Team Jesus. News hit the Jerusalem squad, and they sent Barnabas, the OG encourager, to check it out. Dude was vibing with the grace he saw, hyping everyone to stay loyal to the Lord. He was such a legit guy, full of Spirit and faith, that he amped up the follower count big time.

Barnabas then hit up Tarsus to find Saul. Together, they turned Antioch into a year-long Jesus fest, and that's where the term "Christians" first dropped.

Food Drive Vibes

Some prophets rolled into Antioch from Jerusalem. Agabus, one of them, dropped a prophecy about a massive famine hitting the Roman scene, which happened when Claudius was the big boss. The disciples, being the cool cats they are, decided to send some love and support to the fam in Judea, rolling deep with Barnabas and Saul to deliver the goods.

James Checks Out, Peter Checks In (to Jail)

King Herod was on a roll, taking a swing at the church crew. He went all out and offed James, John's bro, which got the crowd hyping. Riding that wave, he snagged Peter too. But the church wasn't having it; they went ham with prayers for Peter.

Epic Jailbreak

The night before Peter's show trial, he's snoozing between guards, chained up, when suddenly, an angel pops up, lights up the cell, and hits Peter with the wake-up call. Chains? Dropped. "Suit up and follow me," the angel said. They ghost past guards, hit the city streets, and poof – the angel dips. Peter's mind is blown. He realizes it's all legit and heads to Mary's house, where the prayer squad's at. He hits up the outer gate, and Rhoda, the help, recognizes his voice. She's so hyped she leaves him hanging at the door and bolts in to spread the news. They think she's lost it, suggesting it's his guardian angel or something. But Peter keeps knocking. When they finally check, their jaws hit the floor. Peter's like, "Shh, let me spill." He tells them the whole angelic breakout story and is like, "Make sure James and the crew get the memo." Then he bounces to lay low. Meanwhile, Herod's losing his marbles, no sign of Peter. He grills the guards and, not one for loose ends, has them taken out. Then, he peaces out to Caesarea to chill.

Herod's Epic Fail

Herod was beefing hard with Tyre and Sidon. They smoothed things over with his buddy Blastus and were like, "Let's chill, we need your snacks." Herod, feeling himself in his bling-bling robe, gave a TED Talk that had the crowd hyping him up as a god. God wasn't having any of that glory-stealing, so he sent an angel to give Herod a wormy exit offstage. RIP, dude.

Cyprus Road Trip

Guided by the Spirit, they dipped to Seleucia then sailed to Cyprus, dropping truth bombs in synagogues with John as their roadie. They bumped into a magician Bar-Jesus, who was throwing shade with Sergius Paulus, a brainy official. But Saul, also rocking the stage name Paul, filled with the Holy Spirit, called out Bar-Jesus's nonsense, and boom, temporary blindness! Sergius Paulus was shook and became a believer, mind blown by God's teaching.

Leaving Cyprus, the crew landed in Perga (John bailed back to Jerusalem). Next stop: Pisidian Antioch. After chilling in the synagogue, Paul stood up, signaling it was storytime. He took them on a historical ride from Egypt to King David, leading to Jesus, the main event. Despite the hometown crowd rejecting Jesus and hitting him with the ultimate cancel, God had the last word, bringing Jesus back from the dead. Paul was all, "Yo, this salvation jam is for everyone!" He warned them not to sleep on this like their ancestors. As they bounced, the crowd begged for an encore for next Sabbath.

Gentile Encore

Next Sabbath was lit! Almost everyone in town showed up. The local Jews were salty, throwing shade at Paul. But Paul and Barnabas clapped back, "We offered you the VIP pass to eternal life, but you ghosted. We're taking this show on the road to the Gentiles." The Gentiles were all about that life, celebrating and spreading the word. Despite getting kicked out by the haters, Paul and Barnabas left them on read, dusting off their kicks and heading to Iconium, with the squad staying hyped and Holy Spirit-filled.

Iconium's Buzz and Fuzz

In Iconium, Paul and Barnabas dropped some truth bombs in the synagogue, lighting up the faith fuse for both Team Jesus and Team Tradition. But, plot twist, the non-believers started a smear campaign, making things spicy for our bros. Yet, they hung tight, throwing down miraculous mic drops until the city split like a bad breakup. Facing a stoning RSVP, they ghosted to Lystra and Derbe, keeping the gospel playlist on shuffle. Lystra was wildin' when a never-walked-before dude got up dancing post-Paul pep talk. The crowd lost it, fan-girling over Paul and Barnabas as if they just landed from Olympus. They were all, "Zeus and Hermes in the house!" Local Zeus fandom prepped a BBQ in their honor. Our humble apostles weren't feeling the god vibes, though. They crashed the party, ripping their robes like, "Yo, we're just regular dudes urging you to vibe with the real MVP, the Creator!" Despite their efforts, the fanfare nearly turned into a misguided worship fest.

Plot Twist: Stoned but Not Gone

Some haters from Antioch and Iconium slid into Lystra, stirring the pot till Paul was stoned and left for dead. But surprise – after a quick power nap, he was back on his feet, making a comeback tour to Derbe with Barnabas. After turning Derbe upside down with the good news and netting a bunch of new followers, they circled back, hyping up the believers. They were all about setting up the squad with local leaders before hitting the road again, spreading the "tough love equals kingdom keys" message.

The Big Debate in Antioch

Back in Antioch, a theological throwdown kicked off when some Judea dudes rolled up claiming, "No snip, no salvation." Paul and Barnabas entered the chat, leading to a Jerusalem-bound road trip to settle the beef. They made stops, sharing the Gentile glow-up stories, and sparking joy all the way to the big church family meet-up in Jerusalem. But then, Pharisee gang dropped a, "But actually, Moses though?" bomb, stirring the pot on the whole Gentiles needing to jump through the old-school hoops debate. The squad and the OGs gathered to hash out the big question: "To snip or not to snip for the Gentile crew?" After some spicy debate, Peter stepped up like, "Yo, remember how the Big Guy upstairs didn't play favorites and showered the non-Jews with Holy Spirit awesomeness just like us? Why we trying to make them jump through hoops we couldn't even handle?" Silence. Then Paul and Barnabas took the mic, spilling the tea on all the epic God-powered stuff they witnessed among the non-Jews.

James Drops the Mic

After the duo's tales, James chimed in, "Listen up, fam. God's been scouting the Gentiles to join the squad from day one. So, let's not trip them up. Just slide into their DMs with a 'No to idols, keep it classy, and chill on the blood menu' message." They all nodded, 'Aight, cool,' and penned a peace-out letter to the Gentile peeps, rolling with Barnabas and Paul to drop the good news.

Antioch Vibes and Goodbyes

Back in Antioch, the crew threw a reading party for the letter. Instant mood booster. Judas and Silas, doubling as hype men, pumped up the crowd with some hearty talks. After a bit, they peaced out back to Jerusalem, but Paul and Barnabas stuck around, dropping more truth bombs and beats about the Lord.

Bromance on the Rocks

Then Paul's like, "Road trip round 2?" But when Barnabas wanted to bring John Mark, the sequel vibes turned sour. They split over creative differences – Barnabas and Mark hitting up Cyprus, while Paul snagged Silas for the next chapter, blessed by the homies for whatever's next. And off they went, fortifying the fam across Syria and Cilicia.

Paul's Squad Picks Timothy

In Derbe and Lystra, Paul found Timothy, a young gun whose mom was all in with the faith, but his dad was a Greek. The local fam gave Timothy big props. Paul, wanting Timothy on the team, got him circumcised to keep the local Jews chill since they knew his dad was a Greek. Rolling through the towns, they dropped the Jerusalem council's mixtape for the peeps to vibe with. The churches got hyped in faith and their numbers blew up daily.

Euro Trip for Jesus

The crew hit Phrygia and Galatia but got ghosted by the Holy Spirit on hitting up Asia. Tried to roll into Bithynia, but the Spirit was like "Nah." So they skirted Mysia, hit Troas, and Paul had this wild dream about a Macedonian dude begging, "Yo, hop over here and help us out!" Taking it as a divine DM, they booked it to Macedonia to spread the good news.

Lydia Vibes with the Message

Landing in Philippi, they chilled there for a bit. On Sabbath, they found a prayer spot by the river, talked to the women there, and Lydia, a purple cloth boss from Thyatira, was all ears. God tuned her heart to Paul's track, she got baptized with her crew, then invited the gang over, "If you think I'm legit, crash at my place." And they did.

Paul and Silas Jailhouse Rock

On their way to pray, they met a slave girl, a psychic making bank for her owners. She kept shouting, "These dudes are dropping the ultimate salvation guide!" Paul, totally over it, cast out her spirit in Jesus' name. Her owners, seeing their cash flow cut, dragged Paul and Silas to the main square, got them beaten and tossed in jail, locked tight. Midnight hits, and Paul and Silas were throwing a praise party in jail, with inmates tuning in. Earthquake! Doors flung open, chains dropped. The jailer, thinking he lost his prisoners, almost clocked out for good until Paul was like, "Chill, we're all here!" Blown away, the jailer's like, "Fellas, how do I hit save on my soul?" "Trust in Jesus," they said, and boom, his whole house gets baptized, throws a feast, and celebrates their new faith family.

When the Cops Say "My Bad"

At the crack of dawn, the big wigs sent the fuzz with a message, "Yo, let those dudes go." The officers were like, "The bosses wanna set you free. So, like, you can hit the road in peace, yeah?" But Paul was having none of it. "Nah, they embarrassed us in public, didn't even give us a trial, and we're Roman citizens! They think they can just shoo us away quietly? As if! They gotta come and walk us out themselves." The cops relayed this back, and hearing Paul and Silas were Roman, the magistrates nearly peed their pants. They came, all sweet talk and apologies, walked them out, and were like, "Please leave our city." After bouncing from the slammer, they hit up Lydia's place, hyped up the crew, and then dipped.

Thessalonica Gets Lit

Next stop: Thessalonica. Paul hit the local synagogue, spending three Sabbaths dropping truth bombs from the Scriptures, showing that the Messiah had to get roughed up and come back from the dead. He's like, "This Jesus I'm talking about? He's the real deal." A bunch of them were vibing with Paul and Silas, including a solid crew of woke Greeks and some influencer women.

Thessalonica Loses Its Chill

But the local Jews weren't having it. They got a posse of troublemakers, stirred up chaos, and went hard at Jason's place looking for Paul and Silas to drag them into drama. Not finding them, they grabbed Jason and some homies instead, hauled them to the city bigwigs yelling, "These guys are flipping the world upside down, and now they're causing mayhem here! Jason's hiding them, and they're all dissing Caesar, claiming there's another king named Jesus." This got everyone all riled up. After squeezing some hush money out of Jason and the gang, they let them go.

Berean Vibes

Under cover of night, the squad sent Paul and Silas off to Berea. They hit the synagogue and found the locals were total class acts, eagerly checking the Scriptures every day to see if Paul was legit. Loads of them believed, including some top-tier Greek ladies and dudes. But when the Thessalonica Twitter trolls caught wind Paul was preaching in Berea, they came down to start beef. The Berean bros quickly sent Paul to the coast, but Silas and Timothy hung back.

Paul's Athens Adventure

Chillin' in Athens, Paul was majorly bummed seeing all the idol swag everywhere. He got into it with both the synagogue crowd and the market folks. Even had a rap battle with some Epicurean and Stoic philosophers who were like, "Who's this wannabe?" or "Sounds like he's peddling some foreign gods." They were curious about his Jesus and resurrection talk, so they invited him to the Areopagus for a TED Talk, asking, "What's this fresh spiel you're dropping? You've got our ears, spill the tea." Basically, Athens was the OG Reddit, with everyone always on the lookout for the next big thing.

Paul's Epic Mic Drop in Athens

So, Paul's standing in the middle of Athens' hippest debate club, the Areopagus, and goes, "Yo, Athenians! I can't help but notice y'all are super into your spiritual vibes. Strolling around, I even spotted an altar that's like 'To the DMs of an Unknown God.' Well, guess what? I'm here to spill the tea on this mystery deity you've been unknowingly hearting. This God, the OG Creator who did the whole universe and everything in it, doesn't crash at temples you've crafted or need anything from us; He's the one giving us life, breath, and all the goodies. He made us all from one fam to chill across the globe, hoping we'd go seeking Him, and, spoiler alert, He's not playing hide and seek. Like, we're literally living in His vibe. Even some of your own hype poets have been like, 'We're His kids.' So, if we're God's fam, let's not think the Divine is some DIY project made of gold or stone. Time's up on ignoring this stuff. God's calling for a cosmic reset from everyone, everywhere. He's got Judgment Day on the calendar, with this dude He's handpicked, and He's given us the receipts by bringing Him back from the dead." The crowd's reaction was a mixtape - some LOLed at him, but others were like, "We gotta slide into your DMs about this later." So, Paul peaced out, but not before snagging a few new followers like Dionysius, Damaris, and some cool cats.

Paul Hits Up Corinth

Next, Paul rolls into Corinth, links up with Aquila and Priscilla (because #TentMakersUnite), and hits the local synagogue to drop some truth bombs every Sabbath. When Silas and Timothy show up, Paul goes full throttle, convincing peeps that Jesus is the real MVP. But when some start throwing shade, Paul's like, "Your bad, not mine. I'm outie to the Gentiles." He then dips next door to keep preaching, with even the synagogue's head honcho and his squad getting baptized. God hits Paul up in a dream: "Don't sweat it, keep talking. I've got your back, and I've got a squad in this city." So, Paul camps out for a hot minute, schooling them on the word.

The local Jews try to cancel Paul, dragging him to court. Gallio, the judge, is like, "This is a family matter. Sort it out yourselves." So, they rough up Sosthenes (new synagogue boss), but Gallio couldn't care less.

Paul's Farewell Tour

Paul, now rocking a fresh shave for a vow, waves goodbye to the Corinth crew, and with Priscilla and Aquila, sets sail. He makes a pit stop in Ephesus, throws down some more wisdom, but dips out despite the encore requests, "BRB, if the Big Guy says so." Hits up Jerusalem, then Antioch, and after refueling his spirit, he's back on the road,

hyping up the disciples across Galatia and Phrygia.

Apollos: The OG Ted Talker of Ephesus

So, there's this dude named Apollos, right? Dude's from Alexandria, and he's got words smoother than your favorite Spotify playlist. He's all about the Scriptures and knows his stuff, but he's only got the demo version of the Jesus story — just the John the Baptist remix. He's in Ephesus, dropping knowledge bombs in the synagogue, when Priscilla and Aquila, the ultimate power couple, pull him aside. They're like, "Let's upgrade your understanding to the full gospel experience." And boom, Apollos becomes an even bigger help to the faith fam, schooling the Jews with mad skills, showing them Jesus is the real deal.

John's OG Fans Get an Upgrade

Meanwhile, Paul's on a road trip, ends up in Ephesus, and finds these twelve guys stuck in the baptism beta version — all they know is John's splash-and-dash. Paul's like, "Guys, you're missing the main event," and upgrades them to J.C.'s name. Instantly, they're speaking in hashtags and dropping prophetic tweets.

Epic School Sessions with Paul

Paul then hits the local synagogue, trying to win debates for three months until some folks start throwing shade at the Way. So, he takes his crew and turns the lecture hall of Tyrannus into the hottest club in Ephesus, where he drops truth tracks daily for two years. Now everyone in Asia's tuning into Paul's gospel beats.

Ephesus Goes Viral with Miracles and Drama

God's pulling off epic miracles through Paul, turning handkerchiefs into healing merch. Then, these wannabe exorcists, the Sceva bros, try dropping Jesus' name like they're featuring Paul, but the evil spirit's like, "Jesus I stan, Paul I fan, but who the heck are you?" and gives them the beatdown of their lives. This goes viral in Ephesus, boosting Jesus' rep sky-high. After a magic book bonfire party worth millions in views (or fifty thousand pieces of silver), the word of the Lord goes full-on trending across the region.

Ephesus Goes Wild: The Big Fan Riot

After Paul decides to take a "Been There, Done That" tour through Macedonia and Achaia with a finale in Rome, drama unfolds back in Ephesus. Enter Demetrius, the silver souvenir king, freaking out because Paul's "Gods-R-Us" talk is bad for business. He rallies the artisan guild for a town hall rant, sparking a mega-fan uproar for Artemis, their homegirl goddess. The city's vibe turns from chill to chaotic, with Gaius and Aristarchus, Paul's squad, getting an unplanned amphitheater tour. Paul's like, "Let me at 'em," but his crew and even some VIPs are like, "Nah, bro, sit this one out." The scene turns into a confused mess, with everyone yelling about Artemis for a two-hour marathon. Finally, the city clerk plays the voice of reason, reminding everyone about the legal ways to settle beefs and avoid being hashtagged #RiotCity.

Paul's Eurotrip: Macedonia to Greece to Near-Riot

Post-Ephesus drama, Paul hits the road to cheer up his peeps across Macedonia and Greece, dodging a Jewish plot twist by rerouting through Macedonia with a posse including the OG Berean Sopater and others. They regroup in Troas for a weeklong truth-spilling session. At a Troas house party, Paul goes on a preaching marathon until Eutychus, snoozing on a window ledge, takes a three-story tumble. Paul pulls a "He's not dead" move, hugs the lad back to life, and keeps the convo going till sunrise, leaving the crowd shook but stoked.

Sailing Diary: From Troas to a Tearful Miletus Meetup

Skipping Ephesus to avoid drama and make Pentecost in Jerusalem, Paul's crew sails from Troas to Assos to Mitylene to Chios to Samos, and finally, to Miletus. Paul, the ancient world's busiest missionary, is on a tight schedule, looking to wrap things up before the big Jerusalem season finale.

Goodbye to the Ephesus Crew

Paul hits up the Ephesus squad from Miletus, spilling the tea on his journey: lowkey moments, highkey dramas, and all the emotional rollercoasters in between. He's like, "Ya'll saw me doing the Lord's work, tears and all, dodging those hater plots." He drops a truth bomb about heading to Jerusalem, not knowing what's gonna pop off, except for some spoiler alerts from the Holy Spirit about upcoming challenges.
He's all about finishing strong, spreading that good vibes gospel, even if it means he won't be dropping by Ephesus again. With a heavy heart, he's like, "Guard the squad and keep the vibe check high 'cause some shady characters are gonna try to mess with the harmony post-me." It's a teary farewell with hugs all around, and a prayer sesh that's all feels.

Jerusalem or Bust: The Tearful Goodbyes Tour

The squad then sails off, hitting up Cos, Rhodes, and Patara, before catching a ride to Phoenicia. They do a flyby of Cyprus, then dock in Tyre to unload some cargo vibes. The local believers try to persuade Paul to skip Jerusalem, but he's on a mission. After a heartfelt beach prayer meetup, it's bon voyage again.
Next stops: Ptolemais for a quick hello, then down to Caesarea to crash with Philip the OG evangelist. His daughters are dropping prophecies left and right. Then Agabus rolls in, snagging Paul's belt for a dramatic prophecy performance about Paul's upcoming Jerusalem saga. Despite the squad's tears and pleas, Paul's determined to face whatever's waiting in Jerusalem, all in for the Lord Jesus. They finally hit the "God's plan" button and prep for whatever comes next.

Epic Drama in Jerusalem: Paul's Big Entrance

So, Paul and his squad hit up Jerusalem, bringing some hype from Caesarea. They crash with Mnason, an OG disciple from way back. The next day, Paul rolls deep with his crew to meet James and the elders, dropping the deets on the epic God moves among the Gentiles. But here's the tea: The local believers are hyped on Paul's stories but spill that there's some major side-eye from the Jewish believers. They're convinced Paul's throwing shade on Moses and telling folks to ghost their customs. To chill everyone out, they hit Paul with a plan: Join some dudes in a purification vibe and show you're still down with the customs.

Temple Tension Turns Up

Paul's down for the plan, heads to the temple, but then some drama-seeking Jews from Asia spot him, crank up the mob, and chaos erupts. They're all, "This dude's trashing our culture and sneaking non-Jews into the temple!" The city flips, they grab Paul, and it's looking grim. Just as they're about to turn Paul into a human piñata, the Roman squad rolls up, saving him from the beatdown but slapping him in chains. The crowd's still losing their minds, shouting for Paul's head.

Paul Pulls the Citizenship Card

As they're dragging him away, Paul's like, "Yo, can I get a word?" The commander's shook Paul speaks Greek and mistakes him for some notorious rebel. But Paul's like, "Nah, man, I'm just a scholarly dude from Tarsus. Let me holler at the crowd." Given the green light, Paul stands up, drops the hand signal for silence, and switches to Aramaic, instantly snagging their attention. He starts his spill: "Fam, listen up. I'm one of you, schooled under Gamaliel, super zealous. I even threw believers in jail. Got the high priest's cosign and everything. I was on my way to Damascus to round up more when things got wild." And so, Paul begins his legendary defense, ready to drop his transformation story on them.

Paul's Wild Ride to Damascus and Beyond

Yo, peeps, gather 'round 'cause Paul's about to drop the sickest throwback story. So, Paul's cruising to Damascus, right? Middle of the day, and BAM! Heaven's spotlight hits him harder than a double espresso shot. Hits the deck and hears this celestial voice, "Yo, Saul, why you gotta be like that, chasing me down?" Paul's all, "Um, who's asking?" And the voice goes, "It's me, Jesus. Surprise! You're on my team now." Mind blown, right? His buddies see the light show but don't catch the convo. So, Jesus is like, "Hit up Damascus, I've got plans for you." Paul's blind as a bat now, so his squad leads him by the hand. Enter Ananias, top-tier believer, who's like, "Bro, Jesus sent me. Time for your superhero origin story." Boom, sight's back, and Paul's dunked in water, sins washed away, full reboot.

Fast forward, Paul's back in Jerusalem, vibing in the temple when he zones out into a vision. Jesus is all, "Bail on Jerusalem, ASAP. They ain't buying what you're selling." Paul's like, "But, bro, I've got street cred here!" Jesus insists, "Nah, you're globe-trotting. Gentiles, here you come!"

Paul's Roman Flex

Now, cut to the Jerusalem chaos. The crowd loses it, screaming for Paul's head. Mid-meltdown, the Romans swoop in. They're about to whip Paul when he pulls the ultimate "Uno reverse" card - "Yo, is this how we treat Roman citizens now?" Mic drop.

The commander's shook, realizing he's messed with a Roman. Next day, Paul's thrown into the theological Thunderdome, AKA the Sanhedrin. He plays it cool, "I'm all good with God." High priest gets salty, orders a slap, and Paul claps back, "God's gonna get you for that." Realizes he dissed the high priest and is like, "My bad, didn't see you there."

Noticing the crowd's a mix of Team Pharisee and Team Sadducee, Paul chucks a theological grenade, "Yo, I'm Team Pharisee! It's all about that resurrection life!" Instantly, the room's more divided than the last slice of pizza. Pharisees and Sadducees go at it. The commander's worried Paul's gonna get ripped apart in the debate club gone wild, so he rescues him. That night, Jesus slides into Paul's DMs, "Chin up, buttercup. You've repped me in Jerusalem; next stop, Rome." And that's the tea, folks. Paul's saga's just getting started. Stay tuned for more adventures – it's gonna be epic.

Paul's Conspiracy Thriller

Alright, strap in, 'cause things are getting spicy. Imagine this: Paul's chilling in the slammer, and over forty peeps are like, "No brunch until we ghost Paul." Hardcore, right? They slide into the chief priests' DMs with this wild plan to ambush Paul. Plot twist: Paul's nephew catches wind of this and goes all secret agent to spill the tea to Paul. Paul's like, "Yo, centurion, I got a hot tip for the boss." So, the nephew tells the commander about the ambush waiting to drop. The commander's like, "Mum's the word," and whips up a midnight express with soldiers, cavalry, and the works to scoot Paul off to Governor Felix in Caesarea. Big move, right?

Dramas in Court

Cut to Caesarea, Paul's facing the music. High Priest Ananias rolls up with his squad and this slick lawyer, Tertullus, who starts buttering up Felix. But when it's Paul's turn, he's all, "Check the receipts, I was just vibing in the temple." Claims he's clean as a whistle and just doing his thing for the Big Guy upstairs.
Felix, feeling the heat, hits pause on the whole circus, "We'll see when the boss man from the barracks drops by." Meanwhile, Felix has these low-key chats with Paul, hoping for some hush money. Two years zip by, Felix peaces out, leaving Paul on read for his successor, Festus, 'cause Felix wanted to keep the peace

with the Jew crew. And that's how Paul turns a conspiracy into a cliffhanger. Stay tuned for what's next in Paul's wild ride.

Paul's Big Move: The Caesar Challenge

Alright, peeps, buckle up 'cause Paul's story is getting a major upgrade. Just three days into his new gig in the province, Festus hits up Jerusalem and, boom, the top dogs and big wigs of the Jew crew hit him with the 411 on Paul. They're low-key begging for a solid, hoping to get Paul transferred to Jerusalem. Why? 'Cause they've got this sneaky plan to yeet Paul off the mortal coil ambush-style on the way. But Festus is playing 4D chess, keeping Paul parked in Caesarea, and he's like, "If you've got beef, come down and spill the tea." Fast forward, Festus is back in Caesarea, puts Paul on the stand, and it's like a courtroom drama without the evidence. Paul's all, "I'm clean, fam. No cap." Festus, trying to score some brownie points with the Jew crew, is like, "Jerusalem trial, yay or nay?" Paul drops the mic: "I'm taking this to the top. I appeal to Caesar!" Festus huddles with his squad and is like, "Caesar it is." Enter stage left, King Agrippa and Bernice rolling into Caesarea with all the bling. Festus dishes the dirt on Paul, mentioning the whole kerfuffle is about some dude named Jesus who's apparently not as dead as advertised. Agrippa's intrigued and is like, "I gotta hear this guy."

So, they set the stage for Paul's big moment with Agrippa and Bernice making a grand entrance, military brass and city VIPs in tow. Festus plays the hype man, but admits he's kinda stuck on what to write to Caesar 'cause, technically, Paul hasn't done anything post-worthy. Agrippa's spotlight is on, hoping this chat will give Festus something to tweet about to Caesar, 'cause sending a man without a hashtag just ain't it. And there you have it, Paul's epic saga turning into a full-blown imperial affair. Stay tuned, 'cause this is where the plot thickens and the stakes get as high as Paul's faith.

Paul's Mic Drop at Agrippa's Crib

King Agrippa gave the mic to Paul and was like, "Bruh, the floor is yours." So, Paul, being the OG he is, starts spitting straight facts. He's like, "King A, you know the drill with all these Jewish vibes and beefs, so lend me your ears."

Paul goes, "Back in the day, all the Jewish homies knew I was the Pharisee MVP, living that strict life. Fast forward, and here I am, getting dragged 'cause I'm all in on this promise God made to our OG ancestors. And what's the deal with folks tripping over God doing God things like raising the dead?"

Paul admits, "Not gonna lie, I was on a major haterade against Jesus of Nazareth, locking up his squad and even cosigning their death sentences. My rage game was so strong, I was hunting them down in foreign zip codes." Then, Paul flips the script about his road trip to Damascus, where this epic light show from heaven had him and his crew eating dirt. A voice hits him up in Aramaic, calling him out, "Saul, Saul, why you hating on me? You're just bashing your head against the wall." Paul's like, "Who dis?" And boom, it's Jesus saying, "You're beefing with me, fam. But chill, I've got major plans for you. You're gonna be my rep, spilling the tea about everything you've seen and will see. I'mma snatch you from your peeps and the outsiders to flip the script for them—turning them from team darkness to team light, from Satan's squad to God's fam, hooking them up with forgiveness and a VIP pass among the holy crew by faith in me." Paul's all, "So, King A, I wasn't about to ghost on that divine DM. I hit the ground running in Damascus, Jerusalem,

Judea, and even to the non-Jews, preaching the turn-up for God and get-your-act-together gospel. That's why the Jews got salty and tried to off me in the temple. But yo, God's had my back up till this hot sec, helping me stand tall and preach to the high and low about nothing but what the OG prophets and Moses said was gonna drop—that the Messiah had to take an L, be the first to bounce back from the grave, and shine a light on our crew and the outsiders." And that's how Paul laid it down, straight fire, in front of Agrippa, spilling his life story and the glow-up from being a hater to headliner in God's epic comeback story.

As Paul was laying down his truth bombs, Festus lost it and was like, "Bro, you're tripping! Too much bookworming is frying your brain." But Paul clapped back, "Nah, Festus, my dude, I'm all about that truth life. King A over here knows the score; nothing's been low-key. Yo, King, you vibing with the prophets? Bet you do." King Agrippa threw a curveball, "Paul, you think you can flip me to Team Christian just like that?" Paul's like, "Deadass, I pray to God that not just you but everyone catching this spill turns out like me—minus the bling (chains)." Post-chat, the squad— King A, Festus, Bernice, and their clique—peaced out, and they're all, "Man, this dude's not about that criminal life." Agrippa hits Festus with, "Could've let the man bounce if he hadn't name-dropped Caesar."

Sailing for Rome

So, the powers-that-be decide it's Italy time for Paul and some other unfortunate souls, passing them off to Julius, head honcho of the Imperial Squad. Hopping on a boat from Adramyttium with Aristarchus from Thessalonica tagging along, we're off. Next stop, Sidon, where Julius is all gentlemanly, letting Paul catch up with his peeps for some TLC. The journey gets real as we try to dodge Cyprus thanks to some gnarly winds. After a scenic route past Cilicia and Pamphylia, we park at Myra in Lycia. Julius finds an Alexandrian liner headed for Italy and it's all aboard. The cruise was anything but smooth, crawling past Cnidus and then hugging Crete's side to dodge the wind. Landing at this chill spot called Fair Havens, near Lasea, we're debating winter plans.

Ship Got Yeeted by Storm

So, the crew caught a vibe from a soft south breeze and thought, "Aight, we got this," and dipped close by Crete. But nah, this wild wind, dubbed the "northeaster," came outta nowhere and had us like, "Welp." Straight up couldn't sail into it, so we just went with it, passing by this tiny spot called Cauda.

We barely saved our little boat, then strapped the big one like it was wearing a belt 'cause we were scared of hitting the Syrtis sands. Next thing, we're throwing cargo overboard 'cause the storm was owning us. Day three, even the gear got yeeted. No sun, no stars, just storm. Everyone was pretty much giving up hope.

Paul's Pep Talk

Paul stood up like, "Yo, should've listened to me. But chill, you won't die, just the ship's gonna be toast. Some angel dude told me I gotta hit up Caesar and that you're all part of the package deal." He was like, "Bet, we'll crash on some island." Two weeks in, floating around the Adriatic, the sailors felt land was near. They checked, found it deep, then less deep, and freaked we'd hit rocks. Dropped anchors and wished for morning. Some tried to dip in a lifeboat, but Paul was like, "Nah, everyone stays, or we're donezo." So, the soldiers cut the lifeboat loose. At dawn, Paul's like, "Eat, fam, you'll need it."

Broke bread, gave thanks, and started munching. Everyone got hyped and ate. We were 276 souls onboard. Post-snack, they dumped the wheat to make the ship lighter.

Epic Shipwreck

Daylight hit, and they saw a chance to beach it. Cut the anchors, let 'em go, and tried to hit the beach but ended up stuck on a sandbar, ship breaking apart.

Soldiers wanted to off the prisoners to prevent escapes, but the centurion was like, "Not on my watch, we're saving Paul." Ordered swimmers to bail first, rest to grab whatever floats. Every single person made it to shore, safe and sound.

Malta Vibes

Found ourselves on Malta. The locals were top-tier, lighting fires, welcoming us cold, wet peeps. Paul's making a fire, and boom, a viper latches onto him. Locals were like, "Oh, he's done for." But Paul? Just shook it off into the fire, no sweat. They waited for him to drop dead or puff up, but when he was chillin', they decided he's not a man, he's a deity.

Chillin' in Malta

223

So, right next to where we crash-landed, there was this big-shot named Publius who was like, "Yo, come over." His pad was lit, and he hosted us for three days. Turns out, his dad was laid up with some nasty fever and dysentery. Paul just strolls in, hits him with a prayer and a high-five, and boom, dude's up and running. After that, everyone on the island with a sniffle or worse lined up, and Paul fixed them up too. They loaded us up with props and supplies for our goodbye.

Finally Hitting Up Rome

Three months later, we hopped on this ship from Alexandria, rocking the Twin Gods as its hood ornament. Made a pit stop in Syracuse, hung out for a bit, then caught a breeze straight to Puteoli. Found some fam there, crashed for a week, and then made our grand entrance into Rome. The local squad heard we were coming, pulled up to meet us, and seeing them got Paul all pumped. Once in Rome, Paul got his own place but with a plus-one Roman soldier.

After chilling for three days, Paul calls up the Jewish bigwigs. He's like, "Look, I'm not here to throw shade at our peeps or traditions, but got nabbed in Jerusalem and handed off to the Romans. They checked me out, found zilch, and were down to let me bounce until the local Jews threw a fit. Had to hit up Caesar, but it's all good. I'm just here 'cause I'm repping Israel, and now I'm all chained up." The Jews were like, "We haven't heard squat about you. No bad vibes from Judea or anyone else. But we're all ears about your take, 'cause everybody's got some tea on this sect."

The Tea Gets Spilled

They set up a meeting, and from sunrise to sunset, Paul's laying down the truth about God's kingdom, trying to get them on board with Jesus using the old school scriptures. Some were vibing with it; others, not so much. As they're dipping out, Paul drops this truth bomb: "The Holy Spirit called it—y'all got eyes and ears, but you're not seeing or hearing anything. If you did, you might get it and get healed. But hey, this God gig is now rolling out to the Gentiles, and they're here for it." Paul posted up in his own spot for two years, door's always open. He's talking kingdom of God, schooling them on Jesus, no holds barred, no one stopping him.

CORINTHIANS

Slide into Corinth Like...

Yo, it's Paul on the mic, called to be an apostle of the big JC by the big G's plan, rolling deep with my bro Sosthenes. Shoutout to the squad in Corinth, you're all holy rollers in Jesus, called to be VIPs, just like everyone hitting up JC's hotline, wherever you at.
Bless up with some grace and peace from Daddy G and the main man, Jesus Christ.

Giving Props

Big ups to God for hooking you up with Jesus' swag, making you all kinds of rich in words and smarts. Christ's story got grip because of you, so you're not missing any spiritual bling while you're on the lookout for JC's epic comeback. He's got your back till the finale, so you'll be looking fresh when our Lord Jesus hits the scene. God's legit; He called you to chill with His Son, Jesus Christ, our Lord.

Squad Goals vs. Squad Squabbles

Alright, fam, let's get real in the name of our boy Jesus. I'm all for team spirit, but you gotta be on the same page, no cliques, no beef, just one big happy crew. Got wind from Chloe's peeps that you're throwing shade at each other. Like, "I'm Team Paul," or "I roll with Apollos," or "Cephas is my guy," and "I'm just here for Jesus." C'mon, is Jesus split up? Paul didn't go on the cross for you, did he? You weren't dunked in my name, right? Thankful I didn't splash any of you except Crispus and Gaius, so no one can say you got the Paul baptism special. Oh, and the Stephanas fam too, but that's it. Jesus didn't send me to start a swim club; I'm here to drop the gospel, no fancy talk, so Christ's cross stays lit.

Christ: The Ultimate Clout

The message about the cross is like, "What?" to those hitting the self-destruct, but for us getting saved, it's God's power-up. It's like the script says, "Gonna ghost the know-it-alls and cancel the brainiacs." Where's the wise guy? The bookworm? The hotshot debater? God's playing 4D chess with the world's smarts. In all His big brain energy, peeps didn't get to know Him through being smart, so God was all about saving believers through what sounds like a joke. Jews are all, "Show us something wild," and Greeks are like, "Hit us with that big brain energy," but we're just here

hyping up Christ on the cross –
a total trip for Jews and
nonsense to Greeks. Yet, for
those getting the invite,
regardless of the crew, Christ is
where it's at – God's muscle and
God's genius, 'cause what looks
like a facepalm to God is still
outsmarting the smartest, and
even God's "weakness" is
benching more than human
brawn.

Flexing in the Lord

Yo, peeps, look at yourselves:
not many brainiacs, not many
high rollers, not many blue-
bloods. But God picked the stuff
that makes the world's brainiacs
feel basic, and the weak sauce to
flex on the strong. Picked the
nobodies to cancel out the
somebodies, so nobody's got
room to brag. It's all Him –
you're in Jesus, who's God's
brainwave for us – making us
right, setting us apart, and
hooking us up. Just like the
script says, "If you're gonna flex,
flex about the Lord."

Paul Drops the Mic in Corinth

Yo, when I rolled up to your
hood, fam, I wasn't flashing my
vocab or dropping wisdom
bombs. Nah, I was all about JC
and that cross life. Came at you
all weak-kneed, shaking in my
sneakers, straight-up. My talk
wasn't about dazzling you with
my smarts but showing off
Spirit's vibe, so your faith's all
about God's mojo, not some
human brain flex.

Secret Wisdom Vibes

For real, we do get deep with
those who are on the level,
talking about God's secret
wisdom stash. This isn't your
run-of-the-mill wisdom or what
those big shots of the now scene
are into, who are basically
yesterday's news. Nah, we're into
the OG wisdom God had on
lock for our glow-up, stuff the
high and mighty couldn't even
sniff out, or they wouldn't have
ghosted our Lord of bling. But
hey, it's like the script says,
"Eyes haven't seen, ears haven't
heard, hearts can't even," but
God's got the hookup for those
who are down with Him.
We're in the know 'cause the
Spirit's like our deep dive into
God's own thoughts. Who
knows what's up with a person
except their own inner vibe?
Same with God. And we got the
Spirit, not the world's vibe, so
we're tuned into what God's
handing out for free. We're not
using those basic human words
but Spirit's lingo, explaining the
feels to those who get the feels.
But if you ain't got the Spirit, it's
like trying to explain a meme to a
rock—just doesn't click. Spiritual

peeps get it, though, and they're like off the charts, but no one can pin them down. It's like, who can school God? But yo, we're rolling with Christ's mindset.

Baby Steps in Christ

Look, squad, I couldn't talk to you like you were spiritual OGs but like you're still in the crib, sipping on that spiritual milk 'cause you weren't ready for the solid food. Heck, you're still not. You've got that petty drama and beef like it's high school all over again. Pulling that "I'm with Paul" or "I'm with Apollos" – come on, we're all in this together.

What's the Deal with Apollos and Me?

So, what's Apollos? And who am I? Just God's delivery guys, doing our bit so you could hit up that faith. I laid down the groundwork, Apollos watered it, but God's the one making it all bloom. Planting, watering, it's a team effort, but God's the MVP here. We're all on the same squad, but we'll get our props based on the hustle. We're God's crew, His field, His high-rise. I got the foundation laid out like a pro, thanks to God's hookup, and now it's your turn to build. But keep it legit 'cause Jesus is

our foundation. You can go all out with your build—gold, silver, or some basic materials. But it's gonna get real when the quality check comes through the fire. Make it through, and you're golden. Get torched, and you're lucky to escape with your shorts on fire. Don't you get it? You're God's crib, and His Spirit's chilling with you. Mess with God's crib, and you're asking for trouble 'cause it's sacred turf, and that's what you all are.

No Cap Wisdom

Aight, peeps, don't fool yourselves. If you're vibin' with this era's smarts, time to hit the noob button and start fresh to get the real wisdom. 'Cause all that high IQ play? God's got it looking like yesterday's meme, He's all about flipping scripts on the smartypants crew. So, stop flexing on human creds. Whether you're team Paul, Apollos, or whoever, it's all good – everything's yours. You're rolling with Christ, and that's rolling with the Big G.

Real Talk on Being God's Squad

Look at us as Christ's crew and secret-keepers of God's dope mysteries. What's key? Being solid. You trying to judge me or throw shade? Save it. I don't even slide into my own DMs. It's God's call in the end. Hold off on those clapbacks till the grand reveal, when God's gonna highlight everyone's true colors. Then, it's kudos from God Himself.

Keeping It Humble

So, I used me and Apollos as examples, so y'all stop getting all high and mighty, picking faves. What's got you feeling so extra? Everything you're flexing with, was it not a gift? So why the glory hogging as if you didn't get it handed to you? You're acting all kinged up, wishing we could be on that throne life together. But real talk, God's got us apostles out here like last call, sentenced to the spotlight, clowned by the world, angel and human. We're the festival fools for Christ, but oh, you got it all figured out, right? We're on that struggle bus for real – hungry, thirsty, raggedy, getting tossed around, crib-hopping. We bless when dissed, we chill when hunted, we stay polite when dragged. Basically, the world's doormat.

Dad Vibes

Not tryna make you feel bad, just spittin' straight facts like a concerned dad. You got tons of guides, but not many dads. I put you on this Jesus wave, remember? So, mirror my vibe. That's why Tim's heading your way – he's my ride or die, gonna remind you of my Christ-like ways, which is the same beat I drop in every church. Some of y'all are getting puffed up thinking I won't show. Bet. I'll be there if God's down, ready to check the realness of the ones talking big. 'Cause God's kingdom? It's not about that talk game; it's about that power play. What's it gonna be? Me rolling up with the discipline stick or with love and chill vibes?

Church Gone Wild

Yo, for real, it's getting messy over there. Heard there's some next-level sinning, like soap opera stuff – dude's with his stepmom? And y'all are just chilling with it, all proud? Nah, that's twisted. You gotta cut him loose for his own good, let him hit rock bottom so he can bounce back when Jesus does His thing.
You're all hype, but don't forget – a bit of bad vibes spreads fast. Time for a hard reset. Jesus, our Passover, got the job done, so let's feast not with the old crusty vibes but with the gluten-free goodness of sincerity and legit truth.

No Chill with Bad Vibes

Yo, I slid into your DMs earlier, telling y'all not to vibe with peeps who are all about that shady life – especially those pretending to be squad but are actually about greed, idol flexing, trash-talking, getting wasted, or scamming. That's a hard pass. And yeah, I wasn't talking about cutting off every Tom, Dick, or Harry in the world who lives like that; you'd have to ghost the whole planet. Nah, it's about those faking the fam vibes while living like they're in a reality show. Don't even grab a bite with them. It's not my job to police the outsiders, but we gotta keep our house clean. Outsiders? God's got their number. Inside? That's on us. Kick the bad apples out.

Court Drama Gets the Side-Eye

Seriously, taking fam squabbles to the streets? Getting Judge Judy on your bros and sis? Nah, fam, we're supposed to be the ones calling the shots in the end, not airing dirty laundry where it doesn't belong. Got beef with the fam? Sort it in the fam. Taking it public's just asking to lose face. Why not just take the L and move on? Why do you gotta play dirty?

Real Talk: VIP List for Heaven's Club

Don't get it twisted – living that shady life won't get you on the guest list for God's kingdom. No backstage passes for the morally bankrupt, the idol fans, cheaters, or anyone living that #Problematic life. Some of y'all were in that club, but you got that glow-up – washed clean, set apart, legit in the eyes of Jesus and the Spirit.

Your Body's a No-Scam Zone

"All good for me" doesn't mean "all good," period. "I do what I want" ain't the motto when it can get you hooked. As for the munchies and other appetites, they're temporary; but your bod? It's for rocking it for the Lord, not for hook-up culture. God's got a power-up for us, just like He did for Jesus. Mixing up Christ's crew with someone just for the night? Big yikes. Hooking up means you're blending souls, fam. Stick with the Lord and keep it 100. Bounce from anything sketchy. Remember, your body's the VIP lounge for the Holy Spirit, courtesy of God. You're not self-owned; you were bought with a price tag – so let your life be a rave that honors God.

Marriage 101

Heads up on your questions about keeping it single or mingling: Flying solo's cool, but with all the thirst traps out there, locking it down with your own boo is key to keeping things legit. Husbands and wives, don't leave your other half hanging. Your bodies are mutual territory. Taking a break? Only if you both hit pause for a prayer sesh, but then it's back to regular programming before you trip up. This advice? It's a maybe, not a must. Wish y'all could be chill like me, but hey, everyone's got their vibe from God. Single or hitched, do you, but if the heat's too much, better to put a ring on it than play with fire.

Marriage Deets: A Modern Guide

Alright, peeps, here's the 411 straight from the Big Guy upstairs – if you're hitched, stay hitched. But if you gotta bounce, stay single or patch things up. Now, for the mixed-vibe couples, if your other half isn't about the Jesus life but is cool living with you, don't hit the road. You might just turn their heart. And if they peace out, let 'em. We're all about that peace life, fam. You never know, you might be the reason they find the light.

Life Vibes: Do You

Stay in your lane, folks. Got a life scenario when God called you? Rock it. Whether you're tatted with your faith or not, it's all good. What matters is keeping it 100 with God's commands. Freedom or not, you're all VIPs in Jesus' squad. Remember, you're too priceless to be anyone's plus-one, so keep it real wherever you're at.

Single or Ready to Mingle?

No cap, I've got no divine DMs about staying single, but here's some wisdom for free. Given the crazy times, it might be chill to stay as you are. Tied down or flying solo, don't sweat it. If you lock it down, no shade – but brace yourself for some extra realness. Life's short, so maybe don't get too caught up in the feels or the deals.

Solo Dolo with No Distractions

Here's the deal – single folks can go hard after God's heart without the drama. Married folks, you've got a tag team going, but keep your eyes on the prize. Ladies and gents flying solo, you've got that undivided focus to be all in for the Lord. Not trying to fence you in, just spitting facts for living that best life without the buzzkill.

When You Know, You Know

Feeling the pressure with your boo? If it's getting real and you're both on board, go ahead and put a ring on it. No harm, no foul. But if you're chillin' and holding off feels right, props to you. Both paths are solid, but going solo might just have that extra sprinkle of chill.

Foodie Vibes and Idol Nosh

Alright, squad, let's chat about grub offered to those no-vibe idols: We all got the brainwaves, but it's love that levels us up. Someone might think they're the head honcho of knowledge, but if they're not vibing in love, they're missing the mark. For those who heart God, you're on His VIP list. So, munching on idol snacks? Here's the tea: Idols are basically nada in the grand scheme, 'cause there's just one Big Boss, our God. Now, for the real ones, there's only one Lord, J.C., running the whole show with Dad. But, not everyone's up to speed on this. Some peeps, fresh off the idol worship train, eat these snacks and feel all kinds of guilty. Remember, what you eat doesn't make you any more God-approved. But don't

let your freedom trip someone else into feeling bad vibes.

Paul's Legit Life Hacks

Yo, am I not free? Am I not one of Jesus' squad leaders? You peeps are my proof in the Lord. Here's my defense against the haters: Got no rights to grab a bite or sip something? What about rolling with a faith partner like the rest of the Jesus crew? Or is it just me and Barnabas who gotta hustle 24/7? Who throws down in battle on their own dime? Who's got a vineyard and doesn't get to enjoy the grapes? Exactly. And hey, it's not just me talking; the Big Book backs me up. We're planting spiritual seeds; a little love in return isn't too wild to expect, right? But here's the thing—I'm not about that "give me, give me" life. I'd rather go through anything than block the good news about Christ.

And for the record, I've been rolling without using any of these rights. But don't twist my words—I'm not hinting for some perks. I'd rather ghost than let anyone strip my bragging rights in spreading the gospel free of charge. If I'm preaching, it's not for the 'gram; it's 'cause I've got this burning mission. And yo, if I didn't share the good news, I'd be in all kinds of trouble. But if I'm all in, I'm looking at some heavenly rewards.

For the Gram or For Real?

You know the drill: we're all in this race, so run like you mean it. Everyone in the game keeps it tight to snag that fleeting crown, but we're after the one that lasts forever. So, I'm not just shadowboxing here. I keep my body in check, training hard, so after I've hyped everyone else, I'm not benched.

Throwback Lessons and Idol Eats

Yo fam, let's not forget the OG squad, our ancestors. They all had that VIP cloud pass and beach party through the Red Sea, all rocking the same spiritual snacks and drinks. They were sipping on that spiritual rockstar, Christ. But, real talk, most got ghosted in the wild 'cause they weren't vibing with God. Let's not hit replay on their playlist of no-nos. Like, don't be those peeps who parked it to eat and then turned up too hard. And don't even start with that swiping right on every temptation or getting salty like those OG complainers. These throwback fails? They're our heads-up so we don't trip on the same stones.

Idolatry? Swipe Left

Alright, peeps, let's keep it 100: idols are just fancy nothings. There's only one Boss, God, and one MVP, Jesus. But check it, not everyone's up to speed, and for some, that idol grub is a major guilt trip. Remember, it's not about what's on your plate but about the vibe you set. So, if munching on certain eats sends someone spiraling, let's pass on it. No dish is worth tripping up your crew.

Paul Dropping Real Talk

Now, onto me: Am I not free? Have I not met Jesus? You're my proof that the gig is legit. But here's the deal: I've got rights, but I'm not about flexing them if it messes with the gospel vibe. And about those sacrifices to idols? Big yikes, they're basically sending RSVPs to demon parties, and that's not our scene. Mixing up Lord's vibes with low-key demon hangouts? Hard pass. We're not about stirring up divine FOMO or thinking we've got the upper hand on God.

Keeping It Chill for the Gospel

"Everything's chill," but let's keep it beneficial. It's all about building up, not just doing you. So, when you're dining at the non-believer's pad, don't stress the menu unless it's explicitly idol noms. We're playing it cool for conscience' sake, not making a scene over freedom rights. Bottom line: Whatever you're up to, eating, TikToking, or whatever, make it a shoutout to God. No stepping on toes, whether they're from our squad, the outside crew, or God's own circle. I'm all about making everyone feel welcome, aiming for that big save.

Be Like Me, Be Like Christ

And hey, about those head coverings: Let's not get twisted. Christ is the head honcho, and we're just rolling in His squad. Guys, keep it breezy without a cover. Ladies, if you're chatting with God, maybe throw on that headgear. It's all about respect and order, with a nod to the angels. Now, when it comes to the Lord's Supper, it's more than just a snack time. It's a heart check and a flashback to what Jesus did for the squad. So, let's not turn it into a hot mess with divisions and side-eyes. Remember, this meal's about unity and remembering the ultimate sacrifice. So, before you dive in, do a vibe check. Make sure you're all in with the right heart, 'cause messing this up is no joke. And if you're feeling peckish, grab a snack at home so

our gatherings stay lit and judgment-free. Stay tuned for more deets, coming your way soon.

Spiritual Swag Drop

Yo squad, let's talk spiritual swag. Back in the day, y'all were jamming to some silent idols, but now we're tuning into a whole new beat with the Spirit. Quick heads up: if anyone's throwing shade at Jesus, that ain't the Spirit talking. Only with the Spirit can you drop a legit "Jesus is the boss." We've got a variety of gifts, but it's the same Spirit DJing the whole party. Whether it's dropping wisdom tracks, faith bangers, healing vibes, miracle mixes, prophecy flows, spirit discerning beats, diverse tongues, or translation tracks, it's all coming from the same divine playlist.

Squad Goals with a Diverse Cast

Picture this: we're all parts of one banging body, the Christ Crew. Baptized into one squad, no matter our backgrounds. Imagine if we were all just one giant eyeball—where would the hearing drop? Or if we were all ears, where would the smelling be at? Nah, every part is crucial, even those you might not see front stage at the concert. If one of us hits a low note, we all feel it. If one of us scores a win, we're all turning up. We're one crew, but with mad diverse roles: from headliners like apostles and prophets to the behind-the-scenes heroes with healing hands, support staff, and those rocking the tongues tracks.

Hitting the High Notes with Love

Now, if I can speak every language, even angelic, but have zero love, I'm just making noise. If I'm all about prophecies, got all the knowledge and faith to do the impossible but ain't got love, I'm nada. Even if I give away everything, even take a hit for the team without love, it's a big fat zero. Love's the real MVP. It's chill, it's kind, it doesn't flex, doesn't diss, doesn't hog the spotlight, doesn't lose its cool, and doesn't keep score on the fouls. It doesn't cheer at fails but vibes with the truth. It's down for whatever, believes the best, keeps the hope alive, and rides out the tough times.

Love's the track that never skips. Prophecies, they'll wrap up. Tongues, they'll chill. Knowledge, it's got an expiration date. We're all about that partial vibe now, but when the full album drops, the singles are history. Back in my noob days, I was all baby talk and kiddie thoughts. Grew up, and all that kid stuff got shelved. We're kinda peeking through a foggy mirror now, but one day it'll be 4K ultra HD, face to face. Right now, we're catching glimpses, but then? We'll see the full picture, crystal clear. So here's the deal: Faith, hope, and love are the forever crew, but love? Love's the headliner.

Hype on Spiritual Vibe Check

Alright, fam, diving into the spiritual deep end, we're not leaving anyone in the dark about these spiritual gift drops. Back when y'all were vibing with those silent idols, now we're all about that Holy Spirit connection. Heads up: Dropping a "Jesus is cursed" is a no-go with the Spirit, but shouting "Jesus is Lord" is straight-up Holy Spirit territory.

Drop Beats Not Just Words

Chatting in tongues is cool and all, hitting direct convos with God, spilling mysteries. But, prophesying? That's where it's at, talking straight to the heart, pumping encouragement, strength, and comfort. Speaking in tongues is your own spirit's workout, but prophesying is like building the whole squad. If I roll up speaking in tongues without dropping some revelation, knowledge, prophecy, or a fresh lesson, how's that gonna vibe with you? Imagine instruments not hitting their notes or a bugle spitting out confusing sounds, nobody's getting ready for anything. Same with tongues, without making sense, it's like talking to the air. So, if you're all about those spiritual gifts, aim to be the top builder of the squad.

Keep It Real and Respectful

Speaking in tongues is a sign, not for the crew but for the outsiders. Prophecy, though, that's for the crew, building everyone up. If everyone's speaking in tongues and an outsider strolls in, they're gonna think we've lost it. But if all are dropping prophecies, and an outsider or someone unsure steps in, they're gonna be hit with the truth, seeing God's real talk in action.

Squad Meetings Must-Have Playlist

When we squad up, everyone's got something to share: a hymn, a lesson, a revelation, some tongues, an interpretation. Keep it all about building up. Speaking in tongues at the meet-up? Keep it to two or three tops, and let's have an interpretation. If not, let's keep it on mute. Let a couple of prophets speak, and let others weigh in. If a revelation hits someone sitting down, first speaker, hit pause. We're all about taking turns, so everyone gets to learn and get lifted. Remember, the Spirit of the prophets is under the prophets' control; we're not about chaos but peace.

Ladies, Gents, and Respect

Now, about the ladies speaking up in the meet-ups, let's stick to the script as all the holy squads do. Got questions? Save it for home discussions. It's about keeping things graceful and orderly. And for everyone, if you're all about prophecy or speaking in tongues, don't hold back on the prophecy and don't ban tongues. Just keep it classy and in order.

Resurrection: The Core Beat

Rolling into the gospel you're standing on, the one saving you if you're holding tight unless you missed the beat from the start. I dropped the headline news first up: Christ took our sins down with him, was buried, rose on day three, all according to the script. Showed up to Cephas, then to the squad, even rocked up to 500+ at once, most still here, though some have hit the final sleep. Made an appearance to James, then all apostles, and even me, the latest drop. I'm the newbie apostle, not even on the original lineup because I was on the wrong team. But grace flipped the script, and now I'm all in, working double-time, not on my own, but it's all grace. So, whether it's me or the OGs dropping this truth, this is the vibe you believed.

Real Talk on Resurrection Vibes

Yo, squad, let's get this straight: If we're out here saying Christ bounced back from the dead, how's anyone gonna say, "Nah, dead folks stay dead"? If that's the vibe, then Christ is still chillin' in the grave. And if that's the case, we're just spitting in the wind, and y'all's faith is like a phone with no signal—useless. And yeah, we'd be straight-up lying about God, saying He raised Christ when He didn't— if, you know, raising the dead isn't His jam. No resurrection means Christ is still down for the count, and that's a big oof 'cause then we're all stuck in our mess, and all the peeps who took a dirt nap in Christ are just outta luck. Basically, if our hope in Christ is only for the now and not the later, we're more pitiful than someone who missed the last bus home.

But Wait, There's a Twist

Boom, plot twist: Christ did rise up, leading the pack for those catching Z's. Death got the boot through a dude (Adam), but through another dude (Christ), we all get a pass back to life. It's all about timing: Christ's the headliner, then when He hits the stage again, His crew follows. After the show, He's passing the mic to God, squashing all beef, and putting every power trip in check. He's keeping the throne warm until He's got all His haters making carpet impressions with their faces. Death's the last one to get booted off the island. When everything's under His feet, Christ's gonna be like, "Yo, Dad, your turn," making sure God's everywhere, doing all the things.

Why Even Splash Around If It's All for Nothing?

And what's the deal with getting dunked on behalf of the ghost squad if the dead aren't getting a comeback tour? Why are we even catching hands every day? I'm practically a dead man walking here, bragging about you guys to Jesus. If I'm throwing down with beasts in Ephesus for kicks, without any hope of a resurrection, might as well just hit up the buffet and call it quits. Don't let the bad vibes drag you down. Wake up, clean up your act, 'cause some folks are clueless about God—I'm facepalming here for you.

Resurrection Glow-Up

So you're wondering, "How do the dead get their comeback? What's the new look?" C'mon, think! What you plant doesn't sprout until it hits the dirt nap first. And what you're planting isn't the plant with all the Insta likes, but just a plain ol' seed, maybe wheat or something. God's got the upgrade plan, giving it a body as He sees fit—each seed gets its own custom fit. Not all living things rock the same vibe; humans, animals, birds, fish—we're all rocking different genres. Celestial bodies, terrestrial bodies, sun's got its bling, moon's doing its thing, and stars? They're all about that variety pack. Just like that, resurrection's got its own makeover: planted busted, raised dope; planted a "meh", raised a "wow"; planted weak sauce, raised powerhouse; planted basic, raised on that spiritual level.

Stay Woke, Be Solid, Love Hard

Alright, lock it down, stay woke, keep the faith, be brave, stay strong. And yo, let love run the show. Big up to Stephanas and the crew, Achaia's VIPs, who set the bar for helping out. Give it up for the real ones, and anyone getting their hands dirty. Stephanas, Fortunatus, Achaicus—they're the real MVPs, filling in for you, giving my spirit (and yours) that energy drink boost. Recognize the peeps who refresh your soul.

LOVE... ALWAYS!

Made in the USA
Monee, IL
17 April 2024